THE UNHURRYING CHASE

D1355694

THE
UNHURRYING
CHASE

by

H. F. M. PRESCOTT

London

EYRE & SPOTTISWOODE

First published (by Constable & Co. Ltd.) 1925
Second, third and fourth impressions under same imprint
Second edition (published by Eyre & Spottiswoode) 1954

This book is printed in Great Britain
for Eyre & Spottiswoode (Publishers) Ltd., 15 Bedford Street,
London, W.C.2, by Butler & Tanner, Ltd., Frome and London

To

M. P.
J. M. P.
and
J. C. P.

I

THE 22nd day of May, 1176, broke grey and remained grey till late afternoon. Then the clouds thickened, growing close and heavy like a pall, muffling both light and sound while everything seemed to wait, blind and hushed, for some event. The light turned yellow and sickly, till in the thick-walled rooms of the castle at Angoulême the torches were lit one by one, and in the Count's own chamber the tall candles of yellowish wax. In the houses of the poor folks round about the foot of the castle, and in the narrow dark and twisted streets of the town there were no lights except the red glow of a fire here and there, for candles and even torches were for the wealthy. The poor folk waited idle, neighbour talking to neighbour, but all quietly, and watching the laden sky that seemed to be bowing down to smother the earth.

Then in the quiet a wind sprang up, that wind which has an evil intent, and is fierce against trees and houses and everything homely and familiar. It sprang up suddenly and from nowhere; it flung itself through the quiet streets, clapped doors to and fro, and shrieked round the towers of the castle. The banner which had hung like a dead thing on its staff leapt and struggled now for liberty, and the watchman holding his hood close under his chin, and looking towards the east where the woods began, saw all the branches tortured and beaten like the waves of a stormy sea.

To a man riding wearily through those same woods it seemed as though either he or the world had gone mad, so wild and demented was the confusion of the tossing branches straining this way and that, creaking and grinding in their struggle with the wind. He was so tired that the noise and movement seemed to be inside his brain; his eyes ached in his head, and he was stiff and sore from head to foot with riding for so many hours. His horse was as tired as he, and seemed to meditate each slow step before he took it.

At last they came to the edge of the wood, and the man, lifting his chin from his breast, peered up through the gloom at the city and castle above him. He could see the lights in the windows and was almost sure that a darker, wavering patch against the dark sky was the Count's banner set on the highest tower. If so, then the Count was in Angoulême and he had not much further to go. He tightened the reins and kicked up the horse to a better pace, and so came through the deserted fields to the dark gateway. The gate was open, since, for all the darkness had come down, it was not yet sunset.

Within the walls it was darker still, but though the wind tore over the tops of the houses, it was quieter in these close lanes than out among the fields, and once inside, as though this breathing space set him free to think of his own business, the horseman let the reins fall on the beast's neck, and leaving it to find its own way, rode gripping the saddle with his hands, and staring straight before him. His face had a weary, beaten look, and yet he seemed to be forcing his mind, in that dull stare, to contemplate without intermission something painful, or something which he did not understand.

When they came to the gate of the castle the horse stopped of its own accord and stood with its head drooping, shaking all down its legs. The rider sat there for a moment looking down at the guard who had crossed their bills before him, as though he did not know what they were, or found it difficult to give up the contemplation of that thing on which his thoughts were so distressfully fixed.

At last, with an effort, he spoke:

"The Count . . ." he said, and his voice croaked so that he stopped, cleared his throat, and began again:

"The Count is here?"

Even before he had finished the words, one of the men lifted his long bill with a laugh.

"Why, it's Messire of Rifaucon!" he said, and then turned again to stare at the rider, and meeting his eyes, began to excuse himself. He might have spared himself the trouble, for the man on horseback took no notice; when his way was clear he drove his heels into

8

the sides of the horse, and the two went on again at the same slow pace.

When, leaving his horse standing in the yard, the rider opened the door of the great Hall, the light and noise struck him almost like a blow on the face. He leaned against the door for a moment, and then started crookedly across the room to a door on the far side.

A fair-haired man stood there in the opening with his back to the Hall, but he turned as the new-comer's hand twitched his scarlet sleeve, and turning, stared at the man who accosted him. He had turned angrily, but his stare was of pure surprise.

"Yves of Rifaucon!" he cried, and came from the doorway into the Hall still staring at the three days' growth of beard, and at all the disarray of the man whose hand clutched his arm.

"Why?" he went on, "where in the devil's name have you been? The Count hath been wroth – of course he needs must call for you, and when they could not find –"

The man he called Yves broke in as though he had heard nothing:

"I must see the Count," he said, and moved his left hand very slightly towards the door as if he were too tired to lift it. "Is he here?"

The other stared at him again, then nodded.

"Shall I go in first and say ye're come?" he said, and he meant it kindly.

"No," said Yves and pushed past him. He could not afford to waste words.

The room he entered was small, hung round with cloth of Arras, and lit with twenty or so wax candles set in silver candlesticks picked out with bright enamels, the work of a craftsman from Limoges. There, in the mellow light, a dozen of the greater sort took their ease.

At the centre of the table sat Count Guilhem Talifer himself, long-faced and sour, his faded hazel eyes with their yellowish whites fixed moodily on the board. On his right was his eldest son Vulgrin, who even in his father's lifetime was known as "the Young Count," and who helped Guilhem to rule that rich and proud country of Angoulême. Vulgrin had ridden in only an hour before, and now, stripped of his hauberk, he sat in shirt and breeches with a loose robe of clouded yellow wrapped about him. He was a shorter man than his father, but had the same length of face and feature, only his look was alert and his greenish eyes had a twinkle in them. By him sat his wife, whom troubadours called "the Golden Countess." On the Old Count's left hand sat his third son, Adhemar, in whom again the family type prevailed. He was as tall as his father and had already the same stooping shoulders, but his hair was dark, and but for its length his face would have been handsome, for he had a fine commanding nose and dark eyes. Just now his full mouth was petulant, and he fidgeted with the silver cup that held his wine, running his thumb to and fro along its edge. The second son, Guilhem, was not there; Yves noticed it, and was glad, for he had no love for the younger Guilhem.

No one spoke as Yves crossed the room. He came up to the table and went down stiffly upon one knee before the old Count, but when he was down he had to lay a hand on the edge of the table to steady himself.

The Old Count looked at his hand and said sourly:

"Stand! Ye may stand!" and his lips drooped at the corners.

Yves pulled himself up, and his face hardened. The Count raised his eyes and looked him over in silence for a moment, and you would have said that he found Yves a disgusting sight, for his long nose seemed to grow more disdainful and his discontented mouth more bitter. At last he said:

"Well, what do ye want?" and then, without giving time for a reply:

"I thought they called you Yves the Clerk because of your shaven face," and he pointed a finger at the half-grown beard.

None but the Old Count would have known the nickname, and none but he would have troubled to notice what he did now; but he was always as curious as a magpie. The esquire at the door, listening and watching, gave an exasperated sigh as he heard the words. "Old Horseface!" he muttered to himself; for that was one of the esquires' nicknames for the Old Count. Yves, however, seemed to find neither absurdity nor annoyance in the Count's remark; his hand moved slowly up as if to feel his chin, then he shook his head vaguely, and let his hand fall.

"I have news," he said, and stopped again, for the Old Count was

10

leaning over the table wagging a long, knotted finger at him, and his face was creased with malicious laughter.

"News, Yves of Rifaucon?" he said. "News? I'll tell thee thy news. There is a certain Richard, Count of Poitou, Duke of Aquitaine, and my dear lief overlord, and son to Henry King of England, Duke of Normandy . . . and the rest. . . . God defend him, or the devil take him; which ye will! And ye come to tell me that this same Count Richard is come against me, and hath passed the Lusignan border and is by now knocking at *my* gates." He stopped and laughed at Yves' face.

Vulgrin, the Young Count, fair-haired ruddy and kindly, leaned over the table and interrupted:

"Have you more news?" he said, and smiled. He was the darling of the soldiers and he knew how to make men love him.

Yves turned his head slowly and looked at him.

"I think I have," he said uncertainly, "but I know not. . . . I know not how much is known here. I . . ." He stopped and looked at the Old Count as though he expected him to speak.

Guilhem stirred in his chair, and shifted his shoulders impatiently.

"Oh! tell your tale," he said, and turning away snapped his fingers to one of the hounds. The dog lumbered up from the rushes and leaned its head on the Count's knee, who seemed to forget Yves in playing with its ears.

Count Vulgrin was the one to ask the questions.

"Tell us," he said, "what other news. Anything ye have heard. We know nothing yet of where ye have been, nor why."

Yves fixed his eyes on the wall behind the Count's head and his fingers tightened on the buckle of his belt; when he began to speak it was in a rapid low tone as though he hurried over a lesson he feared to forget.

"Count Richard came from Poitiers into the Lusignan lands. They said at Ruffec that he hath taken Pamproux there, and some say Rouille too."

The Old Count looked up at that, and Yves hurried on:

"But ye know that, lords –" The Old Count smiled, and turned again to scratching the dog's ears.

Yves' eyes went back to Vulgrin, and he continued, but more

disjointedly now, either because the Old Count had disturbed him, or because his brain was too tired to think connectedly for long; or perhaps because he was coming to something he found difficult to say.

"I was on the hills near Sauzé, and I saw him down in the valley. He was coming away from it then . . . and I knew nothing. . . . I saw his banner and I thought it was men of Ruffec and Confolens coming south to fight for us . . . and it was Count Richard."

The Old Count sat up suddenly, pushing the dog off, and Yves, as if it was a reminder, went on more hurriedly.

"He went to Charroux and took that; a three days' siege; and then he went east again and took Saint Saviol – stormed it – there is nought left of it, but it smokes yet. . . . I was there two days ago."

He paused, because neither of the two Counts was listening. Vulgrin had leaned along the table and now they whispered together, while everyone else sat silent.

Then the Old Count looked up.

"Where did he go after?" he snapped.

Yves shook his head.

"I followed no more then," he said. "I rode for Angoulême."

The Count shrugged impatiently, but Vulgrin was kinder.

"That is news to us, that he was at Saint Saviol. It is good service to us, Yves," he said.

The Old Count looked up again suddenly, peering at Yves with his eyes half shut.

"You followed the Count from Sauzé?" he said.

Yves shook his head.

"I saw him down in the valley," he said, harking back to the same words he had used before, as if he could only tell his tale one way. "I saw his banner . . . and then I went on to Rifaucon." His voice shook so that he paused a moment, and the Count spoke for him.

"And found he had it. We know it." Thus, shortly and indifferently, did he state that thing before which Yves' mind stood stunned.

Yves looked at him heavily.

"Aye," he said, "he hath Rifaucon." His voice dragged on the words. "It is half a ruin. . . . I did not know. . . . I found it. . . . It is half a ruin."

The Old Count said nothing, but dropped his eyes to the table edge,

12

and sat hunched and brooding in his chair. It was Vulgrin who gave what comfort he could.

"Rifaucon can be won again," he said. "But your father –?"

"He is dead," said Yves almost casually. "One of the serfs told me ... in the woods next morning. . . . Count Richard hath given Rifaucon to Raymond of Scorbé Clairvaux, he said. . . . He saw my father die. . . ."

"Alas!" Vulgrin murmured. "God rest his soul." He bent his head and said a prayer under his breath, then crossed himself and began to question Yves more closely as to what he knew of Count Richard's doings.

They let him go at last. He reached the door and turned for the courtesy due from esquire to lord, but though he was the Old Count's esquire, it was Vulgrin who acknowledged the obeisance; Count Guilhem had crooked his finger to an old sergeant of his who stood behind his chair, and now was whispering him behind his hand. Yves lifted the curtain and passed out.

As he came into the open courtyard he found to his surprise that it was still light, with a colourless sky veiled by one unbroken stretch of cloud. His brain was so bemused that he had to stop to wonder why it was strange to him – the faint cold light, and the silence. Then he remembered the portentous wind which had died without any storm fulfilling its threat.

As he stood there, someone came up behind him and touched him on the arm. It was Count Guilhem's old sergeant, and over his arms were draped a long scarlet cloak, and something green, while a sleeve of reddish brown trailed almost to the ground from among the other clothes.

"Here," he said, holding out the things towards Yves. "Here, take, keep! These from the Lord Count," and he tumbled them into Yves' arms.

"Why ... what ... what are these?" said Yves.

"Can ye not see? . . . Fine gear forsooth . . . too fine, say I, but then . . . they're none of mine. They are gear for you to wear," and the old fellow sniggered. He was privileged because so much in Count Guilhem's confidence.

13

"But," persisted Yves, holding the clothes still in his outstretched hands, neither accepting nor rejecting the gift. "But why . . . Ye say the Count . . . the Old Count? But wherefore?"

The old man leaned forward and pointed his words by tapping with his finger on Yves' wrist.

"By cause he does not like to see his esquires go about as scarecrows," he said, and with that, and a cackle of laughter, he turned away and left Yves standing.

The esquires of the Old Count and of his sons lived, when they were neither on duty, nor eating, nor otherwise occupied, in a room on the second floor of a tower opposite the door of the big Hall. Thither Yves climbed slowly, with his arms full of the ungracious gift of the Old Count, and as he climbed a confused noise of voices came down to him and a glow of light, which, with the noise, grew clearer as he ascended. The door of the tower room was, of course, open; it was always open because no one took the trouble to shut it after him though each sometimes cursed his fellows for the same carelessness.

Just below the door Yves halted, because the clamour inside was so great that he was unwilling to plunge into it, tired as he was. As he leaned against the rough stone wall, fragments of talk, like foam upon the waves of the noisy sea of talk and laughter, came floating out to him.

First it was Simon's loud, deep voice:

". . . And so I had him down, and by Saint Christopher, if. . . ." The rest was lost.

"Nay, nay! Give it back to me, ye thieving jackdaw!" That was young Robert the Boaster, so called not for any habit of boasting but on the strength of one tale; but once is sometimes enough for a nickname.

Then Yves heard Folquet's high voice with its distinctive lisp:

"Heh! Pons of Jarnac! This knife is yours. 'Ware heads! . . . Catch!" Something flew across the doorway and fell with a clatter.

Yves moved at last, making up his mind to go in. As he climbed the few remaining steps he was wondering in a vague way who Pons of Jarnac was. The name was new, and yet it was only a few days since he had slipped away from the other esquires on the banks of the little river Boutonne; and yet again, what other things had happened since that time!

As Yves pushed into the room there was a sudden, short silence, in which the voice of Robert, who stood with his back to the door, seemed ridiculously loud.

"Oh! your hawk is but a . . ." His voice was drowned in a renewed babel, everyone crying Yves' name first, and then questions, one after another without a pause for a reply. Yves did not attempt to speak, but went slowly over to his pallet bed, flung his burden down and then himself sat down as stiffly and carefully as an old man. Everyone in the room crowded round him, still hurling questions over each other's shoulders, but gradually the noise died down.

"But where *hast* thou been?" Simon made himself heard after many commands for silence.

Yves looked up into the big heavy face, with its pleasant blue eyes, as though he had never seen it before.

"Rifaucon," he said and bent to unclasp his shoes.

"Then –" shouted Robert the Boaster, before Simon had time to stop him, "then Count Richard hath not taken it!"

Yves did not look up, but spoke to the floor as if he were ashamed of the words and would hide them:

"Aye – he hath taken it," he said, and there was silence for a moment before he spoke again:

"He hath taken Charroux and Saint Saviol too," he said. "That is all I know, so let me be," and he lapsed into an obstinate silence, from which he could not be shaken. After a few efforts they left him to himself and began to discuss the news he brought, meagre though they found it. Only Simon stood watching him with a puzzled frown on his face. Finally, since Yves took no notice of him, he sat down on the pallet alongside. Yves looked up and away again.

"See here," said Simon quietly. "It is time for us to begin the vigil, but what will ye do? Ye are too forwearied to watch." Yves had been busy taking off his sword-belt; it took him a long time, for his fingers seemed clumsy, but now he laid the sword down with the belt twisted round it.

"Vigil?" he said stupidly. "What vigil?"

Simon stared.

"Why, to-morrow is Pentecost," he said. "Have ye forgot? Ye should do vigil to-night with me and Jehan and Folquet and Robert the Nutcracker. If ye do not the Old Count cannot make you knight this Feast; and . . . well . . . perhaps. . . . But what will ye do?"

Yves stood up and began to pull off his tunic.

"There's naught to do," he said.

"But," protested Simon, "he may not make knights again for long enough."

"I cannot help," said Yves heavily. "'Tis no matter neither. Get off my bed."

Simon gave him up with a shrug.

Gradually the room grew quiet. The four eldest esquires had gone off to the chapel, carrying hauberk, lance, shield, spear, helm, and sword, for their night's vigil. The younger lads went one by one to bed, but long before they had ceased talking, Yves was fathoms deep in an ocean of sleep. He lay with his knees drawn up and the gay cloak pulled close about his shoulders, which were broad almost out of proportion to his short stature. His cheeks were sallow, and the dead, lustreless black of his hair fell straight and thick over his brow, like a dark feather, throwing a shade that seemed almost a frown. Even in sleep his hand was clenched upon the folds of the cloak and his mouth set in a hard line, that told, with the short, high-bridged nose, of a stubborn strength and pride. Yet it was not the face of a plain fighting man, nor of one who could win to an easy happiness. There was a kind of austerity behind the hardness; and tempering, or contradicting that, a hint of some delicacy or gentleness which was not merely due to the mystery of sleep.

II

Urbs in portu satis tuto
De longinquo te saluto;
Te saluto, te suspiro,
To affecto, te requiro.
                    LONGFELLOW.

THIRTEEN years before, Yves had come to Angoulême, a little lad, just old enough to be a page, riding beside his father, very curious and excited and a little afraid. It was one of the privileges of Rifaucon, small border fief though it was, that its heirs should be trained to arms and courtesy in no less a household than that of the Count of Angoulême, from whom each should, in due time, hold the land.

So, on the feast of Saint Martial in the year 1163, Elie of Rifaucon had ridden into Angoulême with five mounted men-at-arms, a sumpter horse laden with yellow cheeses – part of the service which he owed to the Count for Rifaucon – and his only child, Yves.

When Yves looked back to that far-off day that had seemed so important and unforgettable in anticipation, but which now was misted over in his memory and contracted by the perspective of time into a mere moment, he could remember clearly only three things, and two of these were trifles.

The first was the dismounting at the gate. He was riding for the first time on a real tall horse, instead of the pony which he used at home, and when the time came to dismount, his heart was making a noise in his chest for fear he should slip or do anything foolish to disgrace Rifaucon before the lounging, staring servants and men-at-arms, who, he thought, were all watching to see if he had learnt to dismount properly. He managed it creditably, except that he bumped his nose on the saddle as he slid down, but that could not have been noticed.

The next memory was still more trifling, for it was only that of a huge pastry built up in the shape of a castle, carried across an angle of the courtyard by a panting cook; it was so heavy that the man went

17

with short heavy steps, almost running. Yves had never seen such a pastry before.

Last of all, he remembered how angry his father had been when he said good-bye to Yves some time that afternoon. He came out from the Count's room with his face as red as the setting sun, gnawing his black moustache and muttering words unpleasant to hear. In his hand he carried two small squares of parchment, one new and creamy-white with a beautiful green seal, the other as yellow as the cheeses he had brought to Angoulême, and dangling from it by faded silk cords a jagged, irregular piece of yellow wax.

In spite of his anger he put the two away very carefully in a little goat-skin bag he carried round his neck, but when he had finished, and tucked it away inside his tunic, he turned to Yves, and, regardless of the dozen or so of knights, men-at-arms, and servants who stood about, regardless of anyone who might pass, or of anyone who might be listening at the windows, he said his say in a voice that filled the courtyard.

"Eh! son," he cried, dropping his big hand on Yves' shoulder, "this Count of ours, God rot him! he is a thief! a rank thief! I would I had the hanging of him. . . . He would have none of the old charter because forsooth the seal is broke, and I must needs buy a new one . . . and at his price too!"

He looked round, not as though he was afraid of being overheard, but with a challenging stare that sought contradiction:

"And the feet and the chair on the old seal are clear to see . . . and hath he not known me, and his father my father . . . ? Blood of God!" he growled, and then something else which Yves could not hear. Then at last:

"Farewell, son Yves! Serve this . . . this jackdaw Count as well as ye may. Yea, and listen! He would have set you as esquire to some other, but I told him the law and the custom of it, and there were those there that said it was so. . . . Ugh! . . . this Count Guilhem . . . !"

He had broken off there, kissed Yves angrily and hastily on both cheeks, thrown himself on his big chestnut horse, and ridden away, turning only to wave his hand as he passed through the gate. After him went all the Rifaucon men, and they too had turned and waved their hands to Yves, and he had answered, but had not dared to stir a foot lest he should run after them and beg to go home.

Home-sickness is the same all the world over and all time through, but with Yves it was especially painful, for even in those days, when he was quite a small boy, Rifaucon was a passion with him. The red falcon rocks over against the shining curve of the river; the woods sloping down to a sandy edge where there were conies; the castle itself, built of the same ruddy stone as the cliffs opposite; the mill with the swift musical water running by; every stone, every inch of land was almost painfully dear to him. It was not that, when he grew old enough to understand, he thought it more beautiful than any other place; but it was different, it was his, it was the first, and so the test and measure of all other places. Rifaucon was the norm; everything else was to be judged by that standard.

As he grew, his love for what was his own grew with him, and he never felt that Rifaucon was only a parcel of land; woods, river, rocks, and castle. It was far more. It possessed him as much as he possessed it, and because he was one of those who must always make an abstraction of what they love, it meant to him his place in the world, his work, and his honour among men.

It made no difference to this love that he seldom saw Rifaucon, and was never there for long together once he came to Angoulême. Indeed it was his affection that kept him away (apart from the fact that Count Guilhem also had a say in the matter), for as Yves grew up a jealousy also grew between him and his father. Yves always counted Rifaucon his. Elie thought the same for himself. Besides this, though Elie would not marry again after Yves' mother died, he kept a woman from the village, a mere churl's daughter, at the castle. She was coarse and loud-voiced, but he tricked her out in cloaks of fine blue cloth, and scarlet gowns, and gold rings and brooches. Yves hated the thought of her at Rifaucon, and could not bear to see her there, so he stayed away. In fact, for four years he had not been once at home, and that he went at last was the result of what is called chance. Yet chance is nothing but the inter-action of two forces – the innumerable actions of men, and the infinite adapted variations of God's plan, by which variations we may suppose He corrects the damage done to His purpose by ignorant and wilful men, thus uncontrollably disposing all things towards their designed and perfect end.

This, then, is how it came about that Yves went to Rifaucon in the month of May, 1176.

At the beginning of the month Count Guilhem had left Angoulême with his household for the usual summer progress through his lands. He himself had taken the northern direction, Vulgrin, the Young Count, with his wife and his household, had gone towards the western parts of the Angoumois, while the two younger sons, Guilhem and Adhemar, had gone south.

Each year, when the summer came, the Count was accustomed to set off on this regular progress from castle to castle, for he had dues of all sorts – corn, wine, pigs, beer, cattle – which he must seek for himself, and eat in this manor or that; and in addition there was always the necessity of visiting the great castles of the Angoumois, those strong places set along the rivers and astride of the great roads, and guarding the entrances to the County.

This year, however, there was something else to give a reason and a spice of excitement to the ordinary round. Everyone knew that before very long there was to be war – war against Richard Count of Poitou, of whom Guilhem held his land; that same Richard whom we know as Cœur-de-Lion, the second son of Henry II of England, himself to be king though no one yet dreamt it, and the great Crusader.

Rumour, then, was very busy in this month of May, though not very much of it was true. Everyone had known, since a short time after Christmas, that there was a league of some sort between Count Adhemar of Limoges, a faithful enemy of Richard of Poitou, and the two Counts of Angoulême. Messengers from the north, with the badge of the Lusignans on their coats, came and went so frequently that any man might guess that, whatever was afoot, they were in it too. But, though everyone, down to the lads in the stables, had his own opinion as to what the Count's plans were, only a very few knew the truth from the mouth of Guilhem himself, or from Vulgrin, and that the day assigned was the first Sunday after Pentecost. Not even Guilhem and Vulgrin knew that Count Richard had also set a day, and that his day fell a fortnight before Pentecost.

When the Old Count set out on his progress, his household hummed with excitement. "Now," they said, "we shall see something." Some noticed that there were more men-at-arms attached to the household in this progress than was usual. As a matter of course every knight and esquire carried his armour with him, strapped behind him to the saddle, while pages and sergeants followed with the spears and the great war-horses, but behind all these came fully as many armed horsemen, while ahead was another company, and riding at large about the path of the whole cavalcade, a score or more of scouts.

At every castle where the Count stopped there was slaughtering of oxen, and sheep, and fowls; cooks laboured almost to death over their huge fires; casks were opened, straw and sweet-smelling rushes were strewn. There was shouting and laughter in the courtyards and in the streets of the town, as the men-at-arms amused themselves; there was laughter and singing too in the great Hall among the squires and knights; dancing with such ladies as the castle afforded; talk with this or that one in the deep window-embrasures; pleasant confusion every-where, excitement, interest, variety.

And always in a room apart, the Old Count and the Young would sit closeted with the lord or castellan, and what they spoke of would gradually and mysteriously filter through to the less important folk. The Counts of Angoulême were calling up their host, and this man must serve with ten, this with fifteen, and another perhaps with forty knights or men-at-arms behind his banner.

It was not, of course, by any means the first time that Yves had followed Count Guilhem on his progresses, but for him, as for every-one else, the rumour of war made this different from the rest, and in addition he had a personal reason for an interest and enjoyment greater than ordinary. Only three weeks more, and on the 23rd of May, that is on the Feast of Pentecost, he was to be made knight. It was the know-ledge of this which, more than anything else, made each day seem the opening lines of a story of chivalry, since on the threshold of knight-hood anything might be expected to happen. If nothing happened (and each day was perfectly uneventful) at least every sunset brought nearer that wonderful day of wind and flame from heaven, which was to see Yves enter, by the gate of knighthood, into the world of men.

At Aulnay, as Yves knelt before him with a basin of brass filled with water for the washing of hands before meat, the Old Count, looking sourly down at his esquire, said, as if he grudged the words:

"I shall pass by thy Rifaucon when we go from Chef-Boutonne."

Yves looked up quickly, and then down again at the water, shaken into rings by the drops from the Count's fingers.

"Well?" said the Count.

Yves did not raise his eyes again.

"My lord will be welcome. Shall I ride on and bid my father prepare?"

The Old Count gave one of his short laughs.

"Oh no!" he said. "I had liefer come unforeseen."

Yves remembered the churl's wench, and a slow flush came up to his face, for he thought that the Old Count knew of her, and was mocking him. He did not love Count Guilhem, and it was little wonder, for since the day he had come to Angoulême and heard his father rage against the Count, he had listened to many tales of the same kind. Of all the numerous ways in which Guilhem extracted money from his vassals there were few which were not crooked, at least in the judgment of the victim. But in addition to all this the Old Count's gibing tongue, his uncanny knowledge of other folks' business, and his exasperating use of that knowledge, made any liking for him difficult. Yves, in common with all the other esquires, would, at one time or another, rage against him for some unforgivable mockery directed against himself, or some story of trickery which had got about, though they sometimes admitted that, on the whole, he was neither unjust, nor entirely unkind, to themselves.

The news that the Count was to pass by, and therefore to lodge in Rifaucon, raised Yves to a dizzy height, since, whatever his faults might be, Guilhem was his lord, whom to entertain was to receive honour. All heights, however, have their fears, and Yves thought of the woman there, and when he did so it spoiled the anticipation. Still, he said to himself, his father might have wearied of her, and at least he was going home, and a week afterwards he would be made knight. The visit fell in perfectly with that great fact, as though it were part of a wonderful plan, or a romance of chivalry in which all events marched

22

orderly to a splendid end. When he was alone he tried to put his reckless happiness into rhyme as the troubadour poets did, and fit it to snatches of tunes that he had made. He was sure of knighthood now; this visit to Rifaucon, so wonderfully timed, seemed to give assurance of all he hoped, and to set a seal of divine approval upon it. He need no longer remember that thing in his mind which was not even a fear, only an intermittent uneasiness. It was gone – it had never been. He was going to Rifaucon, would perhaps do homage after his father for the lands that were to be his, and then, a week after, he would be made knight; all his thoughts came back to that. So he planned and dreamed, silent among the other esquires.

They left Aulnay, and riding eastward, plunged soon into the wet and shadowed woods, where the light seemed to be turning back to darkness. In a couple of hours, they would reach the banks of the little Boutonne, running swiftly in its shallow, pebbled channel, and there they would cross it, and turn north into the open country. From the ford it was a matter of a day and a half of easy riding to Rifaucon.

As they rode through the woods Yves strained his ears to hear, above the trampling of the horses in the soft soil of the track, above the creaking of leather, the jingle of bits, the voices of men talking and calling to one another, above the soft, steady mutter of the rain on the young leaves, the sound of running water which would tell him that they were near to the ford. Once across the river his face would be set for Rifaucon.

Absorbed as he was in listening, he hardly spoke a word all morning to Simon, the eldest of Count Guilhem's esquires, by whom he rode; and Simon, finding that he would not even answer questions, twisted himself in his saddle, and rode thus with his head turned over his shoulder, talking to Jehan and Folquet, who were behind. Yves frowned at the sound of their voices, for every unnecessary noise, even if it were only the scream of a jay in the woods, made his listening more difficult, and when a mounted man-at-arms came galloping up from behind, shouting as he came, all along the column of march, for room to pass by in the narrow track, Yves was angry indeed. Even when the noisy fellow had passed, and the crowding and confusion were over, conversation began up and down the line, as everybody began to discuss what had been his business. Yves pushed his horse as near as he could to the edge of the track and turned his face to the trees, but the noise defeated him – he could hear nothing, although he knew that they must be near the river now. It was a small and childish thing to be put out by so little, and Yves knew it, but the knowledge only increased his ill-temper. When at last he did hear the sound of the river, and turned, smiling and ready to talk, he found that the others had caught his ill-humour, and pointedly excluded him from their conversation; indeed Simon dropped back half the length of his horse and left Yves riding almost alone.

They came to the edge of the trees, and to the green banks of the shallow river where the road crossed it from south to north but when Yves looked at the ford he could not believe what he saw.

Instead of being crowded with men and horses, as it should have been if the head of the column had led the way across it towards Rifaucon, it lay empty and shining in the pale sun that now came reluctantly from behind the shredding clouds. The Count could not have passed over already, yet where was his banner? Yves looked to the right where the trees ran back from the river, and saw it dip and sway along the road that led south, and after it trailed the long, bright procession of armed men.

"Lo!" cried Folquet behind him. "Were we not going north, and now –"

Yves turned.

"Yea," he said. "He told me to Rifaucon. That's not the way." He was troubled and angry but he got no sympathy.

Simon laughed.

"I wager he did it for a jape against you!" he said, and seemed to find it a good one."

Yves only answered by a scowl, and turning his horse towards the river he muttered something about "giving the beast a drink." He expected no answer and got none. Simon and Jehan looked at each other in silence and shrugged their shoulders; Folquet took no notice whatever, and they all rode on without a glance behind.

The noise of the cavalcade died away as though it had either sunk into the wet earth, or been drawn up by the thirsty sun as the clouds were being drawn up, reduced to a film, and at last to nothing at all. Yves, sitting still in the saddle while his horse drank, listened to the failing sounds and then to the deep silence; he remained there even after he had pulled the beast's head up from the water, so entirely motionless that a heron, sweeping down in fine circling flight, dropped to earth and settled on the bank close by him.

Meanwhile Count Guilhem was pressing forward for Angoulême. There was every reason for speed, since he had just had word that Count Richard had been beforehand with him, and was no more than a few hours' march away. The only thing to be done was to hurry back to Angoulême, there to complete the preparations which Richard had interrupted, and make fresh plans in place of those which Richard had spoiled.

As for the man who had brought the news from Aulnay, and whose noisy passage had so much annoyed Yves, he rode home slowly and cautiously by another way through the woods. Yves and the heron were undisturbed.

III

Ah! is Thy love indeed
A weed, albeit an amaranthine weed,
Suffering no flowers except its own to mount?
Ah! must –
Designer infinite! –
Ah! must Thou char the wood ere Thou canst limn with it?
FRANCIS THOMPSON.

A MAN on foot, wearing the dark gown of the monks of Saint Benedict, and swinging a long, stout staff with which from time to time he flicked at the loose stones in the track, came out from the trees and walked rapidly down to the river. He was a small man with a thin, quiet face, insignificant enough at the first glance, although his quick movements hinted that he was one who would do everything vehemently. He came on with his head bent and a little frown between his brows, as men will who live mostly in their own thoughts, and yet he stepped with the spring and neatness of some small, swift animal.

Yves, sitting hunched in his saddle with his eyes on the water, his face darkened by a frown, and his mouth set hard, took no notice of the interruption, but the horse threw up its head and moved restlessly.

The monk raised his eyes at the sound, and they rested on Yves with the fierce probing stare of the hawk. They were strange eyes for that quiet, rather worn face; sandy-brown flecked with green and very much alive, with quick glances that would harden now and then into a concentrated stare. At once hot and keen, as though they had in them something both of flame and steel, they seemed to shine in his face, and no one who saw them could ever again call him insignificant.

He passed Yves by, and took to the water without pause or hesitation, his skirts gathered in one hand, his staff prodding the river-bed before him for a safe crossing. Yves roused himself to watch him, splashing on knee deep in the water, then, urged by the common courtesy of wayfarers, he shouted:

"The ford is good right across, Father. It goes no deeper. It is paved."

26

The monk stopped with his skirts bunched in his hand, and the quick water running past his knees.

"I thank you, son," he shouted, and waved his staff. Then he turned and splashed on to the other bank.

Yves watched him out of sight, and with a sigh went back to the consideration of his own problem. Rifaucon was near; it would be easy to go there after all, but if he went, asking no leave and slipping off without a word, the Old Count would be very wroth. Yves, however, was angry too, for he considered that the Count had merely mocked him, so he set his teeth and his face took on an expression of mulish obstinacy. He straightened himself in the saddle, tightening the grip of his knees, and the horse lifted its head, and began, slowly and idly, to cross the river.

Half a mile further on he overtook the monk, and, since he had put care behind him and was bound for Rifaucon, he turned in the saddle as he passed, and smiled. The monk's quick eyes took in the change that the smile made in Yves' face; as sudden sunshine on dark water, it was almost like a half-shy caress. He was still thinking of the young man as of one seen for a moment and gone for ever, when he came to the top of the hill, and there, in the middle of the road, saw the rider bent over his horse's off hind foot. When Yves raised his eyes he was not smiling.

The monk stopped.

"A shoe dropped?" he said, though it was self-evident, since Yves held it in his hand.

"Yes," Yves growled, and let the animal's foot fall.

"Did he wrench it off? Let me see," said the monk, and bent down.

"I do not know," said Yves, and he tossed the shoe away and dusted his hands together. "I forgot to look at his shoes this morning," he added. He had been too busy thinking of Rifaucon and knighthood that morning to trouble with such matters.

The monk shook his head and straightened himself, running his hand in an understanding way down the smooth, shining flank of the horse.

Yves became a little less surly.

"Well," he said, "I must needs tramp it till I find a smith," and slipping the bridle over his arm he fell into step along side the monk.

They walked steadily, speaking little. The monk said he was for Eymoutiers in the Limousin, and Yves remembered to have heard of a great abbey there. In return he said he was bound for Rifaucon, but no more, since he was in no talking humour. Presently the monk tucked his staff under his arm and fell to his beads, so that Yves was practically alone again, walking as he did beside a mere body, the mind and spirit of which had departed to an infinite distance.

At last the monk dropped the beads with a pleasant clicking noise to their place at his girdle, and began to talk.

He had travelled from La Rochelle, he told Yves, having come thither in a ship from Spain. He chuckled to himself as he spoke.

"Oh, that ship! a sorry sick monk was I!" he said.

"Spain!" said Yves, suddenly interested. "What did you make there? Was it pilgrimage?"

The monk shook his head, smiling again his quick fleeting smile.

"Nay, I was not searching after the holy saints but after heathen Jews," he said.

"Jews!" said Yves, and spat in disgust, as a good Christian should. "Those evil dogs! . . . but why?"

The monk laughed outright.

"Silly lad!" he said, and Yves could not resent it. "They are not all bad. . . . Alas! poor souls! But good or bad they know their Hebrew tongue, and there are many learned doctors among them in Spain."

"Then," said Yves amazed, "ye know the Hebrew?"

"Aye. Needs must a man to understand Scripture. Greek got I in Paris. Hebrew in Spain."

"Holy Mother of God!" murmured Yves, and fell silent again, looking sidelong at the monk from time to time as at someone marvellous.

Soon the monk was talking again, about his own life; but merrily, not boastfully. He was a serf's son, and thought no shame to tell Yves of his father, that slow, honest man, and the four brothers that had their wives and youngsters and drove the eight-ox ploughs and laboured at their lord's harvest. With just the same candour he told Yves that he was on the way now to Eymoutiers, where he had been bred up, to be

28

made abbot – he, a serf's son, tramping afoot across France, and learned in Hebrew, Latin, Greek.

At the hottest hour of the afternoon they came to a small village set in a crinkled green cup between five low hills, and there they found the smith at his forge. Yves would have said good-bye to the monk at the door of the shed, but he would not have it. He leaned against the door-post while Yves gave the horse over to the smith, peering into the half-darkness, and seeming to see everything. Gradually, as the work went on, he was drawn further in; first he moved to the wall just inside the door, then he went and stood by the fire, finally, with a laugh, he rolled up his wide sleeves, and putting the smith's man aside, took his place. The smith, who never spoke if a grunt would serve, looked hard at him, and smiled, half unwillingly. They worked in silence, as though the "clink clang clink clink clang" of the hammers and the roaring breath of the fire were enough expression for the restless heart of man.

When they had finished, the smith laid his hammer down carefully, rubbed his hands together, and said, as though he had long meditated the words:

"Y're a good smith."

The monk laughed.

"Good enough," he said, and seemed pleased. "I was the farrier at my monastery."

The smith's unusual loquacity was not yet exhausted.

"Where are ye for?" he said, and to include Yves in the question he tipped his head slightly in his direction.

"I for Limoges; this young lord for Rifaucon," replied the monk.

It seemed to satisfy the smith. He nodded, held out his hand for payment and gave back half of it without another word.

They had not gone a dozen paces from the forge when they heard his voice.

"Hi!" he called, and then, as they did not turn, unwillingly he called again. "Hi! Father!"

He came after them, swinging upon bandy legs, grimed and shaggy and swart, with a skin as tough as his leather apron; a strange sight in the sunshine, as some beast might be, which, made to hunt in the dark, had left its den in the daytime. He seized the monk by the arm.

29

"Take the steep path," and he sheered the air with his right hand, ". . . beyond the stream by a piece of rock. . . . A runnel of water down it. The path goes straight," he jerked his head towards the hill they faced. "Then," his right hand swept round again, "by a big clump of gorse. He'll get to Rifaucon to-night that way. Saves yon valley. Shorter for you too." He had said as much as he would and as little as he could, and, with a crab-like gesture of his hands, he turned and left them.

On the brow of the hill they stopped, with one accord, to take breath and look back over the village. Only the last houses could be seen, and one of the three great fields, striped with lighter and darker green like a breadth of rayed cloth where the grass balks ran between the villagers' strips of land.

Turning, they looked down the side of the hill to the valley road, which, but for the smith, they would have taken, and both gave an exclamation. With the monk it was of mere surprise, but with Yves of understanding and satisfaction.

Far down the valley, between the pale green nut bushes, came a clump of horsemen, riding very close. Behind them was a short space of road, white in the sunshine, and then again another block of men, helmets and spear-points flashing, the coloured cloaks of the knights like so many flowers in a garden. Before them went a drooping banner, dark red with perhaps a device in gold, but it was too far off to be clearly seen.

Yves smote his hands together so that his horse, startled, threw up its head and danced aside, jingling bridle and bit, and banging the helmet against the saddle bow.

"Ha! look!" he cried triumphantly. "There go the men of Angoulême that the Count hath called up against Richard of Poitou. Ha! the good company!" He laughed, and then was suddenly silent.

"This is secret," he said and stared hard at the monk, who nodded.

"No fear. I am not Count Richard's man," he said.

They turned to continue their way, but Yves dropped behind for a minute, and drawing his sword, raised it to the salute. Then he hurried after the monk.

"They are all gone by," he said as he fell into step beside him.

30

Down below in the valley, hidden now from the two above by the gentle contour of the hill, another company passed between the hazel bushes, and yet another, and another. But these were not companies of knights. There was no gay colour here, only the monotony of leather and harsh steel, for these were the dreaded, hated Routiers, the mercenary soldiers, cursed by the Church at every council, and still swarming over the whole of France in the pay of the great lords. Like a cloud of foul, stinging insects they followed the gay banner – *gules* a lion rampant *or* – the banner of Count Richard of Poitou.

. . . . .

When they had crossed the ridge, and the path began to drop steeply down to the valley beyond, the monk stopped and looked about him.

"I grow hungry," he said. "It's past noon, and too hot to go further empty. Look!" he pointed along the side of the hill to a little clump of pines. "There is shade."

Yves shook his head, though he was very hungry.

"I have nought," he said, "I must get me on to the next village."

"Nay, nay," protested the monk. "Here's enough for both – bread and cheese and a little wine – let's eat together merrily. Lonely eating is as ill as fasting. Come now, there's no nay!"

He smiled at Yves as he spoke, and Yves smiled back, and they turned off towards the trees, better acquainted by that slight thing. Over the bread and cheese and wine they grew friendlier still, and more at ease. The monk had a quick, merry tongue, and before long he had lured out Yves' lurking wit; they laughed together, Yves lying on his face, chin in hands, staring over the warm, green country, the monk leaning back against the trunk of a pine tree.

Presently, during a pause, Yves, without knowing what he did, began to whistle a tune between his teeth, and then to sing the words softly to himself. The monk turned to him quickly:

"Ye know it? Sing! Sing!" he said. "That part where Roland first blows the horn:

> 'Roland ad mis l'olifant a sa buche,
> Empeint le bien. . . .' "

He sang the words in a small high voice, and then broke off and waited for Yves to begin.

Yves rolled over on his side and sat up, laughing softly, as though he were glad at something, and throwing back his head, began to sing.

The monk, watching his eyes kindle and his face glow, forgot the music for a few minutes; then the swing and lift of the chanted lines caught him, and he gave himself up to them, and to the voice which had in it something of the compelling, sombre resonance of a great bell, or of the hollow mountain echoes of the pass of Roncesvalles.

Yves sang on, verse after verse of the tramping music of the song of Roland, beating time for himself with one hand while the other lay clenched on his knee. When he stopped suddenly it was not because he knew no more.

"Ha!" he cried softly. "Very soon I shall be a knight!" and he stared straight in front of him with a little smile.

"If God wills," murmured the monk.

The impulse to avert disaster by some such deprecation after a too-confident forecast of good, is as old as humanity, and this, strengthened by his own deep-seated habit of mind, was the only motive behind the monk's words. Therefore their effect on Yves astonished him. If in the midst of a feast a sudden arrow should strike into the table and there stand quivering, the effect on the guests might be much the same.

The glow faded from Yves' face, leaving it bleak, and he turned slowly and rigidly, like a man who fears what he may see.

"What do you mean?" he cried, and his voice was sharp, as though the monk had laid bare some old, secret misgiving. Then, leaving no time for the reply, he went on:

"Would He have every man a monk?"

The monk, still amazed at the effect of his words, answered only by another question:

"Son," he said, "why are you angry?"

Yves would not look at him.

"You speak as if. . . . Is not knighthood an high and holy thing? I have my land . . . and must I. . . ." His voice, loud and angry at first, trailed gradually away into silence, and his head dropped on his chest. The monk had to lean forward to catch the next words:

32

"I am afraid. . . . What does He want of us . . . of me? . . . How much?"

"Shall I answer?" said the monk, very low, but his voice had the shaken sound of a thrilled bow-string.

"Yea," said Yves. He raised his head and they faced one another like two swordsmen who probe each other's eyes for the lurking intention of the next attack.

The monk spoke:

"Thou sayest – 'How much?' and I say – 'All'!"

Their gaze remained locked, as though neither swordsman dare withdraw, but Yves muttered, hardly seeming to move his lips:

"He would have me a monk?"

The monk shook his head ever so slightly.

"That is not enough. That would not content Him."

"Ah!" cried Yves. "Speak plain! Leave these dark words!"

The monk was silent a moment, and his eyes seemed to try to pierce through Yves' eyes to the soul behind.

"It's this contents Him," he said at last, "it's you, you yourself He must have . . . without a will except to do His will . . . bound hand and foot for Him to unloose."

As he watched he saw Yves' face change. The mouth set hard, and the eyes narrowed, like a man who faces, but will not flinch from a blow. Then he knew he had been right when he counted on a quality he had divined in Yves – an austerity that would shrink from nothing and be satisfied with nothing but the most naked and harsh truth.

The tension relaxed, and each turned away. Yves stared again across the sweet valley, but his eyes were blind to everything there, as he thought of the choice which the monk had put before him. It was not a choice between the knight's sword and the monk's cowl but something greater.

Without looking round again he said:

"And if I will not?"

The monk stirred and sighed before he answered:

"He is a Hunter which never tires," he said.

.   .   .   .   .   .

When they took the road again the monk began to talk resolutely, in spite of Yves' heavy silence, and gradually Yves forgot to think of those things which man is too weak always to contemplate, and spoke, freely enough, of life in Angoulême, of hawking, of next year's harvest, and such cheerful, simple matters. But when they struck the road leading eastward to Charroux and Civray the silence that preludes a parting fell upon them, for, not half a mile further on now, Yves would turn aside to gain the valley of the clear little river Pérouse, and so, through miles of woodland, to Rifaucon.

Already the trees crowded close on the road, and through their branches the sun, westering now, splintered his rays into millions of golden shivers, and the birds began to tune their voices in the taller trees. Yves and the monk were shut, as it were, into a long, cool room roofed with blue and tapestried with green, for where the road turned to the right the trees formed a wall across it, hiding everything beyond.

They came to the bend of the road, and there saw something which pulled them up short. Just here the trees ran back a little, leaving a small patch of fine turf, and in the midst stood a roadside Calvary, black cross and pallid figure clear against the soft green of the trees behind. But it was not this which made the two halt.

Against the feet of that figure, leaning back at his ease, lounged a man, an untidy fellow in a leather coat very worn and shiny, with a mustard-coloured hood pushed back from his tousled hair – a Routier soldier, to judge from his looks. His very pose was a mockery of the image, but that was not all. On the bowed head of the Christ he had set his steel cap, while from one of the nailed hands dangled a pack, from the other a sheathed sword.

Shame, as though he was disgraced even by seeing such a thing, held Yves motionless for a second; then he started forward, but the monk was quicker. Without a word or a cry he flung himself across the open space, and the Routier, although he was as quick as a cat, had only time to roll aside and scramble up, before the monk was on him. He dodged, trying to reach his sword, but the monk snatched the steel cap from the head of the figure, and hurled it full in his face. The pack followed, and before the Routier could recover himself, the sheathed sword came

34

down like a thresher's flail on his head and shoulders. He leapt aside, spitting curses, tried to run under the sword, and failed. At last he gave it up, and bending low, with both arms up to guard his head, he bolted for the trees.

The monk stopped, breathing hard through his nose, and waited till the swaying undergrowth was still. Then he turned, picked up the pack and steel cap, and pitched them after their owner. The sword followed, spinning clumsily. It crashed against a branch and fell.

There was no need of Yves. He and the monk stood awhile, listening to the Routier plunging about in the undergrowth as he collected his gear, but the man did not show himself again, and gradually swore himself out of hearing. When all was quiet the monk turned away and crossed the open space to the Crucifix. Yves saw him kneel down, saw his quick hands go out, and heard him sob.

He could not watch, and so drew back to the edge of the wood, and began to pace up and down, peering into the shade from time to time lest the Routier should have crept back unheard. But though his eyes were on the wood, and his hand ready on his sword, his thoughts were set on something far different.

He listened again in his mind, himself both judge and prisoner, to the monk's demand – "All!" and found him a terrible advocate.

When they came to the place where their roads parted Yves went down on his knees in the dust.

"Bless me, Father," he said.

The monk blessed him. "Benedicat te omnipotens Deus; Pater et Filius et Spiritus Sanctus. Amen." Then Yves rose, and the two faced one another again. For a moment they stood so, each striving to enforce his thoughts to speech, and each silent.

At last Yves gave a little, helpless gesture, and turned abruptly away. He caught at the bridle, struck the horse on the flank with his clenched fist, and leapt up as the beast started off. Once in the saddle he turned with a brief gesture of farewell, then gave the horse a spur.

As the beast plunged and broke into a stormy canter the monk took a quick step forward.

"Wait!" he cried. "Wait! His will may be to give you all your desire."

The words had come too late, for already the rider was out of earshot. The monk stood watching for a moment until horse and man vanished round a bend and dip in the road, and the dull sound of drumming hoofs ceased.

IV

Per me si va nella citta dolente
per me si va nell'eterno dolore;
per me si va tra la perduta gente.

. . . . . .

Queste parole di colore oscuro
vid 'io scritte al sommo d'una porta.
DANTE.

FOR a little while Yves rode blindly and fast, seeking only escape, though he did not rightly know from what he fled; but when he had gone a couple of miles he let his horse slow to a trot, and finally checked it to a walk. All about him lay the woods, in the perilous beauty of young green and low golden sunlight. The air, musical with the song of many birds, seemed itself to be green and golden, and he caught his breath, as his heart leapt at his throat, and because his voice was not like that of the birds he muttered to himself the songs he dared not sing.

He knew that he had wasted enough time already, but still he dallied, staring about him, while the sun sank lower and became fiercely golden, and all the western sky turned the colour of burnished brass. He came to a cross track running east and west, and pulled up to look down it, his back to the sun, and looking, could hardly believe his eyes. Every trunk and bough, the pale copper-coloured fallen leaves, the trampled track itself – all were dipped in a flame, and glowed, ruddy and fiery; and yet, as he looked back over his shoulder, the sun was gold and the sky like burnished brass. He looked, and wondered and rejoiced, lifted far above fear in a confident and unreasoning ecstasy. The terrible monk had broken down every door of his mind and soul, and now, as they stood open, Beauty marched in with banners and trumpets, and he shouted for joy in his heart, and cried to Beauty for help against Holiness, summoning God to aid against Himself.

As he lingered he remembered that he had been here once before, and remembered too how a hind, felling trees near by, had shown him a pool at the eastern end of this glade, where he had watered his horse, and how, as he had ridden back, Lord Thibaut of Saint Saviol – it was his land hereabout – had come sweeping down the ride with a merry company of huntsmen, dogs baying, horns blowing, all hot upon the scent of a great hart. He turned his horse, making the excuse to himself that the animal needed water, and rode slowly towards the pool. He reached the screen of trees that shut in the end of the glade, and bending his head to shield his eyes from the low, swinging branches, he came out suddenly upon the clearing, which at its further end widened out into good pasture land, where Lord Thibaut and his serfs grazed their kine, and where some strayed even now, not yet driven home for the milking. In the midst of the clearing lay the little pool, the hither end in shadow, the further transparently clear where the sun's rays lit it. But that was not all.

Yves reined in his horse and sat still, looking across the pool, and he smiled, for here again was beauty. Beyond the pool stood a little hawthorn tree, its trunk twisted like some carved pillar, its boughs laden with the creamy blossom which the sun now tinged to rose. Upon one of the topmost sprays a thrush was singing, its notes as liquid as the shining water, and below the tree stood a girl, her back turned towards him, her face lifted, her russet gown dyed crimson by the light, her hair a tide of molten gold that fell below her waist. He kept himself very still because the tree was lovely, the bird's song lovely, and the girl, listening as unconscious as a nymph and clothed in light, the loveliest thing there.

She must have thought that Yves' horse pushing its way through the trees was one of the cattle coming back to the herd, for it was several minutes before she turned regretfully, and with a sigh, away from the tree. That thrush would have made a pleasant addition to the pot, but she had no sling.

Then she saw Yves. For a moment she stood, ready to run, but he let the reins fall on the horse's neck, and it moved lazily on towards the water. She thought that she had nothing to fear, but there was no telling, so she started off for the trees, walking slowly, her staff trail-

38

ing behind her, nothing more than a bare-footed, round-faced peasant wench, never guessing that Yves had seen her glorified.

He watched her as she went, saw her cross the line of shade that lay clear and cool upon the grass, and saw her gown fade to a plain russet, her hair cool to a clean pale gold. It was as though something flaming had been quenched in water. He pulled up his horse's head, and rode off without a backward look, but he did not forget.

He had regained the track that led north, and was riding steadily, his mind divided between thoughts of Rifaucon and the passing glories of that high mood which seemed to fade with the sinking sun, when a wild, long-drawn scream sheared the silence. It came from the direction of the little pool, and he reined in his horse and sat, straining his ears in the silence for any other sound.

For a moment he heard nothing but the little trickling noises of the wood: the light stirring of the leaves, a woodpecker at work, the sound of a twig falling, and then, startling him though he listened for it, another scream, but this time cut off short. He did not wait for more. Swinging his horse round in the narrow track he thundered off the way he had come.

The curtain of trees at the end of the ride hid from him whatever was going on in the clearing. He pulled up cautiously, peering through the crowded leaves, then gave his horse the spur, and crouching low in his saddle as though he were at the joust, and shouting with the full strength of his deep lungs, he exploded into the clearing, unexpected, and with all the advantages of surprise.

He did not need much advantage, for there were only four ragged and wild-looking ruffians there. One of them held the girl, but with difficulty, for she was a big girl and strong: he had clapped a dirty hand over her mouth and she fought to wrench it away. The others, armed only with stout, heavy bludgeons, were rounding up the cattle, which, terrified, jostled together, stamping, backing, thrusting this way and that, with a confusion of tossing horns and wild eyes.

It was over in a very few minutes. Only one of the thieves attempted to fight, and on him alone Yves used the edge of his sword. For the others, the trampling horse, the sudden onslaught, and the flat of the broad heavy blade were enough. Two with broken crowns, one

39

unhurt, and the last, and staunchest, with a slashed shoulder, broke away into the shelter of the woods.

Yves turned his horse's head, and rode back to the girl, and as he came he was laughing. He did not guess that his laugh hurt her, nor could she have told him why it did, but she had seen him ride shouting across that little space of green, like Saint Michael, as strong and swift and terrible – it did not trouble her that he was a strange swarthy fellow for the Captain of God's Host – and now he laughed. What would the Princess Sabra have felt if Saint George had come back laughing after his fight with the dragon? The worshipper of a saint naturally expects that he should take himself seriously and live up to his high calling.

But she could not be angry. In a moment she was kissing his green leather shoe, clinging to the stirrup leather, and crying over both.

Yves shifted his sword to his left hand, and patted her back, as clumsy as any man must be when a woman cries, and he cannot, or will not, cure her by kissing.

"There! There! child," he jerked out. "There's no ill done. The kine are all safe. He hath not hurt thee." Her hair under his hand felt warm, as though it held something of the sun, and he took to stroking it.

After a gulp or two she was composed again, and began to thank him, but stumblingly, like a child.

"Pfiu!" He waved the thanks away and turned to sheath his sword. "'Tis nothing." He addressed the words to the hilt and the scabbard. "Lord Thibaut is a very good friend to my father. Besides, it's the business of all us lords to guard the serfs that feed us. Why else are we for?"

Even such simple philosophy as this was beyond her; besides, his words seemed to her a tissue of mistakes. She could not explain, nor even herself understand that it was not thanks she wished to give, but praise. However, she could set him right about Lord Thibaut.

"Lord, I'm not Lord Thibaut's serf," she said.

"No?" said Yves. "Then you'll belong to the Holy Sisters at Savigné?"

She shook her head.

"I'm Lord Elie's of Rifaucon," she said.

Yves stared.

"Nonsense!" he said almost angrily. "What do you mean?"

She lowered her eyes because he was angry.

"It's truth though," she protested. "He hath a-bought the manor from Lord Thibaut a week gone by."

Yves laughed.

"Saints!" he cried, and at the change in his voice she looked up. "Then am I at home before I looked for it, yea, and have saved mine own cattle."

It was her turn to stare, and so she did, with such wide eyes, and so hopelessly puzzled, that he laughed now at her.

"I am Yves of Rifaucon," he said. "Lord Elie is my father. That is all." Then he turned to the practical issue.

"Where is your village?"

"Yonder!" she answered, and pointed to the woods on the east.

"Hm!" he said, and rubbed his chin with one finger. "Those rievers went that way." He considered for a moment. "Drive the cattle on, child!" he said. "I will be your warranty through the wood."

She obeyed at once. Picking up her staff she called to the cattle, and they, docile once more, ordered themselves into a long procession, and moved off with their lounging, meditative gait. The girl, as much a creature of habit as they, took her usual place by the side of the leader, her hand on the animal's ridged back. At the end of the line came Yves, and as they entered the wood he drew his sword, and rode with his eyes searching the undergrowth. Every now and then he would catch a glimpse of the girl's face turned back to watch him, and once or twice he nodded reassuringly, not knowing that she needed no reassurance. Had the devil himself stood in the way she would have pushed past him without a qualm:

"There comes one behind!" she would have said.

The strange procession – the girl, the slow kine, and the mounted man – came at last to the further edge of the trees, and Yves looked down into a wide valley, that sank gently to a willow-marked river-bed, and rose as gently to a low ridge of hills opposite. He left the last cows to their own slow pace, and rode on at a trot, past the line of switching tails and gently nodding heads, though an air all fragrant with the promise of milk, to the head of the procession.

The girl must have heard him coming, but she did not look round till he drew up abreast of her. Even then she only glanced up at him quickly and away again, saying nothing.

"Whither now?" said Yves, looking down at the crown of her head.

She raised the staff and pointed up the valley to their left.

"How far?" said Yves.

"Nigh on a mile, lord."

"Hm.... I will ride along with you, and get me on to Rifaucon after."

"Ah! lord," she said softly. "But I shall be safe," and turning away from him entirely, she ran her hand down the side of the cow.

"You will," said Yves, "for I shall go with you.... Quite safe.... And the cattle," he added.

Presently he began to ask questions.

"What's your name child?"

"Madeleine, lord."

"And how old are you?"

"Fifteen, lord."

"And not married yet?"

"Nay, lord."

"And your father is a serf?"

"Yes, lord."

"And sisters and brothers?"

"None, lord."

"Child," said Yves solemnly, "look at me!" and when she obeyed: "Open your mouth," he ordered.

She opened it a little and shut it quickly.

"Yea. You have a tongue like other wenches," said Yves, and smiled at her.

That child's jest made her laugh, and Yves laughed too. After it she was at ease, and began to chatter a strange mixture of simplicity and woman's wisdom, of little doings in the village and the gossip of neighbours, and a great deal about the house of Grey Nuns at Savigné.

"Did he know that house? ... There was a garden ... she had seen it through a gate ... it was lovely."

He knew it. In fact the abbess was of his kin. She was his mother's

42

sister. The girl grew silent at that, awed by such a conjunction of heavenly bodies in her firmament.

Yves reached out, and gathered up a handful of her hair. He was ordinarily shy and tongue-tied before women, but this was no more than a child, and a serf's child at that. For him she was only part of the enchantment of the evening.

"You should have a troubadour to sing songs about your hair," he said, and he laughed and let it fall. "He should call you . . . call you. . . . I have it! Golden Mantled!" He mused a moment, looking down at her, still faintly smiling.

"Perhaps," he said, half to himself, "when I have learnt the craft . . . I shall to Toulouse when I am made knight, for there are no troubadours come to Angoulême. . . . Perhaps I myself will make a song to you."

Her eyes, which had been raised in a startled, half-frightened glance when he touched her hair, came up again now, round with wonder.

"Oh!" she said. "You make songs, lord?"

"Badly, right badly!" he said and laughed at her. "I must learn the craft; but I'll make you your song, child."

They came to the village green. Cows and cowherd were perfectly safe now, and had been so for some time past, but Yves sat silent on his horse while the serfs came up and parted the cattle. When it was done he rode up to Madeleine. "Ye said the bailiff was at Civray Fair?" he said.

"Yea, lord," she answered.

"Then," said Yves, "I will sup with you before I go on," and he swung down from the saddle, and stood by her, half a head shorter than she, and as swarthy as she was fair.

She led him, suddenly shy again, to a little hut of mud and wattle, where in the corner of its single room a big sow dozed and grunted below the roosting perches of a dozen sleepy, puffed-out hens. A hugely fat woman with a red face and sharp blue eyes was stirring the iron pot which hung over the fire. Madeleine ran to her and began to whisper, but she put the girl aside, looking at Yves with unconcealed suspicion and anger in her small eyes.

"What have ye done with the wench?" she said, and came towards him, as if she threatened.

43

"By our Lady!" began Yves, "I've done naught, except –"

"Except what?" cried the woman, her voice hard and shrill, but Madeleine caught her, put a hand over her mouth and whispered again. The girl was no more squeamish than most people in those outspoken times, but such questions were *lèse majesté*.

Apparently she satisfied her mother, though the woman still looked at Yves grudgingly. He was put to sit in the doorway, while the two of them busied themselves about supper. Madeleine went down on her knees and blew the fire until her cheeks were as red as the elder woman's, and all the while, although she clutched it to her bosom to keep it from burning, the ends of her lovely hair lay trailing in the dead ashes. Her mother, standing firmly with bare feet well apart, stirred the pot slowly, and every now and then cast a doubtful glance over her shoulder towards Yves.

Presently he got up, and carrying the three-legged stool, came over to the fire, and sat down there.

"I am ever a-cold," he said, suddenly boyish as he smiled up at the old woman, and held out his hands to the blaze.

"Na! Na!" she said, and all at once her voice softened. "Blood should be hot at your age, lad," and she smiled down at him as if he were a spoilt child. That made them friends, and they talked, while Madeleine listened.

He asked for news of Rifaucon, but she could give him none. The woodland tracks were very bad, so that few from the village ever went so far; besides, just now all the free men were at Civray Fair. She had seen Lord Elie, though, when he came to buy the manor from Lord Thibaut, and a lady with him in a blue cloak, so fine – Yves changed the subject quickly.

Presently she gave him a wooden bowl full of the hot stew, greasy and rank with garlic, and he took it, balancing it in his hands till it cooled a little, and as he waited he smiled across at Madeleine.

"When will the wench be married?" he said, turning to her mother.

The woman frowned, and threw a fresh, unnecessary log on the fire before she answered.

"This year, I wot," she said, and looked at him, almost hostile again; "since she must be wed, I suppose," she went on. "If she's not wed already it's because. . . . Well, it's thus . . . though it's no gain to talk of it . . . we're serfs. . . ." Her face hardened into the lines of harsh, resentful endurance that come to the poor as the scars of their deadly war. "We're serfs . . . but we used to be serfs of the Grey Nuns at Savigné, and I'd vowed her . . . she's the only child I've borne and I vowed before ever she was gotten. . . . But they sold the manor to Lord Thibaut. He lacked serfs and so. . . . Oh! I say naught. It's his to say yea or nay. But I always wanted it . . . and the lass."

Yves turned to stare at Madeleine. This simple, bright-haired child wanted to be a nun? She wanted that from which he shrank?

She nodded, her eyes on his face, and then, before he knew what she would be after, she was on her knees at his feet, her hands upon his wrists.

"Ah! lord, I pray you. . . . Ye're our lord now . . . or your lord father. Ah! let me be a nun!"

He tried to draw his hands away, but she clung to them.

"Ye want it?" he said stupidly. "But why?" The question was strangely urgent, but she could not have known how he longed for her answer to enlighten the great darkness in his mind. She tried to find an answer, frowning, as her dull and empty wit groped helplessly. Why did she want it? It had always been set before her, and one of the nuns had petted her, and she had seen their garden where they seemed to pace all day long with hands folded . . . and they ate beautiful white bread . . . and . . . and the abbess was of his kin. As she thought of so desirable a life her face shone.

"Oh! I can't tell why. . . . I don't know. . . . Only I should be happy," she said very softly, and Yves dropped his eyes because he could not look at her any more than he could look at the monk before the Crucifix.

"You shall, child," he said, as quietly as she had spoken. "I will move my father to it."

Before he could prevent her she had kissed his hands, and then, when he had freed himself, he found that the older woman was crying. Poor soul! She was brave enough to face familiar hardship, but at this unexpected happiness she broke down, and luxuriated in tears. Nor would she be comforted, seeing that she was enjoying herself.

45

In the midst of it all the serf himself came in, a dreary-looking man with limp, straw-coloured hair, and there were more explanations, more tears, and much confusion. Yves said that he must go, for it grew late, and even the last twilight had all but faded, and the serf, after trying listlessly to persuade him that it was already too late to start, was bidden by his wife to go along and point out a short way to the woods.

Yves kissed the woman on her cheek as she tried to curtsey, and then hesitated, half turned on one heel to go to Madeleine. Whether she saw the hesitation or not, she helped him. Crossing the little room swiftly, she went down on her knees before him, and bent over his feet, her hair all about her face, murmuring:

"Your shoe latchet, lord. It is undone."

He touched her head very gently with his hand, because she was holy.

The serf plodded along leading Yves' horse by the bridle for a couple of miles before he thought fit to leave him to find the way himself, then took the money Yves gave him, said a mournful "God w'ye," and slouched away into the darkness.

Yves rode on soberly. "Straight on, down by the brook, past the Grey Sister's House, and then a track – a very bad track – in the woods." These were the serf's instructions and Yves followed them mechanically.

He was thinking far less about the path than about the girl he had just left. She had laughed, and hugged her father when she had told him she was to be a nun. A nun! And that meant . . .? All that the monk had said. And she was merry and simple . . . and she said she would be happy.

He lifted his head suddenly and stared into the darkness. Was it this way, then? he thought. Was it as simple and easy as this? "Caritas, pietas, hilaritas." That old motto for monks came across his mind, familiar as daily bread, but now it seemed new. For a moment he was sure that this was the answer, and that the terrible dilemma could be solved with a smile. A sudden waft of sweetbriar seemed to mingle with and bless the thought. He looked up again, and saw that he was riding by the long wall of the garden of that House of Nuns, and all the air was perfumed; yes, he was sure that this was the answer.

46

He left the garden behind, and the certainty lessened as the distance increased; but still it might be so.

In a little while, remembering Rifaucon, he ceased to think even of the uncertainty; he whistled at first, and then at last, lifting up his head in the darkness of the woods, he sang, one song after another, and all at the top of his voice.

It was black dark when he reached the river below Rifaucon, for the moon was not up; but it did not matter, since he was on ground which both he and the horse knew. He had left the road, and taking a little path down through the woods, crossed by a ford he knew, since this way would save him half a mile or so, taking him straight to the castle without going through the village.

Before him, though he could not see it, the castle rose up on its small rocky hill. It was not till he was actually on the path that crept up under the threatening walls that he could see its bulk, dark even against the darkness of the sky.

There was no light anywhere, for it was late, and no one but the watchman would be awake now. He pulled up on the edge of the moat before the gate, and putting his hands to his mouth, shouted :

"Holà! Holà! Holà! Open me the gate!" But there was no answer.

"Asleep, are ye?" he muttered, and shouted again, and again waited. In the profound silence and darkness a little movement of air, less than the least breath of wind, touched his face, bringing with it a faint smell, so faint, and so soon gone, that he did not even try to think what it was, especially as his horse, suddenly restive, fidgeted and snatched at the bridle.

He lost patience, swung out of the saddle, and began to grope in the roadway for a stone to fling at the door. He would wake all the castle if need be; so he fumbled for one heavy enough to satisfy his ill humour. The horse, still uneasy, backed away, dragging the bridle from his hand, and Yves, with a muttered word, let it go.

He found a stone, heaved it with both hands from its place in the track, and with all his strength hurled it at the gate. The crash would be enough to wake the dead.

No sound! He might as well have thrown a puff-ball.

47

Then, after what seemed an endless pause, he heard the lifeless, dull thud of the stone falling on soft earth, and just at that moment, creeping to him through the blank and gaping doorway, came another puff of wind, stronger this time, and bringing with it that same carrion smell of rotting flesh.

V

Quan vei pels vergiers desplejar
Los sendatz grocs, indis, e blaus,
M'adoussa la votz del chavaus
Elh sonet que fan li joglar
Que viulan de trap en tenda,
Trompas e corn e graïle clar.

BERTRAN DE BORN.

YVES, waking at Angoulême the morning after his return, came painfully out of a deep sleep to an immediate realisation of all that had passed. There was no blank pause before recollection flowed back, since even in his sleep he had never escaped from the inexorable memory. It had darkened his mind all night, and now, waking, he saw it plain.

He got out of bed, padded across to the window, and leaning out, saw by the shadows that it was close on noon; as he lingered he heard a far sound of shouting, softened and made beautiful and sad by distance, and remembered that this was the Feast of Pentecost, and that he himself should have been striving lustily at the tourney beyond the walls, in all the pride of fire-new knighthood. He drew in his head quickly and stepped back into the room, but he could still hear the shouting, or fancied he could, and stood in the middle of the floor, listening unwillingly, till at last the chill of the stone-walled room roused him; he found that his teeth were chattering, and realised that he had not yet dressed.

As he struggled into his shirt the door creaked, and the long face of the Old Count appeared at the opening. It was his way to come like that, stepping softly and then peering; indeed that was one of the means by which he got his knowledge of other folks' business. But, thought Yves, as he waited with a respectful expression for the Count to come in, what does he want here now?

When the Count spoke it was to ask the same question of Yves, but crossly.

49

"It's nigh noon," he added. "Why were ye not there to take your knighthood?" He looked at Yves with his eyebrows raised and his lips dropping at the corners.

"I slept," said Yves. The Old Count always drove him to take refuge in his surliest manner.

Guilhem snorted.

"It's well ye care so little, since if ye had come I'd not have made you knight. What have ye now to bear the charges? Landless men can't be knights even if ye think it."

Yves was staring at the Count. He had not thought of that before, but now, thanks to Guilhem, he knew everything, and the worst at once. He stiffened to meet it.

Guilhem turned, and with a peevish gesture slammed the door.

"And all the others are gone mad over this folly of tourney," he said. "I can get no work done for me." He jerked each sentence out more angrily than the one before, as though he suspected Yves of wishing to contradict. "And you think I have nought to do!" he ran on. "And we ride to-morrow! And you young puppies wasting sweat and horse-flesh at a game."

Yves waited in silence for the Count's impartial reproaches to cease, but silence did not save him, for when Guilhem had reached the window he turned on Yves.

"What are you waiting for?" he cried. "Get you dressed. Don't stand there like a fool." He went over to one of the beds, poked it with his finger as though he feared some treachery might lurk there, and sat down, still watching Yves without looking at him.

Yves was angry. He dressed quickly, splashed noisily as he washed face and hands, and gashed his chin as he shaved. He was smouldering with rage when he came back to straighten his bed, but all the time Guilhem had said nothing.

When Yves came to the bed the first thing he saw was the gay scarlet cloak under which he had slept, and remembering whose gift it was he turned half round, hesitating. He felt he could not fold and lay it out under the Count's very nose without giving him thanks.

But Guilhem prevented him. He jerked himself up from the low bed.

"Oh, yea," he said. "You can say your 'Pater Noster,' but say it smartly. I cannot wait the lee-long day," and he stalked across the room and out. A moment later his head came round the door again.

"Come to the Chancery room," he said, and was gone.

When Yves reached the Chancery room he found both Guilhem and Vulgrin, and half a dozen clerks. Guilhem fell on him at once, sent him off with a wooden tally and a knife to the granary to count the sacks of corn; when he came back drove him out again, this time to the master-armourer's store, to number the arrows brought in by the fletchers of Angoulême; when that was done thrust a bundle of parchments into his hands and bade him read out the lists thereon.

"Ye can read," he snapped, challenging Yves to deny it.

Yves began to read.

So it went on, all afternoon, till Yves wished the Count in the lowest depth of the Pit; but he had no time to think of Rifaucon.

At last Vulgrin turned to his father.

"One of us two, at the least," he said, "must go to dinner."

"Why?" said Guilhem angrily.

"Pentecost. State must be kept," replied Vulgrin.

"Go then! Go! I'll not come. These fooleries!"

Vulgrin turned back at the door.

"And the clerks?" he said.

"Oh! let them go." The Old Count turned on them fiercely. "But come back betimes!" he added.

Vulgrin still paused and looked first at Yves, then at his father.

"No! He shall serve me. I must eat, and I shall want him after," said Guilhem, and grabbed another parchment from the table. Vulgrin shrugged and went out, for it was useless to say more.

So, when a serving-man brought in the Count's dinner, Yves served him, in great anger, and yet with a growing respect, for Guilhem at work was no longer the railer who blew hot and cold and girded at everything. He knew what he wanted and saw that it was done quickly, and Yves understood that even Vulgrin was only doing what he was told.

When Guilhem had finished he brushed the crumbs from his gown, peered into the half-empty wine cup, and stood up.

"Now fill thine own belly," he said, and sweeping up a confusion of parchments from the table, he went over to the window and began to pore over them. Yves, as he fell to on Count Guilhem's leavings, ravenously hungry after a long fast and hard work, heard him muttering to himself over the figures, but for once he left Yves entirely alone. He did not even try to hurry him, and it was Yves himself who, when he had finished, asked the Old Count what was to be done now.

After a while the clerks came back; and then Vulgrin, who said that a man had ridden in, sent by the younger Guilhem to say that he would be in Angoulême in an hour or so. The Old Count kept everyone working long after the candles were lit and the clerks yawning from ear to ear, but at last they finished; all was ready for the start next morning, and now there was no more to do.

The Old Count drove the clerks away at last, as angrily as though it were they who had kept him at work. Vulgrin had gone some time since to talk to the master-farrier, and now the Old Count was left alone with his esquire. Guilhem yawned and stretched his arms above his head so that Yves heard the joints crack.

Without any warning the Count turned on him.

"You want to be a troubadour," he said.

It was useless to deny anything which the Old Count's curiosity had ferreted out, so Yves said:

"Yea."

"Ye read . . . and write?"

"Yea."

The Count grunted.

"Poetry is foolishness but some men are fools," he said ungraciously, then:

"Bid someone fetch me Messire Guiraut of Cabreira."

Yves stood quite still, staring at the Count, who was apparently looking at the ceiling. Did he mean that Guiraut of Cabreira, the Catalan, famed as a troubadour in France as well as in Spain, was here in Angoulême, or was it one of his crabbed jests?

The Old Count spoke again without moving his head.

"Leave staring like a half-blind owl, Yves of Rifaucon," he cried, and Yves, with a start, turned to do his bidding. When he came back he took up his station behind the Count's chair, but his eyes were fixed on the door. It opened at last and Guiraut of Cabreira came in.

He was a tall man, broad-shouldered, and walked with an easy swing and his head held high. His ruddy-brown hair shone in the curls with a golden tinge, and his eyes too were of a golden brown, and, so Yves learnt when he knew him better, changed easily from merry to soft. He came in smiling, and seemed to know that he was a handsome fellow, yet his easy, pleasant confidence was far removed from a swagger. He was dressed in green with a long-tongued red belt, from which hung a red purse fringed with white and gold. He was a very fine bird indeed, and shone in the little room.

Even the Old Count could not resist him, but smiled, and if there was a spice of mockery in the smile it was only to be expected, since mockery was a habit with him.

"Messire Guiraut," he said, "this young cock," and he waved a hand towards Yves, "would be a troubadour. I know nought of what it needs to make a rhymer, but I know he can make a great noise halloing of other folks' songs."

The troubadour looked across at Yves, and if his face was serious now, his eyes twinkled.

"We shall see," he said, and then, speaking to Yves as courteously as though he were already a knight and a famous singer, he said:

"What is your name?"

"Yves of . . . of Rifaucon."

The Old Count turned quickly in his chair.

"Why 'of . . . of Rifaucon,'" he mocked. "Has never a man before lost his land and got it again?"

Yves became sullen, and made no answer. The Old Count left him alone and turned again to the troubadour.

"Now hearken, Messire Guiraut," he said. "It is your pleasure to go with me in this war. I think you a fool for it, but it is your affair. I'll lend you this fellow as esquire until we come back and then I'd have you teach him to sing or rhyme or . . . or . . . whatever you troubadours do. Is it your pleasure?"

Yves was so much surprised at such courtesy from the Old Count, that he forgot to wonder at him taking the pains to make the arrangement.

Guiraut of Cabreira smiled frankly into the Count's gloomy face.

"What I can I will," he said. "Now I thank you for a good esquire, and after, if the Saints will, for a good troubadour."

The Old Count waved his hands before him as though he were tired of the whole matter and would push it away.

"Enough! Enough! Take him with you," he said.

Yves came round from behind the chair, and went down on one knee, but before he could speak the Old Count forestalled him.

"Nay! Nay!" he cried, pulling his cloak closer about him, and looking anywhere but at Yves. "Ye need not thank me, nor yet tell lies, and say ye'd be no man's esquire but mine."

"I'll not!" said Yves, and glowered at the old man's averted face. He had been grateful, but the Count made gratitude impossible.

The Count turned suddenly. The sour droop of his lips did not alter, but in his heavy eyes there passed the faint flicker of a smile.

"I thank ye!" he said.

The watchman leaning against the eastern battlement of Count Guilhem's castle of Moulin Neuf saw the sky overhead turn from pale blue to paler gold, and knew that in a short time the sun would heave himself up from behind the woods. The man pulled round the horn which hung at his back, and blew three long, hoarse notes, then, trailing his spear behind him, he went to the nearest tower, smote on the door with the haft of the weapon, paused to listen for an answer, and receiving it, went on and down the steps, leaving his place on the wall to be taken by the newly wakened men in the tower.

Meanwhile the three notes of the horn had been echoed all round the circuit of the walls. A trumpet down in the town blew, further off someone beat on a drum, and a stir began that grew into a bustle. There were shouts and hurrying footsteps; horses' hoofs rang on stone or thudded on the soft earth; and ten minutes after the watchman had put the horn to his lips the whole of the little town and castle was awake and alive.

Late last night Count Guilhem and his sons, with the host of Angoulême, had poured into Moulin Neuf, filling the streets with torchlight and clamour. The two Counts and most of the knights had gone up to the castle, the rest had found a lodging, as best they might, in the town. For all the order had been – "Arm and saddle at dawn!" and that was early enough, since it was only four days now till Midsummer Day.

Guilhem Talifer of Angoulême was about to try his last chance. Driven from place to place before the battering of Count Richard of Poitou, if he could yet win through to Angoulême all was not lost, since he had left the city well stuffed for a siege and the walls were strong. So, marching early and late, he had come to Moulin Neuf, and now would press on again in spite of jaded men and horses.

The courtyard of the castle gradually filled with armed and mounted men, who ranged themselves knee to knee, and waited in a close-packed mass for the coming of the Counts and the word to march. Behind Guiraut of Cabreira Yves sat stiffly on his horse, his sallow face with its narrowed eyes seeming all chin and hard-set mouth. Count Richard had beaten Angoulême at every turn, and Yves was full of a very bitter anger.

Guiraut of Cabreira turned suddenly in his saddle.

"'Tis too fair a day for all this sweat and coil," he said, as he raised his face to the sky and laughed.

Yves grunted, but the words roused him to look up. Above, the sky was a clear, deepening blue, and the sun already touched, changed, and made beautiful the tops of the towers. A few pigeons wheeled in the air above the horsemen, rising and falling with giddy tumbles that ended in a whirl of spread wing-feathers, an instant's hovering, and a swift upward flight. The clack of their wings was quite audible, so quiet were the tired men and horses in the courtyard. Yves, with Guiraut's light words still in his mind, turned almost angrily from watching the birds, and added another item to Count Richard's score. Such idle happy things as those were not for him now; he began to look over the buckles of sword-belt and shield-strap, the lacing of his mail gorget, and the leather thongs that held his steel head-piece in place, and when that was done he looked about the courtyard. Guiraut's broad shoulders prevented him seeing anything in front, but, looking right and left, he saw everywhere the lean, bare shafts of the spears, close as standing corn, the cold, colourless gleam of chain, or scale, or mascled mail, and the varied gay colours of cloaks and surcoats and painted shields. Many of the surcoats were torn and stained, the shields hacked and battered, with the painted devices half defaced, but there was enough colour left to make a brave show.

There was a stir in the courtyard, and all heads turned one way. Count Guilhem and Count Vulgrin had come out of the doorway of the Hall. There was a murmur, then someone shouted, and at that the whole courtyard burst into a roar.

"Angoulême! Talifer! Angoulême!" they shouted, and with a long, swishing sound, as of some great scythe cutting its swathe, every sword was drawn.

The Old Count walked heavily, burdened with his chain hauberk. The only answer he made to the shout was a slight gesture of his hand, and his face was hidden by the painted, flat-topped helm, that suggested some grotesque abortion of nature, with a dark horizontal slit instead of eyes, and perforations where should have been mouth and nose. Count Vulgrin indeed raised his hand and smiled an acknowledgment of the salute, but the smile was strained, and he turned immediately to let his esquire cover his head with the big helm, while his younger brother, Adhemar, crossed over to his horse and mounted without once raising his bent head. Of all the Count's sons only Guilhem the younger seemed undismayed; he stared this way and that with his challenging, wild-bull stare, and smote his gauntleted hands together.

When the Count and his sons had mounted, the trumpets sounded, the banner of Angoulême in the gateway gave a jerk, a plunge, and moved forward, its heavy folds hardly stirring from the staff, and now the whole courtyard was full of noise and stir, while the gateway arch echoed with the clatter of hoofs. When the last horseman had gone and all was quiet again, the pigeons returned to their play in the sunshine.

It was a bare three miles from Moulin Neuf that Count Richard fell on the army of Angoulême. The vanguard of his host topped a hill half a mile to the left of Count Guilhem's march, halted, and then, with a sound of trumpets and horns that carried clearly in the still air, swept down the hillside.

The whole army of Angoulême wheeled to meet it, those on the right wing spurring hard to come up with those on the left. Down went the lances to the charge, and then with a long, rolling crash the ranks met. White shivers flew from the broken lances, here and there a horse went down, or a man was torn from his saddle and thrust into the fatal confusion of trampling hoofs, and now the swords were out, and flickered like a grey, changing mist over the battle, filling the air with an insistent grinding sound like that of a heavy surf upon a pebble beach.

The two front ranks pierced each other and mingled, and the fighting became a blind confusion. Yves saw the horse in front of his go down, and realised that the man who still bestrode it, feet planted wide apart, shield well up and big sword swinging, was Guiraut of Cabreira. He shouted and drove his own horse forward, saw from the corner of his eye a sword flash, threw up his shield to guard his head and shoulder, and failed. A fierce pain seemed to rise to swallow him up, he choked as if he were drowning, and after floated down through a confused and noisy dimness, in which there was for a while – he could not tell for how long – one single clear object. It was the wild, distended, shining eye of a horse.

That, so far as Yves was concerned, was the end of the great campaign against the Count of Poitou. There followed for him an indefinite period of pain and delirium through which came and went Guiraut of Cabreira, and another person whom Yves' bemused brain could not recognise. Then came two empty days of delicious sleep, during which the stranger seemed to have vanished with other delusions, and only Guiraut, kind and smiling, appeared from time to time.

On the evening of the third day Yves woke to find Cabreira beside the bed.

The troubadour sat down carefully at the foot and smiled at him.

"Now, friend Yves, for all those questions ye would be asking."

"Nay, Messire," said Yves. "Tell me everything!" and Guiraut, crossing one leg over the other, and nursing his foot in his hands, began to tell the tale in his own way.

"Count Richard," said he, "is gone; ridden out just now with all his men, and the two Counts go to Angoulême to-morrow, and I with them. But they stay only to prepare for their journey to England, and then away thither to King Henry, for Count Richard hath bade them make their peace with his father or he'll not be satisfied."

"But, Messire!" cried Yves, "I do not understand!"

"Peace! Peace!" said Guiraut, teasing. "Everything in mine own time. Ye said everything?"

"Yea . . . but . . ." protested Yves.

"Ah me! . . . then for the beginning," said Guiraut. "Know then, fair friend, that Angoulême hath had a fair trouncing. . . . Nay . . . that's not the beginning neither. Listen, then!

"Ye fell off your horse with a slit in you as wide as a plough-furrow, but by the favour of the Saints ye fell off on the side where I was. I thought ye were dead, and I said – or I would have said if I'd had time to spare – 'There's one singer less in this naughty world.' But ye'd left your horse, and I caught it. Then I thought – 'Little courtesy to borrow a man's horse but if he be dead,' and so I stood over you till by came two of Count Guilhem's squires – Pons of Jarnac was of them. That gave me space, and I hoisted you up like a sack of corn, and across the horse, and time it was, for ye had taken a kick on the head was as bad as the sword-stroke."

Yves began to speak but Guiraut bore him down.

"We had our belly-full of fighting that day," he said, "and always going a-back. Angoulême had never a hope, though that old man – Count Guilhem – he laid on like a woodcutter! And Count Vulgrin strikes a good stroke, too, but – there's naught serves against yonder Richard of Poitou. Fair friend," and Guiraut's voice rose in his excitement, "he's the best knight in the world!"

"Ah! Messire, enough!" cried Yves, but Guiraut took no notice.

"As swift as a hawk he is!" he ran on. "I saw him strike poor Elie of Saint Martin, God rest his soul! Elie had his shield up, but the Count's stroke cut it like cheese, and Elie's helm and head – yea, shore him to the nose. And a troubadour too . . . he sang the other night in Hall; and merry and open-handed . . . and courteous withal. He said . . ."

Yves brought his fist down upon the bed so that the pain leapt through him again.

"Let be! Let be!" he cried. "Why will ye speak of him? I will not hear! Let be, Messire Guiraut!"

Guiraut stared.

"Why . . . why . . . ? What ails . . . ? Ah! I have it. Call me a fool! He hath taken your fief and castle!"

He looked anxiously at Yves.

"Well-a-day!" he went on ruefully. "But Pons will have a word to say to me!"

"Pons," said Yves, smiling, but rather wryly, to reassure Guiraut. "Who is . . . ?"

"Nay, nay! Ye must say no word more. I'll tell you of Pons. . . . Though ye should know, seeing he is one of you . . . one of the Old Count's esquires. A big man . . . ye cannot have forgot. He hath had all the tending of you. . . . Good! you remember?"

He smiled at Yves, encouraging him, as he saw the puzzled expression fade, and Yves nodded, remembering how, the night he had come back to Angoulême, he had stood on the threshold of the esquires' room and heard the new name, and wondered at it. He guessed, too, that the big, silent visitor, who had seemed to be part of his delirium, had been this same Pons.

"But he hath not been here these two days," he said.

"Nay," replied Guiraut. "The Count keeps him busy these last two days because they are his days for service. But he hath mixed the draughts for ye to drink, and right foul they taste, I wot. . . . Yea, he's a right good doctor . . . more monk than knight; for they say. . . ." But he broke off and turned as the door behind him opened.

A big man, as tall as Cabreira, but more heavily built, came in, carrying in one hand a wooden bowl. He paused before he crossed the room, and shut the door gently and deliberately. He had a broad, pleasant face, very composed in expression, with frank, light blue eyes set wide apart, and fair, straight hair cropped close to his head; it needed only the tonsure to make him look like some stout-hearted monk. "Ah! Pons," said Guiraut. "Come hither, thou learned clerk! Tell us where it was ye got your knowledge. . . . Paris . . . Chartres?"

Pons came forward slowly and sat down on a stool beside the bed.

"Chartres," he said, without looking at Guiraut. His eyes were fixed on Yves' face.

59

"Humph!" he muttered to himself. "It's well I came!" Then to Yves, "Drink this," and he held the bowl to his lips.

He did not stay long. When Yves had drunk all, Pons stood up, looked down for a moment at him, and then turned to Guiraut of Cabreira.

"I must go," he said, but the tone meant more than the words. Guiraut took the hint and followed him to the door. As they reached it Yves stretched out his hand towards them:

"Messire Guiraut!" he cried.

Both stopped, but Pons, after an instant's pause, went out, frowning. Guiraut came back across the room.

"Ah! Messire Guiraut," said Yves. "Of your courtesy come hither! Close!"

Guiraut did so, and stood, smiling. Yves' hand went up, searching, and found the hilt of Guiraut's sword.

"Messire," he said, "I am your man to do what ye will, save against my lord. By Christ and the Holy Cross!"

"Messire Guiraut," said the minatory voice of Pons at the door – "I stay for you."

VI

Love in her sunny eyes doth basking play:
Love walks the pleasant mazes of her hair:
Love doth on both her lips for ever stray
And sows and reaps a thousand kisses there.
In all her outward parts Love's always seen –
But ah! he never went within.

COWLEY.

THE two Counts had already left Angoulême when Yves and Pons rode in from Moulin Neuf. Going leisurely across France, and briskly across the crisp waves of the Channel before a fair breeze, Guilhem and Vulgrin found King Henry at Windsor. There he received them with fury, rated them, bound them over to peace by fearful oaths, and then, relenting, rode out hunting with them through the mellow days of a perfect September.

In Angoulême the Old Count's younger sons, Guilhem and Adhemar, managed the business of the great fief. The town was quieter than usual, there were fewer knights and men-at-arms about the castle, but the months passed pleasantly for those who remained. For Yves it was a good time, because of the friendship between him and Pons, which, first begun at Moulin Neuf, grew now into a very fine and comely thing.

Pons was different from all the other esquires. He seemed to bring with him from the cloisters of Chartres something of the calm of the men of peace who debated there only of immutable things, beside which the rude jostling of knights, kings and pawns seemed idle as the moves in a game of chess. He came with his head full of the sayings of great clerks from Aristotle to Abelard, a silent, thoughtful fellow, and of a mild temper: in many things a very monk. Had he stayed at Chartres he would probably, in due time, have become priest and bishop, and a notable captain in the Church militant, as a man not quarrelsome, yet unyielding; merciful, yet fearless; no great scholar, and yet wise in his own way. Now, since his elder brother had died suddenly, one green unhealthy Christmas, and since his father was lord of a very great barony that guarded one of the gates of the Angoumois, Pons, his minor orders annulled by decree from Rome, had been sent to Angoulême to learn to be a knight, and guardian of that same gate when his father should die.

What Pons had done for Yves at Moulin Neuf, Yves could now repay – though there was no thought of debt or repayment in their friendship – by helping Pons to make up for the years of training and use in arms which he had missed at Chartres. They spent hours together in the tilt-yard, Pons frowningly intent, Yves eager, and yet unwontedly patient.

At first it was:

"Ha! Haste! haste! Pons. . . . Nay, I'd have had you there . . . keep your shield higher." This from Yves, as they fought with the blunted swords.

Or, when they rode a course against one another, Yves would cry as they came close:

"Lower in the saddle! Lower! Drop your helm!" and after the crash he would rein in his horse to explain:

"Ye sit firmer so, and see the better too."

After a time Pons became more formidable, till at last their constant practice was a benefit and a test for Yves himself. Pons' weight in the saddle, his length of arm, and his great height, gave him initial advantages, but in addition he was stronger than Yves, though not so well breathed, and his apparent deliberateness masked a precision that was as deadly as any speed.

One evening in April, several months after the return of the two Counts, Yves and Pons, neither being on duty, left the younger esquires to their noisy mock-fighting, and went off together, in their usual way, for an hour's practice in the tilt-yard before the light failed. Even when they were forced to stop because they could not be sure of their strokes, they did not return at once to the castle, but finding a stableman, gave their horses over to him, and stood a moment watching as he trotted them off, with the helms dancing at the saddlebows and the grey hauberks hanging limp over the saddles.

Yves pushed back the leather coif that covered his head, and unlaced the leather tunic at his throat.

"Fair friend," he said, as they strolled off towards the ramparts, "the Saints forbid I ever meet thee in anger. I'd liefer a smith's hammer than thy hand."

Pons laughed, but neither spoke again till they reached a part of the southern wall where it ran back in a shallow curve, with a tower to right and left, and below, the fading plain, and the long curve of the river, shining coldly here and there. They leaned against the battlements, silent still for a while, till Yves moved restlessly, and leaning further out, peered down at the ground at the foot of the wall.

"What scores of coneys," he murmured, and then, with hardly a pause, but in a very different voice, he went on:

"Count Richard hath my Rifaucon, or I should not have to devise what I should do. . . . I have thought. . . . Each man hath his place as rivets in a hauberk – serf, priest, lord, and his lord again – but I – none! And so . . ." He paused and turned suddenly on Pons.

"Pons, what would ye do?" he cried.

Pons leaned both elbows on the wall and kicked his scabbard aside with his heels before he answered.

"I wis not what ye would have me say," he said cautiously. "What would I do an if . . .?"

"If ye were me?" said Yves.

"But for ye to do how . . . when?" Pons asked, still dubious.

Yves smote his open hand on the stone.

"How can I tell?" he cried. "But I have no place and so must make choice. . . . Messire Guiraut laughs at me. . . . He calls me a fool when I. . . . But how can I leave thinking of Rifaucon, and let Count Richard be? And yet I could be a troubadour and the friend of every great lord, and pass endlong and overthwart France in peace. There it is!"

He stopped, because, having stated the practical issue, he found his mind turning towards a thought he feared, and as he fought to prevent it, he hardly listened when Pons began to speak.

"For me," said Pons, and turned his head away from Yves to watch the fussy, uncertain flight of a bat – "for me, I think to go overseas on Crusade. It seems a right fair thing for a knight to do." He paused, and then, as though he had made a boast, hurried on, excusing himself.

"Mine uncle hath a fief in the Kingdom of Jerusalem. He saith that land is ever hungry for knights."

Yves broke in as though he had not heard, and yet it was Pons' words which had driven his mind still further down that road whose end he dared not see. So he hurried into speech.

"There's Rifaucon," he said. "It should be mine . . . the folk there are mine. . . . I would be good lord to them. . . . If I go overseas. . . ." He seemed to push that thought aside – "But Guiraut saith – Messire Guiraut of Cabreira – he talks of what the 'gaye saber' teaches. He saith life is a good thing, and a man is best when he taketh pleasure and keepeth measure in all things . . . like good tune to good words in a song. . . And he saith poetry is the fairest thing. . . . And there's so many fair things to sing. . . ."

He stopped, having once more avoided the monk's choice, although his mind was still aware of the near presence of that dark thought. Pons, however, helped him to drive it away.

"As for Messire Guiraut –" he began, and it was easy to guess from his tone that he attached little importance to the troubadour's advice.

Yves answered the tone, and he was angry.

"Ye're wrong, Pons. . . . He is. . . . I took oath to him against any but Angoulême. . . . I am his true friend and servant."

But it was difficult to prevent Pons if he had made up his mind to speak.

"As for Messire Guiraut," he began again, "I think he talks too much. The Old Count calls him an empty pot that makes a loud, sweet sound. He doth not like him neither."

"The Old Count!" cried Yves. "Whom doth he like? Not thee, nor me, and will ye take his words? Ye're a fool, Pons." He turned his back and flung away.

Pons let him go a little way, and then followed. Ranging up alongside, he was silent for some time, then began to talk peaceably about a hawk which Yves was training.

Guiraut of Cabreira had, it is true, been at some pains to convert Yves from what the Spaniard considered a needlessly discomfortable view of life. He had argued a little, and laughed more, but the most

64

powerful persuasion which he had used, and he had been quite unconscious of it, was his own magnificent self. "Was not the world a fair
enough place?" said Guiraut, and Yves, seeing beauty everywhere,
must needs agree. "What more then could a man do than enjoy it?"
Yves had no answer.

During one of their lessons, Guiraut, who was singing over the verse
of one of his own chansons which he was teaching Yves, broke off
suddenly.

"See here," he said, "I gave promise I would teach you to be a
troubadour, and so I will. I have told you how the duty of such is, in
the gay science of love, how he must choose a lady and serve and sing
her and her only, and ye will not, because forsooth ye care to make
nothing but songs against that Count Richard of yours."

He sprang up and stood at his full height, then, stretching out his
hand, caught Yves by the throat and threatened him, laughing:

"Find you a lady before I see you again, and bring me a song ye
have made her – 'chanson,' 'alba,' 'serena' – what ye will, so it be of
love, and so I have a rest from your 'sirventes'!"

Next day Guiraut met Yves in the Countess' garden. Yves had been
sent to bid Count Vulgrin go within to his father to speak of a weighty
matter, but when he had given his message and Vulgrin had turned
towards the gate, Guiraut stepped before Yves, barring his way in the
narrow path.

"Yea, then?" he said, and Yves knew what he meant, and laughed.

"Ah! fair friend. . . . No. . . . I have not chosen." He looked round
about the square, walled garden where the Countess' ladies were walking. "But if I must," he shut his eyes, swung round on one heel, and
stopped, his hand stretched out.

There were three of the Countess' ladies standing together near a rose-
bush, and Yves' finger happened to point direct at the midmost of them.

"Who is yonder?" he said, with his eyes still shut.

Guiraut burst into a huge laugh.

"Oh! graceless face!" he said. "It is the Domna of Segonzac, and you
might have chosen a long shot worse!"

He laughed again and then seized Yves' arm.

"Come with me," he said, serious again. "And you shall see the fairest lady of the world. You know her well, but ye shall watch and learn from me how a good troubadour must bear himself towards his lady." As he talked he dragged Yves with him to the little space in the midst of the garden where there were two curved stone seats, and between them a lazy, tumbling, little fountain.

The Countess sat there, embroidering at one corner of a big half-circle of white samite, which was to be a cloak for Count Vulgrin at the next Christmas Feast. While Guiraut sat down by her Yves took up his stand, as a good esquire should, a little behind his betters, where he could watch and be ready lest they should want him, and yet not seem to be there at all. From where he stood he could see the back of the Countess' head; the fine soft silk of her wimple, the colour of springing corn in June, when it is neither blue nor green. She had paused in her stitching and her arm lay along the back of the seat, the wide sleeve hanging down like a great wing of true azure, and Yves looked at the colour and it pleased him; but for the most part he watched Guiraut's handsome face as he bent towards her, and he saw a light in it which he had not seen before.

His attention wandered; the sun was sweetly warm, and called out all their perfume from the flowers and shrubs. Now and again there came a waft of scent from the sweetbriar, or, like the sonorous thrum of a deep lute-string breaking in upon the flowing notes of a flute, the odour of the evergreens, warmed in the sun, mingled with the scent of the hyacinths which filled the garden.

Yves heard his name spoken, and looked again at Guiraut.

". . . Yves of Rifaucon, he will be a troubadour and I am teaching him his craft. He has but now chosen his lady. Come here, fair friend Yves," said Guiraut, turning round.

The Countess turned too, so that her back was towards Guiraut; she tilted her head over her shoulder to look at Yves as he came forward, and as he moved he kept his eyes fixed on her face.

It was a matter of six paces or so to the seat. He saw the gold of one of the long plaits that clung as though they loved it to the softness of her cheek, and kissed her neck as they fell down to rest on her bosom. He saw her face, of which Guiraut himself sang that it had been made for love alone, of white and red, like summer flowers. He had seen it

66

all a hundred times before, and never till this day. Only six paces, and he stood behind her shoulder looking down into heaven, and he was dizzy as though he had stood on the extreme verge of the world, and seen the stars below his feet.

Her head was poised so that he saw below him her blue eyes like pools, and her sweet chin, and the lovely line of her throat, and all lay as open as a flower to kisses.

"So, Messire Yves," she said, "you have chosen a lady to serve," and while she spoke, and he still stared down at her, he saw a tinge of colour flow from her cheeks up to her hair, and spread to the whiteness of her throat.

"Yea," said Yves, and his eyes said something more.

The Countess blushed more rosy, and her lips moved. She turned back to Guiraut, and as she turned there was a fresh and dewy softness in her face, for she was a woman who loved to be loved, and came very near to loving those who loved her. She looked at Guiraut for a moment, and because she was one of the Queens of Hearts, she conquered, slew, and beatified him afresh in that look, and without a word. Then she turned back to Yves.

"How didst thou choose?" she said.

For a moment Yves could not answer, for he was watching her lips, as lightly and tenderly laid together as those of a child. Guiraut, whose eyes never left the Countess, answered for him:

"He shut his eyes, and pointed his finger, and said 'Who is she?' and it was my Lord Robert of Segonzac's wife, Domna Alais, and I say he was lucky enough."

The Countess looked again at Yves, and when Guiraut could not see her face there were little bubbling springs of laughter in her eyes.

Cabreira went on with hardly a pause:

"To-morrow he will have to bring me a 'chanson' to Domna Alais. I have suffered many 'sirventes' at his hands, and full unwillingly, for I care nothing for 'sirventes' and the doings of kings. So now at last I will have a song of love!"

The Countess poked her foot out from under the hem of her dress, and pointed it this way and that, watching it as though she judged it, and its scarlet shoe.

"He will make a song?" she repeated thoughtfully. "But he could write it now and sing it to me. And if I think well I can say a word for him to the lady he so much loves." And she looked first at Yves, and then at Guiraut, so that both could see the ripple of laughter in her eyes.

Guiraut laughed, and taking out his wax tablets thrust them into Yves' hand.

"Go along now! Rhyme it as you like – y'are free for once. . . . And take the lute. There is a corner by the apple-tree yonder; go and beat it out there."

Yves came back after a while and went down on one knee before the stone bench. The Countess' face had been before him all the time that he was making the song, but now that he saw it again, he thought that he had only just perceived its beauty.

She turned from Messire Guiraut, looked at Yves, and blushed and smiled, a baby smile that she hid again as soon as ever it peeped out.

"Messire Guiraut," she said, "shall we call my women to hear this song too?" Before he could say yes or no, she had clapped her hands and called to them.

"Hearken, wenches!" she said as they crowded round, laughing and curious. "This is his first song to his lady."

'Yves began the song: "La boc' ia muda, ai! non puosc cantar":

> My throat is dumb, I cannot sing –
> Like a poor lark before the spring
> > Has freed the earth
> > And his sweet tongue,
> > Because her worth
> > May not be sung.
> Alas! How should I sing her heavenly courtesy?
>
> I cannot sing, since all fair words
> And all sweet notes, like little birds,
> > Are gone to play
> > About her face.
> > Nought can I say
> > Unless her grace
> Give them to me to sing her heavenly courtesy.
>
> Yet even then I dare not praise
> Her face, the sun of all my days,

68

> Nor could I sing,
> Nor any man,
> That fairest thing
> Since time began –
> Herself, herself, that is right Heavenly Courtesy.

So Yves sang, with his eyes on the Countess, and Guiraut watched her as she listened. The women looked at one or another of the three, as fancy led their eyes, but the Countess herself looked only at the little shining needle with its tail of red silk, held between her idle fingers.

When he had finished, Yves dropped his eyes and fingered the lute-strings in silence, waiting for her to speak, but she did not. The women spoke: some of them clapped their hands, and then they all broke out in comment or praise, and began to look about among themselves for the lady of the song, and guess, and laugh.

One, a woman in her middle age, spoke above the others:

"That is a song well sung."

"But," cried another, a girl with the laugh of a brook in her voice, "it might be an hymn to Our Lady in Heaven. 'Tis all of Heavenly Courtesy. . . . And the sad tune! I have no list to be sung in that manner wise."

"Nor need ye fear," broke in a dark girl with a quick, tart way of speaking. "It's full unlikely. But I think it a right fair way to . . ." She stopped suddenly and flushed an angry red.

"Oh! thou, Audiart! Aye, thou wouldst like it. We all know Domna Audiart of Rouillac!" the other cried, and then, as though she feared Audiart's tongue, she turned to Cabreira, pouting:

"Is it not a strange song of love?" she said.

He laughed.

"Fair, gentle friend," he said. "Verily, yea! The man is half a monk, but he will learn better wit."

The Countess, who had been watching Yves, interrupted them:

"Now go your ways," she said, "and leave Messire Guiraut and me to devise together what the song merits."

She waved her hands, and as though a wind had scattered it, the little circle of chattering, laughing women broke up, and left the three alone again.

Yves rose from his knees, but still he dared not look at the Countess.

69

She had turned to Guiraut, the laughter in her face misted over with tenderness.

"What do you say of the song, Messire Guiraut?" she said.

"Not ill done, for the first," he said and smiled at Yves. Then, seeing him so shamefast, he went further, praising him as he knew how to praise, with voice and smile as well as words. Yves looked up at that, and even dared glance at the Countess.

"But," went on Guiraut, "it doth not seem to me that you said much that was in especial right for Domna Alais. I should not have known that it was she. A troubadour should, by hints ever so light, show which is his lady, unless there be reason good he should not. . . . But ye will learn."

"I . . . it . . . but . . ." began Yves, and stopped, because it was so difficult to speak of his great presumption. The Countess checked him with her hand, and turned to Guiraut. "Oh! dullard Guiraut!" she cried. "Have you no better wit than that? Ye say the song doth not fit Alais of Segonzac. Of course it doth not, seeing that he sings another lady."

"But," broke in Guiraut, "he always – he never said –"

The Countess held up her hand daintily.

"Nay – how should he say? She will have bade him be secret. Oh! not in words, perhaps, but a look – it's enough. And then, when you would have him choose someone, how could he say? He is hiding her in the song."

She looked from one to the other, her lips pursed as though she held truth between them and would prevent him slipping out. Guiraut was silenced, but he was still puzzled. He had known often enough of these hidden loves, and yet –

The Countess may have been watching him, for she turned to Yves. "Is it not true? Every word I said?"

Yves said "Yea," looking at her as though she had saved him from a great peril – at least that was how Guiraut read the look.

"Oh! go to! go to! Thou false traitor!" he said, and laughed.

VII

"Love is the perfect sum
    Of all delight."
I have no other choice
Either of pen or voice,
To sing or write.
                    ANON. (17th century).

THE delightful secret which had begun in the garden that day
remained a secret for months. Domna Alais of Segonzac accepted
her position as a jest, and though she and the other women teased Yves,
they did not seriously try to discover the lady of his songs. Such secrets
were considered honourable, and what gentle and courteous man or
maid would wish to play the part of the evil tale-bearer in a new
Romance? Yves' habitual shyness and taciturnity helped, but it was the
Countess herself who did most. She loved the whole play, and would
be so amazingly bold in her teasing, and go so near to the truth, that no
one could dream that it lay there.

One afternoon in early winter Yves was called by one of her pages
to go and amuse her and her women. He found them in her bed-
chamber, four or five of them sitting on the big bed, the Countess herself in a chair by the fire, the rest of the women scattered about the
room, some on the chests, some on cushions on the floor, and in the
midst of them a big brazen trencher heaped up with red and green
apples. When he came in there was a merry clack of tongues, and some
of them looked up to greet him, but he saw only the Countess.

When he knelt on one knee before her, she stopped her sewing and
leaned a little towards him, so that they seemed private among all the
chattering crowd.

"Messire Yves," she said, "I would have you sing or tell us some
story – what you will. But," and she looked about the circle of women
and laughed, "let it be of love. Domna Audiart of Rouillac hath been
telling us tales of Godefroi of Bouillon, and of all the heads he split
asunder . . . naught of love. . . . And we are only women, after all."

"Yea," cried a girl in tawny yellow who leaned against the Countess' chair. "But if Audiart could borrow her an hauberk and helm she would away overseas Crusading! Beware! Messire Yves," and she laughed, pointing with her finger. "Yonder is our champion!"

They all turned to look at Audiart of Rouillac, sitting a little apart from the others, though not so much as to be quite alone, and in spite of the shadows everyone could see the blood come up in her face.

"Forsooth," she answered, and her voice was sharp. "Forsooth, who would not be a man rather than bide among such chattering pies? But if I were a man," she went on, including Yves among her tormentors although he had not spoken, and giving blow for blow, "if I were a man I'd not sing of naught but love, as Messire Yves does now-a-days. Thunder of God!" – her father's oath came out strangely in her high voice, but as red-hot as ever he had made it – "is there naught else to think of but kissing and clipping?"

She became silent as suddenly as she had spoken, and frowned down at her hands lying tightly clenched on her lap. The Countess turned to Yves;

Fair friend, can you answer this woman of mine? Or is love foolishness?"

Yves dared to look at her for a second, then dropped his eyes to the fire.

"I am unskilful and right unworthy to answer in so . . . in so great a quarrel," he said in a low, halting voice, and paused, while a dark flush rose slowly under his sallow skin. "But I have learned. . . . If a man serve his lady he serves the greatest lord of earth and finds the perfect way. . . . He cannot serve a greater lord than Love . . . and . . . Ah! fair, gentle ladies, forgive my stumbling tongue . . .! But bethink you how a man finds all worship and honour in that service . . . and such joy. . . ." He threw his hands wide in a despairing gesture. "Ah! I cannot," he said, and turned towards the Countess.

She smiled at him, softly.

"Ye have said enough for me, fair friend," she said, and then, as laughter peeped out of her eyes, she looked round at Audiart.

"And enough for thee, wench?" she said.

Audiart blushed again from the neck of her blood-red gown to the roots of her dark hair, but her brown eyes flashed as the women laughed.

"I am not a troubadour like Messire Yves," she answered – and her tone said "God be thanked!" – "I have no fine words . . . but . . ."

"Ah, Domna," Yves broke in, turning to her almost pleadingly, "this service is the fairest thing. See! . . . the knight must choose for his lady one already wife to another lord, so that no thought but of true pure service cometh to him. He serves her. . . . If so be she is gracious to him his soul is nigh to Paradise. . . . He is hers entire, and no thought of gain. . . . He doth not. . . . Alas!" he broke off with the same help-less words, "I cannot! . . . But I will sing. Hearken ye to another more able than I."

He snatched up his lute, and without even the prelude of a chord began to chant that lovely Romance of Tristan, turning to it as to a revelation of truth which made argument unnecessary.

As he chanted, thrumming gently on the lute from time to time in the manner of minstrels, both he and his audience forgot the dispute, and while some of the women paused in their work and sat dreaming, with fingers idle, others bent their faces over their stitches to hide from the glow of the firelight the tears upon their cheeks. Yves kept his eyes on the ground, for the Countess had told him long ago, teasingly, sweetly, that he must not look at her when he sang; but she could watch him, and she did; and the sorrows of Ysolt were nothing to her but a pleasant sweet sound:

> Amis, je fail à mun desir
> Car en voz bras quidai murir,
> en un sarcu enseveili. . . .

She smiled, so slight a smile it could hardly be seen, and her glance wandered over him, from his straight black hair and shadowed eyes to the plain hem of his green gown and the sober buff leather of his shoes.

When he finished, and laid the lute down, one woman sighed, and another laughed with a catch in her breath. The Countess pushed a cushion forward with her foot.

"Sit here, Messire Yves," she said, and when Yves seated himself cross-legged at her feet, "Give him an apple now."

"Ah!" said one damsel after a short silence, wiping her eyes daintily on the end of her trailing sleeve. "It is a very sad tale!"

"There are no such lovers now to cry for," said an elder woman tartly. "Men now-a-days take all love as light as merry-making."

"Well, what is love but pleasure?" cried the girl with the laughing voice who had teased Audiart in the garden, and she threw her arm round her neighbour's waist, and pinched her so that she squealed.

"Messire Yves does not think so," said a pert girl with flaming hair, Geralda of Fouquebrune. She had tried in vain to make Yves look at her, and now she succeeded, but though she was ready for his eyes she could not hold them.

"Nay," he said softly, looking down at the Countess' slipper. "That's foolishness, to say love is naught but pleasure."

"But," cried Geralda, and she was very cross, "Messire Guiraut of Cabreira said so. I heard him say it. Did he not, Domna?" she said, turning to the Countess.

"Ah! . . . but Messire Guiraut . . ." said the Countess.

. . . . .

It was not many days after this that Yves happened to come back from the tilt-yard with two other esquires, Guy of Chabannes and Adhemar of Las Tours, down the cloister-like covered way along the walls, which led from the tilt-yard, by the postern gate, past the door of the Chapel, to the main courtyard of the castle. They were coming back from tilting, deliciously tired, their helmets hanging by the chains over their shoulders, the mail gloves pulled off but dangling at their wrists. Pons, who had been with them, had stayed behind to have a rivet fastened at the armourer's shop, so they strolled slowly, laughing a little, and full of the contentment which exercise brings to healthy bodies.

As they turned the corner near the Chapel door they saw coming to-wards them three of the Countess' ladies, Almodis and Agnes of Brives, and Audiart of Rouillac. All stopped suddenly, for the passage was narrow, then Guy, laughing aloud, sprang forward and seized Almodis round the waist.

"A capture! A capture!" he cried, and lifting her in his arms, ran on, stumbling under his burden. They heard Almodis protesting, but with

74

a laugh in her voice, and a smothered answer from Guy before he turned the next corner.

Adhemar turned to Yves.

"There's still a maid for each of us," he said, and snatched at Agnes, but she slipped by him, and bunching up her long yellow robe in her hands, she fled, her blue wimple flying out behind her and Adhemar in hot pursuit.

Before Adhemar had gone a couple of strides Yves had decided to take his advice, but Audiart was ready for him. She backed against the wall, standing there, dumb and fierce; when Yves caught and dragged her forward, she struck out at his face, and as he lowered it, at his head, struggling like a mad thing.

Yves had followed the examples of Guy and Adhemar thoughtlessly and lightly, but Audiart's resistance changed that. At first he was merely brutally angry at her blows, then, feeling her so weak for all her fierceness, anger went down before an impulse equally old and terrible. She ceased to struggle for a minute and he threw back his head so that the chain hood jingled lightly, and laughed, and drew her closer, so that to escape his lips she must strain her head away, her terrified eyes watching him aslant.

He paused, smiling because he was so completely master, and as he smiled he saw her eyes change, and something he could not understand pass like a shadow over her face. All her resistance ceased, and her eyes clung to his, crying to him, so he thought, for mercy.

He stared at her for a moment, his face still bent over hers, then loosing her abruptly, almost pushed her from him. They stood for a moment close to one another, both silent and incapable of movement or even of thought, as the spent wave fell back. Then Yves bowed his head, muttered something unintelligible, and left her.

Without knowing where he went he made for the ramparts and strode along them blindly, noticing neither the chill, drizzling rain which the wind blew into his face, nor the weight of his mail coat. He had forgotten Audiart too, had forgotten her the moment he left her. It was to the Countess that his thoughts leapt – hounds whose leashes Audiart had only served to slip. Away down the wind went that wonderful love which he had praised; those hounds were baying upon a different, hotter scent. A fig for Heavenly Courtesy, and the love which sought no gain. The Countess was a woman, he, a man. That was the lesson he had learnt.

Two nights afterwards there was high revel in Angoulême, since heralds and knights had come from Lord Adhemar of Limoges, and must be feasted before they were sent home again with presents and fair speeches, and who knows what secret words to repeat to their lord about a new league against Count Richard.

Some of the greater knights sat at table with the Old Count and Count Vulgrin, and drank after them from the great gilded cup called Galdemar, round whose brim the jewels winked in the candlelight. The other messengers sat, according to their degree, among the knights and men-at-arms of Angoulême, and everywhere the scullions, with their tunics looped up, scurried to and fro carrying the great platters, while from time to time some specially dainty or curious dish would be carried up to the Count's table with horns and trumpets blown before it, and little drums beaten.

After the meal was ended Count Vulgrin beckoned to a page, and putting into his hands the great cup Galdemar, sent him down the hall to Guiraut of Cabreira, who sat among the knights. The lad whispered in his ear, and Guiraut, rising, drank to the Counts, set the cup down, and sent the lad off for his viol.

During the pause everyone settled themselves more comfortably in their seats, elbows were rested on tables, chins on hands. Count Vulgrin leaned aside and whispered the Countess, who looked at him and laughed. The Old Count threw himself back in his chair so that his face was in shadow, and folded his dark blue samite cloak, with its embroidery of tripping stags, more closely round him. At the lower end of the hall the men-at-arms talked behind their hands to one another, and the scullions bestirred themselves to clear away the last trenchers and the squares of black bread which would serve the common folk for their next meal.

Yves, standing among the esquires behind Count Guilhem's chair, watched Cabreira as he stood, his handsome head thrown back, his ruddy brown hair curled and shining. The troubadour's broad shoulders were covered by a cloak of azure, and the tunic below was of hunter's green. He was evidently thinking of what he should sing, for his eyes were fixed absently on the smoke-blackened rafters, and his fingers beat out a measure on the golden belly of Galdemar.

The lad came back with the viol, and Guiraut tuned it carefully, and began to sing. He sang first a song of Bernard of Ventadour, then that lovely chanson which Jaufré Rudel made to his "amor de lonh," the princess far away, and all the while Yves' eyes were on the back of the Countess' head, while the music clamoured in his heart. Then Guiraut drew the bow again across the strings and Yves raised his eyes, for he knew this prelude. It was a new song, made by Guiraut himself while the Countess and Lord Vulgrin had been away in the southern parts of Angoulême. Yves had seen the troubadour working on it, crouched over the brazier in his tower-room, trying out the melody on a lute, and drumming the metre with his fingers on his knee. Yves knew all about it, knew to whom the sweet notes cried, and could not bear to hear it. He said nothing to anyone, but passing behind the Count's chair he reached a little door that led from the hall into the garden. He closed it behind him, shutting himself out from the sound of Guiraut's voice, and stood in the frosty faint moonlight in a sudden great silence.

Only three people in the Hall took any note of his going – old Count Guilhem, the Countess, and Guiraut of Cabreira.

Walking up and down the straight paths, Yves saw, after a time, the lights put out in the Hall, and felt himself now entirely alone. The only sound in the garden came from the little fountain and he was drawn towards it as though it companioned him. For a while he watched the dark, tumbling water, then turned and sat down on one of the stone seats. His hand touched something there, and a faint jangling sound mingled with the clear water-noise of the fountain. Someone had left a lute lying on the seat.

He picked it up and played with it idly for a time, not thinking of anything, but only shaken and torn by a tumult of desire. Then, as his fingers thrummed idly on one string or another, he first began to listen to the notes, afterwards gradually to order them to a melody, and at last his distress found a channel and an outlet.

77

Perhaps because it was the saddest of all, he chose in that night of faint moon and starlight the 'Alba,' the dawn-song of the Provençal poets, which deals with the parting of lovers. He tried his tune over once or twice and then began to sing – "Sobre la tor la gaita guarda" –

> The watchman on the tower looks east,
> The grey light creeps along the sky,
> The chill dawn wind goes softly by.
> Yet there's no colour in the flowers,
> No sound is there from man or beast,
> No wakeful eyes or lips but ours . . .
> Ah! dearest lady, make this kiss
> An endless infinite of bliss . . .
>   "Away! It is the dawn!"
>
> My dearest lady lifts her head;
> She hears the clear note of the horn
> That tells us of a new day born.
> Ah! friendly watchman, do not mark
> The waking east that flushes red,
> 'Tis deep night still, the west is dark.
> "Nay, lord, look up, day storms the sky!"
> Alas! my dearest love, good-bye!
>   "Away! It is the dawn!"

Rough and of necessity inadequate as the song was, it eased him for the moment. He laid the lute down on the stone bench and buried his face in his hands.

Suddenly he felt fingers touch his hair. He sat still, still as death, knowing, beyond all reason, that it was the Countess; then he bowed his head lower, slipped off the seat and to his knees, and bending down to her feet, he kissed them. He heard her give a little gasp; she stooped, and caught his hands in hers, and now he was looking up at what to him was all of heaven.

"Yves," she said softly, "was that song for me?" but she knew that the question was needless.

He whispered "Yea" and his voice shook.

She loosed his hands slowly, and lifting her own put them together below her chin, laid lightly together as though she prayed.

"It was a right sweet song, well made and well sung," she said in a voice that gave tenderness to the formal praise; then made as though to turn away. Yves, suddenly and desperately bold, threw out his arms and

78

caught her about the knees, like a suppliant. She swayed over him, and one long plait brushed his cheek as he looked up at her.

" 'Ah! dearest lady!' " he said, and no more.

The Countess stood quite still for a second, then with a movement as graceful as the flight of a swallow she stooped, took his face between her hands, kissed him once, lightly, and was gone.

VIII

By God that sends the master maids
I know not whence she came,
But the sword she bore to save the soul
Went up like an altar flame
Where a broken race in a desert place
Call on the Holy Name.

HILAIRE BELLOC.

AUDIART of Rouillac had not long since come to Angoulême and she hated it, but, since she was the Count's ward and a woman, she had had no choice, when her father died, but to obey the Count's messenger, and come to Angoulême, leaving Rouillac in the hands of one of the Count's stewards, a fat, pursy, straw-haired man whom she mistrusted at first sight, and on no grounds whatever.

Life in Angoulême among the Countess' ladies she found almost insupportably dull, since there seemed to be nothing but needlework and chatter, and all the time she fretted to be back in Rouillac. She thought of a new fishpool she would make, and a clearing in the woods; of all sorts of little matters that were mightily important to her, and then she raged because she could do nothing.

Her only comfort was a truant pleasure. She would slip off sometimes, making an excuse about a sick hawk or some such thing, and make her way to the stables, there to linger as long as she dared, watching and sometimes talking to the serfs working there. It was in this way that she came to know old Peire Bersin, one of Count Guilhem's stewards, and a quaint friendship grew up between them. Peire had been one of the Count's sergeants when both were young, and now, small, frail and dry, he spent his time riding about, on a very fat bay horse, from manor to manor on the Count's demesne, overseeing the farming of the lands. When he came to Angoulême he could almost always be found near the stables or the cow-shippens accompanied always by a big old hunting-dog, yellow-toothed and lean, with a dusty coat worn with age.

For some time Peire was Audiart's only friend in Angoulême, and she came as often as she dared to talk to him and to listen to him talking. There was no part of his business that wearied her in the telling, and there was little of it that she forgot. The selling price of hay; how to choose which cattle to kill and salt at Michaelmas and which to feed in the shippens through the winter; the different ways of thatching; the planting and thinning of trees; to all these things and a hundred more Audiart would listen eagerly, asking question on question, and storing it all up in her mind against the time when she should have Rouillac to order.

One day, between the hay and corn seasons, she found Peire in the stable yard watching the breaking in of a fine young chestnut colt. She made her way round the trampled circle and smiled at him.

"Hath a good pace and holds his head well," she said, nodding towards the colt as it swung by.

"Aye," said old Peire, and no more, watching the animal through narrowed eyes. Only when it was led away did he turn to Audiart and begin to talk. There was a lack of straw just now, since last year's harvest had been short in the stalk. This would be better, please God, if they had not too much rain. He had seen as good a field of grain beyond Saint Michel as ever in his life days.

Audiart listened, and reaching out her hand pulled the old dog towards her by one of his short and shabby ears. She took his nose in her hand, shaking his head from side to side, and because she was a friend of his, he took her roughness politely.

"Ah, Saints!" she cried, when Peire stopped, "I would I were at Rouillac. A year ago we had a right good crop there when all about was blighted . . . and the vines. . . . My father. . . . Alas! when he was alive I did not idle away my days with a needle among a pack of fools."

Peire looked her over as he had looked at the horse.

"I knew Lord Gilles of Rouillac," he said. "And he was a wise man . . . a good judge of cattle and corn. . . . But it is not often a wench mells in such matters. I wonder sometimes he let ye. . . . Not that ye don't know a fair deal. . . . Aye," he chuckled and rubbed his ear with a knotty finger, "I am thinking ye'll not need a steward in your fief to tell ye how nor why."

Audiart's plain face changed at that.

"Ah! Pierre," she said, "indeed I love the ordering of a fief. . . . I do myself think I could as well as any man. . . . Better than Lord Jaufré of Châteauneuf. . . . God rest his soul," she added perfunctorily.

"Lord Jaufré . . . who be he?" said Peire.

"Did ye not know. . . .? Nay, ye would not. I was troth plighted to him. But he had a fall at a tourney and lay a-bed for a year, with no strength in his limbs and then he died. That was no more than two months back and so I am free again. Dear Saints!" She sighed impatiently. "When shall I get me another lord and be wed?"

Peire Bersin turned and looked at her narrowly.

"Nay, then," he said doubtfully. "Are ye so hot for love?"

Audiart shook her head.

"Not I," she cried almost angrily. "But to be wed. They two are not the same at all, at least with us lords. I know not how it goes with the common folk."

Peire shook his head. Such a convention was strange to him, and being a simple man in a simple age he spoke plainly about child-bearing.

"Oh! as to that," said Audiart, and shrugged, putting the question aside. She was not offended, but the subject did not interest her.

"But when I am wed then I can go to Rouillac, for only maids must needs be fools," she said.

This was Audiart as she had always known herself until the moment when Yves pushed her from him and left her standing in the passage by the Chapel. Then she found herself a stranger. For a moment she stood watching him vacantly, and then, hearing laughter and the voice of Agnes of Brives, she looked wildly round for shelter, saw the door of the Chapel close by, and slipping in, closed it softly behind her.

The little Chapel was very dark after the outdoor light. Colour, form, and the heavy scent of incense seemed all subdued to one dimness, while a priest's voice rose and fell in strange, hollow cadences as indistinct and deep as the colours in the gloom. She turned back to the door, pressing her forehead against the hard wood, and felt all the more by contrast how alive her flesh was with the pulses of her leaping blood.

She gave a shuddering sigh, and lifting her hands strained them against her breast so that she might feel again his linked mail biting into the flesh, and shutting her eyes she tried to make herself believe that this time he would kiss her.

In the empty pause shame and confusion came to her, and she snatched her hands away, and turned to look over her shoulder, fearing that she might have been watched. Even when she knew herself unseen she was ashamed at this sudden strange thing. The rejoicing blood fled up to her face and she covered it with both hands, but even so she could not hide herself from herself.

Then because she was a brave girl she lifted her head.

"I will not!" she muttered through her teeth. "I will not! It is an evil thing. . . . It must be evil."

"And lovely! . . . and lovely!" sang her blood, and she felt his arms round her again, and forgot everything else in remembering that. But he had not kissed her, and she ached at the want of it. Oh fool! fool! she cried out on herself within her mind. How could she have been so slow to learn that . . . that . . . ? She shook again with the remembrance of the sudden realisation, which, as his lips drew closer to hers, had taken all strength deliciously from her and raised her eyes to wait upon his.

She crushed her knuckles to her mouth, and again reaction came, and drove her now towards the altar. She went down on her knees beside a pillar, and put her palms tight together, but she did not pray, and one would have said that between her straining hands there was no room for even the least of God's fingers stretched out for her to cling to.

There she fought to be master of her desires, and untouched, since that had always been her unconsidered creed; and, when she had almost won, something which was no less herself laughed at her, and, wordless, and needing no words, overwhelmed her denial. But she would not yield.

At last the tumult died down, and by ways I cannot show, comfort came. She did not herself know how it was, since thoughts change like water ripples, and it does not need a new thought to bring enlightenment. When she got up stiffly from her knees she looked from under frowning brows at the altar with its steady lamp, and crossed herself. The gesture was at once a pledge and a prayer.

83

"But," she raised her chin, and muttered the words half aloud to the Presence there. "I love . . . him. . . . That is not the same."

The day after Yves had sung his "Alba" in the garden, Audiart, with a basket on her arm, went down through the orchard which had been planted in these times of comparative peace between the wall and the moat on the townward side of the castle. It was a sweet and quiet place, sloping so steeply that even the bare branches were enough to make the lower part private from the wall and postern above. Beyond the moat there was another orchard and a little stackyard belonging to one of the burgesses, and beyond that the brown huddle of houses that was the town.

Audiart had left the Countess and her ladies waiting for Yves of Rifaucon to come to amuse them. The Countess had sent a page off to find him, or, failing him, Guiraut of Cabreira. Audiart sat still till the lad had been gone a few moments and then she sprang up.

"Give me a basket. I will get some apples. I saw some good late ones in the orchard. I am thirsty." So she talked herself from the room, giving far too many reasons, if anyone had troubled to listen to her. Now, she stood in the postern gateway a moment, swinging her basket and looking about her. She knew just where the best apples were to be found, but there was no hurry; she did not want to go back yet, since he would be there. Her throat tightened at the thought of going into the room and being looked at. He would look at her. She called herself a fool for running away, since if she had stayed she would at least have been inconspicuous.

She started off impatiently down the slope, and then habit prevailed upon her mind, so that she forgot her trouble and noticed only the condition of the trees, and catching a glimpse of the stackyard between the branches, saw that the stacks were well made and thatched – a good harvest.

Half-way down the slope she stopped suddenly, and a rude hand seemed to snatch at her heart and shake it. At the foot of one of the trees Yves sat crouched. One arm was flung round his up-drawn knees, the other rose and fell monotonously, but with a suppressed ferocity in the movement, plunging his dagger again and again into the ground be-

84

side him. Audiart could not see his face, but without that she might have guessed that he was not in a mood to welcome any interruption.

She might have guessed, but she did not, since that shock of the heart which the sudden sight of him had caused was making it difficult for her to breathe, impossible for her to think. She hurried towards him, not knowing what she would say, but only that she must reach him quickly or run away; and coming up behind his shoulder she stood a moment, one hand nervously swaying a branch where hung two pale yellow-green apples. He did not turn, although her shadow fell on the grass before him, and she must wait a moment before she could get breath to speak.

As she paused, he burst out suddenly, but still without looking at her.

"Tell my lady the Countess that I cannot come," he said, and Audiart hardly recognised his voice.

"I am not from the Countess," she said, and was suddenly jealous. She had not cared nor thought before that he was the professed servant of some woman, although she had known it. Now that she knew whom he served she became cruelty incarnate. It was not the Countess she hated and lusted to hurt, but Yves, and if she had held a knife she could have killed him to satisfy her rage.

"Ah!" she said after a long pause, and her voice was as strange as his had been. "It is the Countess!"

Yves' hand stayed in the monotonous movement which he had not interrupted even for her coming.

"What is the Countess?" he said, and if she had not been so angry she might have been afraid.

"That you. . . ." She could not say "love," and a fresh spurt of malice drove spiteful words to her lips. "That you run after like a little dog," she said.

"Will you begone?" said Yves through his teeth.

Audiart laughed, but there were tears of rage in her eyes.

"Why should I begone, Messire the Courteous?" she mocked. "Is the orchard yours?"

Yves got up so suddenly that she started back.

"If ye will not, then will I," he said, and turning his back on her, tramped away, his head bent and the dagger swinging in his hand.

85

Audiart stood perfectly still for as long as one would take to count ten; she turned her head slowly to watch him, then, as abruptly as he had left her, she clutched her long skirts and fled after him. She had seen his face as he turned from her, and understood at last that he was in trouble.

She caught him up by the edge of the moat.

"Messire. . . . Stop!" she cried, but he took no notice, and she had to put herself in his way with outspread arms before he came to a stand.

He had been angry before, but her persistence drove him to fury.

"Can you not let me be? Get out of my way!" he said and raised his hand, but she did not move.

"No! no! no!" she cried. "I will not. . . . I must know . . . the Countess . . . hath she been unkind?"

"Death of God!" cried Yves. "No!" and his hand went out in a furious gesture to strike her aside.

Audiart gave a little gasp as she saw the dagger flash, but desperately brave, in the way of women, she snatched at his wrist, caught it, and clung with both hands. The sudden check held Yves quite still for a second, then he growled something in his throat, and began to tear at her fingers with his free hand.

"No! No!" she cried again, her voice rising higher as he hurt her. "Ye shall tell me . . . what is amiss . . . ye shall!"

Without any reason or warning all Yves' fury left him, and his hand fell to his side.

"Nay . . . let me be . . . Domna . . . let me go!" he said.

His voice caught Audiart by the throat and choked her, but she clenched her teeth and stared at his averted face, so that when he raised it, he saw only that her mouth was stern, and her eyes as clear, intolerant, and fearless as a boy's. He looked at her stupidly for a second, then dropped his head again.

Audiart snatched her hands back from his wrist and put them behind her lest they should go out to fondle him like a hurt child, and her throat ached with tears so that she could not speak.

Yves had lifted the dagger again and was staring dully at the blade.

86

"I must. . . . I cannot. . . . I have sworn. . . . I may no longer serve her," he muttered.

"But how?" cried Audiart. "Wherefore? Hath she said. . . . Is Count Vulgrin wroth . . . ?"

Yves shook his head.

"Nay . . . none of those. . . . But I cannot tell you. . . . Only I must not go nigh her nor sing . . . nor. . . . And she . . . and yesterday. . . ." His voice failed and they were both silent, and if he was wretched so too was Audiart, for pity can be a wild beast and tear the heart.

Then, since she could not take the short way to comfort him, she tried reason, though without much hope.

"But I do not understand – but I have heard of such haps before, in the stories. . . . And the lover, he served his lady without seeing her . . . not ill content. And Messire Guiraut of Cabreira saith –"

Yves broke in with an ugly laugh.

"Let be what Messire Guiraut said!" he cried.

"But . . . surely . . . ye believe the same . . . ye are his friend . . . ?"

"Am I?" said Yves and laughed again.

"But," persisted Audiart, "I heard ye say yourself that love is –"

Yves raised his head and what she saw on his face held her silent and sent the blood up to hers.

"Love?" he said. "I want her!"

Audiart came suddenly back to reality, and ceased to argue.

"Ah!" she said in a low voice, speaking only to herself. "It is no wonder the priests say it is an evil thing." She was thinking of the knowledge she had got of herself in the little chapel two days ago, and suddenly she smote herself on the breast.

"Up, beast!" she cried. "Up from thy foul mire!"

Although Yves entirely misread her intention and took her words to himself, he did not fail to recognise the fierce urgency of her tone. It awakened him, and, as though an archangel had shrilled to him from the midst of a blinding light, that sudden trumpet call of fierce austerity brought him to a stand.

"Yea," he said slowly, and after a long silence. "A beast I am. . . . And yet. . . ." His voice rose to a cry of pain as he remembered again the golden Countess. "No! By God Himself! it is not that . . . not that only. . . . It was not all foolishness that I said. . . . And how shall I forego all that fair thing . . .? There is none better!"

He met Audiart's eyes and thought them inexorable when they were in fact merely desperate.

"There is," she said; "many a better thing. Love is weakness."

He turned from her and looked down at the green, still moat, and watched the movements of a small company of ducks which came smoothly into sight, and passed, with now and then a sideways dart, trailing lovely lines of water-ripples behind them. He remembered those ducks for years, and yet all his mind was set on Audiart and could not escape. Nor, indeed, did he wish to escape, since all the monk in him which underlay the troubadour answered her summons.

As for Audiart, she did not care, being a woman, that she had spoken treason against love. She was in no way concerned with Love in the abstract, nor, properly, with any love at all – only with her man.

Yves turned to her at last.

"What can I do?" he said, as simply as if she were a saint or his mother, and she had to put violence on herself to answer him without weeping.

"Why," she said, "there are other things a-plenty for a man. There is honour to be got in knighthood, and . . . there are the Holy Places to defend . . . and thy land to rule."

He looked up at her slowly, and she had to turn away biting her lips and winking her eyes to keep the tears back. She dared not cry, since if she did he might be offended – worse, he might guess. . . .

"I am a landless man," he said. "My land is lost."

When Audiart spoke, her voice was hard, and seemed even hostile.

"I must go," she said.

Yves had been busied in idle play with the dagger. He started at her sudden words, and then gave an exclamation. She turned back to him.

"It is nothing," he said, showing her a clean cut across the thumb of the thick leather hawking-glove he wore.

"There is blood," she said, but he shook his head, and pulling the glove off, sucked at the shallow cut, while she watched him hungrily.

"It's nothing," he said again, taking his hand from his mouth and

88

smiling at her. It was the first time that his smile had been for her, and it brought tears smarting to her eyes. She looked down at his thumb and longed to have it to tend but did not dare to say so.

"The glove is done," said Yves ruefully, and spread it out for her to see. She gave up hope of being allowed to do anything for his hand, and turned her attention to the glove.

"It could mend," she said, and halted on an offer to do it for him. Yves laughed.

"No use! The bird's claws would find it out. Nay, it's done," and he threw it carelessly over his shoulder.

Audiart watched it fall, then moved nervously.

"I must go," she said again.

They went slowly up the sloping path together, Audiart keeping far from Yves lest she should touch him. For a wonder he noticed that trifle, and it seemed to him to be of a piece with all her fineness. Before they reached the gate she stopped.

"I came to get apples," she said, without looking at Yves. "Farewell, Messire," and without another word she turned and left him.

Yves looked after her, watching her red gown as it trailed behind her. "She always wears that sanguine colour," he remembered, and then blotting out the trivial thought came loneliness, because she had left him to his tormentors. He set his teeth and strode on, ashamed of the weakness which she would have scorned.

When Audiart reached the bank of the moat she stopped, and looked all about her, but not for apples to gather. There was no one to see her, and the glove lay close to her feet. She stooped quickly, and snatched it up, and peering round again, held it hidden for a moment in her hands.

Then she raised it slowly, but the blood ran up suddenly to her face, and she let her hands fall. She dared not kiss it, even here where there was no one to see. Perhaps in the dark . . . yet even there. . . .

For a moment she stood with the glove hanging from her hands. She must hide it, and so, having spied about her again, she drew a deep breath, folded it hurriedly, and slipped it into her bosom, drawing the ends of her wimple together over it, as if the trees themselves were pointing at it. Her face flamed again, and she covered her eyes with both hands.

It was twilight before she came back to the Countess' room, and she had judged it wiser not to bring any apples, since they would be a reminder of how long a time she had been absent.

IX

"I marvel much, pardy (quoth she) for to behold the rout,
To see man, woman, boy and beast, to toss the world about;

. . . .

Yet are they never friends indeed until they once fall out;
Thus ended she and her song and said, before she did remove,
The falling out of faithful friends renewing is of love."

RICHARD EDWARDES.

IT so happened that Count Vulgrin stood at one of the windows of
the Chancery tower when Yves came up from the orchard after
leaving Audiart. Vulgrin watched him go slowly by, stop short half-
way across the ward, and stand, staring at nothing, only to start away
again like a horse touched with the spur. He watched Yves till he was
gone and then turned back into the room with a heavy frown on his
face. The Old Count sat bowed over the table, busy with a list of corn
dues from the demesne. He muttered crossly to himself over the parchment, and worried the end of his quill pen with his teeth.

Vulgrin looked at him angrily for a moment as though he were
somehow to blame, then he stalked across the room and stood beside
him. The Old Count did not look up, and Vulgrin, snatching up a pen,
began to jab at the table with it. For a few minutes the old Count took
no notice of his fidgeting, but at last:

"Away from my light! I cannot see," he snapped.

Vulgrin started, and then, as though the words had freed his own
tongue, he burst suddenly into speech.

"See here, fair lord father! That esquire of thine . . . that Yves of
Rifaucon. . . . My wife . . . he. . . . And it's not him only, that cursed
Guiraut of Cabreira . . . he too. . . ."

The Old Count had listened in silence, still bent over his work, but
now he raised his head with the suspicion of a crooked smile on his lips.

"Son! Son!" he said. "Dost not know that it is great honour for any
lady to be sung by a troubadour so famous as Messire Guiraut. . .? At
least they tell me so."

91

"I care not," cried Vulgrin. "And if he is famous, the other is nothing – a landless esquire. . . . Cabreira perhaps . . . but I'll not have the other here; he shall out to-night and sing his songs to the bramble-bushes. . . . Aye, and thank God his throat isn't tightened in a noose!"

The Old Count huddled lower in his chair.

"Eh! now! Eh! now!" he muttered half aloud as he drew inky patterns on the table with the squeaking quill and wiped them off again with one long finger. "Eh! now! What a dutiful good son! He will hang mine own esquire or drive him forth; all to save the old man trouble!"

Vulgrin brought his fist down upon the table with a sudden crash, and the Old Count clapped his hands to his ears, and began a testy remonstrance, but Vulgrin bore him down:

"I'll not have it, I say. . . . If he be your esquire, call him off . . . then I'll be satisfied."

Guilhem took his hands from his ears.

"Ye need not shout," he said coldly. "What hath he done?" He met Vulgrin's eyes as he asked the question, and they dropped.

"I . . . I do not know . . . not for sure . . . but in her garden . . . the other night. . . ."

"Oh!" said Guilhem. "Ye saw that?" and he chuckled.

Vulgrin looked up again with rage in his face.

"You laugh?" he cried. "You. . . ."

"That is naught," said the Old Count.

"Naught? Then have you seen more? By –"

Guilhem sat up suddenly in his chair.

"Y'are a fool. Be silent," he said, and angry as Vulgrin was, he obeyed.

The Old Count relented.

"More . . ." he said, and chuckled again, "but no worse . . . no harm." And as though the matter was finished he picked up his pen again, and tried it on his nail.

Vulgrin watched his bent head furiously for a moment, then he flung round the table and sat down opposite him.

"I have wondered why ye had such a favour to him – to Yves of Rifaucon," he said after a minute.

Guilhem crackled the parchment as though to remind Vulgrin that he was busy.

"Must I give account?" he mumbled, and then with a sudden harsh chuckle he looked up at his son.

"Nay . . . ye're wrong in what ye're thinking. It's not for that reason neither," he said, "for I never saw his mother in my life days."

Vulgrin frowned as though the Count had mistaken his meaning, he did not dispute it, and stretching out his hand, drew towards him the squared reckoning board with its counters and picked up a notched tally from the heap that lay on the table.

"Well!" he said, as he fell to work. "Call him off then, and I'll say no more. . . . But I shall watch . . . and Guiraut of Cabreira shall pack too if I. . . . Do ye hear?" he challenged his father.

The Old Count only grunted.

Vulgrin had said that he would watch; the Old Count had said nothing, but it would have been strange if he had not set himself, with an equal though different ardour, the same task. So here were two watchers, but had there been a hundred, and each of them eyed like Argus, they would all have seen the same thing. No hermit ever fled the company of women more persistently than Yves of Rifaucon. No lover was ever more assiduous than Guiraut of Cabreira.

It was quite clear to Count Vulgrin that his father had given Yves warning, and he soon lost interest in that direction, and even helped Yves in some of his evasions, with a good-humoured tolerance, as of one in the secret. The Old Count, however, was hot on the track of another secret. Yves had had no warning from him, and none, he was sure, from Vulgrin. Why, then, this sudden change? He watched, he listened, he lay in wait to entrap in their talk any who might be in the secret, but, for a time, it was all in vain. He tried Yves, and was met with a blank face and a stolid sullenness that baulked him. He tried the Countess, but she was as puzzled as himself, though she did not manage to conceal it so well. He tried Pons, and there again had no success, for Pons knew less than any other about the business.

Guilhem might have hit on the truth sooner if he had not been busy over other and greater matters. The Limousin ambassadors were still in

Angoulême, and, if it was a mere visit of courtesy except for some business to do with the rights over certain beechwoods, the courtesy must have been peculiar, or the beechwoods valuable, for there was no talk yet of the men of Limoges departing.

One chilly day of east wind, when the sun shone through a veil of cloud as coldly luminous as a cat's-eye stone, the Old Count was stalking along the broad walk that led under the lee of the castle wall to the steps by which he meant to mount to the archers' gallery along the top. The wind, uncertain here because of the sheltering walls, carried along with it a little bustling crowd of newly fallen leaves. They ran after him like children, leaping and dancing, then sank down dead, and then up once more, faster and faster, to rise in a circling whirl and fall flat again as the wind drew away.

The Old Count turned as he heard the rustling of the following leaves, and made a grimace at them as they sank. He climbed the creaking stairs slowly, and at the top stood for a moment to take breath while the thin wind flattened the skirts of his long gown against his legs. As he lingered, habit drove him to glance over the battlement into the narrow street which ran below this side of the castle. He expected to see nothing, but chance favoured him.

Down below two of his esquires rode soberly by with hawks on their fists. They were Adhemar of Las Tours and Pons of Jarnac. That was simple enough; they had leave to go and the Count did not care for that. What held him still peering over the wall was the sight of Yves of Rifaucon coming down the narrow lane in the opposite direction. Guilhem was quick and missed nothing. He saw how Yves hesitated, then went doggedly on with his head bent, and how Pons drew his horse sharply to one side as they passed. Neither spoke to nor looked at the other, only Adhemar called over his shoulder to know if Yves would go hawking with them. Yves answered with a surly "No," while Pons rode on without even turning his head.

When they were gone the Old Count continued his way along the ramparts. He was going to see for himself if the new stock of bows had been properly greased and stacked in a dry place, but as he went his mind was busy with Yves' affairs.

"Why had Yves given up his suit just when the Countess...?"

94

Guilhem chuckled to himself, then frowned again at the puzzle. And Cabreira . . . had he anything to do with it, since Yves' loss was his gain . . . ? And now there was something amiss between Yves and Pons of Jarnac, those two friends . . . and Yves in the devil's own mood all the time.

The Old Count vented his exasperation at the silly puzzle upon the man who had stored the bows in a corner where the rain might drive in on them.

On the feast of All Hallows, in the early morning, Guilhem Talifer, Count of Angoulême, made four new knights. Three were esquires from Limoges – the fourth was Pons of Jarnac. When the business of bathing, clothing, and knighting was over, the four new knights went off to eat after their vigil, and then to arm for the tourney, which would be the last before the winter season, and only possible because of the long spell of fair weather which had made October seem like a softer June.

The Old Count meanwhile departed to his room in the Bear Tower, where he would first eat alone, and after be dressed for state, since, when the tourney was over, the Limousin ambassadors would take formal leave. When Guilhem left the Chapel he called for Yves of Rifaucon to attend him, and the other esquires sighed with relief, and grinned as Yves went off after the Old Count.

"Old Horseface always will have Yves," said one.

"Aye – Saints be thanked," said another with a laugh.

"I wish them joy, each of other," put in a third, "for Rifaucon is like a curst dog on a chain now-a-days."

It was true that the Old Count would send for Yves more often than for any of his other esquires, and in general Yves did not rebel against the extra duty; indeed, although he hardly knew that it was so, the Count's room had become a sort of refuge for him. To-day, however, he went unwillingly, for his eyes were heavy for lack of sleep, and his temper was like a frayed bowstring stretched tight. He was glad therefore, when, before even he had brought the ewer for the Count to wash his hands, the door burst open suddenly, slamming against the wall, and Count Vulgrin came in, very red and angry.

Vulgrin was usually courteous and kind to all, but to-day he merely glared at Yves, pointed his finger at the door, and said:

"Out! I must be private."

Yves, leaning against the wall of the narrow stairway outside, supposed that it was some hitch in the Limoges business which had made Count Vulgrin so angry, but whatever the cause he had no interest in it. Presently he heard some man coming up the stairs, and went down a few steps to stop him, but the sight of Guiraut of Cabreira's broad shoulders checked the words on his tongue. He put his hand out in silence, barring the way, and Guiraut paused, looking up at him, and seeming to find words equally difficult.

Yves spoke first.

"The Counts are private, Messire. None goes in." He spoke in the formal, sing-song voice of the well-trained esquire.

"I am wanted. They wait me," said Guiraut.

Yves turned and struck on the door.

"Messire Guiraut of Cabreira," he cried loudly, and laid his ear to the wood. Then he turned to Guiraut.

"Pass in!" he said, and pushed open the door.

Ten minutes or so went by before Cabreira came out, and then he nearly stumbled over Yves, who was sitting on the steps, half asleep. Cabreira stopped with an exclamation, and seemed about to speak, but Yves turned from him and pulled to the door of the Count's room. When he looked round again the troubadour was at the bend of the stairs. Next moment he was gone.

When Vulgrin had departed Yves was called in again, and the Old Count bade fetch in his meal. He ate it in silence except for a few muttered orders and the usual peevish comments, of which Yves as a rule took no account. To-day, however, they pricked him like burrs.

At last the Count stood up.

"Get me my gear," he said. "And let's be fine for Limoges to see." His eyes followed Yves as he opened and bent over one of the big chests where lay Guilhem's state robes.

"Well," said the Old Count, watching the back of Yves' head, "thy friend Pons is a knight now."

If the slightest jerk of Yves' head was an answer, then Guilhem's words were acknowledged, but nothing more.

96

"I'll have you wanting to be his esquire!" said Guilhem with a short cackling laugh, as though he had made a jest.

Yves said nothing at all, and shut the chest very carefully, as if a noise would have broken something fragile in the room. He laid the gay embroidered cloak and surcoat over the back of a chair, and the great sword on the table. It was a very fine sword in a red leather scabbard worked with gold. The hilt was gilded too, and there were in it, besides the jewels, two of the hairs of Saint Mary Magdalene, which made it very precious.

Yves went down on one knee before the Count, with the gold spurs in his hand, and Guilhem put his foot on Yves' other knee. Yves was slow, and the Count fidgeted.

"Haste! Make haste!" he said. "Ye're as slow to-day and as owlish as if ye'd kept vigil with the knights."

Yves' finger found the buckle opening and he pulled the strap tight with a sudden tug.

"Auch! Fool! Too tight! Two holes back!" cried Guilhem.

Yves bent over it again, and was very clumsy, but Guilhem said nothing more till he had both spurs on, and the surcoat, and Yves had left him to fetch the sword with its long, embroidered belt. Then, as Yves came back to him, he spoke, his eyes looking at the wall just above Yves' head:

"Ye and Pons of Jarnac should have been made knights the same day, seeing ye are such friends."

Yves stopped short suddenly as though the bowstring had snapped.

"Blood of God!" he cried. "Does it need I tell you? I swear ye know it well enough. . . . And ye jape at me that I should be made knight . . . and call Pons my friend."

With a sudden violence, he lifted the sword in both hands and dashed it down at Guilhem's feet. The heavy blade crashed on the stone floor, and both stared at it for a second. Then Yves turned away and went slowly towards one of the windows.

"I struck him in the face," he said. "He'll not forgive it."

"But why?" said Guilhem.

"Oh!" cried Yves, "what odds why I did? Because he chid me for discourtesy to Messire Guiraut of Cabreira. That's why."

The Old Count let him go, and stood for a few minutes biting his nails. Then he stooped stiffly, picked up the sword, looked the hilt over, and began to gird himself. He was unhandy at it, and Yves, as though he could not help it, came quickly over to him and knelt down, taking the ends of the belt into his own hands.

"I ask pardon," he said gruffly, and Guilhem, having got what he wanted, was satisfied with that.

"There's no harm done," he mumbled.

When the Old Count went outside the town to the place fixed for the tourney, Yves walked beside him, leading his horse by the bridle. The Count chose to watch from a little hill beside the lists where wounded and dismounted knights could take refuge for a time. Before them the fighting swayed, broke, and re-formed, like shifting cross-currents in the sea at a point where the waves meet. A party of the knights from Limoges took possession of a barn near by, and there was a great noise of shouting and battering on the doors before they were driven out. During the fight for the barn more and more men kept coming up to take part, so that all the tide seemed to set in one direction. A knight with a very new surcoat of white silk over his armour went by riding on a big war-horse, close to the place where Guilhem and Yves stood.

"Pons!" cried Guilhem. "Pons of Jarnac!"

The knight swung his horse round and rode slowly back. The Old Count greeted him strangely.

"Put off your helm, Pons," he said, and when Pons had obeyed: "Clerk you were, knight you are, so answer me some questions wisely, knight and clerk!" said Guilhem.

Pons, as always, grew red before the Count's jeers, but he set his square chin, and looked down at the old man.

"Say then, Lord Count," he said.

"First then, for I can be clerkly too," began Guilhem, with a sliding glance at Yves, who was gazing blankly before him, "why did Yves of Rifaucon leave singing to my lady the Countess?"

He got a startled look from Pons for this, and a muttered: "I knew not even he . . ."; from Yves he got nothing but a jerk of his hand on the bridle. Guilhem went on:

98

"Second. Why did Yves of Rifaucon mis-say Guiraut of Cabreira?"

Pons looked involuntarily at Yves and lowered his eyes quickly.

"I know not," he said.

"A wise clerk!" sneered Guilhem. "And the last – Why did he strike you in the face?"

Pons grew redder yet.

"I know not that neither," he said.

Guilhem laughed.

"Is this what learning doth for a man? Doth he know nought but A and B?"

Yves turned suddenly, and spoke as it were to the Count's saddle without raising his eyes to the Count's face.

"Messire Pons doth not nose about in other folks' affairs," he said.

The Old Count looked down at the top of his head.

"Meaning that I do?"

Yves looked up quickly, then straight before him once more.

"As you will, lord," he said.

Pons waited for the Count's anger, but instead there came only a sort of cold flicker at the corners of Guilhem's mouth. He turned again to Pons.

"You know nothing of these matters?"

"Nay," said Pons.

"Fair lord," struck in Yves again, "do you?"

Guilhem did not trouble to look at him, but he reached his foot forward in the stirrup and poked Yves gently in the back.

"Yes," he said, "all! I ask no questions till I know the answers." He looked from one to the other as though he wanted applause, and his lips drooped crossly when none came.

"Now listen to me, Pons of Jarnac," he said, "and I'll give you the answers. First, then – Guiraut of Cabreira made Yves of Rifaucon forego the service of his lady, because Yves at Moulin Neuf had been fool enough to swear an oath – and swear it unasked if I have got it right. Second . . . Nay, now! I bethink me there's but one answer to my questions. Ye have it."

He watched Pon's face for a minute with his usual sour smile, then gave a sudden chuckle. Pons started at the sound, clapped his helm on again, fumbled with the strappings, and without another word snatched up his reins, wheeled his horse, and rode again into the press. It swallowed him as water swallows a stone.

When the fighting slackened, and all were beginning to think of dinner, Pons came again to the Count upon the little hill. Yves was no longer there, for Guilhem had sent him away to get himself armed and horsed, since, he said, he was weary of seeing so black a face.

Pons rode up to the Count without ceremony and so fast that he had to pull his horse back almost upon its haunches to bring it to a stand. He spoke, too, without troubling to put off his helm, so that his voice sounded strange and muffled.

"Where is that man – the troubadour – Cabreira?" he cried.

Guilhem looked at him delicately.

"How should I know?"

"But he fights with them of Limoges, against Angoulême, not with us?" said Pons.

"Doth he?"

Pons put up both hands and tore his helm off, emerging suddenly with a grimed face running with sweat, and damp streaks of hair that strayed out from under his steel cap and mail hood.

"Lord Count, where is Messire Guiraut of Cabreira?" he said.

Guilhem smiled at him coldly.

"He is gone," he said.

"Gone?" cried Pons, and the Count still smiled.

"But where? . . . Why? . . . Why did ye not tell me? How long since he went? . . . Whither?" Pons broke out furiously.

"Here is great plenty of questions!" said the Count. "Hear now if I can answer! He went two hours back; where I know not, but that he will keep clear of Angoulême; and as for telling you . . . why should I? Why do ye want the fellow?"

Pons frowned at him, but he spoke more calmly.

"He would take back that oath, if I got him," he said.

"What a fine new knight he is!" said Guilhem. "It's well for Cabreira he got away, and" – his voice changed and he looked queerly at Pons – "and for Yves of Rifaucon too!"

Pons stared, but Guilhem would say no more unless he was urged.

"What do you mean, lord Count?" said Pons.

Guilhem put up his chin, and looked at Pons down his nose.

"It's well for Yves of Rifaucon," he said, "that he gave that promise, and he'd best keep it still. . . . Ye know forest law – lopping or maiming or hanging for trespass. . . . Well, see you keep Yves out of that wood. . . There's a Count of Angoulême forester there. . . . Oh! no – not I. . . . Nay!"

Pons looked in the Count's eyes, and nodded. They came nearer to liking each other in that moment than at any time before or after.

That same afternoon, in the stable, Pons found Yves cleaning down his horse, and there the friendship was made again, and they kissed each other, and not being ashamed of tears, cried together.

Then Pons drew back, still holding Yves by the arms, and looked at him.

"Yves," he said, "I am ashamed!"

"Nay," cried Yves. "Nay – it was I –" and their self-reproaches might have begun all over again, had not a new idea come suddenly to Pons.

"Yves," he said, interrupting him, "let us take the oath to be brothers in arms, thou and I."

Yves turned from him and seemed to be interested in the dark corner of the stable.

"Nay," he said. "Not till I am knight. It would not be fitting for a knight and an esquire. And I cannot be knight till I have wherewith to bear the charges."

Pons answered his voice rather than his words.

"Alas!" he said. "Alas! that ever I kept vigil and took knighthood without thee!"

Yves gave a queer shaken laugh.

"I was there . . . behind ye. . . . I too . . . I kept vigil," he said, and he kept his face turned from Pons because those were very bitter hours to remember.

"Alas!" said Pons again, and smote his chest with his hand. Then he was silent, seeking for words to ask a question, and stretching out a hand began to stroke the shining quarter of the horse.

"Yves," he said at last, "was it true . . . that the Old Count said . . . about the Countess?"

Yves nodded.

"Yea," he said, and then, answering a question which Pons would never have asked, he went on:

"I could not tell you. She . . . she bade me be secret."

Pons found speech still more difficult, and when the words came they seemed to be jerked out of him.

"And . . . do ye still?" he said.

"Yea," said Yves, and would not look at him. "And I think sometimes I ever shall."

Pons sighed and might have said more but Yves went on after a little pause:

"But she said . . . she said Love was weakness . . . and I have thought – Oh! I have thought a great deal, and she is right. . . . I know it though I cannot help but love . . . the Countess."

Pons broke in, utterly bewildered.

"But she . . .? Who said . . .? The Countess?"

"Nay, nay," said Yves impatiently. "Domna Audiart."

"But who . . .?"

"Oh! Of Rouillac. She is . . . one of the . . . of the Countess' women. But . . . she is right. Without I had seen her . . . and she had counselled me, – I doubt I would. . . . Nay, I know not what I would have done. . . . I . . . it. . . . She said, 'Up, beast, from thy foul mire!' "

He was silent a moment, brooding over things which were hidden from Pons. Then:

"I remember," he went on, "a monk said me once that God was a Hunter. . . . It's true. . . . It was His beaters turned me back from that covert. But oh! Pons!" He turned suddenly and caught Pons by the arm and his voice grew sharp – "I must have Rifaucon – I must get it again. How can I do aught without it? 'A man without land, a shoe without a sole, a mill without a sail.' Ye know – nay, ye do not, but I do. . . . I must have Rifaucon, and then I will do whatever . . . yea, anything. . . . But I must have it. . . ." His voice dropped to a whisper so low that Pons could not hear, though he thought he caught the word "afraid." Then it rose again, but changed and burdened with a heavy anger:

"Whilst I have been so . . . so alone, I have thought of Count Richard that hath my Rifaucon . . . and I have thought sometimes that if God should damn my living soul I should not cease from following after, nor forgive him – Richard of Poitou. I swore it last night by Christ Himself on . . ."

Pons laid a big hand across Yves' mouth.

"Stop!" he cried. "Do not speak so! Ye are mad!"

Yves pulled the hand away, but when he spoke it was in a tired voice.

"I have been," he said.

Pons looked hard at him for a moment till Yves grew restless under the stare.

"Yea, Pons?" he said.

Pons shook his head.

"I know not. . . . Ye seem someways . . . different. . . . I know not," he said doubtfully, and then, as if he gave the puzzle up, he went on:

"Now promise me we'll swear the oath to brotherhood."

"Nay! nay!" said Yves, and his voice was troubled. "Your knight-hood –"

"But yea! yea!" interrupted Pons, unusually urgent, and then stopped, struggling for words. "Knighthood . . . it's a good thing," he said, "and high, but not . . . not so good nor high. . . . We are two friends. . . . That is the best."

He finished, very red, and almost stammering, and then, seeing the answer in Yves' face, he cried:

"Ye will! To-morrow, then!" and putting both hands on Yves' shoulders he looked down at him.

"And hark ye, Yves," he said. "There's another matter. My father, God keep him, he is old . . . he cannot live long, and I shall be lord of Jarnac . . . and then ye're no longer landless. . . . Jarnac is broad enough."

Yves laid his arms round Pons' neck.

"Ah! Pons," he said, "I cannot say what should be said of thy courtesy and gentleness . . . for of all knights thou are the most gentlest."

"Tchk!" said Pons. "Speak sense!" and they smiled at each other.

X

Viola.   Aye; but I know.
Duke. What dost thou know?
Viola. To well what love women to men may owe.
                              Twelfth Night, Act II, sc. iv.

THAT same afternoon Audiart came into the dark, dusty-smelling building which flanked the long line of stables and housed the fodder and seed, sack after sack in neat rows. She could hear through the ill-fitting boards of the partition wall the murmur of men talking in the stable beyond, the low steady sound of the horses champing, and the occasional sharp click of some impatient hoof on stone. The granary, however, was empty, and with a casual glance around, she went over to the place where, she knew, stood the sacks of this year's seed corn. Peire Bersin had hoped much from this harvest, and she was anxious to see how it had turned out, and also to find Bersin himself if she could.

As she stooped over one of the sacks, unknotting its stiff hairy cord, she heard someone come in from the stable.

"Is it thou, Perie Bersin?" she cried and turned, and saw Yves of Rifaucon. "Ah!" she said, and that was all. Yves, as surprised as she, only shook his head and muttered "Nay" in unnecessary answer to her question. Then they stood in silence peering at each other in the gloom, tongue-tied by the recollection of their last meeting in the orchard.

At last Yves moved, and coming over to the sacks near Audiart, laid down the wooden measure that he carried, and began to fumble with the knots.

"This one is open," said Audiart, and moved aside.

He gave a glance at her, picked up his measure, and thrust it into the sliding grain.

"I want oats for my beast," he muttered.

Audiart forgot herself at that, and snatched his hand away:

"What?" she cried. "It's seed corn! The oats are there," and she pointed. "Surely ye should know!"

Yves looked at the half-full measure, and at the pale gold inside the mouth of the sack and he flushed a little.

"I thank you," he said with a stiff and offended humility. "I am a fool. But," he added obstinately, "the oats should be here; they're changed."

He turned his back on her and went off to the oatsacks, and Audiart watched him miserably. If only, she thought, he had not come in so suddenly, she would have thought what to say, but now . . . he was angry. And yet, she thought again, with a sudden spurt of annoyance, seed corn was seed corn, and she could not have let him take it. The consciousness of well-doing gave her courage to speak.

"The sacks at the far end are the best, Messire," she said. "They're oats from Rochefoucauld, and Peire says the best of all the Angoumois."

She meant it as peace-making, but he took it badly, barely turning his head over his shoulder to say,

"I thank you."

Audiart was nettled.

"Have ye done with the seed corn?" she said spitefully, and turned to tie up the sack, angry with him and with herself, and very unhappy. She was a practical girl, little given to day-dreaming, but she had rehearsed in her own mind a dozen meetings with him, and what she would say, and how he would answer . . . and now – this!

She started when she heard his voice close by her.

"Nay. I'll knot it again," he said. She saw his hands come near hers and drew back quickly, and stood aside looking down on his bent head, with all anger gone from her, but as helplessly silent as ever.

Yves, stooping over the knots, said something which she could not catch.

"Ye said?" she questioned.

"I said," muttered Yves without raising his head, " 'Ye will think I am ever and always discourteous.' "

"Why . . .?" said Audiart. "What . . .?"

He finished the knots and stood up, his face still a little flushed.

"When you . . . in the orchard that day," he said, "and . . . and . . . that other day before."

"When?" began Audiart doubtfully, and then turned her face away quickly because it flamed. "Oh!" she said and was silent.

Yves went on doggedly, staring down at the dusty floor.

"Yea . . . then . . . I pray you . . . I did not ask pardon . . . I did not think. . . . But now. . . ." He looked up at her as though he sought forgiveness in her face, but she kept it turned from him. His thoughts wandered from penitence and fixed themselves upon her. He stared at her for a moment groping for words, and could find none that were fitting. "You were right," he said at last. "What you said that day . . . when I told you, in the orchard."

That seemed so ridiculously inadequate that he stopped, wishing that she would say something, but she was still silent and a shadow of disappointment crept across his mind since she did not seem to care — perhaps had even forgotten.

He moved away from her, but slowly and unwillingly, and even then Audiart could not speak. How could she say, "Have you foregone the Countess? Are you unhappy?" What right had she to ask? But he was going and she longed to know . . . or, if that were impossible, at least to keep him a little longer.

"What I said?" she repeated stupidly.

Yves stood still.

"Yea," he said. "But if you've forgotten I need say naught else."

She heard the hurt tone in his voice and it almost freed her tongue.

"I have not," she cried, and Yves knew that her voice was different, and was glad without knowing why. "I am . . . I. . . . Tell me."

Her stumbling ceased there, for Pons of Jarnac's big voice burst in on her suddenly:

"Those oats are long a-growing!" he said as he came through the door behind Yves, and then seeing, Audiart, he stopped short, and all three fell into a quagmire of distressful silence. Pons recovered first.

"I thought ye had been lost," he said, and the stupid remark rescued them all.

"Nay," said **Yves** and strode over to the place where he had left the oats.

Audiart frowned at Pons, and answered his look:

"I came . . . my hawk is sick," she said, and then, remembering that the hawk was clearly anywhere but there, she frowned the more heavily, and was only saved the necessity of thinking of a better excuse by another interruption.

A flaming red head, with heavy plaits hanging from under a green wimple, came round the outer doorway.

"Audiart! Audiart! Pest on the wench! Ah! there ye are!" and in came Geralda of Fouquebrune, reckless, ungovernable fifteen-year-old woman. She saw the two men almost as soon as she saw Audiart, and her green eyes sparkled.

"Ah!" she said, and laughed.

Yves, already at the inner doorway, turned. He looked at her for a second with a hard stare, and then both he and Audiart spoke together.

"We waited for you, Domna," said Yves to Geralda.

"I said ye not to wait for me," said Audiart.

Geralda laughed again. She was as quick-witted as Yves, and playfully malicious too.

"Come, wench," she said, "since I have waited. You can't stay here. The Countess would be angry if she knew it."

Through the tail of her eye Audiart saw Yves move, though ever so slightly, at the Countess' name, and that, with the young chit's tone, roused the devil in her; but because of Yves it was a silent, sullen devil.

She sat down on one of the sacks of corn.

"I wait for Peire Bersin," she said and frowned at Pons and Geralda. Geralda shrugged.

"So!" she said. "But I will not," and she held out her hand to Pons. He, remembering his manners with a start, crooked his fingers to receive hers, and they moved side by side towards the door.

Yves came closer to Audiart.

"Domna," he said, in a low voice. "Indeed it is not fit. The Countess –"

He said no more, for Audiart lifted her head quickly.

"Get you away!" she cried furiously. "I care not what she saith. She's a fool. . . . So are ye all. I hate Angoulême!"

Yves' hand, stretched out to receive hers, dropped to his side, and he turned away, and strode after Pons.

Pons had halted at the door and Audiart heard him say:

"How? Will she not come, Yves?"

She heard Yves' answer too, and his laugh, which was worse.

"Nay. But ask her yourself if you will. I've my bellyful."

When they were gone she sat still, biting her lips, her throat aching with tears that she was too proud to allow. Her eyes, wandering round the granary, lit on the measure of oats that Yves had forgotten. She stared at it for a few minutes and then sprang up.

Yves' horse did not lack his oats, and, being a gentlemanly beast, he bore courteously with her caresses, and even with a few tears. As for Peire Bersin, returning to Angoulême full of pride in his harvest, he missed Audiart, wondered for a time why she came no more to the stables, and then forgot about her as he had had to forget many things in his long life.

When Audiart reached the Countess' room that day, Geralda was on the look-out for her.

"Ha! Audiart," she cried, above the cheerful hum of talk. "Couldst thou not find the silk? I should not have troubled thee." And, as Audiart stared, she turned to her neighbour.

"It was a scrap of silk," she ran on. "Blue silk that she had, wrapped about an ouch, and I begged for a piece."

She watched Audiart make her courtesy to the Countess, turn her back on the crowded room, and move over to one of the window embrasures, but for a few moments she went on sewing diligently. Then she laid her work down, yawned, stretched, and stood up.

"I believe the rain is done," she said, and humming a song as she went, crossed the room and stood beside Audiart.

"Alack!" she cried dolefully, turning her head over her shoulder. "It rains still," but she did not go back to her place. Instead she rubbed her head against Audiart's shoulder, very much as a cat does, but Audiart did not turn – only she drew a little further away. Geralda moved closer.

"Audiart," she said. "I' faith I've an ill tongue, and I love to tease . . . but I like you, Audiart."

Audiart turned to stare.

"What do you want?" she said bluntly, and Geralda laughed aloud.

108

"Nay. It's the sad truth," she said. "I hate women . . . but I like you. You never tell what anyone saith to you . . . do you?"

"I do not. . . . Why should I, though?" said Audiart, and Geralda laughed again at her genuine surprise, and putting up a hand tickled Audiart's cheek.

"Nay. I knew it. But some do. . . . I do," she said, looking sidelong at Audiart, and putting an arm round her waist drew her further into the window embrasure between the two stone seats.

For a few moments they stood, looking down into the garden below, Audiart saying nothing, and keeping her body stiff and unyielding within Geralda's arm. Geralda with her free hand took the end of one of her own long copper-red plaits and began to brush her lips with it thoughtfully.

"I wonder . . ." she said at last, "if you have any servant who loves you."

Audiart held herself still, and stared rigidly out at the dripping garden.

"I have none," she said.

"And yet thou art far older than I," went on Geralda with a good show of simplicity. She believed Audiart, though she would not have believed another; but disappointed of a secret, she could at least turn the conversation towards herself. Audiart, however, was too stupid for her.

"How should I have servants?" she said. "I am not fair." She had recovered herself, and turned to Geralda with a smile of tolerant and half-amused scorn.

Geralda pounted, because she must either speak without being questioned or else be silent.

"Folquet of Vignolles," she said at last, "prayed me for my favour the other day." She glanced up at Audiart to see how the news was received, but Audiart was looking down at her clasped hands.

"But keep me the secret," added Geralda. A dozen people knew it already. Audiart, not knowing this, smiled. She half liked, though she did not trust Geralda, and for once she asked the right question.

"And did ye promise him?" she said.

Geralda frowned because she was pleased.

"Nay! Not I! I am a maid unwed, and he . . . he's a boy. . . . I wait till I be married and then I shall have my lord and a lover as the great ladies do."

"Nay, and I hope," said Audiart, "that you'll have a lord will whip you well and keep you from mischief." But although she meant it, she smiled as she spoke.

"Oh, fie!" said Geralda, and laughed. She leaned her head out of the window and drew it back suddenly, her finger to her lips. Audiart leaned forward.

Below them, only a few feet away, Yves of Rifaucon went by, his head bare, his shoulders hunched against the rain. Audiart could not draw back, because Geralda, peering out beside her, held her there. They watched him in silence till he was out of sight, but Audiart hated sharing him with Geralda.

When he was gone, Geralda sighed.

"If I have a lover I had lief he were like Messire Yves of Rifaucon," she said.

Audiart made no intelligible answer.

"It is because he is so strange . . . no talker nor japer," continued Geralda. "And he is strong. . . . Have you ever watched him jousting?" She gave a little excited laugh. "I think he is like Lancelot or one of those great knights. What dost thou say?"

"He is no knight, only an esquire," said Audiart, but she could not check Geralda.

"Shame on you!" she cried. "He hath lost his land and cannot be knight. And ye know it and ye flyte at him for that. Did not Sir Ysumbras the same? Nay then, I think he is like some great lord or prince in disguise that lacks his kingdom only a while."

Audiart lost all patience. If she could she would have boxed the child's ears.

"Well!" she snapped. "It's a right good disguise!"

Geralda was not put out, since opposition gave her opportunity to say more.

"Nay, nay!" she said and smiled. "But in sad truth, what think ye of him? Do ye not like him right well?"

Audiart left the second question unanswered.

"I think he is a strange little fellow," she said, and shrugged; but within herself she smiled teasingly at her thought of Yves, as though he were really there and knew the joke. "Thou dear!" she said to him.

Geralda broke in on her thoughts.

"No," she cried. "He is comely . . . and a singer. And likely to be as great a knight as any."

"Well! he's not proved yet," said Audiart, and smiled again in her mind at the foolishness of her own words. As though she cared whether he were proved or no!

"Nay, but he will," persisted Geralda. "He may go on Crusade and win a kingdom. Men have done it."

Audiart laughed derisively, so angry with Geralda that she was almost angry with Yves. Then she frowned suddenly and her lips drew into a straight line. She shook off Geralda's arm, turned back into the room, and picking up her neglected embroidery, bent over it.

For a long time, however, she did nothing more than run an un-threaded needle back and forth through the curving stalk of a half-finished leaf, since all her mind was occupied in torturing itself. She had never thought of it before, but now she was sure that he would go on Crusade, and it seemed to her, in her foolishness, that she herself would have sent him, by those cruel idle words which she had not even meant. And yet – her thoughts rose to glory in him – it was his fitting work, seeing that it was the best a man could do, and he . . . she was down on her knees before him. Then a new thought came, and it was terrible. She saw him fighting in the blinding sun, bruised, sweating, parched with thirst, borne down, dying, dead. The image was so dreadful that she cried out – or thought she did – and came suddenly back to reality. Yet when she looked round furtively no one was watching her, and she knew that she could have made no sound. She threaded her needle and began to stitch away feverishly at the horns of a trotting stag.

Immediately after Christmas news came to Count Guilhem that the burgesses and serfs of his town of Chalais had set on his bailiff, hunted him through the streets, and when he took refuge in a little chapel of Saint Anthony, had smoked him out by burning damp straw to wind-ward. When he came out choking, they had made it final by a rope over the bough of a neighbouring oak tree. The Count bit his nails, blinked his eyes, and turned from the messenger in silence, but twenty-four hours after he and all his court were on the way to Chalais.

Count Guilhem called it a progress, but it was very different from the ordinary summer progress, and vastly more uncomfortable, though the hard frost made fairly good going for the horses and pack-mules. It was bitterly cold, and everyone rode muffled in their cloaks and blowing on their frozen hands. The Old Count, out of pure malice it seemed to them, had insisted on taking the whole court, so that the Christmas festivities might not be broken off. The women grumbled, for only the Countess had a litter, and they must ride, so there was very little mirth, since they were far too cold even to chat with the knights and esquires who rode before and behind. Towards evening, to make matters worse, a thin, bitter wind sprang up, and brought with it showers of stinging sleet that made it necessary to hold hoods below chins in spite of nipped fingers.

When, therefore, one of the Countess' women pushed her way out of the ranks, and stopped, fumbling with her stirrup leather, only a few of her companions called to her, and even they took no notice of her answer. After the women came the knights and esquires, every head bowed against the driving sleet. Audiart looked up and about as if she sought help, and at that moment one of the esquires broke the line and came out to her.

"What's amiss, Domna?" said Yves, and stooped to look at the leather.

"It's nigh breaking," said Audiart. "I told Gaultier last night to put a new one in, and forgot to see if he'd done it." She spoke crossly because she was angry with herself, and then, raising her head, she smiled because he had come to help her; but as he was still bending from the saddle he missed the smile and only noticed the curtness of her voice.

He paused for a moment, then swung down from his horse.

"You must get down," he said and took her bridle. She obeyed without question.

The long procession of knights went by them hardly noticing their existence. One reined aside to ask the same question – "What's amiss?" but Yves, his head under the knee-flap, answered curtly:

"Naught but a worn stirrup-leather. Ye need not stay for us." The knight rode on, and no one else spoke to them.

Yves took the strap from the saddle and looked at it; then he went over to his own horse and began to unbuckle one of the stirrup leathers.

"What are you doing?" cried Audiart, though she knew perfectly well.

"It won't mend. Ye must have a stirrup," said Yves.

"Nay!" Audiart put out her hand to stop him. "I can ride without. Let be!"

Yves pushed her hand away and lifted the skirt of the saddle.

"So can I too," he said gruffly.

"But –" began Audiart, and got no further, since she could think of nothing to say.

"Ye will hate me," she muttered, but he did not hear. She thought that he had heard and only spared her the truth, so when she heard him swear under his breath she flushed, and clenched her hands together.

He stood up with the leather in his hand and took out his knife.

"Your buckle is half an ell too narrow," he growled, and began to pare away the edge of the strap. "My leather will not pass."

"In Rouillac," she said, with a miserable little spark of anger, "they make them always so."

"Maybe," he said, and shrugged.

Audiart looked about her desperately. The baggage mules had passed, but after them, though almost out of sight, went a few grooms and men-at-arms.

"See!" she cried, pointing to the last horsemen. "I can get a leather from one of them."

Yves looked up, then turned back to his work, scowling, and tried the strap again.

"Ye'll have my stirrup-leather for now. After ye can have any other man's. I care not," he said, and Audiart was silent, thinking with a kind of dreary anger that he might either have left her alone or else put himself out for her more cheerfully.

It took some time to finish, for the leather was tough, but he worked in silence, and at last slipped the strap through the buckle and ran it up to the holes. Then he bent to see if the stirrups hung even.

"It is right," said Audiart hastily, and without giving him time to help her she mounted. He did the same, and only then turned and spoke.

"We had best take a track to the left," he said. "I remember one near here. It strikes the road soon. It's bad but short, and we'll sooner catch the others." Without waiting for her answer he pushed the horse forward.

Audiart hung back.

"It's an ill time to go by small tracks. The beasts are hungry after this long frost. There are wolves abroad," she said.

Yves did not even turn his head.

"Go then how ye list," he said.

Audiart followed him.

They rode on in a fierce silence, and it was only five minutes later that Audiart remembered she had not thanked him; but it seemed too late now, and besides she was afraid both of his, and of her own temper. Worst of all, her stirrups hung unevenly, so that riding was uncomfortable, and she dreaded lest he should turn and see it, and set to work again upon the leather.

The track grew worse, for a stream had overflowed and then frozen, and the horses floundered. Audiart saved hers with difficulty after a long stagger, and Yves pulled up and looked round.

"I'll lead –" he began, and stopped. His eyes went down to the stirrup iron, and he leaned aside to look at each in turn. Next moment he was standing at her horse's head.

"Get down!" he said. "They hang uneven."

Audiart, stamping her feet upon the creaking ice to warm them, turned from him, trying to believe she did not care, and moved away down the path.

Yves, left to himself, pulled angrily at the leather, and hacked it with his knife, being in a very black temper indeed. When his own horse suddenly backed into him, and Audiart's threw up its head and danced aside, he swore aloud.

"Blood of –" he began, but the oath was never finished.

As he turned to strike at his horse, he saw coming, down the twilight path, a great, lumbering dark body. It was a bear.

For a second he stared, then, dropping his knife, snatched at his sword, and taking three strides towards the animal, stood still and shouted, waving his arms. The bear paused as if doubtful, swinging its little pointed head from side to side, then it came on again, and Yves knew that nothing would stop it now.

"Get on your horse and away!" he shouted, not daring to turn his head, and went forward again, stepping slowly, his eyes fixed on the bear. The beast had got up on its hind legs, and came nearer, swaying clumsily. It was so close now, that Yves could see bare patches in the fur, and his last clear thought was that the beast had been hunting flesh. Then thought faded before the intense concentration of the surface mind which ruled his muscles for the stroke, while below that there was nothing but a savage rage, so blind in its ferocity that it did not even know its own cause.

He gritted his teeth together, gripping the sword-hilt so fiercely that his hand shook, then, as the bear came within reach, monstrous, reeking, his great paws swinging for the blow, Yves gave a sort of cry, and leapt, and struck. It was a thrust straight from the shoulder, a stroke he loved, and deadly if it found its mark.

Next moment the weight of a mountain seemed to fall upon his sword, tearing the hilt from his hand, and he was borne back, staggering. As he reeled against a tree he snatched at his dagger with a choked curse, found the sheath empty, and started forward again, ready to fight with bare hands. Only then he realised that the bear lay in the pathway, spitted by the sword through throat and skull.

For a second surprise emptied his mind, as he stood staring at the great dead bulk. Then rage came sweeping back. He laughed softly, set one foot on the head and wrenched out the sword, laughed again to see the blood pour out, and did not guess how that laughter twisted his face.

Then he turned to Audiart.

A little later, Pons, riding with the knights, found Yves beside him, and grunted a welcome to which Yves made no reply. After a while, however, Yves spoke.

"The curse of Hell!" he muttered, so sudden and fierce that Pons turned.

"Why?" he said. "What is it then?"

Yves drew a long breath.

"Naught . . . that matters," he said. "I know ye're not her friend. . . . Domna Audiart's."

"What hath she done?" said Pons.

"Naught," growled Yves again. "Only laughed at me when. . . . She makes me a fool ever. . . . Ah!" he bit off the rest between clenched teeth.

Pons nodded slowly.

"Aye, she hath an ill tongue. I –"

"She hath!" broke in Yves.

Pons finished his verdict:

"I hate that manner women," he said.

Yves let the matter stand there and said no more. After a while he dropped behind, and it was only when they could see the lit windows in the towers of Montmoreau, where they would spend the night, that he pushed his horse close up to Pons.

"Here I am," he said, as though to draw Pons' attention.

"Yea, then?" said Pons, and wondered what next.

Yves rode in silence for a few minutes and then began to speak quickly, in a low voice.

"I was wrong . . . thou too . . . she is not . . . I do not. . . . Other wenches . . . but she is different. . . . After all, I was a fool to take that track." He said no more for a few minutes and then broke out again. "Pons! she had my knife in her hand, and she'd have stood if . . . if the beast had. . . . By God!" his voice dropped almost to a whisper. "She's the bravest wench alive! She laughed. . . . I don't know why I was angry with her for it then. . . . It was the beast. . . . If it had . . ." he drew in his breath sharply through his teeth and his face hardened again into something the same expression that Audiart had seen when he turned from the dead bear. Then he frowned and shook his head.

"I don't know . . ." he said doubtfully. "But when she laughed it was . . . it was like . . . ye know how it feels, jousting, when you take a big buffet and go over your horse's tail. It was like that when she laughed."

Pons interrupted heavily.

"Do not think of her," he said.

Yves turned on him fiercely but checked himself before he had said anything, and his face became troubled.

"I wish . . ." he began, and sighed. "After all's done, I've little to boast of . . . no cause to be proud of myself. She is right."

"Grr!" said Pons under his breath, but Yves did not hear him.

In the crowded courtyard at Montmoreau, the business of dismounting was long and tedious. Audiart, riding listlessly, had lost her place with the other women, and came in among a crowd of knights and esquires who were too tightly packed to make way, so that she had to wait till the confusion lessened for her turn to dismount.

Since she had rejoined the rest of the women and seen Yves ride off without a word, she had gone over in her mind, again and again, every detail of what had passed between them, trying to understand. If he hated her, why had he stopped to help her? That was the question she could not answer.

When he had seen the bear he had called to her to get away – as if she would have left him! – and she had caught up his knife from the ground, and watched him as he went to meet the bear. She shook again as she remembered the tumult of fear and exultation that had filled her as she saw him go towards the animal, stepping delicately, swaying his sword in his hand, and so strong. . . . So strong, and yet. . . . Dear Mother of Heaven, protect him! Protect him!

Then afterwards he had turned, his face distorted into an animal's snarl, and to cover her sick faintness of reaction she had laughed, a very shaky laugh, and had seen his face change to another sort of anger. And after that. . . . Oh! why, why, why would he not be friends?

She was so tired now, however, that she had ceased to wonder, and all the miserable questioning had lapsed into a dull weariness that longed only for rest, and, with a sort of homesickness, for familiar kind people.

As she sat bowed in the saddle, an eddy shook the crowd. Her horse backed suddenly, another came on and pressed her close. She looked up dully, half dazed, into a face both familiar, and it seemed, kind. She smiled, as simply as a child, before she realised it was Yves; and he smiled too. At that she remembered, and her hand went up to her throat as if

117

she had passed a great danger, but she was too wildly happy now to be silent.

"What a press!" she said, and laughed.

"We're as tight as cheeses," said Yves, and they laughed again, together. Then the eddy carried them apart before either had said anything more than mere foolishness; but for all that both felt that something which had been wrong was now set right, and both were causelessly gay.

XI

IN the spring of 1179 Count Richard began to stir once more. He had got wind of the transactions between Adhemar of Limoges and the Counts of Angoulême, and between these three and Geoffroi de Rançon of Taillebourg. He did not wait for his enemies to strike, but before April came in himself struck, stormed Pons on the Seugne, and marched north-east, taking Richemont within the week. From there he pressed on, leaving behind him as he went a line of castles, stormed or surrendered – Gensac, Marcillac, Gourville, Anville – which would serve as a wall to cut off the Counts of Angoulême from that other rebel, Geoffroi de Rançon. Then he turned his back on Angoulême and hurled himself against Taillebourg.

What the Old Count thought of it all, whether he took it as a mere warning or as a threat, no one knew. He did not waste his strength battering upon Richard's wall, but drew back to Angoulême with all his hosts and his newly hired Routiers, and sat down to wait, perhaps because he counted upon the strong and triple walls of Taillebourg, fabled impregnable, to break Richard's teeth.

For whatever reason there was a lull at Angoulême during the last week of April and the first of May, so that it was almost possible to forget that there was such a person as the Count of Poitou, and be gay because of the coming of spring.

To folk who lived in castles winter meant smoke and foul air, or else fierce draughts that swung the arras to and fro, and blew the rushes along the floor with little tickling noises. It meant long evenings in which one tired of all one's friends and of all the old, re-told stories. Spring, therefore, came as a release almost from captivity, and especially so for the women, for in the winter the men would often be out hunting as long as the short daylight lasted, and then be heavy and sleepy all evening after.

When May came then, even in this year of war, the ladies of Angoulême would have their way, and the men had no wish to deny them. So, very early on the morning of the 1st of May, between fifty and a hundred knights, esquires, maidens, and dames rode out into the clean country, as others were doing all over France and England too, to play in the sun, to gather the may, and to come back laden with green and flowery branches, laughing and pleasantly tired, having entered into the lordship of a new summer.

They rode five miles out from Angoulême to a little hill where the hawthorn bushes were so laden with scent that they made the air drunken. All one side of the hill was creamy-white with the bloom, but the top was bare and green except for the daisies. There they unsaddled and left the horses to graze, and there they sat down to rest after their ride, some two by two, others in large companies, till the whole hillside was gay with the colour of their gowns, and the air with the sound of their laughter.

Geralda of Fouquebrune was the first to tire of the pleasant idleness. She turned her head over her shoulder and looked over the country-side, then back to the crowd with whom she had been chattering.

"I would we could dance," she said to no one in particular.

One very young knight, that same Folquet of Vignolles who had sought her favour when he was only an esquire, and who still watched for the crumbs which fell from her table, snapped at this.

"Dance, domna?" he said. "Why not?"

Geralda looked at him down her pretty nose.

"And how shall we dance without music?" she asked derisively.

Folquet grew red at her scorn, and angry at himself for growing red.

"We could . . . there is . . . someone could sing," he said, sullen and fierce at once.

Geralda startled him by a sudden graciousness.

"Ah! fair dear friend," she cried gaily, and her hand just touched his shoulder. "Verily yea! someone shall sing and we will dance."

She sprang up, laughing, and shaking out her skirts.

"Fair friends," she cried, and clapped her hands, "who will sing for us that we may dance. . .? Oh! la, la, la, la." And she paced a few pretty steps to her own singing.

Folquet leapt up and put his hands to his mouth.

"Oyez to the herald!" he cried. "Who will sing that this fair gentle lady may dance?"

Those round about laughed at him, and some suggested one name and some another, but Geralda clapped her hands again and turned to Folquet.

"Ho! herald!" she said. "Cry me Yves of Rifaucon. He can sing."

The herald did as well as his strong lungs allowed him, and as if it had been the palace of a great king, the word was passed from group to laughing group over and around the hill.

Yves, lounging at full length with Pons of Jarnac and a few non-amorous knights who kept apart from the ladies, heard himself called by several voices at once.

"Oh Saints!" he said. "What do all these pies want?"

"Come and sing that we may dance!" cried someone, and because it was not courtesy to refuse, Yves stood up obediently, but as he climbed the hill he looked back ruefully. Then, remembering that the dancing might bring Audiart from the crowd of women among whom he had last seen her, and perhaps give him a chance of speaking to her, he went on more briskly.

Audiart, sitting a little apart in the shade of one of the incense-bearing may-trees, saw him coming, and because she had been watching for him, now he was here she shrank back lest he should see her.

Geralda met him at the top of the hill.

"Oh! Messire Yves," she said, dimpling at him. "Will you sing, then?"

"I will well," he said, but Audiart was pleased to see his eyes wander from Geralda's face and go searching for someone – Pons, she supposed. Then the merrymakers crowded round him so that she could see him no longer, though she could hear his voice.

"Sing us the Harvest Song," cried someone.

"Nay, nay, not that!"

"It's a good dance!"

"Sing Thomas the –"

"Oh peace! peace!" shouted Yves above the clamour. "I'll sing what I will. Make place! Stand aside!"

"Place! Place for my jongleur!" cried Geralda, and Audiart frowned, but when the crowd parted and she saw Yves again he was not looking at Geralda. He had turned to speak to one of the knights; Audiart saw him smile, and because she so loved that rare smile of his she was glad that it was not for Geralda.

"Now peace!" she heard him cry again. "I'll sing 'The Miller and his Wheel,' " and he led off at once with the jolly, jog-trot tune, and the crowd melted into lines and circles, and swung to the rhythm of the song. Audiart, safe now in her gazing, leaned forward, her hands clasping her knees, forgetting everything but Yves. When she found her view suddenly cut off by a man standing before her, she drew back, angry at the interruption.

"Domna," said he, smiling down at her. "Why do you not dance? Come with me and we will break in." It was that same Robert the Nutcracker who had been knighted three years before at Pentecost.

Audiart shifted her position so that she could see Yves again, and then, angry lest she should have given herself away, answered crossly: "I have no will to dance."

"Oh! Domna!" he persisted with a teasing, rueful smile. "Have pity on me!"

Audiart found herself craning her neck to see round him, and she grew more angry.

"Not I," she said, and then lied defensively as women will. "Do but let me sit in the sun. You hide it from me."

Robert moved away with a shrug, and Audiart, glad of his departure, looked about her with relief before she returned to her gazing, and saw Pons of Jarnac sitting a few yards away. That spoiled her content. She could not watch now without feeling that Pons was watching her; besides she was afraid of him. He stood so near the throne that she craved for his approval, but she knew, without any reason for knowing, that he did not approve. So she grew embarrassed, watched him from the corner of her eyes wondering if she should speak, decided that she would – and did not.

Presently she heard someone come up to Pons with a quick rush of feet.

"Fair dear friend," said a child's voice. "Will you play at knights?" It was a little lad called Guilhem whom the Old Count would have about the Court; people said that his mother was a baker's daughter in Angoulême.

Audiart looked round and saw Pons heave himself up on an elbow. "I will," he said. "Where are your knights?"

"Here they are," said the little lad, holding out a tightly clasped handful of ribwort plantain heads which children now call "conquerors." Breathing hard through his small nose he divided them, scrupulous to give his adversary the exact half.

"Which of us shall begin?" he said, looking up into Pons' face.

"Fair sweet friend," said Pons solemnly, "you shall begin."

The child took his stand, feet planted far apart and very firmly. He lifted the "knight" he had chosen, and then paused.

"Your knight is too tall," he said, and taking hold of Pons' big fingers in his little ones, he loosened them and pushed back the stalk of the plantain till the head stood out only a couple of inches. Then he was satisfied, and struck. The head of Pons' knight fell off.

"Oho!" cried Guilhem in a very deep and manly voice. "He is down! He is dead!"

"Alas the poor man!" said Pons, and chose another.

Audiart, who had been watching them sideways, spoke suddenly: "I did always love that game," she said.

Pons looked up at her and then down at the child's knight. He lifted his own and struck before he answered.

"It is a strange game," he said coldly, "for a girl to love. It is for boys."

Audiart forgot that he was Yves' friend.

"Nonsense!" she said sharply at this plain absurdity, and turned away, leaving Pons confirmed in his opinion of her and angry too – all the more angry because he knew that he was not entirely fair. Soon after he carried young Guilhem off with him to look for water-boatmen in the stream.

Audiart saw them go with a mixture of relief, annoyance and regret,

123

and next moment forgot all about them, since she saw that the dancing was over and that Yves was looking about him. Because she wished so much and so hopelessly that he would see, and come to her, she must needs turn away, and when he flung himself down at her feet she pretended to start.

"You did not dance," he said, tipping his head back over his shoulder to look at her.

Audiart was afraid that he might guess why she had not danced, and she blurted out clumsily:

"How did you know? There were a many dancing."

"I saw you," said Yves, and because she flushed, he thought she was angry, and looked away. Both of them were silent, but Audiart watched his hand lying relaxed on the ground, and she was content for a while, until the silence grew so long that she feared he might leave her.

Then, just as she thought she could bear it no longer, Geralda's voice broke in, and she looked up to see the girl standing a few yards away, as daintily poised as a bird on a spray, her red hair fairly ablaze in the sun.

"Ah! Messire Yves," said Geralda with a pout and a lisp. "There are king-cups down there by the brook," and her wide green sleeve swept out like a wing as she pointed. "And I want to gather them."

Yves, propped upon one elbow, looked at her, screwing up his eyes because the sun was behind her head.

"Yea, Domna," he said, "I have seen them."

Geralda pouted more, and forgot her lisp.

"Well – uncourteous – must I go alone?"

Audiart gripped one hand over another and bit her teeth together as Yves sprang up.

"Nay – I'll see to that," he said fervently, and then turned from her.

"Folquet! Folquet!" he shouted. "Hi! Hither!"

Folquet of Vignolles broke from a group near by and came towards them.

"Messire Folquet," said Yves, and there was more than a spice of malice in his smile as he looked at this very young knight, whom as esquire he had thrashed more than once, and not so long ago. "Messire

Folquet, here's a fair lady errant wants to gather king-cups. The adventure is yours, sir knight. I'm but a squire." He louted low before Geralda's flushed angry face and Folquet's offended dignity, and dropped once more upon the grass.

When the other two had gone he turned to Audiart with a glint of laughter in his eyes.

"Oh! these wenches!" he said and grinned like a schoolboy.

Audiart laughed, then checked herself suddenly, and went very red; but Yves was not looking at her, and having spoken to her then as he would have spoken to Pons, would never have guessed, even if he had seen her flush, that she had taken his words as a smiling, careless rebuke to herself.

The silence lengthened. He was happy enough in it, but Audiart was not. "Oh! these wenches," she kept saying to herself, and each time the words hurt her again.

Yves reached out idly, tore off a long grass stalk, and began, as idly, to tie it in knots.

She seized that as an excuse for speech.

"Give it to me," she said suddenly, and held out her hand.

Yves looked up surprised, but obeyed.

"I'll show you a knot will never run nor pull," she said, leaning towards him. "They use it at Rouillac – the carters that bring in the wine casks. One of them taught it me – Grey Follo they called him. Look!"

Her quick fingers made the knot as if by magic.

He laughed.

"Do it again. Slowly," he said, but he watched her hands more closely than the knot.

She untied it and gave it back.

"Now tie it," she said, and he tried, clumsily.

"Nay! nay!" she interrupted him, and for a moment laid her fingers on his to direct them, then drew back as if she had pricked herself. Yves looked up surprised.

"Nay, ye'll never learn," she said ungraciously, and left him wondering why she was so curt. He frowned and threw the grass away, and they were silent again, but Audiart was remembering his words – "Oh, these wenches!" and wondering if he thought ... no, if he *knew* that she had longed to touch his hands.

At last she forced herself to speak, for only in that way could she convince him that she was not one of "these wenches." It did not matter that she was one of them so long as he did not know it.

"Messire," she said, "show me how your Rifaucon goes."

He turned and stared at her.

"See! here's a bare patch without grass," she continued. "Scratch me the lines with a twig."

Some gentle angel surely inspired the idea. Yves' face changed, and he plunged at once into the fascinating subject, and she with him.

"Yea – half a mile from castle to village. . . . No, here lie the woods. I would make a new holding there. It's good land."

"But have you enough villeins to spare? It needs a good man for a new holding."

"Oh! aye, unless . . . well, perhaps not . . . but see here . . ." and so on. They were both happy, so happy that they forgot themselves and remembered only each other, and Rifaucon.

Yves rode home with Pons. He would have liked best to stay near Audiart, but dared not, and she did not know how to keep him with her. So they rode apart, but neither could be unhappy after such companionship and so fair a day.

Yves was silent most of the way back, and Pons, never over-anxious to talk, had something on his mind.

At last Yves spoke:

"She says if I drain the Low Acre and cut it often, I'll rid it of the flea-bane. . . . Domna Audiart of Rouillac, I mean," he added.

Pons knew quite well whom he meant but he was silent, and Yves turned suddenly.

"Say it!" he commanded.

Pons shook his head.

"I cannot speak in this business," he said.

Yves looked at him soberly.

"Pons," he said, "we are brothers, and will you not speak?"

Even then Pons would not answer at once, but at last he blurted out:

126

"I fear she will do you a shrewd turn. . . . She hath a sharp tongue. . . . I would have a woman kind and meek."

Yves flushed a little and looked straight before him.

"You mistake," he said. "I do not love her 'par amours' . . . as a lover. . . . I don't ask her for kindness. . . . But I am her servant with most pure entire heart. . . . Oh! Pons!" he cried suddenly with a different note in his voice, "she is . . . she is. . . . I . . . I see God in her!"

He stopped suddenly and looked askance at Pons as if he had said too much, and after that they were silent till they reached Angoulême. But it was because he had said too little rather than too much that Yves flung that sudden suspicious glance at Pons, as though he had been an enemy, for he knew now, and the knowledge was both utterly strange and utterly familiar, that, in every way in which a man may love a woman, he loved Audiart. It did not come into his head to wonder how she thought of him. To-day she had suffered him kindly, and that was enough, since he had set her so high that her mere forbearance was a bounty.

XII

Nay . . . said Palomides, I never espied that ever she loved me more than all the world, nor never had I any pleasure with her, but the last day she gave me the greatest rebuke that ever I had, the which shall never go from my heart. And yet I well deserved that rebuke. – *Mort d'Arthur*, Book X, Chap. LXXXII.

THAT night as Yves served the Count he could do nothing right, and Guilhem did not fail to tell him so. Yves' head, however, was in a golden cloud which hid the common earth and only let him see above it the vast sky spaces and pure snows of unscaleable peaks. He did his service with a vacant look and a half smile that might well infuriate the Count, and his obliviousness to rebuke spurred Guilhem on to greater effort.

At last, when they were alone together in the Bear Tower, one word among the Count's spiteful mumblings caught Yves' attention.

"And Rifaucon!" the Count was saying. "Four castles lost this year, and you ask me to get you your penny-worth fief. . . . You're a fool . . . you're . . . Why don't you answer?" he snapped. "Stop smiling at me!"

Yves frowned instead.

"I did not ask," he said.

Guilhem snorted.

"No! you're content to be nothing . . . to hang about the Court. . . . What do ye think ye're for? What good are ye to any without ye have land?" He subsided again into inaudible mutterings but he had wakened Yves.

"What good was he to – Audiart – without land?" He asked himself the question now, and forgot his late content.

Guilhem, glancing up, caught his troubled, resentful look, and his eyes glinted. He had scored a hit in his favourite game of baiting.

"And now," he went on, moving his head restlessly from side to side. "Now I suppose ye'll have heard that before Count Richard hath gobbled up Taillebourg, that man Geoffroi of Lusignan – I hate him, half wolf, half fox – he will be with us, and Talleyrand of Perigord – he's a slow cow, a fool too . . . and that we'll chase Richard merrily away to his Poitou. . . . I suppose they'll have told you that, or something like it. . . . And that Taillebourg can't be taken. . . . They talk so! blabbing fools! What fool was it that told you?"

Yves gave him a straight stare.

"Lord Vulgrin," he said.

The Old Count looked at him for a moment in silence and then gave a sudden laugh, much like a dog's bark.

"Ho!" he said. "Even so –!" and paused. "Well!" he said, and his voice was almost conciliatory, "Taillebourg is down. . . . That's the news . . . and hold your tongue on it! But I shall pack off the women to-morrow to La Rochefoucauld. . . . Idle mouths. . . . I don't want them in Angoulême while we stand siege. . . . Ho! there's a merry time coming!"

He ended with a laugh that seemed to mock both himself and Yves, but when he spoke again it was in a voice so changed and strange that Yves could do nothing but gape at him, finding no words, no thought even, for an answer.

"Yves of Rifaucon," said Count Guilhem, "I'm an old man. . . . I'm tired of it."

Next morning as the Countess and her household and a score or so of knights and men-at-arms – all that the Old Count could spare – rode under the eastern gate of Angoulême, Yves was running his fastest through the narrow, twisting passages that burrowed between the low houses and under sagging archways, forming an intricate web all over the town, only to be used by those that knew them well. Yves knew them, and had chosen this way because the Old Count – curse him! – had kept him till it was almost too late, and these lanes were both shorter and less frequented than the main streets. Run as he might, however, when he burst out into the street before the gate, he saw that already almost all the household of the Countess had passed.

He stood, hesitating whether to run forward or to wait, and trying to get his breath. One or two of the women waved to him, and laughed, calling out jests or farewells that either he did not hear or did not heed, since he looked only for Audiart. Then, as he stared, he caught the glance of Geralda of Fouquebrune, and she pulled up her horse beside him, looking down with green eyes questioning.

"Messire Yves –" she began, but he interrupted her roughly.

"Domna Audiart of Rouillac?" he said, and did not care that her face changed, and her lips tightened.

"Now why," she said softly, "why do ye want Audiart?" and when she saw his eyes stray from hers to search among the last few women as they rode by, she smiled, but not kindly.

"Well!" she said, as he turned back to her, frowning, "as ye see, she is gone. She was among the first. She always is ready . . . not like other women," and she looked at him with her head on one side.

Yves hesitated, unable to decide whether he should not, after all, run out after the riders, ridiculous though he might look. His silence gave Geralda her chance.

"No," she went on, speaking, as it were, regretfully. "No – and I marvel much ye should run about after her, Messire Yves, seeing how cruel she jests at you."

She would not notice Yves' start nor the sudden darkening of his eyes.

"I'm your true friend," she continued. "I said when she jeered at you for a landless man that it was shame to do it. . . . But she hath a wit. . . . She loves to mock. . . . Oh! perhaps it was all in jest, but I'd not speak so! And when one said (women talk foolishly among themselves, Messire Yves) that they thought you comely, and forbye landless, like some great lord or prince that goes unknown and disguised, Audiart said, 'May be, but it's a right good disguise,' and called you a strange little fellow."

Yves tried to harden his face to a mask of stone behind which his pain might cower unseen.

"Yes?" he said, and felt that his lips were stiff.

"Oh!" said Geralda, and laughed. "Perhaps I was wrong to tell you. . . . But if you don't care . . . I thought ye believed she had a favour towards you."

He shook his head.

"No," he said, driving each word out with an effort, "I did not think it. . . . Why should I?"

130

"I am glad of it," Geralda said, and almost purred. "I'm right glad. . . . I should not heed her. . . . Maybe you've done something to make her mislike you so, for she's always fleering at you. . . . I said to her that ye would go on Crusade, and prove yourself, and be a great knight after all –" (It was a bitter little stab from a fresh quarter, that "after all," just put in to let him know that others beside Audiart – even Geralda herself – might find something lacking in him.) "I said so," she went on after the slightest pause that gave time for her words to sting. "And Audiart laughed . . . as much as to say she knew you would never go."

As though Yves did not rightly understand what she was saying, but only caught the echo of her words, he spoke, looking up and down the empty street:

"If you do not go," he said slowly, and he might have been thinking out a difficult thing, "you will never catch up the others. . . . You must go."

Geralda straightened herself in the saddle, looking down at him still with eyes very hard and intent behind their brightness. Was he angry, or indifferent, or –? She could not tell for certain, but what he said was true, and she tightened the reins.

"Farewell, Messire Yves," she said, looking back as the horse moved on. "The Saints be with you."

He did not smile or move, but she heard him say calmly:

"I thank –" and then no more, for the noise of her horse's hoofs drowned whatever came after.

When she looked back again he had turned away and was walking slowly up the street. She put her horse to a canter and soon joined the others, but for a while she rode apart, unsatisfied because she could not be sure that she had hurt him, uneasy because she was almost sure she had.

"I thank –" said Yves as Geralda's horse moved away, and then, because he would have to raise his voice to make her hear, he stopped. It was not worth while even to hold up the mask any longer. There was nothing in the world that was worth while, nothing in the world except a pain that seemed in his breast and in his head – that, and Audiart.

He turned away and went slowly up the street, careless as to the direction he took, but forcing his mind to keep his steps straight . . . so that he should not stumble . . . so that no one should look at him . . . so that he might get clear away. He was like a sick animal slinking off to find solitude.

A baker's man, coming shouting round a corner with a tray of loaves balanced on his head, made him look up and step quickly aside, but the effort was too much for his mind, and he stopped, looking about him as though he had found himself suddenly in a strange town.

Above him towered the great west wall of the Cathedral, its five arched recesses like caves hollowed from a cliff-side, but swarmed all over with carving. He stared, moved a pace or two doubtfully, and then, like a fox bolting to earth, made straight for the great doorway and plunged in. Homeless he was, lost, beaten, betrayed, and utterly undone, and here – there was no thought in his mind, but he knew – here was home, refuge, shelter. His hurried steps slackened, he reached a pillar and stood, his hand feeling comfort in the still but potent stone, his eyes finding the dim light itself merciful.

For a moment, no more, the place eased him, then thought came creeping out from beneath the weight of pain; thought that was not one pain but many, and each as sharp as a sword, for each was a memory of Audiart. Audiart in the stable; Audiart in the wood with her dark hair dishevelled; Audiart in the orchard; . . . Audiart a little kind . . . very wise . . . angry . . . hard . . . cruel. . . . Cruel and hard? Yes! but always right. She was his good. He had seen God in her, and now she had turned her face from him and blotted out his light.

He moved, restlessly and aimlessly, away from the pillar and across the empty nave. Opposite the door in the stone screen he stopped and took a few quick steps forward, staring at the red lamp in the darkness of the sanctuary. God was there.

"Oh Christ! Merciful!" he whispered, desperately importunate, as if he could compel the mercy he needed, and stood still, gazing. God was there, but was He merciful? Would He give refuge against even Audiart, or was He like her – good, just, cruel? Yves strained his eyes to see, but the sanctuary was dark, and the lamp a mere shining jewel of light that revealed nothing. His need was to see the Face of God, and there was only darkness and the unanswering, steady gleam.

He turned at last and went out. There was no help here.

Count Richard, having left Taillebourg like a beaten dog, turned on Angoulême. One morning the burgesses and knights watching from the ramparts saw the fields about the town swamped by a cold wave of steel, with here and there the bright colours of the banners floating upon it. After the host came the pack-mules, and after them the ox-teams, dragging behind them the swaying siege engines.

Two days after the coming of that army with its banners and trumpets, the Old Count rode out to make a fresh submission. Count Vulgrin did not go, because he was ailing these days, being ague-shaken. Yves of Rifaucon did not go either, but sat on the battlements looking down upon Count Richard's camp. He watched the banner of Angoulême got out, blowing bravely on a free wind, and then turned away and drew patterns in the dust with the steel shoe of his sword-sheath, tasting upon his tongue the dregs of a bitter wine. Defeat, final and irreparable, was the wine that wryed his face and drew lines about his mouth, but the dregs were more bitter still; he thought of Audiart and of God, and the bright sky turned black.

When the Count of Poitou had sung his *Te Deum* in the Cathedral of Angoulême – (Yves was nowhere to be found on that day) – he departed, the richer by some mule-loads of silver, a jewelled reliquary, and the sworn oath of Guilhem Talifer, the Old Count, that he would, within three months, leave Angoulême and go on a pilgrimage to Jerusalem.

So, on June 30th, the feast of Saint Martial, Guilhem went down to High Mass at the Cathedral to receive the pilgrim's blessing, and Yves walked beside him, leading his horse by the bridle. Inside the church he stood behind the Count, carrying the scarlet satin cap of the County, and listened to the hollow sad chanting of the priests as the office drew to its climax. Then, at the appointed moment, the Old Count left his place, and alone, moving heavily, passed into the sanctuary to make his offering and receive the blessing.

Yves watched him go and clenched his hands till the nails bit into his palms. Something was approaching which he feared to meet. He would not think of it, but ground his teeth together and began to fortify himself against his fear by telling over in his mind the score which he had against Count Richard of Poitou.

The buzz and murmur in the crowded church died suddenly away, and Yves, turning, saw that the Old Count had come back from the altar, and stood, his hand raised to command silence.

"Is there any man," he said, "who will go with me on this holy pilgrimage?"

Yves gave a little gasp, for the thing he feared was upon him, and he and it stood face to face. There was an empty hush that seemed to him to last long slow minutes, but which was really only a matter of seconds. Then a peasant in a rough lamb's-wool coat pushed his way from the crowd at the far end of the great church, a knight brushed past Yves, another followed. There was a shuffle of footsteps from one side and another, and in all about thirty men, gentle and simple, passed up into the sanctuary. Last of them all went Pons of Jarnac, hanging back and looking about him as if he sought for someone. He gave a last look round, then turned, and followed the others.

It was done! Yves was breathing as if he had been fighting for his life, but it was done, and he had made his choice. He did not think now why he had so chosen; he had not thought when he moved aside to avoid Pons' eyes. The blind will that is the root and core of each soul had chosen; circumstances and character, desires and aspirations, all those burdens which a man can never shed because they are part of himself, all those, laid upon the pans of a balance, had swung exactly even. And the will, the ultimate will that is the self, unpersuaded and free in its choice, had put out a finger and pressed down one of the pans of the balance. He had chosen.

When they returned to the Castle Count Guilhem went up to his room in the Bear Tower with Yves following unwillingly. The Count lowered himself heavily into his carved chair, bade Yves bring him a platter of strawberries that stood on one of the carved hutches, and then sat, silent and huddled, staring out of the window. From time to time he stretched out a groping hand to take a strawberry from the dish, and soon there was a sprinkling of the frilled stalks on the wide sloping

134

splay of the window, since more fell short than went through the narrow opening. Yves, telling over once more the score against Count Richard, almost started at the Count's grating voice.

"Clear me these," said Guilhem, waving a hand towards the strawberry frills, and Yves moved to obey, collected them, and thrusting his hand through the window, shook them from his palm. When he turned back into the room he found the Count watching him.

"Stand there," said Guilhem, pointing to a place on his left hand, and as Yves went over to it the Count turned in his chair, watching all the time.

"You will not go this pilgrimage?" he said.

Yves shook his head in silence.

"Why not?" said the Old Count.

Yves shook his head again, and moved impatiently.

"I will not. . . . I will not go. . . . Count Richard . . . he shall not send me," he said through his teeth.

The Count peered at him, dull-eyed and frowning, as if he found it difficult to believe that this was the true reason. Then at last he rose stiffly, like a very old man, turned away, hesitated, came back to Yves, and laid a hand on his shoulder.

Yves looked straight in front of him.

"If I could," said the Count, and his voice made Yves' hands clench, "if I could I'd have got thee thy Rifaucon. . . . But now . . . unless I come back . . ." He stopped, because Yves' face shook.

"No," cried Yves in a voice that was almost a whisper. "It's not that only."

The Old Count looked at him, and then quickly away.

"What then?" he muttered.

"I dare not," Yves said. "It means everything if I go . . . the monk said it and I have always known. . . . And I dare not."

"But why?" pressed the Count. He was too wise to say that a pilgrimage was not for ever, and that Yves could come back. He knew that such words would have been mere idleness.

"Why?" said Yves. "I do not know. . . . I dare not. . . . He is terrible . . . and if I give myself up bound. . . . I dare not."

The Count shook his head. This was beyond him.

135

"I'm a man has done little I ought," he murmured, not looking at Yves. "But the priests are always saying He is kind. . . . I believe it."

But Yves had got control over himself and he was thinking of Audiart.

"Is He?" he said in a hard voice.

The Old Count moved slowly away, his head bent, and Yves was left alone. He waited until he felt safe and then hurried out, down the stairs, across the courtyard, and, by the little gallery, up to the ramparts, craving only solitude, for, though the blind choice was made, thought was waking now, and regret, and desire for that which he had denied. He stayed there, leaning against the battlements, and the swallows, flying close, went by with a soft musical whirr and rustle of wings; but he did not heed them, for he was at war.

It was here that Audiart, passing along with another of the Countess' women, came suddenly upon him. She had not seen him, except at a distance, since her return from La Rochefoucauld, and she did not guess how fiercely he had avoided her. To-day, having found him, she must speak, for someone had told her that he was one of those who had taken the vow of pilgrimage in the Cathedral that very morning. He did not turn as she came near, but she paused beside him and spoke, using words which she had rehearsed so often lest she should stumble in them, that they had lost all sound of sincerity.

"I am glad, Messire, that you go on this pilgrimage. I will pray –"

She stopped there abruptly, and stood, smiling pitiably at him, for he had turned, and even before he spoke, his face gave her warning.

"Are you glad?" he said. "Why then? Because I am not going! Now go pray for me if ye list!" He would show her that he cared neither for her cold condescension, nor for her disapproval.

Before the poison of bitterness in his voice she shrank back and fled, dumb, and shaking all over, sick and afraid before something unreasonable as a nightmare, and indubitable as waking.

Yves did not seem to care for the effect of his words, but turned away, leaning his elbows upon the wall, and his chin in his hands. Long after she had gone he remained there, his eyes shut and teeth clenched upon a misery at least as cruel as hers.

XIII

My life closed twice before its close,
    It yet remains to see
If Immortality unveil
    A third event to me.

So huge, so hopeless to conceive
    As these that twice befell.
Parting is all we know of heaven
    And all we need of hell.

                   EMILY DICKINSON.

TWO years later, on the last afternoon of the Fair of St. John, the Midsummer Fair, Geralda of Fouquebrune, now Geralda of Claix, seventeen years old and a married woman, rode down the narrow street that led from the castle to the west gate of Angoulême. Two serving-men rode behind, and two before, and three men-at-arms brought up the rear. She was on her way home now to Claix, having ridden in to the Fair to buy thirty ells of grey woollen cloth for the gowns and tunics of the house-serfs. The big bundles of stuff were roped to the pack-saddle of a mule which one of her men led, while another carried a more precious package – a length of yellow silk that was to be a gown for Domna Geralda herself.

Close to the gate, where the street narrowed to a cart's width and swerved to the left, she saw her two serving-men in front draw to one side, and next moment a man on horseback came round the corner, riding slowly and gazing about him. As he came closer and passed Geralda glanced at him, looked again, stared, turned in the saddle, and then cried:

"Messire Yves?"

The rider stopped and looked over his shoulder.

"Messire Yves as I live!" said Geralda, and laughed, backing her horse. He made no effort to come towards her, but merely waited.

"You did not know me!" she said, and her eyes ran over his face, searching and probing, and trying to understand how he had changed; for he had changed. "And I did not know you, at first," she added.

"Oh, but yea," he said. "I knew you well enough."

Such blank indifference pricked her, though she cared nothing for him now, either to help or hurt, and she remembered an old weapon. She affected to sigh.

"Ye've not forgiven me," she said, "for telling you that I did about Audiart of Rouillac."

He raised his shoulders slightly.

"Oh, that!" he said in a tone which even to her was entirely casual. "You mistake."

There was no sport here, Geralda realised, but she lingered still, since she was still curious. Why had he changed so? Why was she almost afraid of him now? But she liked to play with fear, and so she stayed.

"Ah! then," she said, and smiled at him, "we're friends."

He raised his eyebrows.

"It's too much grace for me," he said, and did not try to hide the sneer.

She vowed to herself she would break this obduracy.

"Nay," she said, and her voice was kind, "I have thought of you. I did not forget. But why did ye not come back when the others came? Have ye been with Pons of Jarnac? Is he returned now too?"

Yves shook his head.

"What are you saying? I do not understand?"

"Why," she said, "when the Old Count died a year agone at Messina – Ye knew the Old Count was dead?"

"Yea," said Yves, "I knew."

"Then . . . when he died they all came home, those who went on Pilgrimage. But Pons, he went on, and now stays in the kingdom, for his cousin hath a fief nigh Jerusalem."

"His uncle," corrected Yves, and then because the words recalled Pons more nearly than he cared, he looked down at his hands upon the reins, and frowned. He was remembering how Pons had told him of that uncle on the battlements looking over the plain, and how he had said neither farewell nor God-speed to Pons.

"Ye have been with him then?" he heard Geralda say. "And is he returned as well?"

Yves looked up, impatient now.

138

"How should I know?" he said. "Ye've got it all awry. I went not with them on that pilgrimage. The Old Count sent me off with Lord Guilhem before ever he started. I've been on the Poitevin March these two years. I am come now with a message. That is all."

"Ah!" she said, and bit her lips because of her mistake. No man likes a woman to be so totally astray about his affairs. She tried another means.

"You'll find much that's strange in Angoulême," she said. "The Old Count dead – God rest his soul – But there's not many will regret him."

"No," said Yves, "not many!" and at the tone of his voice she laughed. He did not laugh, but only looked at her stonily until she grew uncomfortable.

"And now Count Vulgrin!" she said, because she felt she must say something. "Harrow and alas! He is very different!"

"What do you mean?" said Yves sharply.

"What? Did ye not know? He died two days agone?"

"Nay," said Yves, "I did not know it," and he was silent, frowning. Then: "There's none but his little wench Mahaut to take his lordship," he said, and looked hard at Geralda.

She nodded once with her lips pursed, then leaned towards him.

"They're saying –" she began in a low voice. "Well! they're saying she's but a little lass, and that the Count had other two sons beside Lord Vulgrin . . . grown men. . . ."

"Oh!" said Yves, "that is the talk. Lord Adhemar . . . and Lord Guilhem?"

Geralda was quick. "You do not like him? Lord Guilhem?"

For the first time, as Yves looked at her, his eyes were not hostile.

"The shoe is on the other foot as well," he said. "He does not like me neither. . . . I made a song. . . . He heard it." He laughed shortly as if he were both angry and pleased at the recollection.

Geralda clapped her hands.

"Oh, brave!" she said. "But 'ware him! He remembers!"

He knew her coin was false but the chink of it pleased him, and he did not care – not now.

"I will," he said, and smiled. "Now tell your news."

Geralda cast down her eyes.

"I am wedded," she said. "To Uc of Claix. . . . You remember him?"

Yves nodded, and she went on:

"I was wed a year ago . . . and Audiart of Rouillac too, but she's widowed." She could not help watching his face, but it told her nothing and she wondered if there had ever been anything to tell. She leaned towards him again and lowered her voice.

"They say," she said, crossing herself and looking about her: "they say . . . you know she was betrothed aforetime, and he was hurt and lay strengthless for a year and then died? . . . And now this. . . . They say it's witchcraft!"

" 'Tis very like," he said indifferently, and crossed himself, and suddenly laughed.

"What is it?" she asked, but he told her: "Nothing."

"Is she here?" he said after a moment.

"Audiart? Yea. Have a care if ye meet her!" said Geralda, and smiled as people do when they jest of dangers in which they half believe.

Yves looked at her with a grin.

"I will," he said, and then with a wave of his hand and a casual farewell he left her, and rode away past the staring servants.

When he had left his sword at a smith's – part of the grip had broken away so that the tang was bare – he went on up to the castle to deliver his message. It had been a message to Count Vulgrin; now he supposed it must go to Lord Guilhem or Lord Adhemar.

"Where were they?" he asked, and was told: "In the Countess' garden." So he made his way there, more troubled than he cared to own by the familiar places, and by the lack of familiar people. Here the Old Count had stopped him once when he was trying to slip away unnoticed to go hawking in the water meadows. Here Pons – He tried to push the thoughts from his mind and shut them out as he shut the door of the walled garden behind him.

Two figures, one with a scarlet cloak, one with broad green shoulders, were marching up and down the straight path that led through the centre of the garden. Guilhem and Adhemar were taking counsel together. At the end of the path, in the broad stone-paved space below the castle wall – the Golden Countess had her rooms above, Yves remembered – there was a crowd of knights and lords, the vassals of Angoulême, and a sprinkling of esquires, heirs of the greater fiefs. Yves went up to the outskirts of the crowd and stood, waiting and watching.

The sun, declining behind the trees, threw lovely shafts of liquid gold through the branches, so that the grass was dappled green and golden-green. The bees were busy in the tiger-lilies and carnations, and the water from the fountain made a soft little laughing noise in its stone channel. Yves' thoughts went back to the Golden Countess; he looked aside to see the seat by the fountain, and he smiled, but not bitterly, because he had no cause to hate nor fear her.

At last the two brothers stopped in their pacing. Adhemar nodded once or twice, Guilhem made an airy gesture as if he said: "Pfiu! That is no odds." Then they turned once more and came down towards the waiting group, and as they came Adhemar's fingers were spread out to touch the neat heads of lavender beside the path, and he seemed gay; but Guilhem walked sedately, one hand behind his back, the other balancing his sword. When they came close he dropped behind, and Adhemar went forward alone, and stood, facing the crowd.

"Lords and knights," he said in his pleasant voice, "listen and give me counsel. My father the Old Count wist well ye were true loyal men, and so we hold you. Ye know well – out alas for it! – how Angoulême is lordless now except for a little lass, and ye know too what days are these, and who is our overlord. Ye know how ill a lord Count Richard was to my father and to Vulgrin my brother. Ye can guess what he will do when it is a wench rules in Angoulême. He'll sell her marriage to a man of his, and that will be our new lord. Now tell – shall it be this way, or will ye have Guilhem Talifer my brother, and me, Adhemar, that are true sons of the Old Count Guilhem; will ye have us for your lords?"

He stopped and drew back to stand beside Guilhem, who was staring this way and that with his ugly challenging look, as the listeners began to talk softly among themselves. La Rochefoucauld was frowning, but Pierre of Ruffec – plump little man – caught him by the sleeve, whispering eagerly, and his face cleared. Pons of Villebois Lavalette was nodding his head as Simon of Blanzac murmured in his ear: "I think it wise, by Saint Jude!" he said aloud at last, and the Constable said "Yea" and others "Yea," and everyone began to speak aloud. Only one or two were silent, and seemed to withdraw themselves from the group.

Guilhem spoke suddenly as though impatient of further discussion: "The lass cannot complain. It means peace for her."

Yves laughed softly to himself and reaching out a hand twitched the gown of one of the esquires who stood near.

> "Said butchering eagle to carrion raven
> 'Our bellies are truly the lamb's best haven,' "

he quoted, and realised that he had finished the second line in the midst of one of those silences that fall upon companies without reason or warning. In that blank pause his voice seemed inordinately loud; no one could help but hear it, and worse, no one could help but know what had come before, and the application of it, since the doggerel rhyme was part of a fable that each man there must have heard from his nurse.

They turned to look, first at him, and then, almost furtively, at the two brothers. As for Yves, he did not take his eyes off Guilhem, even though it was Adhemar who spoke first.

"What? Who? Death of God! . . . I," cried Adhemar, his voice running high till it broke off into speechless rage.

"Who is he?" he began again, turning to Guilhem. Adhemar had a poor memory.

Guilhem's eyes were on Yves as he answered his brother.

"A fellow of none account . . . an esquire, and penniless. He hath lost his land, but he can string rhymes and thinks he is free to say or sing. . . . I have forgot his name."

Yves had a slow, sullen temper that rarely blazed, but when Guilhem spoke of him as he might have spoken of an ill-bred dog, he caught fire.

"Yea then?" he said, and at the sound of his voice one or two started forward, as if to prevent violence. "Yea then? I am penniless, and have lost my land, and ye have forgot my name? Ye do well, since it's a shame upon Angoulême – for it's Rifaucon! Rifaucon! that Count Richard hath taken, and Angoulême is too weak and coward, for all your fine talking, to win it again!"

142

Guilhem waited for him to finish and then:

"Do ye think thus to get your Rifaucon from us?" he said, and made the simple question brutal.

Yves was reckless now, and careless that he had been in the wrong at the outset.

"Do I think?" he said. "Nay, by God! I do not! I gat it not from my lord the Old Count, nor from Count Vulgrin. I'll not get it now, when Counts are such cheap-jack merchandise that we may buy us two for the price of one."

There was a stir among the men who stood watching; hardly a sound or movement at all, but a something, as there is when a soft breath of wind goes through the leaves of a tree. Adhemar's hand went to his sword and he took a step forward, but Guilhem was too ready and too clever for him. If the veins of his bull-neck were swollen, no one noticed it but Yves, for his voice was easy as he caught Adhemar's shoulder.

"Na, na, fair sweet brother, let be! Hard words break no heads."

There was an audible murmur of surprise and applause among the listeners at such unexpected forbearance. It was no one's business but Yves' to wonder what it masked.

It was of this that Yves was thinking as he left the garden with the others, and he called himself many times a fool for having provoked these Counts-to-be, for nothing. Knowing Guilhem as he did, he understood that the less time he lingered in Angoulême, the better. His message could take care of itself; he could make Vulgrin's death his excuse, and once clear of Angoulême he would leave Guilhem time to forget. It was a fool thing to have done but – He gave a little short laugh of satisfied anger, and raising his head found himself staring into the face of Audiart.

His heart gave a great leap in his breast as though it tried to escape, and then settled down to a pounding beat that shook him; but he kept his eyes steady, and before that harsh stare hers dropped.

When she was past he raised his hand to wipe his forehead, but he did it unconsciously. He wanted her. He needed her. The walls which, during this last two years, he had so painfully built about himself, had

143

crumbled and left him as defenceless as ever, and he knew now that those walls had never been anything but dust. He had tried to hate her, to forget her, to laugh her away; he had said: "Good she may be, but I desire her not. . . . What have I to do with good?" But he did desire her. Though she had turned her back upon him, yet she pursued him, and he could not escape her; and behind her, dimmer and more terrible, he saw the inexorable Hunter Whom also he desired.

He heard a step behind him, and starting aside, he turned, expecting any impossibility.

But it was only a serving-man who pulled up as Yves halted.

"Messire," he said, "Lord Guilhem bade me seek you. He hath a word for you."

Yves stared at him for the least instant, his thoughts astray; then he brought them back to the immediate thing which faced him.

"Go on then," he said. "I follow you."

As he walked back behind the man, his hand went groping at his side for a familiar resting-place and could not find it. He remembered then that he had no sword.

They found Guilhem Talifer in a small round room in one of the outer towers of the castle. It had been his before the death of his father and brother, and he had not yet troubled to move into the greater rooms which they had occupied within the inner walls. It was a pleasant room enough except that in summer, as now, the stagnant moat below the window sent up a heavy poisonous smell. But no one in those days noticed one smell; there were too many.

As the servant backed out and shut the door Yves went down stiffly upon one knee, and Guilhem, sitting in one of the window-recesses, his face invisible against the pale sky behind, stared at him in silence. After a few moments of this unpleasant pause Guilhem rose and came down from the window, gathering his loose, ungirt gown about him. Yves stood up.

Guilhem turned to the table and smiled.

"There lie," he said, "parchment, and ink and pen, and tablets too . . . nothing lacks. Sit down now, Yves of Rifaucon, and write me a song."

As Yves frowned at him, trying to understand what this might mean, Guilhem suddenly let go all pretence of calm.

"And when ye've done," he said, coming closer to Yves with every word – "and when ye've done I'll have my knaves in, and bid them horsewhip the very hide off you."

Yves held his ground.

"That is not law," he said, and knew that he spoke idly. "And if I am landless others are not, and they will see I have right."

"Oh fool!" said Guilhem. "How should they care . . . or even know? But if they know they will not care enough to trouble me. . . . And they need not know."

He watched Yves' face set and grow a little paler, and it pleased him. He went over to the door and turned, with his hand on the latch.

"I give you a half-hour," he said, and shut the door behind him.

For perhaps a quarter of an hour Yves sat at the table, busy with pen and ink. When he left it there were many little scribbles on the corners of the parchment, but only two lines of verse, and two lines of music. He went to the window, and stood looking down over the moat, and humming to himself. A man-at-arms was idling down below in the growing shadows, and once he stopped and stared up at the tower window.

Yves saw that he was in a strong trap.

At last he heard the latch of the door lift, and turned back into the room. Guilhem was standing by the table; in one hand he held a lute, in the other a leather-thonged whip. He leaned over the parchment, peering at it sideways.

"It is full short," he said.

"Yea," said Yves and he smiled now. "But long enough."

"Maybe," said Guilhem, and then he laughed. "But if I had been you, I had made it as long as the Song of Roland!" and he held up the whip to point his jest. He sat down, still chuckling, waved Yves to a low stool before him, and gave him the lute. Yves took and tuned it.

"Begin," said Guilhem as Yves looked up at him, and he leaned back in his chair so that Yves could not see his face for the shadow of the high, carved back.

Yves played a run of mocking, laughing notes, and began to sing, and what he sang was what he had said in the garden.

"Said butchering eagle to carrion raven –
'Our bellies are truly the lamb's best haven!'"

The absurd tune he had made ended with a triumphant twang and a loud "Ho! Ho!" but Guilhem neither moved nor spoke, and Yves, wondering, and laughing within himself, leaned forward a little to see his face.

Without warning, and as quick as a snake in the grass, Guilhem's hand shot out, and before Yves could avoid it, the leather thong of the whip scored his face. He leapt up, staggering back over the stool, his arm up to protect himself, the blood already running warm and sickly into his mouth.

Guilhem came on again, blood-mad and ready to kill, but fortunately for Yves he forgot his sword, and forgot his men outside the door. He wanted only to strike, and there was no more reflection in him than in a charging bull.

Yves dodged aside, feinted, and ran in under the searing thong that caught him again and laid his cheek open, but he had snatched up the heavy footstool, and hurled it. It took Guilhem full in the midriff and drove him back helpless, till he managed to pull himself up against the table. There he stayed a moment, making horrible noises, and then, tearing out his sword, he plunged again at Yves.

There was no distinct thought in Yves' mind as to what he should do, but he found himself at the window. His knee struck the stone sill, his shoulder buffeted against the narrow arch, and next moment he was choking in the slime of the moat, his face smarting afresh at the sting of the water. He came up gasping, struggling to control his breath lest he should give himself away, but there was no need. The place was deserted, and save for himself, absolutely silent.

In the tower room above, Guilhem Talifer lay sprawling close by the window embrasure. He was in a dead swoon, but he groaned and twitched from time to time.

Just as Yves crawled out of the moat, Audiart got up from her knees in the little chapel that stood on the passage-way between the postern

146

and the main courtyard. Half an hour ago she had come here because she was desperate. She had gone down on her knees and locked her hands, and then she had fought with Omnipotence.

"Give him to me! Give him to me! Give him to me! I have tried . . . but I cannot lack him any more. . . . Give him to me!" That was all she said, but she said it over and over, and in a desperate whisper, because she dared not say it aloud, and yet God must hear. Suddenly she became silent and very still, and for the rest of the time she only gazed, dumbly and through tears, at the crowned Virgin and the Child who held the Orb in His hand.

When at last she rose from her knees she was very weary. She stood for a moment, her head bent and hands clasped loosely before her; then she drew a long breath, raised her eyes, and smiled. It was a smile that shone, and made her for a brief second, beautiful.

As she had knelt there whispering her urgency, she had seen, was sure she had seen, the gracious veiled head of the Mother bow itself towards her, and the Son's little hand move in a gesture of august consent. For a moment she had stared, amazed into fear before so wonderful a thing. Then she had been swept by a huge and singing flood into a vastness of light that dazzled her. Joy was coming. It was on the way. God had allowed it.

As she pulled open the heavy, grinding door of the chapel, and saw the cold dimness of the passage before her, she gave a hurried glance over her shoulder towards the altar, as though she needed the promise reaffirmed. There was no sign now. She shut the door behind her, turned to go, and saw Yves.

The passage was dark except for the distant glow of a torch set in its iron ring, and his back was towards that only light, but she knew him at once and as a matter of course, and her heart was in her throat at this terrible swift answer to her prayer. For an instant her only thought was – "Then it is true."

She stopped because her knees trembled so that she could not move, and she dared not look at him.

"Who is it?" he said in a low voice that sounded strange in the vaulted passage.

"Audiart," she answered, and heard him draw his breath. It was coming true! She remembered that it was here that he had nearly kissed her, and here she had learnt she loved him; it was as though God's finger was just completing a perfect circle in this place. She put one hand against the wall to steady herself.

Yves had drawn back from her a little, and he turned his head away, for he felt the blood trickle from the weals on his face, and he would not let her see. He thanked God that the passage was dark.

"Hearken, Domna," he began after a pause that seemed endless to Audiart. "The Countess. . . . Get me to her chamber secretly . . . for . . . for God's Son's sake. . . . I –" He stopped short because he so hated to ask her anything that the sudden movement she made was enough to check him.

"The Countess?" Audiart repeated in a dead voice. "You want her?"

"Yea. Get me to her that none know it. She'll give me the key and then . . . when it is dark –"

Audiart did not let him finish.

"And you ask me?" she cried suddenly, and her voice was strained like a floss of silk over a knife. "*Me*, to get you to her? Shame, shame be with you, knave that you are!" She could not say any more, for this thing went beyond words. It is a dizzy gulf to fall through, that which lies between Heaven and Hell. She heard Yves laugh, and thought she had never before heard such a horrible sound.

"Ye may believe me," he cried, "that I would not ask you if I could get to her any other way, but –" He broke off suddenly, listening intently to a sound of footsteps. They paused, and then receded, but they had reminded him of the need of haste if he was to get clear of the gates before the hunt began.

He caught her wrist suddenly and gripped it hard; hard enough to hurt and frighten her.

"Take me there! Now!" he said fiercely, for he must get his way. She gasped as he caught her and began to struggle.

"I will not. . . . Never!" she cried distractedly, sobbing with pain and misery. Suddenly she left off trying to free her hand; raising the other she struck desperately at his face, heard him give an exclamation that might have been of pain or anger, found herself free, and fled from him up the passage.

148

Less than an hour later Folquet of Vignolles, that same young knight who had been Geralda's slave, knocked at the door of the Countess' room and was bidden enter. There were only four women with her, the rest were wiser than to remain with the setting sun, but the Golden Countess, though thinner now and paler, looked up as he came in, and smiled; it was enough for him. He went down on his knee to kiss her hand, and for once the formal salute was a mask for truth.

"Well?" said the Countess.

"Domna," he said, looking at her with a great pity, "are you brave?" He was sure she was.

She went white and gripped the arms of her chair, and her hands shook.

"Why?... What?... Oh! what must I do?" she cried and her face quivered.

He was surprised, but her fear seemed lovely since it turned to him.

"Do not be afraid," he said. "There's not a thing to fear. But I told you how Lord Guilhem and Lord Adhemar spoke in the garden this afternoon. Then, at sunset, they had us into the Hall to give them final counsel. Counsel!" he growled, and spat aside into the rushes. "It was all shouting and swords out! They yelled 'Guilhem!' and 'Adhemar!' and then 'Adhemar!' and 'Guilhem!' until I thought the roof would split. So they two count themselves lords of Angoulême now.... But I came away before the oath-taking ... and I set to work."

He paused, looking at her gently as if she were a child to be protected, though usually he dare hardly meet her eyes.

"Now, dearest Domna," he said, "I have horses ready, and a pillion for the little lass that's Lady of Angoulême sure enough if only we can get away to Count Richard. He'll see to that."

The Countess stood up, her hands clasped tight together.

"Yea, let us go." Then she sank down again as suddenly. 'Oh, I dare not!" she cried. "To-morrow perhaps.... I dare not ... not now.... We shall never pass the gate."

Folquet looked round towards the women as if for help, and found Audiart of Rouillac watching. He did not like the way she looked at the Countess, and so he scowled at her till she dropped her eyes to her work again.

"Domna," he said, turning back to the Countess, "here's no danger. I have the key of the southern gate. Count Guilhem hath not missed it yet, and we had thought of this when we kept it from the rest. It will be as easy as butter in the churn. See now! I let out Yves of Rifaucon half an hour ago. . . . The guard care nothing, they'll not stop you. Yves went by them muffled in a cloak; he might have been anyone, but they did not care. . . . And Count Guilhem was after him, he said, but the guard said naught as I let him out."

Audiart interrupted him suddenly.

"Yves of Rifaucon?" she said. "Why?" and then, as though she cared nothing for the answer, she bent once more over her embroidery.

"Why was Lord Guilhem after him?" Folquet answered her, half impatiently. "Oh! about this same matter of the inheritance. At least that was how it began. He braved Lord Guilhem in the garden to-day –" Folquet laughed grimly. "He said a thing . . . I marvel. . . . But I think Yves of Rifaucon fears not even the devil. . . . But Guilhem caught him after . . . somehow. He'll carry the marks for a year – Yves will. I lent him my sword . . . and a cloak to hide the blood on his face and –"

"O! O! O!" It was a very low cry, hardly more than an audible shudder, but everyone turned, and saw Audiart peering at her hands.

"What is it?" cried the Countess, angry because she had been frightened.

"O!" Audiart ended with a gasp. Then in a voice that threatened to run up and break: "I ran my needle in. . . . Nothing," and she tried to laugh, and raised both hands to her mouth.

But there was no freshly drawn blood upon any of her fingers; only a little dry clot in the midst of one palm.

XIV

O, that I were as great
As is my grief, or lesser than my name!
Or that I could forget what I have been!
Or not remember what I must be now! . . .
Richard II, Act III, sc. III.

WHEN Yves rode into Perigueux the whole town seemed about to dissolve into rain. Rain fell straight and relentless from the leaden obscurity above. Rain ran in steady streams from gutters and eaves, making a cluttering noise in the miry street. Rain-pocked puddles splashed up as his horse trod heavily through the downpour. The only thing which seemed to have a distinct and vigorous life of its own was a swallow that came with a straight, arrow-like flight down the narrow dark lane towards him, and sheared away and up, as though it had come to give warning and then escaped.

Obeying the directions of a man he had met slouching along under the dripping eaves with a sack over his head and bits of damp straw adhering to his tattered gaberdine, Yves followed the turns of the main street, and came out at last before the gate of the castle. A sentinel stood there, lounging upon his bill in the dry patch under the gateway-tower. He looked at Yves without curiosity and spat.

Yves dismounted and stood dripping in the shelter of the gate.

"Take me to Count Talleyrand," he said shortly to the sentinel who was watching him. The man threw back his head and seemed about to laugh, but he caught Yves' eye, and thought the better of it. Instead he kept silence.

Yves repeated his words.

"Who art thou, gossip?" said the man with heavy familiarity.

Yves looked at him.

"Not *thy* gossip!" he said.

The man wavered, doubtful. This fellow with the mud-splashed, drenched clothes, and the raw weals across his face, did not look like one of the masters – and yet – He compromised.

151

"Ask over there!" he said, and jerked his thumb towards a doorway across the court. Yves swallowed his anger, and went on.

He found the Count at last in a perron in the midst of the garden. There were three men there, apart from the crowd of lesser folk, any one of whom might have been the Count, and Yves, as he went slowly up the steps of the perron, looked hard at each, trying to guess which was to be his new lord, and what manner of man he would be to deal with.

One, dressed very fine in dark green with red hose strapped with blue, and wearing a great gold chain about his neck, sat at a small table of chess. He had silky hair of a darkish brown with light in the waves, and a beard that hid his mouth. Another, sitting opposite at the table, was fair and ruddy, with the build and proportion of feature proper to a generous man, but there was too much calculation in his light-coloured, keen eyes, and too much cold restraint on his lips, for anyone to make that mistake. Yves hoped that this was not Talleyrand. Behind the two stood an older man with a bald head and a careful expression. He looked as though he had spent all his life over affairs and could never be easy.

Yves went down upon one knee before the group, and said, addressing no one in particular: "Lord Talleyrand of Perigord."

All three turned to look at him; the dark man with curiosity; the fair man superciliously, his eyebrows daintily raised; the older man with a worried frown.

It was the first who spoke as Yves paused.

"How did you come here?" he said, and still stared.

Yves took his cue, and spoke to him alone.

"Lord Talleyrand," he began, "I am from Angoulême –"

"Ah! A messenger!" cried the old man and his face cleared.

Yves shook his head.

"Then how did you come here? Who let you pass?" said Talleyrand. "What's your business? Go away!"

Yves stood up. This Count seemed to him to be a fool.

"I came to you, Lord Count," he said, "because the talk is in Angoulême that you will fight Count Richard of Poitou. If that talk is true you will need swords."

Tallyerand, instead of answering at once, sulked over the table, fingering the pieces and frowning in silence.

"Well?" he snapped at last, as Yves did not move.

"Is that true?" said Yves.

The Count, looking round, caught a half-suppressed smile on the fair man's face, and his frown grew darker. He turned to Yves with a great assumption of dignity.

"You are . . . you are . . ." he began angrily, and paused, seeking a word.

"Saucy!" suggested the fair man, with eyes discreetly lowered. The Count accepted the suggestion with an ill-tempered grunt.

"Well," said Yves without budging, "if that talk is true I desire to serve you."

Talleyrand opened his eyes in a wide stare, turned back to the chess-board, looked at the pieces, and then swept them this way and that with an impatient movement of his hand.

"Is that all?" he cried. "Why then, in the devil's name, should you push yourself in here and interrupt my game, and my lord Saint-Astier's too? Go to Malinvaux! It is his affair."

"Malinvaux?" said Yves. Then, as the Count made no answer and continued to set up the pieces on the board, he went a step nearer.

"Malinvaux?" he said again. "The Routier captain? Death of –" He stopped short because no oath was sufficient.

"Count," he began once more, "I came to you as a knight –" and again anger, and something that was more fear than anger, stopped him.

"Then you may go as a knight!" snapped Talleyrand, without look-ing up, and waved him away.

Before Yves could move or speak Saint-Astier leaned forward.

"You do not look as a knight," he said, ". . . though of course it is raining."

Yves stared at him with a hard eye.

"Are you a knight?" said Saint-Astier gently, and waited with a faint smile for Yves' reply.

"No," said Yves, and went slowly and darkly red, while the smile grew on Saint-Astier's face, and Talleyrand laughed, suddenly and loudly.

"Ho! Ho!" cried Talleyrand, breaking into the conversation again. "Then was I to have had the making of you knight?"

That laughter and the jeer freed Yves' tongue for the moment.

"It would have been no shame to you," he said hotly. "My fathers have been lords and knights as long as yours."

Talleyrand was an easy man in general, and only wished to be let alone, but he was angry now.

"I take no force what your fathers have been, but if you stay longer here I'll ... I'll. ... Go to Malinvaux! ... or the devil! Have your choice." He looked across the table at Saint-Astier as though for approval.

"He will not go to Malinvaux," said Saint-Astier with a sly smile, and Talleyrand, after staring at him for a moment while he hunted for the joke, found it, and gave one of his great laughs.

Yves turned away, hesitated, and turned back. Talleyrand had not enough self-control to be silent.

"Well?" he said impatiently.

"Is it true that you will fight Poitou?" said Yves.

"What in the devil's name is it to you?" cried Talleyrand.

Yves kept silence and waited. Talleyrand looked up. Saint-Astier made as though to interfere, but Talleyrand burst out before he could speak.

"Yea, it is true. Now get you away or I'll have you driven. ... Get away! Get. ... Thunder of God! Get away!"

Yves had to wait half an hour in the deserted courtyard before Malinvaux came from his dinner. Yves heard a light step, and turning, found Malinvaux standing just behind his shoulder, his fair hair, almost white, seeming to have been washed so by the rain, his extraordinary bushy eyebrows, pale as his hair, half hiding a pair of the sharpest and wickedest pig's eyes. Malinvaux had a reputation. People said, that in Gascony, when he had taken a castle, he pledged his prisoners in a cup of their own blood, drinking it to the last drop. Perfectly healthy, with muscles and mind like steel, he caused the same creeping repulsion as a leper or an idiot; a nightmare creature of soft steps, soft flesh, and cruelty worse than a beast's because it was human.

He did not even trouble to stare Yves down, though he could have done it. After a hard glance, eye to eye, Malinvaux looked him all over, carefully and intently, and in absolute silence.

"Hold out your hand!" he muttered, and when Yves obeyed, looked at wrist and forearm, and the sword-hardened palm. Then he nodded.

"You have arms?" he said sharply. "And a horse?"

"Only a palfrey," said Yves as briefly. "And my sword is all I brought."

Malinvaux laughed unpleasantly. He was a churl's son.

"Ah! a poor gentleman?" he sneered, and before Yves could answer he was away with his long, silent stride.

At the door he stopped and spoke to a page who lounged there out of the rain, idly watching the interview.

"Take this fellow –" said Malinvaux, jerking his thumb towards Yves, "take this fellow to Eschiward the steward. Bid him give him arms and food. Do it now!"

The page moved aside, leaving Malinvaux ample room to pass, but when the Routier captain had gone, the boy became pert enough to make Yves long to kick him.

Among Malinvaux's Routiers that served Count Talleyrand for hire, there was a man whose christened name was Constantin. To this, the Routiers added the surname of "The Weasel"; but he himself preferred to say that he was Constantin of Born. He was, in fact, and he never forgot it, the elder brother of that stormy troubadour, that stirrer up of strife between France and England, Bertran of Born. He should have been co-lord of Hautefort with Bertran, but Bertran had driven him out, neck and crop, and here he was, a broken man, a Routier who had once been lord of his land.

In appearance he was personable enough, being of middle height, strongly yet slightly built, so that he walked with a sort of dancing tread. His face was thin, with a long, high-bridged nose and pointed chin, and the colour of his hair was between red and sandy. The Routiers called him "Weasel," but the name was not given on account of his hair.

Because of the similarity of their present position and antecedents, an acquaintance and alliance – it was never a friendship, for each disliked

155

and despised the other and took no pains to hide his feelings – an alliance grew up between Constantin and Yves. Neither knew how it began; when it was at its closest they saw much of each other; when it gradually waned neither could say why, having put up with the other for so long, he should now find him intolerable.

One day in January, when Yves had been in Perigueux close on six months, Constantin caught him up at the gate of the castle. Yves' obvious unwillingness quickened Constantin's faint desire for company, and he ranged alongside with a crooked smile which Yves did not trouble to answer. They walked on, down the street, which lay very bright in the cold sunshine, the wrinkled mud of its surface swept hard, pale, and dry by the thin wind; and for a while neither said a word.

At a turn in the road where there was sun, and also shelter from the wind, they came upon a group of burgesses, solid, comfortable men gowned in sober-coloured cloth tunics and big cloaks lined with marten or coney fur. As Yves and Constantin went by, one of them, a broad-shouldered, prosperous fellow with a sensible, keen face, turned from his talk to watch them past, and with a muttered word spat after them.

Constantin, whose eyes were always wandering aside, saw it, and halted as suddenly as though he had come to the end of a rope. Yves, oblivious, had forged on ahead, but Constantin ran after him and seized his arm.

"Come back!" he cried, and stamped his foot upon the road. "Come back! . . . These fellows . . . these. . . . Let us give them a lesson!"

Yves slackened his pace but he did not stop.

"Wherefore?" he said.

Constantin pulled him to a stand.

"Because . . . they . . . they. . . . Didst thou not see? They spat at us . . . at us! Sons of dogs . . .!"

Yves shrugged scornfully.

"Why the plague should they not?" he said. "Come on!"

Constantin forgot the burgesses in rage against Yves.

"Do ye love to be a Routier?" he cried. "Will ye forget what ye are?"

Yves stood still and throwing up his head laughed at the cold bright sky.

"Death of God!" he said. "But thou art a jester, my Constantin . . . my dainty lad! Nay, the ladies of the Castle should have thee to lap thee in silk and cradle thee soft."

The mockery made Constantin angry, and for the moment it put him off his point.

"Jester?" he cried. "That's thy fool part! God He knows I would not jest as thou dost with these Routier dogs . . . not so good as dogs neither . . . they're swine! I'll not forget I was born lord of Hautefort, and I'll keep myself clean as I can."

"Why for?" sneered Yves. "Who cares what you are?"

"I do," snapped Constantin, and he spoke the truth. It was the last rag of honour to which he clung. "But as for you –" he went on. "Have you no shame?"

"You are a fool," said Yves.

"Nay, but have ye no shame for yourself?" persisted Constantin as though he longed to wring the hated admission from Yves.

"Shame?" said Yves. "None!" and went on to affirm the lie. "Hath the louse shame that she lives in filth? I wot not. She lives merrily, and so do I," and he laughed in Constantin's face.

Constantin was torn between disgust and satisfaction.

"Yea, indeed!" he said. "I might have known it was like that for you. You that go to the brothel house!"

"There's a butcher's wench, Constantin," said Yves. "She dwells near by the shambles."

Constantin flushed.

"It's different . . . and I take my chance of hanging seeing that I'm Routier and her father a free burgess. But as for you . . ." he cried, growing yet more angry. "And ye jest . . . as ye jested of that ye did at Gabillou." He spat the name in Yves' face, meaning it to be venom, but Yves took it calmly.

"Oh! tittle-tattle!" he said. "How thou lovest that tale! God bless thee! Keep thy heart warm with it. I give thee free leave," and with a smile and a wave of the hand he turned away and left Constantin where he stood.

The tale of what Yves had done at Gabillou was forgotten now by everyone but Constantin. In fact, for the ordinary Routiers it had never been anything more than the jest and talk of a day, but to Constantin it was an enduring bitter satisfaction. "Lord, I thank Thee," he said in effect, "that I am not such a man as this Yves – and he was born a Pharisee too!"

Gabillou was one of the smaller fiefs of Perigord, and Archambaut of Gabillou had quarrelled with Count Talleyrand. There was wrong on both sides. Archambaut had taken some cattle from Talleyrand's demesne land at Bouchaud, and Talleyrand had hanged a free man of Gabillou who unwisely came to the fair at Perigueux. Just a month after Yves arrived at Perigueux, Talleyrand decided that not only could he keep the Routiers quiet, and set them to feed on other men's corn, but that he could also pay off old scores at the same time, by sending them out against Archambaut.

It took Malinvaux five days to get into Gabillou, for the castle was strong, Archambaut was as brave as a wild cat up a tree, and the Routiers had no siege engines but the pine-trunks they cut from the near woods, and used as battering-rams, swinging them in slings of oxhide taken from Archambaut's slaughtered cattle. On the fifth day they broke open the gate, drove back Archambaut and a dozen men who met them, and swarmed in.

In the confusion, Archambaut and three men left from his dozen got back across the yard to a small, strong storeroom beside the Hall, and there they went to earth, and barred the door. There was one loophole, high up, and a Routier, climbing on shoulders, clung a moment, and peered in.

"Naught!" he cried, and leapt down. "Naught but the four of them and some corn-sacks. Let 'em be! They'll do no hurt, and we'll waste our time getting 'em out. They'll burn –"

He broke off as he heard above all the din a scream and a burst of wilder shouting from the upper storeys of the big keep. While he lingered here, others had found the women. He, and those with him, turned and raced for the keep doorway, leaving Yves behind them, standing in the horribly echoing courtyard, before the small door. He turned from it after a moment, stared about, and crossed over to a little woodstack that stood beside the gate.

Five minutes later he had set light to a very pretty little bonfire against the door behind which Archambaut and his three men waited. He drew his sword, slipped his hand into the leather thong so that the blade hung safe at his wrist, and going again to the woodstack, fetched back with him a heavier log. Then he too waited, watching the fire as it felt over the tough, iron-bolted surface with soft, wandering fingers, more deadly than any steel.

At last he saw that the door itself was ablaze. He ran forward and swung the log once and twice. The door shattered with a crash; part swung inwards on the softing hinges, part fell into the room. Yves dropped the log and leapt in over it, his sword ready.

Inside that dark small room, where there was no space for sword-play and little light except that which came from Yves' dying fire, he had the advantage. Two of Archambaut's men were already desperately wounded. One of them indeed died suddenly as he stood, blood bursting from mouth and nose without Yves' sword once touching him. The sound man Yves caught in the throat, just where the chain gorget ended. The second wounded man dropped just as Archambaut slashed, missed Yves' shoulder, and laid his arm open.

Yves turned, man to man now, and there were a few moments of silent, furious fighting. Then Archambaut went down slowly on one knee, his hand pressed to his side, his face twisted into a strange expression of rage, and pain, and blank surprise. He tried to rise, but could not, and slipped back into a sitting position, his legs sprawling as he propped himself up on one hand, while the other clutched at that gnawing mouth that tore at his side.

He looped up at Yves, and Yves, standing resting on his sword, looked down at him. The little dark room seemed very quiet, although outside there were still shouts and echoing crashes, and all the confused, ugly noises of a sack.

Yves suddenly smiled and nodded at Archambaut. "That was not such an ill fight," he said. "I thank you for the sport ye've given me. . . It's better than . . . that!" He nodded towards the door.

Archambaut tried to speak, but found it only possible to whisper.

"God requite you," he said, "filthy Routier!" Then, his arm giving way, he fell back, but his eyes still glared up at Yves.

"Nay! Nay!" said Yves pleasantly. "Ye've got your death on a good sword. I'm as good blood as you –"

He stopped suddenly because there was a stir behind him where the corn-sacks stood, and as he turned to look, something rose out of the gloom, and shrieked, and fled, thrusting him aside.

It was a woman, and, though he did not know it, Archambaut's young wife, three weeks wed. She had held still and silent for so long and then her nerve had broken. She fled, but she did not go far. At the door she paused as she heard a yell from the men outside but Yves was after her, and his sword caught her between the shoulder-blades.

He looked at the men across her huddled body and laughed at their blank faces.

"Ye see!" he said. "I must have my sport like as you, but I take it this way . . ye, the other," and without paying them any more attention, he stooped, tore off the white wimple from the girl's head, and tied it round his dripping arm, knotting it with his teeth. Then he turned to the door again, but he hesitated before he went in.

"Hark ye!" he said, bending over Archambaut. "She's dead," and he saw the eyelids quiver up from the grey cheeks.

"God's terrible curse on you!" said Archambaut in a whisper that tore him.

Yves stood up quickly.

"Fool!" he said. "I should have thanks." He grew suddenly angry. "Fool!" he cried again and struck the dying man with the flat of his sword.

Between Archambaut's bloody lips two words came very slow, and only just audible.

"God's curse . . .!" he whispered, his eyes fixed on Yves.

Yves met them, and stooped again.

"You can take this comfort," he said, neither angry nor mocking now, but merely stating a plain and familiar truth. "He hath cursed me."

Archambaut's mouth opened, he stared for a fraction of time in blank amazement at Yves' face, and in that stare his jaw dropped and he passed.

Yves had a certain popularity among the Routiers, not because of his jests, for they could not understand them all, though some were broad

160

and plain enough, but because of his singing. This same thing, too, gave him power with Constantin. Indeed it was Constantin who first found it out. He heard Yves whistling a fragment of music in the stable one day, and he pounced upon him.

"What is that?" he cried.

Yves paused and grunted.

"Song of Guilhem of Agoult," he said, and began to whistle something else.

Constantin came closer, his face changed and eager.

"You know the 'gaye saber'?" he said. "You can sing?" and as Yves stopped to stare at him he went on, as if excusing himself:

"I love to hear music. It's the one thing in Bertran –" He broke off and began again. "I have a lute of his – his favourite it was. I stole it when I came away. It was a little revenge." He laughed spitefully. "I will lend it to you if ye'll sing to me."

He did as he promised, and after this he and Yves spent their pleasantest hours in a deserted place on the ramparts, Yves singing, Constantin feeding his starved soul with listening.

One night – it was the very evening after their quarrel in the street – Constantin, willing to patch up the alliance again, came to Yves in the crowded courtyard after supper, and said,

"Shall we go to the ramparts? Will you sing?"

Yves spun round, stared, and nodded.

They went up separately, and Constantin, when he reached their usual place, found Yves already there, bending over the lute, playing a few strange chords, and singing very softly to himself.

As Constantin dropped down beside him, Yves stopped short.

"What was that?" said Constantin, curiosity awake.

"Naught," said Yves, but Constantin knew from his voice that he was moved.

"Nay, sing it," he said.

"It is not finished."

"Finish it, then, and let me hear. I'll wait you."

Yves laughed.

"It's two years and more," he said, "since I began to make that song, and ye say ye'll wait!"

He remembered the night on which he had begun it – the night of that day when Audiart had said, "I am glad that ye go on this pilgrimage –" and he began to jangle the strings to drown the echo of her words.

"Sing what is made," persisted Constantin, chiefly because Yves refused.

"Not I," said Yves, and his voice was final. "It's for none but one alive."

Constantin knew that more persuasion was useless, but he was willing to be unpleasant. "Ah! then," he jeered. "It's for thy lady, is it? Saints! A Routier's lady!"

Yves disappointed him.

"Nay," he said lightly. "It's for Count Richard of Poitou. I keep it for him. No. It's not that 'Count Richard the Thief' I made the other day. I'll not sing you this . . . but . . . I'll . . . I'll . . . sing you a right fair thing I have made for that lady of mine." He ended with a gasp that he tried to change to a laugh, and snatching up the lute again, broke into a swinging tune, and began to sing.

It was a song such as the Routiers would have loved, since it was almost incredibly foul. There was one line only, the first, which was clean,

" 'Forsooth," said Audiart, "I am a maid!"

After that, the song was not fit for hearing.

Yves finished and there was silence. He leaned over to Constantin.

"What! my lad?" he said. "Laugh! Laugh!" and he laughed himself, and jerked Constantin in the back till he laughed too, but not very willingly.

When Yves was quiet again Constantin spoke, puzzled, incredulous, and disgusted.

"Did she give you her favour and love?" he said. "But is there verily such a lady?"

"Verily yea! Her name was Audiart of – Audiart, just as I call her in the song," said Yves. "Oh! it's true!" He broke off and laughed crazily. "And as for giving me her favour . . . Why, sure she doted! Fifty times hath she prayed me for my love . . . down on her knees . . . hath kissed my hands. . . ."

He stopped, and there was a silent pause.

"Oh! Christ!" he cried suddenly. "Constantin! Oh! Christ!" He stared at Constantin for a moment, then buried his face in his hands, and broke into terrible wild weeping.

Constantin looked at him, and listened for a moment with disgust. He stood up.

"I am going," he said, and went.

XV

. . . Lives there who loves his pain?
Who would not, finding way, break loose from hell,
Though thither doomed? . . .
. . . Let Him surer bar
His iron gates if He intends our stay
In that dark durance.

Paradise Lost.

THE Routiers lived, herded like cattle, in a small court and a big building which had served originally for a barn. From these quarters they were not supposed to stray about the castle, though they were free of the town; but since the courtyard interrupted a vaulted passage which was the nearest way from the postern to the Hall, a good many people passed by on their way to one or the other. That is to say that a good many men passed – knights, serving-men, beggars, even Count Talleyrand himself, but no women except of the lowest kind, and those by stealth.

One evening in March, when the weather had turned suddenly warm, the Routiers were sprawling at ease in the courtyard after their supper. They lay like beasts, dirty, and ragged, and shameless, and above them and the dark square of the courtyard the sky was a faint memory of blue.

A serving-man stopped to light the cresset at the opening of the passage to the Hall, and a few of the nearest Routiers turned to watch him. Someone picked up a bone, and flung it in rough jest.

"A hit! Yves Ner!" cried another and followed it with a handful of filth, for the courtyard was foul with refuse of all sorts. Yves (the Routiers had no worse nickname for him than "Ner" because of his black hair and dark face) laughed, as the scullion fled, his head bent to escape further playfulness.

A little while after a couple of knights went by. They walked quickly and looked straight before them,. for though they themselves were in the light of the cresset, they could see nothing in the courtyard but a dark blur of sprawling figures. They could hear, however, and the jests that came to them out of the shadows were by no means courtly. So they hurried, stepping as delicately as they could, and holding their noses carefully between thumb and finger. When they had gone the shouted jokes ceased, and Yves looked up again from picking at the worn edge of his tunic.

"Yves Ner!" shouted one of the Routiers and wiped his mouth on his sleeve. "Yves Ner! Hollo! Sing to us!"

Yves rolled over on to one elbow and yawned.

"Plague rot you – let me alone. I've no lute. . . . The Weasel hath taken his again."

"Sing without it!" cried another, and several turned to take their parts in urging him to sing.

"Where is the Weasel?" shouted someone. "We'll get the thing out of him."

Constantin of Born leapt up from the midst of a group, with his knife bare.

"Come then!" he cried. "But the lute – I've smashed it!"

"That's truth," said Yves and he laughed.

There was a growl of anger from one or two, and Constantin might have had to use his knife, but some inventive wit cried aloud:

"By—! The cooking-pot! Use it as a drum! 'Ware shins!" and next moment one of the great iron cauldrons out of which had come the broth for the Routiers' supper came clumsily rolling, pushed on by one or another, provoking in its passage both curses and laughter.

"Hollo! Yves! Ner! Here comes the ladle!" cried the same voice, and the long ladle spun over the heads of the crowd and fell at Yves' feet.

He pulled the pot towards him and tried its tone with the ladle. It gave out a clear ringing note. He laughed.

"Roll me hither the other one yonder – the smaller one," he cried, and they did it. He sat back upon his heels and lifted the ladle.

"Silence, beasts!" he said, and grinned round at his audience as the shouting and laughter, the foul words and ugly babel of the Routier courtyard died away to single voices, isolated oaths, a stir, a hush. . . .

"I will sing you 'The Song of Count Richard the Thief,' " he cried, and raising the ladle brought it down upon each of the cooking-pots in turn. The two notes, harsh and plangent, seemed almost visibly to shake in widening circles through the half-darkness of the courtyard. Yves began to sing.

It happened that just as the hush settled over the Routiers, another group of men came from the archway on their way to the Hall, and in the midst of them the little, round, rosy, white-haired Bishop of Perigueux, Peire Monet, with his drooping nose, and quaint, pursed mouth. He was, as always, dressed as finely as any man in Talleyrand's court. His cloak was of fine cloth, lined with vair, his belt was embroidered with red and gold threads, and the cross which he wore about his neck was set with stones more precious than those it had borne in the time of his predecessor; for Peire Monet had a fine taste and was not content with the antique simplicity which he called clumsiness. With him went several of his knights, and a page or two, all gaily dressed according to their lord's taste.

The sudden hush surprised the Bishop. He did not flatter himself that it was due to respect for him. Then came the two sonorous notes, and then Yves' voice. My lord Bishop, who had a knowledge of music, as of every other elegancy of life, laid his hand on the arm of the tall knight who walked beside him.

"Stop! Robert," he said, and stood, listening and peering, his head nodding in tune to the music, while all his knights crowded behind him, staring and listening too.

The Bishop heard it to the very end. Yves' voice had something in it of the fine quality of ringing metal, so that the harsh sound of the beaten iron seemed to echo it; the strong tune tramped to the two single notes; and at the words, which he caught well enough, he was not ashamed to smile. It was a song fit for the ears of Routiers. Dealing with burlesque adventures of a man who was no more than a name to them, it satisfied them because it was outrageously coarse and irresistibly funny. The Bishop, however, although he allowed himself to smile, did not stay so long for these reasons, but because he had found a jongleur.

With the last word of the song Yves brought the ladle down on the bigger of the two pots, and as it rang, laid his hand on it, choking the sound, so that the music seemed to mock itself. He looked about, caught the Bishop's eye, and turned his back on these unexpected listeners.

The Bishop was not to be baulked.

"Ho there! jongleur! Ho! jongleur!" he cried in his high, piping voice.

Yves did not turn, but the Routiers did, and seeing the gay crowd, began to crack their usual jests, only more than ordinarily broad, since they were directed against a man of Holy Church. The Bishop, however, having both pluck and dignity, did not retreat. Instead, he clutched the skirts of his gown in both hands, and picked his way over the legs and bodies of jeering Routiers, to the place where Yves sat, still balancing the iron ladle. Bending down, the Bishop touched him gently on the shoulder.

Yves glanced up, and scrambled unwillingly to his feet. He did not look anywhere but at the Bishop's scarlet boots.

"You sing well enough, fellow!" said Peire Monet. "Do you know other songs less . . . less . . .?" He paused suggestively.

"What does it matter to you?" said Yves, surly as a bear. He could jest and be merry among bestial Routiers, or poke jibes at a broken man like Constantin of Born, because they were in no better case than himself, but the Bishop was neither Routier nor broken man.

"Tut! Tut!" said the Bishop, amazingly dignified for all his small stature. "I take you for a jongleur and would do you a service – have you to sing to Count Talleyrand. . . . It means largesse."

Yves raised his eyes and stared at the Bishop, so astonished at this natural conclusion that he was not even angry.

"You *are* a jongleur?" said Bishop Peire, seeing his astonishment. "You know other songs?"

"Yea," said Yves, but his tone sounded doubtful.

"What then? Whose?" asked the Bishop sharply.

"Oh! The Monk of Montaudan's. . . . Bernard's of Ventadour. . . . Yea, I know others," said Yves unwillingly.

The Bishop nodded, smiling again.

"Good!" he said. "I'll forget how unseemly ye answered me at the first. Come. I'll take you to Lord Talleyrand," and he turned to go.

167

Yves took a step after him.

"Lord Bishop . . . I . . ." he began, but Peire Monet did not hear him. Yves shrugged his shoulders and followed.

When they reached the foot of the steps leading to the great Hall, the Bishop paused, and looked at Yves in the light which came from the open doorway.

"Can you tumble, or swallow swords?" he said.

"I cannot," said Yves angrily.

The Bishop raised his eyebrows.

"Pity! Pity!" he said. "Ye should learn. I speak for your good. The ignorant love these things more than singing. Well! Well!" He began slowly to ascend the steps, but half-way up he stopped once more.

"Robert," he said to the tall young knight with whom he had walked, "he will need a lute. You have one. Go fetch it. And you," he turned to Yves, "wait here for my lord Robert, and I will tell the Count of you." He beamed upon them both, and turning away, climbed the remaining steps and went in, his knights and pages at his heels.

Yves and Lord Robert, Robert of la Chaillot, left together, looked each other over quickly, as two fighting men will always do. Robert was tall; he was young, five years younger than Yves, and still rather lean and angular from his growth, but his shoulders promised strength. His face was not handsome, it was too harsh featured for that, and his stiff hair stood out round it in a ludicrous bush of reddish brown, as rough as pine needles. But his eyes were of a gay blue; Yves' covert watching look, a sort of hooded stare that had grown a habit with him, met them, and found them full of the cruel but friendly merriment of a boy. Yves' face lightened because he could not help it, but he dropped his eyes.

"Shall I wait here, lord?" he said.

"Aye," said Robert, and turning, leapt down the four steps, and swung away across the courtyard.

Yves sat down on the steps to wait, and after a time began to whistle, going over this song or that, in case he should be asked to sing what he had forgotten. As he was thus occupied, his eyes, wandering over the

168

half-lighted yard, fell on a great trough of water, set there for the
hounds and horses to drink, or for the scullions to rinse their hands in.
He got up and crossed over to it, still whistling softly to himself.

When Robert of la Chaillot came back, he found Yves stooping
over the trough with his sleeves rolled up and the neck of his tunic
open, sluicing himself with the clear water. Robert stood watching him
in silence, curious and observant. He saw Yves stretch out a groping
hand along the edge of the trough as he stooped, his face all dripping
and his eyes shut; and watching the unconscious gesture Robert smiled,
but said nothing, and waited while Yves wiped face and hands as best
he could on the skirts of his tunic.

They went together the whole length of the great Hall, Robert leading, his head tipped back as he always carried it, glancing this way and
that, as though wherever he looked might lurk some adventure. Yves
came after him with his eyes on the ground, and when Robert had
waved him to a stand, and taken his own place behind the Bishop's
chair, he waited, standing easy upon one foot, rather like some be-
draggled crow among a crowd of sleek farmyard birds.

Talleyrand was there, of course, and Saint-Astier too, and Yves
would not look at either, remembering the perron in the garden, and
their mockery, which they most naturally had quite forgotten. Yves
was a stranger to them – a mere dirty Routier brought in from somewhere to make sport. Talleyrand leaned over the table; he had eaten
and drunk well, so that his eyes were very bright and his hair disordered. He wished to be amused and Yves did not look the sort of
man to do it, so he became a little peevish.

"Well! fellow," he said, "what is your name?"

"Yves Ner," said Yves, and gave him half a glance.

"You are a jongleur?" said Talleyrand, and Yves nodded. Talleyrand
turned to the Bishop, who, having come late to his food, was now busy
with it to the exclusion of all else.

"He looks more like . . . like a . . ." Talleyrand began, but his in-
vention failed him.

The Bishop, with his mouth full of heron, only shook his head, and
made a gesture that seemed to express confidence in Yves.

Talleyrand turned back.

169

"Can you tumble or dance?" he said, but before Yves could answer, the Bishop laid a hand upon the Count's arm.

"I told you he could not," said the Bishop at last. "But he can sing."

Talleyrand threw himself back in his chair.

"Sing then!" he commanded, but added, grumbling to himself, "I don't believe he can. I'd as lief believe him a troubadour to make songs as a jongleur to sing them. He's got a hanging face . . . ugly dog. . . ." His mutterings subsided and he waved his hand. "Sing – if ye can," he said, and Yves sang.

Talleyrand was never out of temper for long, and when Yves finished the Count beat his hand upon the table.

"Brave! jongleur," he cried. "Sing again!" and the Bishop broke in with: "Whose jongleur were you?"

Yves hesitated.

"Messire Guiraut's of Cabreira," he said. "He had me sing his songs awhile . . . not long."

The Bishop nodded, satisfied.

When Yves had sung three or four songs they set him down at a table among the house-serfs, and the Count bade give him meat and drink. Then, while he ate and drank, they talked over his singing as they might have talked over the paces of a horse, and Yves listened, and laughed at himself because he was glad that, for the most part, people praised him. There was a great deal of noise in the Hall, but no one paid any further attention to him, and so, the wine making him sleepy, he laid his head down on the table and slept.

He was awakened by someone shaking him, and leapt up, his brain all confused.

"Come on, jongleur!" said the serving-man who had roused him. "They want another song," and catching up the lute from the table, he thrust it into Yves' hands and pushed him forward.

Talleyrand had drunk a good deal more since Yves' last song, and now, as he looked at Yves, he held the wine-cup tilted in his hands so that the wine ran down like a little pillar of clear yellow glass from the lip to the board.

"Now, jongleur," he said, and set the wine-cup down with a jar, "sing again!"

Yves paused a moment, and just then Robert of la Chaillot's voice broke in, very eager and clear:

"Have him sing the song he sang awhile back," he cried. "About Count Richard the Thief."

Talleyrand turned heavily to him.

"Eh?" he said. "Count Richard . . . the . . . Thief? I don't know that song." Then to Yves:

"Who made it?" he asked.

"I never heard any say," said Yves, with a spark in his eyes that was not quite a smile.

Talleyrand waved his hand.

"Sing it – sing!" he said and held out his wine-cup to be filled again by the page who stood beside him.

So Yves sang it, and Talleyrand laughed until he cried, and demanded more, and Yves sang again, and again, and then grew weary of it.

"Lord," he said, "I am a poor jongleur . . . I can remember no songs more."

"None more!" cried Talleyrand.

"I must try others over before I sing them before so great lords," said Yves and louted low to Talleyrand and the Bishop.

The Bishop smiled at him.

"God bless thee, my son!" he said in a cooing voice, and made the sign of the cross over the table.

Yves did not trouble to make a leg again; he knew that the Bishop was too well content to notice any omission.

Outside the door of the Hall he paused, waiting till his eyes should get used to the darkness, and as he waited, remembered that he still carried Lord Robert of la Chaillot's lute. As he turned to go back he saw someone standing in the brightness of the doorway, and by the bush of hair he guessed that it was the man he wanted.

"Lord," he said, "I have your lute."

Robert grunted.

"Oh! you're there?" he said, and his hands came out groping for the lute. Then as Yves turned away:

"Wait!" he said. "I have a word," and he pulled Yves aside from the doorway as two knights came out and made their way down the steps; they called out a jest to Robert, and he answered them, and turned back to Yves still laughing.

"Whose was that song ye sang?" he said, "that of Count Richard? . . . Ye said . . .?"

"Raoul . . ." began Yves with the first name that came into his head, and then remembered that he had said he did not know – "la Perron-ière," he finished after the slightest pause. He hoped Robert would not have remembered.

"Ah!" said Robert, "I thought so," and Yves congratulated himself.

Then Robert laughed.

"I thought so," he said, "when ye smiled at Talleyrand, when he asked you. Nay, it wasn't a smile neither . . . but I guessed."

Yves frowned at him in the darkness.

"Give me leave to go," he said.

Robert caught him by the shoulder as though he feared he would escape.

"Is it not true?" he said. "Ye made it yourself?"

Yves stood silent and Robert shook him suddenly as though to shake the answer out of him. Yves tore his shoulder free, and then, unexpectedly, even to himself, he said:

"Yea – it's true," and turned to go.

Robert caught him up before he was at the bottom of the steps.

"Who are you?" he said.

"What –?" began Yves, and stepped back. "Mind you your own mill," he said bluntly, using a proverb of the country-side about Rifaucon.

"Eh? What's that?" said Robert. "Oh! I understand," and he laughed. "Well, you have told me, will you, nill you."

"What do you mean?" said Yves.

"I should have asked you 'what' not 'who' ?" said Robert. "But I know it now from two things." Yves said nothing, but Robert was never shy, and went on – "These two. First of all – when I found you washing – Well, a churl might have washed his face if it had been as

172

dirty as yours," and he laughed disarmingly. "But he'd not have stretched out his hand for a napkin. That's one."

"Did I?" said Yves, and almost smiled. "I was not thinking what I did. . . . I was trying to remember. . . ." Then, because he could not help it: "What was the other?" he asked. Robert had the knack of getting his own way.

"The other? . . . Oh! that? . . . A churl would not have told me to mind my own. . . . What was it? . . . My mill," he said.

"Oh, marvel!" said Yves, and forgot he was a Routier. "You should be a great king's counsellor, and renowned . . ." he mocked.

"So I shall be," said Robert, smiling but serious, and so he might well have been, had he not broken his neck at a tourney not a year after that day.

Yves remembered himself and moved impatiently.

"Is that all your word?" he said, surly again.

Robert caught him by the wrist.

"Nay, nay. It's a grace I have to ask of you. I would not quarrel. . . . But it is good sport to ferret in other folks' business," he added almost as an apology.

Yves only grunted, but he stood still.

"Listen then," said Robert. "I have a lady who is –"

"Spare me that!" put in Yves.

"Then shortly – I can sing, my voice is well enough, but how can I learn songs except from Peirol; that's Count Talleyrand's jongleur? She hath heard all he knows. Oh! he sings them all a hundred times. . . . So," he finished, "I would have you teach me some she knoweth not."

Yves was silent, and Robert waited on him. At last:

"Why in the devil's name should I?" said Yves.

Robert laughed, almost shyly. He was an egotist but he had a sense of humour.

"Ah! well, I could not say . . . except . . . nay, there's no reason," he said.

Yves made up his mind.

"I'll teach you!" he said. "But it will have to be when and how I can. Malinvaux is no great lord to be glad of jongleurs in his company."

The first time they met, secretly, and in an old, half-ruined barn in an unfrequented part of the town, Yves was very much on the defensive, very much the poor jongleur, though he knew that Robert knew it only for a show. It was: "Saving your grace, it goeth this way . . ." or, when Robert sang a false note: "My lord is not yet at his ease . . ." until Robert swore at him, and Yves became merely surly.

As time went on, however, things grew more easy. Entire selfishness is sometimes as light-handed as the most tender consideration, and since Lord Robert, having once discovered the secret, cared not at all who or what Yves was, Yves himself forgot to care. He did not even care that Talleyrand, that "slow cow," would make no move to begin the war against Count Richard, no, nor so much as unleash his Routiers for plunder. Talleyrand had said to himself that Perigueux must be kept safe, and so in spite of letters and messengers from Adhemar of Limoges and the rest, he would not move. Yves' companions cursed, and Malinvaux went about like a mad dog, but Yves did not care, since when Talleyrand sent for him, or he met Robert of la Chaillot by stealth, he escaped from the Routier company, and could let himself forget past and future, and think only of the craft of song.

One night towards the end of March, he and Robert were in their crazy barn. The lesson had not gone well, and Yves stood up, stretched his arms above his head, yawned, and shivered.

"Try it again," he said shortly, and catching up the lute began to pace softly up and down to warm himself, while he played for Robert to sing.

Robert got half-way through the verse, and then failed over a run of notes. Yves stopped suddenly, and stamped his foot.

"Again! Thou – Do I spend mine hours shivering here to teach thee to be a fool again and again?" he cried with his teeth chattering, and flung himself down beside Robert. "Listen! So it goes," he said, and sang it two or three times. Robert tried it again, and got it right, but only after a hesitation.

"Master," he said, and smiled at Yves, not in the least put out, "I may be a fool, but there is a devil of a twist in that song."

"Tchk!" said Yves, but he laughed. "Well! remember it now," and he repeated the melody on the strings.

Robert sang it, and sang it right.

"I have it now!" he said. "And who made the song? Ye did not say."

Yves looked up. "I made it," he said, and bent over the lute again. Robert watched him for a moment, frowning, and then burst out:

"By the Cross! I cannot see . . . no, I cannot see wherefore ye're not jongleur. Jongleur? Not that neither. It's troubadour ye are. And I had forgot, I had forgot, that ye could make as well as sing. Robert!" he cried, and smote himself on the breast, "thou art a fool!"

Yves had turned as though to face an attack, and he would have spoken, but Robert ran on:

"See here, man!" he said eagerly, not to be thwarted if once he chose to take an interest in anyone. "Leave Perigueux. Talleyrand hath a close fist. . . . He's not my lord, the Bishop is mine. . . . *He* would be large if ye'd serve him, but he's sick now . . . I fear . . . he's old too. But there are plenty other lords. Saint-Astier hath praised your singing many times – Well, if ye like him not, neither do I. . . . But go hence. There is Count Richard, he –"

He broke off because Yves made a strange little hissing noise between his teeth. "No!" he said, in a voice so low and fierce that Robert was silent from sheer surprise. "No!" he said again, and began to play the song over once more. He finished a few bars; then his hand crashed, jarring, across the strings.

"When I have seen him dead . . . or dishonoured . . ." he said. "Then . . . I'll be what you will."

"Dead? Who dead?"

"Him. . . . Him you said. . . . Count Richard of Poitou," whispered Yves. "Dead or dishonoured . . . that is all. . . . See! . . . I'm a Routier. . . . I'm . . . I was. . . . But all, all, all from first to last he'll have to answer for . . . He'll have to answer . . . and pay fine. . . . Blood of God . . . I shall see that yet."

There was a pause before Robert spoke.

"But," he said, "there are other lords than he. . . . Raymond of Toulouse . . . King Alfonso in Aragon –"

Yves seemed to find some difficulty in answering. At last he said:

"No! . . . It's not only that . . . but. . . . It's no use . . . I cannot because He . . . He driveth me. . . . His dogs. . . . It's His doing and how

175

can I escape . . . ever. . . ? Besides . . . if I could I would not because of –" he was going to say "her"; though how he thought to please Audiart by remaining a Routier, he did not understand; but Robert broke in.

"What are you saying," he cried, impatient of something he did not at all understand. "You talk foolishness."

Yves shut his mouth on the unfinished sentence.

"Sing it again!" he said abruptly and began to play.

When the lesson was over Yves went to the door and pushed it open. There was a half-grown moon in the sky, so cold, clear and white that the grey dead light which suffused the air seemed rather to come as an exhalation from the earth than from any beams of hers. Yves laid one hand on the door-jamb, looking out while Robert groped on the floor for his cloak and sword, and without turning his head he spoke.

"If I do leave being a Routier," he said heavily, "it will be shame to me. . . ." He thought again of the Hunter, and of Audiart, and because he could not explain his thought he was silent. Robert laughed.

"Shame? To leave the Routiers? You're mad, or a fool born. First you talk of . . . what was it? Someone's dogs . . . and now! –"

He came up behind Yves and smote him on the shoulder with his open hand. "Why," he went on, "use thy plain kind-wit. A troubadour's – yea, and a jongleur's too – is an easy life, and pleasant, and well thought on. A Routier –!" He laughed, and let his hand slip from Yves' shoulder.

Yves stood still. He stared at the ground, which was as grey as the fields after hoar frost, but the grey was only moonlight. It was a strange light, more deceiving than darkness; he could not see, and he frowned, straining his eyes, but what he could not see was in his own mind, which was dimmer, and full of a more deceitful twilight than this little deserted space of grass. He groped and peered. There was a shadow there, it was the Hunter who was also the Judge, and before Him Yves was a hunted beast and an outlaw. His sentence was given, and he supposed the Hunter would execute it. Well! if he chose to be a jongleur would it be worse? There was a warmer light when he looked that way, and music, and yet, as he thought of it, a voice he could not smother cried helplessly and like a lost child, and cried to the Hunter.

He moved impatiently, kicking away a stone that rolled under his foot, and the movement seemed to shake the shadows in his mind and drive them further off. After all, they were no more than shadows. . . . He was a Routier; that was real enough, and the foul taste of it was in his mouth. Robert was real, and his common sense, and if he chose to be a jongleur that would be real.

Then why not? The Hunter? He was nothing . . . or if not nothing. . . . He would forget the Hunter. And still there was a misgiving in his mind. Though he did not understand the reason for it, he knew that if he chose to be a jongleur he would be entirely shamed, and if he let his feud against Count Richard lapse he would have parted with his last pride. He found that the reason was – Audiart – and he started back from it.

Robert, standing behind him, fidgeted with his dagger-handle; his interest in Yves' affairs was dwindling, and he was anxious to go. He began to sing, very softly, a snatch of Yves' song:

Domna pels vergiers . . .

Music is a wine, and makes drunken. Yves, listening, was swept again into the shadows, but they were more real than the ground under his feet. Audiart! He caught his breath. Audiart, and the Hunter! They were real now, and close, and she was implacable. She was angry and implacable . . . and so was God. . . . And he was an outlaw . . . and song was a rebel pleasure – a delight that was a defiance.

Robert stopped singing.

"To-morrow then?" he said, hoping to rouse Yves. "Or if –"

Yves turned on him suddenly.

"I will," he said. "By God Himself! I will." He stared at Robert for a moment, then, throwing back his head, broke into the verse which Robert had left unfinished, and sang it through, not very loud, but so that Robert lost all his impatience to go.

"Saints!" said Robert, when Yves had finished. "Thou a Routier? Thou should'st sing to kings!"

Yves laughed, but a little unsteadily.

"Do me grace," he said, "and say to Talleyrand that I would serve him as a jongleur."

"No need!" cried Robert, and clapped him again on the shoulder. "He talked . . . yesterday I think it was . . . about having you for his jongleur with Peirol, for the same pay, he said, but Peirol makes no songs. O ho! thou wilt ride in velvet before the year is out."

He laughed, so that Yves laughed too, and they went out into the moonlight, but there Robert stopped again.

"There's another thing. Here!" he seized one of Yves' hands. "Take and hold!" he said, and pressed something hard and small into the palm, shutting Yves' fingers over it. "It's my largesse to the troubadour," he added, and dropping Yves' hand, backed away, laughing.

Yves peered down at the thing he held. It was a heavy gold ring with a dark stone in it whose colour was muted by the moonlight to a dimly lustrous grey.

"Nay, Robert," he cried, holding it out to him. "It's a fee for a great lord to give to a great troubadour, not for thee to give to me. Here, take it again!"

But Robert stepped back, and put him away with his hand.

"Nay! Nay!" he said. "I will not. I shall be a great lord some day, and thou. . . . We have said! Besides I do exalt myself by largeness as every other lord – 'The gift to thee, the honour to me.'"

Yves stopped, dandling the ring in his hand uncertainly, and while he hesitated, Robert, with a schoolboy whoop, turned from him and ran.

Yves saw him go. Then he took from his pouch a broken lute-string, slipped it through the ring, and tied it about his neck, tucking it inside his tunic. When that was done he strolled after Robert of la Chaillot, and as he went he lifted his face, and laughed, and was suddenly afraid, horribly ashamed, and once more reckless.

He snapped his fingers at the sky and began to sing.

XVI

Gloster.   . . . I have heard more since.
        As flies to wanton boys are we to the gods, –
        They kill us for their sport.
                     King Lear, Act IV, sc. i.

TWO nights later, as Yves was in the stable watering his horse, a servant came to the door.

"Hi! jongleur!" he called. "Hi! You! Yves Ner! Hi! jongleur!"

Yves looked up and grunted.

"Come away, you!" cried the servant. "The Lord Count calls for ye."

Yves put down the bucket and wiped his hands on his tunic. He looked about the stable with a sort of jeering farewell, and followed the man. They crossed the yard in silence and when the man spoke Yves started.

"Have ye heard?" said the fellow, with a sort of unwilling eagerness in his voice, such as people have when they carry news of a disaster, and long to tell it.

"Eh?" said Yves. "Heard what?"

"About Count Richard?"

Yves stood still.

"What?" he said, and the man stared at him.

"Why, that he cometh hither, yea and is nigh, with a great host. They say he hath a devil . . . keeps it in a coffer and four mules carry it, they say. And it eats children. . . ."

He ran on, with more of this, but Yves did not hear him, and did not even notice when the man left him at the door of the Hall.

Lord Robert of la Chaillot had to search for Yves next night. He ran him to earth at last on the ramparts, at that very place where Yves and Constantin of Born had been used to lurk, half-way between two towers, and a quiet spot. Yves was leaning against the battlements staring out, and did not turn when Robert stopped beside him.

Robert looked at him, and laughed softly.

"Holy Saints!" he said. "What is all this thou hast done? The Castle buzzes with it."

"What do you mean?" said Yves woodenly.

"Why, making a jest of Talleyrand to his face and Saint-Astier too. When they sent for you to sing – I would not believe it, for ye said me ye would serve him."

Yves raised one shoulder.

"What have ye heard?" he said, without troubling to look at Robert.

Robert hitched his sword round so that the hilt did not scrape against the stone, laid down the lute he carried under his cloak, and leaned his elbow on the top of the wall.

"They say that first of all Robert of Saint-Astier would have you for his jongleur – I told you he liked your singing well – and he gives you a ring and ye throw it in his face –"

"I did not," interrupted Yves. "I flipped it back over the table and it rolled off. He hit his own head as he dived for it." He gave an edged laugh at the recollection.

"But why?" cried Robert.

"He . . . he made a jest of me when I came here. I cannot abide him," said Yves.

"But Count Talleyrand too!" persisted Robert. "They say he laughed when you . . . when Saint-Astier. . . ."

"Aye . . . he did," put in Yves. "Saint-Astier came up from under the table as red as a cock's hackle, and Talleyrand laughed."

He lapsed into silence again, and though Robert waited for more none came; so he must continue his questions.

"And then – they say – ye fleered at Talleyrand. Is it the truth ye told him if ye were his jongleur ye'd soon be a scarecrow for hunger?"

"I said, and it's the truth," said Yves, "that I'd never had anything of him for all my singing yet but a platter of meat and a drink of sour wine." He paused, laughed again to himself and then went on: "He said – ye know how Talleyrand seemeth to swell when he wants to look the great Count – he said, 'Fellow! I have given you mine own wine-cup to drink from.' 'So,' said I, 'but there was nought in it.' "

Robert clapped his hands and gave a huge laugh.

"Head of God! Why was I not there?" He stopped laughing suddenly and frowned at Yves. "But . . . I do not understand. . . . Will ye be Routier still . . .? Why. . .?"

Yves moved away from the wall.

"Let that alone," he said.

Robert shrugged.

"So be it. . . . But my song? I have the lute here," he said, and held it out to Yves.

Yves took it slowly and doubtfully.

"I do not know . . ." he began and stopped. "This place is well enough," he went on more briskly, and led the way along the ramparts to a pile of great stones prepared for casting down from the walls in case of siege. Two of the stones had rolled a little apart and Yves sat down on one while Robert took the other. Yves lifted his head and listened a moment.

"None will hear us," he said, but he listened still. The wind had risen, and they could hear how it hurled the big banner on the next tower to and fro upon its staff, so that it seemed to mutter and chuckle to itself. The wind swept smoothly by them from the south, carrying on its tide the light of the moon, cloudless, and almost at the full; and with the light, it brought, from time to time, such small sounds as the step of the nearest sentry, the rattle of his shield, or the jar of his scabbard tip against the wall.

"He'll not hear us," said Yves. "The wind comes from him to us, and there's no one else on the other side until the next tower."

He picked up the lute and fingered the strings, but aimlessly. He began a melody, broke off before he had finished half a dozen bars, and jangled the strings together.

"I have not thought what I would teach you," he said, and tried another, only to leave it half finished. At last he hit on one that pleased him, probably because he had difficulty in remembering it. It was a song of that earliest of the troubadours, Guilhem Duke of Aquitaine, and not much in fashion now because it was so old. Yves had heard it long ago, and only half remembered it, so that he must chase the fugitive melody, and try over first one phrase, then another, before he was ready to sing.

At last he had it complete.

"Listen!" he said, and struck a few notes. Then he began to sing.

Farai un vers de dreyt nien. . . .

"I'll make a song of naught at all."

He never finished that song, and never, in his whole life, tried again to sing it. Before he had finished the first verse an interruption came. A hand reached suddenly over his shoulder from behind, took the lute from him, and brought it down upon his head with a crash of splintered wood, and a complaining discord of strings. Malinvaux was no great lord to be glad of jongleurs in his company.

The sentry on the wall, hearing footsteps behind him, turned quickly, expecting to see Malinvaux returning, but it was another man. He was running, but slowly and uncertainly as though he had outrun his strength. He did not look at the sentry, but the sentry stared at him, and saw a dark trickle of blood running down from his hair.

When he had gone the sentry moved a step or two to follow, then made up his mind that whatever there was to discover, it lay in the other direction. He went off smartly along the ramparts. Close to the pile of stones he came on two men standing facing one another. One was Malinvaux, and the fellow did not wait to see or hear more. He returned quietly to his station.

Robert of la Chaillot was very far from being a fool, but he stood stock still before Malinvaux and could not speak. He was angry, but his tongue seemed tied.

"Ah!" said Malinvaux, after looking Robert carefully up and down, "a lord!" His voice was very deep but it grated harshly. "I suppose I sh'd ask pardon for yon." And he jerked a thumb towards the great blank of air beyond the wall, where an owl called mournfully.

Robert shook his shoulders as if to shake off a restraining weight.

"What did ye do it for?" he cried furiously. "What? . . . The devil! . . ."

Malinvaux shrugged and spread out his big hands.

"How should I know the lute was yours? Or know that you was . . . what you are?" he said, apologising, but with intended discourtesy apparent behind the words. "When Count Talleyrand will let us out

I'll get ye a brave new lute the first castle we sack." The insolence was not even latent now.

Robert took a step towards him.

"You ill-born dog!" he said, and then because rage drove him on to speak: "You come on me – you break my lute . . . and you take and drop it over the wall. . . . While I stand here!" It was not that which had made him angry, but of the real cause he was ashamed to speak.

"Eh?" said Malinvaux. "If ye wanted the thing when it was broke why did ye not say?"

Robert stamped his foot upon the stone.

"Why didn't he kill you? . . . He had a knife. . . . I thought. . . . The devil away with him! Why did he not? Curse him! . . . Why did he not?"

Malinvaux gave a contemptuous grunt.

"Don't ye know a knife is shorter than a sword? He did try." He laughed at the memory.

"Yea!" cried Robert furiously. "But your sword wasn't out of the sheath. . . . You held him off . . . it might have been a broom!"

Malinvaux stopped laughing.

"Am I a fool?" he said. "Can't I keep a man off with a scabbarded sword if I need. . .? I should say yea . . . or I'd be dead often by this." He chuckled again. "But he jumped about like a flea . . . when I poked him . . . and he tried to run in." He moved away, still laughing. "I'll not forget y'r new lute," he called over his shoulder.

Robert watched him go, and raged. He raged against Malinvaux, against himself, against Yves; but chiefly against Yves. He did not understand why he hated even to think of Yves, for, being a young man with a comfortably thick skin, he had never before felt ashamed on another person's account.

However, when he happened to meet Yves at the river-gate, he was sensible enough to put aside his aversion; for the fellow could sing, whatever else he did. So he stopped.

"That song –" he began, but got no further, for Yves' dead face woke for a moment.

"Never!" he said. "Not another note! Never come to me for a

song – never!" and he pushed past Robert without once looking at him.

As he went, and heard again in his memory Robert's cool casual voice saying, "That song –" Yves realised that for the first time Robert had spoken to him as a lord to a Routier. It did not make things worse, but it made them clearer.

That same evening, Yves, after a hard day's work upon the walls preparing for Count Richard's coming, was lounging in the barn where the Routiers lived. It was a foul night of wind and rain, so the big place was full. Yves was occupying his mind and keeping it from straying by watching a game of dice between two of the Routiers. One of the men, nicknamed "the Miller," had laid on the floor a dagger in a fine scarlet sheath, the spoil of some castle away in Gascony. The other, "Creeping Simon," set against it a small silver cup with two handles of interlacing dragons that writhed up the sides and looked in over the lip.

Yves stretched out his hand and drew the stakes towards him. The cup was a pretty bit of work; he rubbed his finger along the scaled back of one of the dragons and laid it down again. The dagger was good too; he found when he slipped it out its sheath that there was a delicate leaf pattern inlaid with gold running down the blade. He tried the edge on his thumb and then began to tap the rim of the cup with it, and listen to the clear, thin note.

There was a change in the noise behind him, but he did not turn, for the play was growing more interesting, and he leaned forward watching it, the dagger in one hand.

A louder shout, a crash, and a sudden silence brought him to his feet, and he looked where everyone else in the room was looking. Malin-vaux stood beside the door, his back to the wall, and his long sword kept a clear half-circle before him. Outside that half-circle three Routiers dodged and shifted, each trying to come at their man. The rest of the crowd, pushing up, made a wider arc, and jostled, and stared, watching the thing as a game, jesting, and laying wagers. There was not one who did not hope to see Malinvaux die.

Yves was in the front rank of the spectators. He did not jest, nor wager, but he watched, and waited to see the stroke that would end it.

But none of the three was doing more than play with their enemy, since each knew that one man at least would probably be the sacrifice; for victory.

One of the three – a bullet-headed fellow with a pug nose, a Norman from Caen – was stooping low, and thrusting tentatively. The second – a Basque with wild hair that hung in startling disorder about his sallow face – had hold of a stool which he used as a shield. He was on the Norman's left, and together they were almost enough to hold Malinvaux's blade. The third – a quaint scarecrow of a man, with straw-coloured hair and loose, slobbering lips – had his own plan; he was creeping up along the wall, to get behind the swing of Malinvaux's arm.

Yves' eyes wandered from the cautious swordsmen, and met those of Constantin of Born, who stood beside him. Constantin grinned.

"Malinvaux tripped over the Norman's foot and struck him for sprawling over the way." Constantin shifted his eyes to look at Yves' hair, matted with blood over his forehead: "He'll not strike a man again," he said. "Your business will be done for you." He did not wait for Yves to reply, but edged away among the crowd.

Yves turned again to the fight.

They were closer now. The shuffle of feet, the long grinding shriek and sharp rattle of blade on blade was continuous, and any stroke might be the last. Suddenly Yves looked down at his hands, as though for the first time he realised that they were not empty. For a moment he stared at the dagger, then with a shout – "Rifaucon! For Rifaucon!" he sprang, slashing right and left as he crashed into the Norman and the Basque.

He found himself grovelling at Malinvaux's feet, but down on the floor with him was the Basque. They rolled together. Yves' head bumped against the wall and the pain was like a dark flame; a hand clutched and tore at his throat, then he got his right arm free, and the gay, damascened dagger went home.

He pushed the Basque from him and stood up to see Malinvaux draw his sword from the body of the straw-haired man. The Norman lay with his shoulder gaping, and groaned dismally. Malinvaux stooped to wipe his sword on the tunic of its victim. He sheathed it, crooked a finger towards Yves, and went out.

There was silence till he was gone, and then a furious hubbub. Someone caught Yves by the shoulder with an astonishing great oath. "Why –?" they cried in his ear, and waved their arms and shouted. He shook the hand off, and elbowed his way through the crowd.

Malinvaux was half-way across the courtyard when Yves reached the door, but he did not look back. Against his will Yves followed, saw him swallowed up by the dark archway of the passage, plunged in after him, and stopped short, for Malinvaux also had stopped, and in that narrow place he loomed up, against the dim light of the further opening, as huge and beastly as the Minotaur in the Cretan labyrinth.

When Yves came near, Malinvaux said one word, the same from which Yves had just fled:

"Why?"

Yves was silent; then at last:

"I do not know," he said. "I do not . . . but . . . you . . . you struck me . . . these fellows are dogs . . . shall not they. . .? And I. . . ." He stopped because he could not make it clear even to himself how the blood of the dead Basque had given him satisfaction.

Malinvaux laughed unpleasantly.

"And you'll come behind me some dark night –" he said.

Yves gave a sort of groan and struck his hands together.

"Would to God you were dead!" he cried. "But I did not kill you . . . then . . . and now I can never."

Malinvaux came closer in the dark passage, peering into Yves' face. They said that he could see like a cat in the dark.

"Good!" he said, after he had stared at Yves for a moment. "You'll be useful."

He took Yves' arm and drew him further down the passage till they were in the blackest darkness half-way between the two arches. "This is good enough a place for talking," he said. "Watch ye yon end; I'll watch this. Now listen, Yves Ner!" He paused to look up and down the passage before he went on:

"This Talleyrand," he said, "I'm weary and sick of him. There's nought to gain in Perigueux but his pence, and they're few. And here's the season wasting. Lo! it's May now, and we might be living fat!" He broke off to curse, and Yves heard him grit his teeth together.

"I'm done with him," he continued. "And I'll take my fellows with me. I know where there is abbeys to plunder and rich men's granges, and the pap-fed burghers' stores. Now –" he paused again and seemed to consider. "Thou, Yves Ner, art a man of knight's birth. . . . Oh! I'm not a fool that I should not know it. . . . And I want a fellow to be my Captain under me. . . . Ye're good enough for that, and I could be sure of ye."

Yves, who had felt Malinvaux's hand go wandering down his side to make certain he carried no knife, smiled, but said nothing.

"Well?" urged Malinvaux. "What d'ye say? Will ye, nill ye?"

Yves hesitated. He could not think yet what this might mean. Then he remembered something.

"But Count Richard . . . to-morrow, they said, he. . . ."

Malinaux laughed suddenly, and put his mouth close to Yves' ear.

"Aye, by—! It's true. He's a day's march off and not a straw more. The devil sends the luck! To-morrow I march out with all our fellows, and because Richard comes speedy he must needs lack men. . . . And there's our bargain made!" and he smote Yves on the shoulder, and laughed.

Yves drew back.

"Richard?" he said slowly, "Richard of Poitou?" He paused a moment because he choked. "Not I, by God!" he cried; "I make no bargain with him till he lies in Hell."

Next day, in the morning, Malinvaux and all his Routiers, except perhaps a score, marched out of Perigueux. In the evening Richard came. Yves, and the others who were left, being on duty on the walls, and only intermittently busy with mangonels and petraries, scanned Richard's host for their late companions, but there was no sign of them. Malinvaux had failed, somehow, to make his bargain. The other Routiers speculated at length as to the reason, but Yves said nothing.

In two days Richard was gone. Talleyrand had a "Te Deum" sung, and High Mass in the Cathedral of Saint Étienne. He boasted very much of the strength of Perigueux, and talked of the great league that was on foot between himself, Adhemar of Limoges, the two Counts in Angoulême, and, greater than all these, the Young King Henry himself –

crowned King without land, and ready therefore to join any league against his younger brother Richard, and his father the Old King. All the early summer Talleyrand rested content, sending off messengers now and then to his fellow rebels, but doing little else. At Midsummer Richard came back, fell suddenly upon Excideuil, and from there came swiftly down on Perigueux, but again he drew off after skirmishing before the gates, and Talleyrand would not move, only he sent out more messengers.

Before the week was out they returned, and Talleyrand gave orders that next day all his knights should be ready to ride out with him, not in arms, but in great state. There were rumours everywhere, and even the truth was pretty well known. It was peace.

That afternoon, as Robert of la Chaillot and another of the Bishop's men – an oldish, grizzled, hardened knight – were strolling through the town towards the castle, a man came up behind them, running heavily, and caught Lord Robert's arm.

"Is this thing true?" cried Yves.

Robert stared down from his great height, and shook his arm free.

"What then?" he said stiffly.

"Answer me!" said Yves, and Robert saw that he shook like a man with the ague. He obeyed.

"It is," he said. "To-morrow the Count surrenders the city."

Yves stepped back a pace.

"Yea! I knew!" he cried. "He hath bayed me in on every side. . . . Fine sport! And He laughs. . . . I cannot go nor this way nor that . . . and He laughs!" He began to laugh himself.

The old knight who was with Robert moved forward impatiently.

"Who is this madman?" he said. "Come on!" and he raised the whip he carried.

Yves leapt aside, turned, and fled down a narrow dark alley between the houses. The old knight stopped to watch him out of sight, and growled in his beard.

"Was he mad?" he said, turning to Robert.

Robert remembered Yves' face.

"Let him be!" he said. "How should I know? God's Death! –"

"He spoke to you. I thought –"

Robert interrupted with another oath.

Next morning when the gates were opened six heralds rode out, wheeled their horses, blew on their trumpets, wheeled again, and rode on. After them came a score of knights fully armed even to their helms, and in their midst the banner of Perigueux. After the knights rode Count Talleyrand, all in rose-coloured samite with a heron's feather in his cap and a big jewel. With him were the Bishop of Perigueux and Lord Robert of Saint-Astier and others of the greater sort, and behind them more knights; these unarmed and gaily clad, with many esquires and some men-at-arms.

They went at an easy pace, for they had all the morning before them. Talleyrand lifted up his face to enjoy the jovial sunlight, and as he did so, a man on a chestnut mare galloped up from the rear, and passed a little wide of the procession. Talleyrand saw him quite plainly – a short man in a leather tunic and steel cap – but hardly knew that he had taken any notice of the fellow until he saw him again.

This time he was on a knoll to the left of the road and had wheeled his horse so as to face the Count and his people. Talleyrand watched him, and the fear of an ambush flitted across his mind. They drew level with the knoll, and then the man moved. He put his two hands to his mouth, and as he shouted every word came clear across the space between, so that many more than Talleyrand could hear.

"Base Perigord!" he cried in a great voice. "Base Perigord! Saint-Astier, thou knave! Traitors untrue!" and before anyone thought to move he had turned his horse and galloped down the further side of the knoll.

Robert of Saint-Astier, very red in the face, turned on Talleyrand.

"Blood of God!" he said, and the words came like stones from a mangonel, "it's that jongleur fellow and he hath my mare. . . . Hath stolen her. . . . He. . . . Nay, ye'll never catch him on that beast."

While Talleyrand sent out a vain pursuit, Saint-Astier occupied himself by biting at the fringes of his leather gloves, and swearing softly to himself.

XVII

Sae rantingly, sae wantonly,
Sae dauntingly gaed he,
He played a spring and danced it round
Beneath the gallows-tree.

BURNS.

TWO days later at sunset Yves found himself on a height over-looking a river valley and a long lake, where, far below, a party of gentlemen were flying their falcons. All round were wooded hills, blind country in which he had spent the day wandering astray. He knew that he had made a circuit to the north-east of Perigueux, but knew no more, since first he could not cross Talleyrand's road because of Richard's men going south to Perigueux, then, when he had crossed it, he had wasted time before he could cross the River Isle, and after that had been driven further eastward by a brush with some outlaws in which, indeed, he had lost nothing and they one of their men. All this had taken time, and he guessed that he was not far from Perigueux yet, for all his riding, but he hoped that perhaps next day he would strike one of the great roads to the south. Then he would make for Gascony, the home of troubles, where a man could always sell his sword.

For to-night, as for the last two nights, he supposed that he must sleep in the woods. He had passed a small abbey a few miles back, and there he would have got shelter had he asked it, but he would not ask; so now he rode on, following the track, since there was nothing else to do. It led him down into the valley, across a ford, and began once more to climb.

It was almost dark when he came out of the trees, and saw on his right a considerable fortified grange. It stood out against the pale, dead, western sky, not properly in silhouette, but with every detail sub-ordinated to the startling clearness of its outline.

For a moment Yves thought it deserted, but as he looked, a faint film of smoke rose and hung above one end of the building, and he saw that the gate stood open. As he watched, a party of horsemen came round the corner of the grange. He guessed, for he saw the hawks they carried, that they were the same he had seen hawking by the river below, and he pressed on, and was just in time to push in after them before the gates shut.

Inside the little courtyard it was dark, and no one noticed Yves. Two men came out with torches, and passed close by him. The mare threw up her head and stepped sideways daintily as though the smoky trail offended her. Then she whinnied.

Someone in the noisy crowd in front of Yves turned, stared, and shouted:

"Head of God! My red mare! And that –! Pull him down! Pull him down!"

Five minutes later Yves found himself sitting on a coil of rope in the musty darkness of a little room by the gate, cursing Lord Robert of Saint-Astier, and feeling his bruises. Just at that moment, Lord Robert himself, very well pleased for many reasons, was standing in the Hall of the Grange. One of his arms was about the waist of a peasant wench he had seen and taken in his hawking that day; he kissed her from time to time, and between his kisses drank yellow wine of Spain from a silver cup.

Next day, after returning from a pleasant morning's hawking, Lord Robert of Saint-Astier sat at his ease, having eaten and drunk his fill. The Hall of the Grange, in which he sat, was in fact more like a large farm kitchen of the old style than the Hall of a great castle like Perigueux or Saint-Astier itself, though instead of the peaceful tackle of the countryside, swords, bows, and bills hung on the walls in easy reach. It was not quite clear of smoke yet though the fire was dying down, and the beams of the barn-like, open-timbered roof were blackened and sooty. The floor was covered with rushes, and in the corners there were greening bones and litters of refuse, but along one side three round-arched, deeply splayed windows, the wooden shutters swung back, let in the soft, warm, sweet-smelling breeze of a Midsummer afternoon.

Saint-Astier lolled in the one chair which the room possessed at a short table set at right-angles to those which ran down the length of the room. The peasant girl, very brave in a scarlet gown far too big for her, sat beside him on a bench, and wriggled her shoulders at the unaccustomed touch of silk. She was very proud of herself in that finery, and quite confident that no one could be finer; but her hair (it was a pretty chestnut colour) stood out around her head in a stiff uncombed bush, as matted as the wool of a sheep, and her bare feet fidgeted among the reeds and dropped bones.

Yves was brought in by two hinds, fellows who kept this grange for Saint-Astier when he was absent. They set him in front of their lord, and then stood, one on each side of him, as mute and unconcerned as two tree-trunks, only that they never let loose his wrists.

Saint-Astier looked at Yves, and Yves looked at the brooch that fastened Saint-Astier's tunic at the neck. The wench looked from one to the other, as restless as a bird, her mouth a-gape and one finger at her teeth.

"Now that I have you," said Saint-Astier gently, "I shall hang you quick and easy. I have high, low and middle justice in my fiefs, and I shall hang you as a thief . . . and that is merciful."

Yves did not lift his eyes, but when he heard Lord Robert say "hang" his heart gave a jump like a startled horse. It was only what he had expected, but it was somehow different now it was a certainty.

"Is there any reason why I should not?" said Saint-Astier, pricked a little by Yves' silence.

Yves looked up, and spoke as he had not intended to speak.

"Aye . . . two things. First you have your horse again; and second I'm too good a jongleur to hang, ye know that." Then, because he was angry with this coward who was himself, he added, "But that will go for naught with you. I look for no such courtesy in you."

Before Saint-Astier could answer the girl had broken in. She leaned forward, and a timid hand hovered above Saint-Astier's wrist, the other pointed a brown finger at Yves.

"Is that a jongleur?" she asked, with her eyes as round as a robin's.

Saint-Astier laughed, and putting out a careless hand, he ruffled her hair.

"Aye, wench," he said. "He is. And a thief and a Routier too! Isn't he a pretty fellow for a rope's end?"

But she was staring again at Yves.

"He sings songs . . . to ladies?" she said.

Saint-Astier nodded, still smiling.

She edged towards him along the bench and leaned her bosom on his arm.

"Oh! make him sing one to me!" she cried.

Saint-Astier laughed again, and fondled her.

"Little fool!" he said playfully, and then over his shoulder to Yves:

"Sing, you!"

Yves shook his head. Then he smiled a little.

"Not for nothing!" he said. "Am not so much your friend. Spare me the hanging and I'll sing."

Saint-Astier pushed the girl away as he would have pushed a troublesome dog, and turned on Yves.

"Spare hanging you because you sing a song? God's Death! Are you Bertran of Born or Peire Vidal? You fool! Aren't there jongleurs a-plenty? . . . If ye were a troubadour –" he broke off and laughed at the idea.

"Take him away, and string him up!" he said, waving a hand to the two hinds, who woke to life suddenly, and began to push Yves towards the door. Yves took two or three steps and then began to struggle, tearing at his hands to get them free.

"What if I were?" he cried. "What if I were a troubadour and could make rhymes?" He became abruptly silent because he was ashamed.

Saint-Astier looked at him and laughed.

"By the Cross!" he said, mocking Yves with his eyes, "by the Cross! if ye were I'd have ye make me a song and go free – if ye were! . . . Farewell!"

Yves, almost at the door, pulled the two hinds to a stand.

"I am! I can! I can make and sing!" he cried, and the two fellows paused uncertain. Saint-Astier turned lazily in his chair.

"Liar that you are!" he said.

"I am not," cried Yves and he stamped upon the ground. "For why should I lie? What would I gain?"

Saint-Astier crooked a finger for the hinds to bring Yves in again, and when they had stood him just below the table, leaned forward staring at Yves as though he saw him for the first time.

"You, a troubadour?" he said. "You midden-rat!"

Yves lifted his head suddenly and looked Saint-Astier between the eyes.

"My fathers were –" he began and then his eyes shifted aside and he stopped. "I am a troubadour," he said without looking at Robert.

"I doubt it's a lie, but I cannot see wherefore," said Saint-Astier. "But ye may try to make your song . . . and if ye do I'll hold to my word. Someone else will have the hanging of you."

The girl broke in again, eager to get her will.

"Shall he make a song to me?" she cried. "Oh! yea!"

Saint-Astier nodded, and then corrected himself.

"Nay," he said. "For I'd not know if he'd truly made it . . . there are so many songs to women." He turned again to Yves.

"Make you a song to mine honour, and see ye show me clear ye have made it, or ye'll hang."

They set Yves down at one of the table ends, and gave him an old lute, very much out of tune, a goose-quill pen, some rusty ink, and a dingy bit of parchment, but he left the pen lying and sat with his right fist clenched upon the table, pretending to himself that he held a dagger, and he did not think about the song. He was ashamed, and he raged at himself. If he had not been a coward he would by this time have been decently hanged, and the whole business would have been over. He was ashamed, and then he remembered Saint-Astier's contempt, and raged against Saint-Astier.

"Well, Troubadour," came Saint-Astier's jeering voice, "how goes it?"

Yves turned slowly.

"Anon," he said, and as he said it, from nowhere an idea came to him, stinging his mind like an arrow, so that he almost started. He swung round to the table again and began to scribble, and to fumble with his left hand among the strings of the lute.

When Saint-Astier called again, Yves was ready, having even

done his best to tune the lute, which he found was cracked and very discordant. So much the better, he thought, and smiled to himself.

As he moved out into the middle of the room a silence fell upon everyone there. Serving-men, knights, and foresters stilled themselves suddenly and waited, so that the room was very quiet. A pair of swifts flew screaming past the window, and in the silence even the beat of their wings could be heard.

Yves stopped in front of Saint-Astier, nursing the lute in his arms, but he did not begin. Instead he turned his head over his shoulder and stared out of the window which gave a hooded view over a valley to the next ridge of hills, crowned with a black line of pines. Above the ridge the sky was a soft blue, lazy with heat, and between the window and the pines, below that lovely vault, the sleepy valley lay in its after-noon midsummer peace.

It was not of the beauty that Yves thought. He was regretting now that he had not made a different use of the time Saint-Astier had given him, but the thing was done, and now, whether he sang the song he had made or none at all, the result would be the same – he would die kicking at the end of a rope. But if he sang at least he would have a little revenge.

He turned to Saint-Astier.

"Fair lord," he said, "hearken to the song I have made!"

He struck a chord upon the lute, and the thing wailed; then he began to sing the "planh," the dirge of Saint-Astier's honour – "Farai unplanh de mort, de dan, e dol":

> A dirge I sing of death, and loss, and pain,
> For honour buried cometh not again.
> Alas! for Robert's honour, dead and slain!
>> Forsworn!

He went on without a pause to the second and third verses, but Saint-Astier, and it is very much to his credit, made no attempt to stop him before he reached the end. When he finished there was a deep silence; no one dare look at Saint-Astier except Yves and the girl, though somehow everyone was aware that he had bitten his lip so that the blood ran down his chin.

When he sprang up, and his chair fell over backwards, the crash seemed as great as though the roof had fallen in.

"You –" he cried. "You. . . . Death of God! You expect me to let you go free after that?"

Yves looked at him and grinned like a dog. He was satisfied now.

"Not I!" he said. "How should I . . . seeing you have sworn it?"

Saint-Astier gulped at something in his throat. He turned aside, kicked a dog out of his way, and marched half the width of the room. Then, as though he had forgotten why he had started in that direction, he stopped, and swung about again, looking round, not meeting any man's eye, but staring above their heads. At last his eyes came back to Yves and he said one word:

"Go!"

The hush broke. A knight moved quickly so that his spur rapped against the leg of a bench; another near Saint-Astier put up his hand and jingled a chain he wore, a man-at-arms coughed and shifted his feet in the rushes, and then these isolated small noises blended into the ordinary stir of life.

Yves looked curiously about him as he went towards the door, and everyone looked at him, but no one moved to stop him. He pulled the door open and stepped out into the sunshine.

The air outside was warm upon his cheek, and over against him the shadow of the outbuildings fell very black and sharp upon the trampled dry ground. A homely clatter came from a low doorway beside the Hall, and a scullion hurried out with a wooden bucket to the well. Yves went over to the gate, unnoticed, and unmolested, but there the porter stopped him. Yves argued, persuaded, cursed, but to no purpose. He was most unwilling to go back, and was at his wits' end, when he heard footsteps behind him, and turned.

It was one of the knights who had stood near Saint-Astier in the Hall, a very young knight, who came across the courtyard with a solemn frown on his pleasant face.

"Open the gate!" he said sharply to the porter, and then, as the man moved to obey, he stood looking down at Yves, while his face slowly flushed to the roots of his smooth fair hair.

"You. . . . They . . ." he began, and stopped because the porter drew near, then came closer to Yves, took him by the arm and whispered:

"Get you away as quick as you can. . . . He – Saint-Astier – will change his mind. . . . They talk even now. Get away while ye may."

"Why tell me?" said Yves, looking at him sharply.

"One man of worship must help another. . . . That is knighthood," said the lad with the quaintest solemnity. "Besides –" he looked round quickly, and then shook his head.

"No matter," he said, and pushed Yves towards the gate.

Yves had not gone three paces before the other caught him back.

"A moment!" he said. "You need a sword."

He began to fumble with his own belt, loosed it, and held it out to Yves, with the sword, a new one, dangling from it. As he put it into Yves' hands he flushed again.

"It is . . . clean," he said. "I was knighted on Saint John's day."

Yves hung back for perhaps half a second, then took it in silence and with a very sour face, and hurried out through the gate.

Once among the trees he slowed down, and went forward at a good walking pace, but without hurry, since whether they came after him or not, hurry was useless. He decided that, and then let his thoughts stray off down very different tracks. He did not think of the pursuit, nor of Saint-Astier and the song, nor even of the young knight at the gate. He was girt about by the most impregnable wall of which man knows, which cut him off from all the world, and left him only a little space of lovely and quiet woodland. Hanging was behind him, a swordstroke or hanging before. Death was the wall that enclosed him, and left him at peace.

The afternoon sun was already westering, and taking on colour after the glare of pure, colourless, noonday light, and the rays came between the leaves, rainbow-tinted against the eye, and golden upon the grass. Now and again a light wind filtered through the innumerable channels among the leafage, filling them as a tide fills all the little creeks along a rocky shore. Yves saw; and forgot – even himself. He paused a moment to watch a herd of the small, white deer down the length of a glade, and laughed at the incessant twinkling of their tails and swaying of their branching antlers. They were more restless than shifting lights in a stream.

Gradually the wood thinned, and he came out upon a high open space where clumps of bramble took the place of trees. A relic of the older wood, a bare trunk blasted by lightning, with jagged branches that seemed to have been tortured before they died, stood over against him in the middle of the space, while round about its roots the brambles grew, thick and high, in trailing prickly masses.

The tree had an unpleasant, deathlike air; Yves looked at it with disfavour, and as he looked, heard the baying of a dog. Something cold crept up his spine, but he moved on soberly, making for the dead tree, and as he went he loosened the borrowed sword in its sheath. He noticed with satisfaction that the bushes were large enough to hamper even a horseman, and he did not think that they would come on horses, for the wood he had passed was in most parts full of undergrowth. He sat down at the foot of the tree, the sword drawn across his knees, and waited.

The noise of hurrying feet grew louder and filled the wood with profane stir, though the dog was running silently now. Then a man burst out from the trees, running his hardest, one hand bunching up the skirts of his scarlet gown, the other holding the leash of a big hunting-dog that galloped and plunged to be let loose to follow the scent at his own speed. It was the young knight of the gate.

He saw Yves, and jerked at the leash to check the dog, but came on still running, blundered round the bramble bushes, and pulled up as Yves flashed the sword before his eyes. He stopped a moment, breathless, waving one hand helplessly. Then, hauling back the straining, snarling dog, he gasped out:

"They're after . . . but I outran them. . . . Saint Christopher!" he laughed breathlessly, "it was a chase. But Marc . . . he's the best dog I ever –"

Yves interrupted him.

"Why for are you come, anyways?" he said, and kept the sword ready.

The young man did not answer till he had unleashed the dog and ordered it off. The animal stood uncertain, then sidled away, looking back to see that he did right.

"Huh!" cried the young knight. "Home, Marc!" and flung the leash after him. The dog made slowly for the open slope, and disappeared.

"I came to help," said the young man and smiled.

Yves' face did not clear.

"You're one of Saint-Astier's knights," he said.

"No," cried the young man. "Not I, by the Cross!" He stepped nearer and laid his hand on Yves' wrist.

"I believe," he said, speaking softly as though he feared even now to be overheard, "I do think he killed my father . . . but there's no proving it."

At that moment another man with another straining dog burst into the open, saw them, shouted, and then stopped doubtfully, looking back in the direction from which he had come. He came forward a few steps, stopped again, stared, and cried:

"Messire, is he your prisoner?"

The young man laughed. He pulled out the sword that he carried and shook it.

"Come and take him if ye can," he called back. Then he turned to Yves.

"I borrowed this," he said, holding out the sword. "They do not know you are armed, and there are not many. It will be a pretty fight." He whistled, very badly, a scrap of a song, and turned again to Yves, overflowing with confidences like an eager boy, which was all that he was.

"I am Bardon of Puyserguier," he said. "Puyserguier may have to stand siege after this, for Saint-Astier will be angry. What sport! And all this for a morning's hawking." He broke off to look. "There comes another with the other hound. The others won't be far behind, but they'll do nought till they're all here. . . . Holà!" he cried, and waved his hand merrily to the two men as they stood together taking counsel. Yves, as the lad smiled at him again, burst out suddenly:

"Here!" he said. "Take your sword and go, you young fool." He pushed the sword he carried into the boy's hand and fairly tore the

199

other from him. "Can't you see," he cried, "I'm all Saint-Astier said? Get hence! I'm a Routier. I stole his horse. Get away!"

He broke off with a bitter curse as three more men crashed into the clearing. It was too late, but still Yves cried "Get away you fool," and scowled into Bardon's frowning face.

The lad shook his head, and they turned from each other just as one man, who was a little ahead of the others, cleared the brambles with a leap. Yves slashed him across the face, and he fell against the trunk of the tree. After that it was a mere confusion of fighting, but it did not last long. Yves heard a sort of cough at his right side, then someone fell against him, clutching at his arm. He tried to get it free in time.

"Let go, you –" he cried. "How can –"

He finished the sentence as he rolled on the ground with another man on top of him. "How can I strike?" he muttered.

When they had tied Yves' hands behind him they turned him over on his back, and one of them, who had a slashed forearm, kicked him before he turned away to look at the wounded men upon the ground. Puyserguier was dead already, of a wide wound in the chest. They turned him over, doubtful how to treat him, then crossed his hands on his breast, and went on to the others. Of these one was dead; the man whose face Yves had sliced would die in a few moments at most; but the other would do well.

They returned to Yves, pulled him up to his feet, and ordered him to march. The wounded and the dead could wait a few minutes. Yves knew what was coming, though no one troubled to tell him, and so he recognised, as soon as his captors, the branch on which he was to hang. It was quite clear to him that it was made for the purpose, thrust well out, gently sloping towards the ground, gay in its leaves, and altogether sinister. He halted underneath it.

He did not look to see what they were doing, for he knew that he had only a few moments now to look at the woods. And yet the woods were nothing to him, for all he saw was fear, and the blank wall of death. Something smacked him sharply on the cheek, and he started away. It was the noosed end of the rope.

One man had climbed the tree to pass it over the bough, and he came down now with a noisy scramble, bringing with him a shower of leaves and twigs. Someone fitted the noose round Yves' neck, and chucked him under the chin so that he bit his tongue. Then they suddenly left him.

He turned in astonishment and absurd hope, and as he turned was jerked off his feet, and swung, kicking, while everything was swallowed up in the hideous thunder of blood in his ears, the bloodshot blindness of his eyes, and the pain that tore his throat.

Then – there seemed to him to be no pause or interval, he found himself lying with his cheek on the cool grass, in a world of loud noises and shouting. When it grew quieter someone came up to him.

"Why!" and an oath followed, "it's not Fat Jehan! The man stirred Yves with his foot. "Who the — are you?" he added.

Yves struggled up on one elbow and plucked awkwardly at the rope about his throat. He recognised the Routier stamp.

"I am one of you . . . Routier," he said in a whisper, and looking about saw that a score or more of men were staring down at him.

"I don't know him," said one of them. "But he might be."

"New joined," said Yves, and grinned shakily. His wits were working fast, as though they ran in a channel prepared for them beforehand. "I've news of a fat abbey hereby," he said. "Help me up. Where's the captain?"

The man who had first spoken brought out a wicked oath and capped it with another.

"I'll carry ye if need is, and that's the news ye have," he said, and hoisted Yves to his feet.

XVIII

Being your slave, what should I do but tend
Upon the hours and times of your desire?
I have no precious time at all to spend,
Nor services to do till you require.

SHAKESPEARE, *Sonnets.*

BUT that Yves had claimed comradeship with the wandering Routiers who so timely interrupted his hanging, it is likely that they would have finished the ceremony on their own account, partly for sport, partly because, having discovered that Yves was not Fat Jehan, they would have felt that they had put themselves out for nothing. The lie tided Yves over that dangerous moment, but he did not trouble to repeat it or to bolster it up, nor was it necessary that he should, since he brought news which made him welcome. The Routier captain – an incredibly dirty and hairy little man nicknamed "the Baker," probably because of his perpetually red face – asked questions that showed him to be no fool, and then bade Yves be ready next morning to show the shortest and safest way to the abbey, and to remember that he would go with a noosed bow-string about his neck.

Once Yves' information was given, everyone lost interest in him, and he was free to do what he pleased till morning. He wandered off to the place where three camp-fires burnt steadily in the still air, and after prowling about for a time, sat down on the outskirts of the crowd, to look about him, and hope for a chance of some supper.

The camp was in a wood, and as he sat with his back against a tree, a smoke-blackened bough, leafless and skeleton, stuck out its stark fingers over his head. He shuddered and dropped his eyes, for it reminded him too clearly of another bough in the forest, and to drive out that thought he began to watch his new companions. The band was neither so large nor in such good fettle as that with which Malinvaux had served Talleyrand of Perigord, but the chief difference was that here there were many women. At Perigueux the Count had refused to feed useless mouths, and the Routiers had had to do without their wenches,

202

but here they seemed almost more numerous than the men. They screamed a great deal, and Yves was not pleased to watch them, but for all that, his eyes fixed themselves on a noisy group close by. There were three or four women and half a dozen men, and he watched them till his eyes became vacant, and his thoughts drifted aimlessly, forgetting what he saw.

He found himself, for no apparent reason, remembering the girl with the golden hair, the girl he had seen . . . how many years ago? He counted on his fingers. It was six years . . . he had seen her just before he came to Rifaucon . . . that very afternoon. What was her name? . . . Madeleine. That was it! He remembered riding past the Nuns' garden afterwards, and the scent of sweetbriar. . . . And the flowering hawthorn tree where he had first seen the girl standing, and the little pool. It was pleasant to think about, and he was very weary. It was a long time since there had been any such pleasant sweet thought in his mind, and it soothed him like balm.

He was still staring, unseeing, at the same group. One of the Routiers had a big peasant woman on his knee, and wished to kiss her, but she struggled and beat him with her clenched fists. The man twisted his fingers in her long hair, pulling her face back, and her hair fell over his hand in long locks the colour of tarnished brass. The crowd around laughed, shouted, and shrieked encouragements to one or other of them.

Yves jerked his head back as if something offensive had been put under his nose. It was Madeleine herself that he was watching; he knew her now. He had to make an effort before he could wrench his eyes away from that woman with the tumbled, coarse hair, and even when he succeeded he could still see her, and could see nothing else; so there was no balm, then, for his mind, no sweet and pleasant thought where he could hide himself even for a minute. He looked hard at her for a moment; there was no toom for doubt, it was certainly Madeleine, and he hated her.

He got up hastily and went away from the fire into the darkness of the wood, and stood, leaning his hand upon the rough bark of a tree, his fingers picking at it aimlessly, and anger sank down because he was too tired to be angry. The shouts and laughter reached him still, and shaking his head as a dog shakes water from his ears, he went on again, further and further yet, till the trees thinned and came to an end, and he could see nothing but darkness, a cloudy sky with a few rifts where the stars looked out only to be smothered, and a blacker darkness where the woods began again.

He sat down clasping his knees, and put his head down on them. There was no light nor hope, nor even the possibility of an end, and he gave himself up to a still and passive despair, as unresisting as a drowned man whose strengthless slack hands move only with the lift and fall of the uneasy sea.

As he sat huddled there, without even a thought, a dog howled in the far woods, with a long-drawn, dolorous cry, as emptily and utterly desolate as his mind. He heard it, and at first it meant nothing to him, but its monotonous repetition disturbed, and finally brought him back to thought, and he lifted his head, listening. Again the beast howled, and Yves knew that Bardon of Puyserguier's dog had found his master. He picked himself up, and went back into the wood until the noise of the Routiers drowned the distant cry. Then he lay down, and, because there is mercy, he slept.

Next day they sacked the abbey of Sainte-Trie and went on again; two days later they pitched their camp in a broad, pleasant valley, about the ruins of a village which they had burnt. Yves, coming back from cutting wood, found a crowd of Routiers round the well in the midst of the village, and as he drew near, he saw that they had a prisoner. He threw down his logs, and went to watch.

The unfortunate was a small, lithe fellow, as slim as a lizard, and very gaily dressed. He had straight fair hair that curled at the ends, and blue eyes, with laughter wrinkles round them; there were the same pleasant tokens round the mouth, but it was drawn now, and though he jeered at his captors, his voice was shrill.

Yves might not have paused longer, had not something lying on the ground outside the group caught his eye. It was a lute, bravely rib-boned. A little further off a tall grey donkey was placidly feeding, and as it moved it shook out a little chime, merry and peaceful, from the bells on its trailing bridle. Yves knew then that the man must be a jongleur, and he pushed his way into the group – but not because he wanted to.

The Routiers were enjoying themselves. They had tied the jongleur's hands behind him, and now they were making pleasantries about well water. He replied with force and pungency, and had the better of it, until one of the men, with a sudden push, sent him spinning towards the well opening, helpless because of his bound hands. He was almost down when another fellow caught him, and while everyone laughed at the game, slung him back across the space to the man who had begun it. Three times the play was repeated, till the jongleur's face was damp with sweat, and blank with fear. The third time the poor fellow tripped on the low coping of the well, and with a scream he could not stifle, pitched in.

As he disappeared the crowd contracted, each man jostling for a place to watch the victim's struggles. They were disappointed. When the splash subsided, the well was still except for the smooth, slowly subsiding undulations of the water. The man must have struck his head as he fell in, and there was no more sport to be got out of him. They hung about for a few moments, then, giving up hope, drifted off to other amusements.

Yves did not follow them. Instead, he went to the edge and looked down, though again he did not want to. There was nothing – only the hard clear square of brilliant blue reflected from the sky, and outside that, the frame of black water. He turned away, picked up the lute, and walked down the village street, avoiding certain things which were unpleasant.

Outside the village, by the smoking timbers of what had been a mill, he found a crowd of drabs, and Madeleine among them. They were skinning a cow that had been killed, clustering round the carcase like flies, pushing one another away, quarrelling and screaming, as they hacked out collops of meat from the bones.

A sick disgust ruffled the apathy of Yves' mind, and then, as he watched, out of disgust grew a fury against Madeleine. He wanted to curse her, to blot her out of life, and did not know why; but it was because she was the measure of his fall.

A passing Routier, seeing how he stared, cracked a jest, and Yves replied with another that made the man crow. One of the women screamed at them, and Yves answered her; then he turned from them, and leaping the broken hedge of the village corn-field, made his way over the trampled, matted ruin of plenty, to a distant patch on the hillside where the grain still stood upright. He reached it, waded a few steps through the swishing heads which were already heavy with goodness, and flung himself down, out of sight and hearing of the swarming village.

The corn was just turning golden ... it was a pure pale gold against the sky as he looked up at it. He had been going to make a song to her ... call her something ... Golden Mantled. He sat up suddenly and pulled the lute out from under his arm, and laughed. He worked at the song, chuckling unpleasantly, for half an hour or so, then seemed to tire of it, for he laid the lute down on his knees and sat for a time with a vacant stare. At last he went back to the village again, walking slowly, the lute swinging from his hand by its red and white ribbons. He sat down on the edge of the well and looked over. The harsh square of blue was the same, but in the dark water at the side there was an indistinct white blur, which even as he looked faded and was gone.

He lifted the lute, held it over the well and dropped it in. When it did not sink, but rolled, floating, he picked up a stone and drove it under. He was still hanging over the shaken water when he heard a voice behind him.

"What are ye after?"

He turned and saw Madeleine.

"Naught," he said, and would not look at her again.

"Why did ye drop it in?" she said.

He threw a pebble after it before he answered, and his voice was listless.

"I'll make no more songs. I was a fool to. . . . I cast me not to sing any more ... not even that one. What use . . . ?"

"What one?" she said.

He seemed to wake suddenly and turned on her.

"It was a song to the Golden Mantled," he said, and the words were as good as a blow, but as soon as they were said he seemed to lose interest again.

"Ah!" she said slowly; and he knew, if he cared to know, that she understood. "Ye remember me. I knew you too – last night I knew you."

He made no effort to answer her, but when she sat down by him he drew away. Yet, when they had sat there in silence for a few moments, it was he who spoke first.

"How long have you . . .?" he began, and left his question casually unfinished.

She turned about as she sat, and looked at him. There had been no expression in his voice – no interest, no anger, no disgust – nothing whatever, and now he sat leaning forward a little, his hands hanging between his knees, his head bent, and his eyes fixed on the ground. She frowned, but not because she was angry. She had been angry with him last night, because of the unaccustomed prick of shame, but she was not angry now, only curious . . . and something else. She began to speak suddenly.

"It's many a year," she said, and kept her eyes on him. "They came . . . Count Richard's men they were . . . they burnt the village. And my father . . . he got hanged . . . there was a many hanged for this or that . . . how was any to know why? Then we . . . those that could, and had got away to the woods . . . we went back. But the Routiers came then. I got away again and my mother . . . and others . . . but it was winter then."

She stopped, remembering how she had lain in the woods that stark winter, more wretched than the beasts, and how she had called on his name and wept, and never doubted that he would come and save them . . . because he was their lord, and she had seen him ride like Saint Michael.

"Why did you not come?" she cried.

That woke him, but only for a moment. His face became blank and empty again.

"I could not," he muttered. "What could I have done?"

She was looking at him again, though he did not see, and there was something in her face which had not been there before. She was not thinking now of what he could have done had he come, and she did not know the thought of her own mind, but as though she had been once

207

more the simple girl of that dead summer, she saw him as Saint Michael – Saint Michael sitting upon the well-edge beside her – a beaten man, she knew that, but still Saint Michael.

He moved restlessly as if he felt her stare at last, and said "Yea?" She hurried on.

"She. . . . Ye know how fat she was, lord . . .?" It did not need her sobbing laugh to explain to him that "she" was her mother. "Well, next spring . . . March maybe because the hollins weren't quite bare, she was as thin. . . . We lived on the rabbits we could catch, and . . . oh! anything . . . but there were too many of us at first. And she died . . . just too hungry to live. And I was hungry too . . . it hurts . . . but. . . ."

He made no movement, said nothing to help her as she paused.

"I came out and followed a lot of Routiers . . . and I picked up scraps . . . what I could get . . . till . . . I was fair enough. . . ."

Again they sat in silence till he turned suddenly as though his patience had broken.

"What are you waiting for?" he cried, and dropped his head again. "Get away!" he said, speaking softly and indistinctly like a man slipping back to sleep, and did not look up even when she had left him.

They left the village behind and came to a country of bare plateaux and pinewoods, and having food enough to last for a few days they left the countryside at peace. During the day they lounged and quarrelled in the camp, but when night fell and the fires burnt low all grew quiet again except for the snoring of the company, as they lay a-sprawl, each man's feet as near to the fire as possible, for nights are cold, even in August.

Yves found them very cold, since he preferred to lie far from the fire rather than among the crowd. He slept badly, waking up now and then to shiver and turn over on the scrubby pine-needles, and one night – it must have been about midnight – he woke up with a start to the knowledge that someone was standing behind his head.

He was used to prompt action, and he took it instinctively. With a sharp twist he rolled aside, turning, as he scrambled up, to face the silent enemy.

It was Madeleine. He stood peering at her in the clouded moonlight, and could see nothing of her face, but her hair as it fell over her shoulders was pure silver gold, and she held in her hands what looked like a great cloak.

"Lord," she whispered, and came a step closer, "here is a coverlet. I remember ye said that day that ye were ever a-cold." As she held the thing out to him he saw that it was one of the sanctuary hangings from Sainte-Trie, a great piece of white silk embroidered in gorgeous colours, with jewels here and there. The colours were dim as a spider's web in the grey light, the jewels hardly gleamed, and the purple cloth that lined it was densely black.

For a short moment he stared at her; then he sprang forward. Big though she was she staggered at his attack, but she was used to defending herself against such advances, and she soon recovered. Moreover she was frantic, fighting wildly, and sobbing as she fought, and it took all Yves' strength to master her hands. He laughed then, and drew back a step, but it was his undoing, for as he moved his foot caught in the trailing stuff that lay forgotten between them, and she, feeling him stagger, gave a last desperate push that sent him sprawling on his back.

He picked himself up, furiously angry, but checked for a moment.

"Why not?" he cried. "Why not? What can it matter to you?"

She spread out her hands in a gesture that had dignity.

"Lord," she said, "it is not I who would be shamed, but thou."

She meant it. There was truth in her voice and he could not doubt, but for a moment his mind recoiled, since it was so infinitely strange a thought, and so abysmally wrong. From sheer amazement he passed through a moment's hysterical desire to laugh because she thought . . . she thought that of him. Then he tumbled back into the gulf. He shook his head.

"That's not truth. You do not know. I am . . ." He threw his hands out helplessly, and turned away from her.

She came up behind him, careless now of anything but his necessity, which, though she did not understand, she knew.

"Lord," she said, "if . . . if . . . ye *did* want me Hugues the Potter would . . . take a price, I suppose."

He did not seem to hear and she came closer.

"Lord," she whispered, and her voice shook, "do ye want me?"

He turned at that, but only to stare at her for a moment; then he dropped his head.

"Yea . . . I know not. . . . Yea . . . if . . ." he said, and stopped.

"Oh! let me!" she burst out suddenly. "Lord, I. . . ." She held out her hands to him, and could say no more, since when ideas had to be spoken she was as dumb as a beast.

More was not necessary. Yves jerked forward as if he tore himself from something that held him back, and next moment he was down on his knees, clutching her dress, his face hidden in it.

The bargain was easily made, for Hugues the Potter would have parted with many women for the sake of Lord Robert of la Chaillot's ring. Without grudging he gave Madeleine over to Yves.

XIX

For so that I your company
    May have, I ask no more.
From which to part it maketh my heart
    As cold as any stone;
For in my mind, of all mankind
    I love but you alone.
                    The Nut-Brown Maid.

SO long as the fair weather held, and that year there was a late, fine autumn, the Routiers moved slowly through the Limousin, like the ten plagues of Egypt, destroying as they passed. Usually they attacked only villages and small open towns, so that they lost few men in fighting and the loss of these was made good by the new recruits who left the burned houses to smoke, and the dead to bury their dead, and joined with the destroyers. It was a safe life enough, but not satisfying, for there was little or no plunder except of cattle and corn, so that when, at the end of October, their Captain, the red-faced Baker, suggested an attack on a small castle which he said was weak enough, everyone acclaimed the idea.

There is no need to tell how they took that castle, partly by surprise, partly by storm, but they did take it, and revelled afterwards in the usual orgy of plundering. When they had done, they set it alight and returned to the camp.

Madeleine, on her knees pounding corn with a sharp stone, heard a shout behind her and the hurrying thud of hoofs. She turned, and saw Yves riding down on her. He shouted like a boy with a new pony, as he pulled the horse back on its haunches beside her, and looked down at her, laughing, and dropped something into her arms. It was a gown of silk the colour of beech flowers, with little circles embroidered all over it in scarlet and gold, but she did not once look at it, only at the horse.

Yves saw her stare, and all his pleasure died.

"Well? What's amiss?" he said angrily, and came down from the saddle. He looked the animal all over, and fondled it; it was a fine bay, well bred and strong. He ran his hand over one of the forelegs, and then turned suddenly on Madeleine.

"What's amiss?" he repeated.

"Naught," she said, and would not look at him, because she had seen him ride up to her again, as he had ridden once before; but this time upon a stolen horse. Similarity had opened her blind eyes to a difference.

He dropped the bridle and seized her shoulder.

"What do you mean?" he cried, and shook her.

She was dumb, but somehow he guessed.

"Must I go afoot," he cried in a fury, "because forsooth I have not always? And if I get me a horse to ride . . . if I get it as Routiers do, will ye . . . will ye cast me in the teeth? Will you, you jade?"

She was neither surprised nor angry when he beat her, for other men had done it, and he had a better right; but after it was over and he had left her, she gathered up the silk gown that lay forgotten on the grass, and crept off to cry in secret.

When she came out of hiding she found Yves very gloomy and tetchy. At first he would take no notice of her, feigned to be sleepy, and in fact sulked like a child, and she bore it, as meek as a slave. At last he turned to her with an unpleasant smile.

"Where's the gown I brought? I suppose ye've spit on it and trampled and torn . . . seeing it was got as the horse was got?"

She looked at him, pleading with her eyes.

"Nay, lord," she said, "I have it . . . I'll keep it ever."

"Ho!" he scoffed. "*Ye* may have such things, but I not?" and she stared at him in silence, amazed that he should make such a mock of such a simple truth.

"I have it here," she said, hoping to please him, and showed the neatly rolled bundle in the big pouch she always carried slung over her shoulder.

"To sell it, I wager," he said, "since ye're too proud to wear it."

"Ah! No, lord," she protested, "not to sell . . . never. . . . I'll keep it . . . always. I . . . it is. . . . Always!" she repeated desperately, for how could she explain that the gown was to her a token of an almost miraculous favour, a tangible symbol of his kindness, and therefore to be treasured as devoutly as any relic?

He shrugged the matter aside, as a thing of no moment.

The Routiers passed the winter in one of the deep, narrow valleys of the eastern Limousin. They built a strong, wooden stockade on a jutting tongue of high land, penned their stolen cattle, stored their stolen corn and sat down to wait for spring. While they waited, the majority spent their time between gaming and quarrelling, but some, and among them Yves, would go out hunting in the woods, more for the sake of the sport than for what they killed.

One evening, a fortnight after Christmas, but the Routiers kept no Christmas feast, Yves came back to the camp, satisfied with a good day's hunting, and ready to be kind to Madeleine. She had been strange in her behaviour lately . . . since . . . since when? No, he did not know since when, could remember no beginning to her strange moods of sullenness and sudden unreasonable anger, after each of which she would fawn on him like a dog, as if to regain his favour. Anyway, it did not matter, since in the main she. . . . He smiled up at the bare jagged branches which, as he rode, seemed to drag themselves quickly across the tarnished face of the waning moon.

He found her in the camp, flung down the heavy body of the buck he had killed, and kissed her. He was glad to see that she was in a pleasant mood, and he twisted her loose hair round his hand, and rubbed it against his cheek.

When they had eaten he leaned his head back on her knee, and drawing her hand down laid it across his mouth and bit gently at one of her fingers. She pulled it away, but let it rest on his forehead.

"I heard news to-day –" he said, and laughed softly. "News of an old enemy of mine – say rather of two old enemies. . . . Ye've heard of Raymond of Scorbé Clairvaux?"

"Yea," she said. "He took your fief, lord. I know."

"Good lass!" he murmured. "Well, the news was of him and of his cursed devil of a friend – Count Richard. But I believe they've noosed themselves this time. Richard he hath had Scorbé Clairvaux from Raymond – exchanged it for some other fief – and hath built a castle

213

there. And it's the Young King's land, not Count Richard's at all. Ye see, wench? And the Young King is wood wroth with both of them. He'll hang Raymond if he catches him, and as for the Count . . . they say even now all the Barons of Aquitaine are leagued with the Young King. . . . So down goeth Count Richard to hell!" He laughed again, and turned his head to look up at her, but she was staring straight in front of her with a set frown and tightened lips.

"Then . . . you will go to him?" she said at last, but it was hardly a question.

"Go . . . to him?" he repeated.

"The Young King."

"Not I!" said Yves. "For why should I go, or what do if I went? No. Let Angoulême and Perigueux and the rest do my business for me . . . I care not. . . . Nor even much if they do not. I used to think . . . but now – I'm happy enough. Let be." He stretched up a hand to tickle her chin, but she jerked her head back.

"Go to the Young King," she said.

He frowned, then laughed.

"I will not," he said. "Ye're a poor fool. Ye don't understand. I tell you I'm happy enough here . . . ye should be glad."

He heard her draw a quick breath, and waited for her to speak, but she said nothing, and he went on:

"Besides, Guilhem and Adhemar of Angoulême are with him. I'd get nought from him – if that is what ye're thinking – with Guilhem there."

Her hands came suddenly together under his chin and she bent over him, and kissed him fiercely. Afterwards she sat silent, brooding and staring, one hand clutching a fold of his sleeve, while Yves dozed contentedly in the warmth of the fire. What he had said was true – he was happy enough.

This time of idleness lasted only till February, for even before that month came in, war was afoot. They moved cautiously northwards, not ravaging widely now, but keeping close, ready for emergencies. The Baker's band was not large enough for him to take service with the great lords as Malinvaux did, or Sancho of Sarrannas or the Moor

Curbaran, but he was quite able to enjoy the pickings left in a disordered country where all old quarrels broke out afresh to be ended only when blood quenched or dead ashes choked them.

News came occasionally of the doings of the great ones. The Young King and his friends were in Limoges; the Old King and Count Richard went there. There was a rumour that the Old King was dead of an arrow shot by the Young King himself, but there seemed no truth in it, for they heard next that the Old King and the Count had retired from Limoges. Whatever was the fortune of the leaders, the Routiers were content, since the war showed no signs of coming to an end. They were content, and so too was Yves.

One night, however, he woke suddenly and painfully from a dream to find Madeleine's arms round him.

What was the matter? she whispered. He had cried out sore in his sleep. What was it?

With his mind still full of the dream he pushed her from him, then sought refuge in her arms, and she petted him and held him fast. For a long time he would not tell her of what the dream had been, but at last he muttered, his face hidden:

"It was of her . . . Audiart . . . in Angoulême," and Madeleine asked nothing more.

Long after she thought him asleep because he lay so still, he was going over the dream in his mind, over and over, not because he wanted to, for every time he remembered it hurt afresh, but because he could not help himself.

He had dreamt that he was standing in one of the courtyards in Angoulême, by the well. He knew that it was Angoulême, though the place was quite strange to him, and he was very happy to be home again. He had a handful of peas, which he was dropping one by one into the well, and watching the splashes they made; strange splashes, very large and full of colours.

Then someone came to him, and though at first Yves thought it was Count Guilhem's old sergeant, he soon became the monk from whom Yves had parted on the way to Rifaucon. The monk seized his hand, emptying the peas from it, and in falling they somehow changed into pieces of meat. Then he said to Yves, as though they had been arguing:

215

"I am her father . . . I know," and Yves answered: "Nonsense!" because he knew quite well that Audiart was not this man's daughter.

But the monk, still grasping his hand, said:

"I am her father. Look! there she is. I told you I was her father," and Yves, turning, saw Audiart. He started to go towards her, turning back to say over his shoulder:

"Perhaps you are right," but the monk seemed to have lost interest, for he was gone.

Yves went on till he was close to Audiart, looking at her all the time, and to look at her made him so happy that he did not notice the expression of her face; he was happier than he had ever been in his life, and he kept saying to himself, "This is right. This is right," but he really meant to say that he had found now what he had been looking for all his life.

Then, when he was quite close, he saw how she looked at him, and he stopped and cried out for pain, because she hated him. He tried to speak, and could not, but she spoke, and what she said was so cruel that he lifted up his hand to shield himself from the blow, and cried aloud again, and woke.

When he woke her words were still in his ears, and as he repeated them to himself they struck heavily on his heart, just as they had done in the dream.

She had said:

"You may have been green once, but now you are nothing but a cow."

Gradually their absurdity, and all the other absurdities of the dream, dawned on him, but that did not matter; the truth of it, and the pain remained. He had only to go through the dream again for the words to strike the same blow, and so, though he lay very still, he did not sleep.

Even next day he could not forget it, but the waking, daylight pain was different from that of the night. He was able, since the Routiers were camped for a few days while the Baker bargained with two neighbouring and enemy lords, to slip away from the camp, and spend the day in the woods. He had made the excuse of hunting, but he came home empty-handed, having spent the time, partly in lying hidden among the hazel bushes, partly in skulking, without any aim but that of concealment, along the sides of a little valley, where yew and holly made a dismal but safe shade.

It was concealment he needed; he knew that, and sought it blindly, trying not to let himself think why he needed it. He felt as a mole may feel when all his little galleries are laid brutally open by the ploughshare, and he wanted darkness, solitude and shelter again; but he did not find them, not even in the gloomy place among the hollies. Instead, the knowledge he wished to avoid came closer, and he knew that he should soon understand. That drove him back to the camp, and to Madeleine. He had been safe and hidden, and now he was discovered and brought to light, so that Madeleine only could give him refuge and shelter.

He went back to her, almost running, wild words crowding upon his tongue, because he must somehow make her understand what was his need. He found her by the brook, filling a bucket, and because she did not hear him, he pulled at her shoulder.

She sprang up and they faced each other.

"Madeleine," he said desperately, "I am.... You must ..." and stopped. It could not be said.

There was no need. She had set the bucket down, and now she came to him.

"Oh!" she said, "your hair! It's full of leaves ... so rough ... like a bramble bush."

Her hands were about his head, touching lightly, caressing him, and she was saying little foolish things as she pulled the dead leaves and burrs away. Then she kissed him.

For about a week he remembered the dream and his fear, then the memory sank back to the shadowed depths from which it had come. He grew careless again and cheerful, and the only thing that troubled him was that Madeleine's sulks began once more. He thought sometimes, in exasperation, that she was never happy unless he was in trouble; he was more right than he knew.

One day in May he woke in the grey of morning, and fumbled to draw closer the gay coverlet, very soiled now, under which they slept. Then he realised that she was sitting up beside him, and he looked up at her sleepily, still groping for the edge of the stuff.

"What was the name of your fief, lord?" she said suddenly.

He was too drowsy to be surprised at the question, only he felt he must answer it. He half sat up, and rubbed his eyes.

"Why," he said, "Rifaucon, surely. Have ye forgot?"

Madeleine moved her head restlessly, avoiding his eyes.

"Nay," she said, and her voice made him turn to stare at her. "But I thought you had."

Yves frowned, then shrugged, and rolled over once more on his elbow. He was too sleepy to quarrel, but she would not let him alone.

"Yves Ner!" she said slowly, as though she savoured the name, and he realised that she had never called him by that name before, nor indeed by any other name but "lord." "Yves Ner!" she repeated, "how would your father, that was lord of Rifaucon – so ye say – how would he like to see you now?"

Yves saw that her intention was to make him angry, but why, he could not guess, and in any case, he would not be angry.

"By God's Death!" he said, and smiled. "He'd like it little, I think."

Madeleine sprang to her feet with something like a sob.

"And what," she cried, her voice suddenly wild, "what would your Domna Audiart . . . your minion in Angoulême –"

She did not finish the sentence, for Yves was upon her, and she had never seen him angry before.

When he had finished he turned from her and flung himself down again.

"If ye say her name to me again I'll beat you so you'll think this was play," he muttered.

She did not answer, and he took no notice of her gasping, muffled sobs, till they stopped so abruptly that he was forced to look round. She was standing behind him, her hair dishevelled, her face marred with tears, and her hands tightly clenched at her sides.

"Oh! you kill me!" she cried, and he started up, because he thought perhaps he had struck too hard, and he was sorry now.

She stepped back.

"Oh! not with your belt!" she said, and laughed strangely.

He was puzzled, understanding neither her unprovoked attack on him, nor these wild words.

"See here, child," he said at last, "why will ye be so curst? But for your . . . your girding at me I could be happy enough."

She interrupted him there.

"Happy? I know it. So ye would. But ye shall not . . . no . . . not here." Her words had broken out sudden and tumultuous and they ceased abruptly.

"But why?" Yves protested. "What harm, since I am here? And it's not so ill a life."

He stopped, because her face was so strange, but she was silent still, her dumb mind travailling with words. Then she spoke, and for a few moments Yves listened to what he must believe she thought of him, and it was a terrible arraignment. He listened in silence, making no effort to interrupt, to justify, or to excuse. Once more he was naked to the prying light, and shelterless – this time shelterless indeed – and he shivered a little as he stood still, waiting for her to finish.

At last she ceased and burst into tears.

Yves took a long breath, and looked about him as though something terrible had withdrawn itself.

"I suppose ye want to go to some other," he said. It was the first clear thought in his mind, though not the most important. "Ye may go."

He had not moved two paces before she caught his hand, and threw herself down, clinging to his knees, and pouring out such a torrent of protests as convinced him at last that she did not wish to leave him. He freed himself, gently enough, almost indifferently, and stood looking down at her as she crouched, still crying, at his feet.

"If ye do not want to go to another . . ." he began slowly, "nor want to leave me. . . . I cannot understand. Why have ye said these things?"

His voice was sharp with pain, and she shook to hear it, since she had wounded him, and now would give no help. What she had said of him she could not unsay, for both knew it to be true, and what she had said to him when she hugged his knees and swore herself his slave, that had been true too, and still less to be unsaid. Nor could she explain herself; how could she tell him that in her mind, what he was stood clear above what he did, wonderful, glorious, and unassailable?

There was no enlightenment for him, and no peace after that. Kind though Madeleine was, invariably kind, she could give him no shelter now. He was not angry, did not even avoid her, but he withdrew behind a dark, impalpable wall of gloomy reserve.

About three weeks after this the Baker, having decided between the two lords, taken the pay of one, and driven the other back within the walls of his castle, began to lay leisurely siege to it. He did not hurry, for there seemed to him to be a chance of another bargain here, and he bore no malice. So the siege hung fire, while the Baker waited for an answer to a message which he had shot into the castle wrapped around a crossbow quarrel.

One evening, as Yves came back from taking his turn in the mine which was being slowly dug towards the foot of one of the towers, he stopped at the brook for a drink, and when he had drunk dipped his face into the water to cool it and wash away the smears of the clay in which he had been burrowing. When he stood up again he saw, beyond the hazel bushes, a man and a woman. The man was the Baker, the woman Madeleine, and as Yves saw them they parted. The man called out a jest, and wiped his lips on the back of his hand. Yves drew his knife half out of the sheath, then drove it back, and strolled after Madeleine.

She heard him and stopped, but he took no notice of her, and they walked towards the camp in silence.

At last Yves spoke:

"I told you ye may go when ye list," he said in a dull voice, but she did not answer. Her silence made him certain, and he stood still. "Ye may go now," he said, leaning upon the pick he carried, and staring at her bare feet in the grass.

Still she neither moved nor answered, and he raised his eyes slowly to find her frowning at him, as intent as a child over a puzzle. At last she burst out, not answering him at all, but taken up with her own struggling thoughts.

"Lord," she said, "I asked him –" and her head tipped a little towards the departed Baker – "I asked . . . because I heard them say last night . . . someone said . . . you were not there . . . but someone said he had gone southward to Uzerche . . . alone . . . or at least without them."

Yves waited, not understanding what she was talking about, but too

220

tired of it all to be impatient. She went on, gradually clearing her mind.

"I asked him – the Baker – to make sure. It's true. He saith they two the Counts of Angoulême, are still in Limoges, and Lord Talleyrand of Perigord hath gone home, but the Young King goeth towards Uzerche. He told me all. . . . I asked him."

"Ah!" muttered Yves, "and what payment will he have for all that?" but he did not look up. If he had done, he would have seen the answer in her face. "And what of it all?" he said.

She went on, twisting her hands together:

"They say that he loveth troubadours and knights, the Young King doth, and that he gives . . . his hands are ever open." She stopped suddenly, drawing a deep breath, and her hands jerked up to her throat as if something choked her, and she must tear it away before she could speak again.

"Ah!" she cried. "Go to him! Go at once! Go . . . quick . . . before. . . . Go!" and then she shivered, and bit her lips.

He was not looking at her, and he had forgotten the Baker.

"It's folly," he muttered. "What have I to. . . ? It's folly . . . unless. . . . They all say he's large with singers. . . ." He raised his eyes to Madeleine, and she saw something change in his face, as though a soul had come back to a dead man's body, and given meaning to its blank eyes.

"It's folly," he repeated, and pitched the pick-axe into the bushes. "By God's Blood!" he cried, and struck his hands together, "I'll try it. . . . It's folly . . . but I'll try it." He was staring at her face, but he did not see it.

"Go now!" she said, but he shook his head and laughed.

"Nay. Supper first," he said and turned towards the camp.

His preparations, once he had eaten, took ten minutes or so. Then he was ready. Madeleine stood by him; she had hardly said a word all the time, and now, when he put his arm about her and kissed her, he found her as unresponsive as an image, and once more remembered the Baker.

He mounted, and turned his horse's head towards the south.

"To Uzerche?" he said.

She nodded, saying nothing, but he edged his horse closer to her and leaned down from the saddle. He felt suddenly lonely and lost, almost frightened without her, and he must know. . . . He laid his hand on hers, which were clenched at her breast.

"Wench," he began doubtfully, and then pride forbade him to ask the question; but he could not leave her without a word.

"Farewell, child," he said. "Wish me fortune."

She moved her head suddenly, shaking back her long hair.

"God and His Mother keep you," she said, and caught her breath at the strangeness of the old accustomed words.

She stood and watched him as he rode away, and saw the sun set his steel cap on fire. At the top of the hill he turned and waved his hand. When he was gone she still watched the empty line of green, and in her mind was no thought, and hardly any feeling, only the beginning of knowledge – the knowledge that he was gone for always.

That night she lay in the arms of the Baker and was feverishly kind to him.

XX

When Sin claps his broad wings over the battle
And sails rejoicing on the flood of Death,
When Souls are torn to everlasting fire,
And fiends of Hell rejoice upon the slain,
O who can stand? O who hath causèd this?
O who can answer at the throne of God?
The Kings and Nobles of the Land have done it!
Hear it not, Heaven, thy Ministers have done it!

WILLIAM BLAKE

YVES rode for ten miles without a pause, then he pulled up, and sat for a time without moving. Before him lay a long mere running up between a wooded hill on one side and a bare grass slope on the other. The pool itself was a shining darkness and very still; the woods were misted with a purplish shade which yet did not hide their sombre green. Above the far end of the pool, where the hills drew together, the sky was a harsh clear transparency, neither green nor blue, and in it floated a fiery cloud of a colour between rose and gold, crossed by a heavy, dull, purple streak. That purple was the only sure colour, and dim though it was, it drew and satisfied the eye. In the dark pool a swan sailed, as purely white as a daytime moon, and as it moved below the lit sky, the ripples were like long trails of thin and fiery beads drawn smoothly after it.

Yves stared at it all, saw it all, and heeded nothing of it. He was thinking of Madeleine. Now that he had left her he seemed to see her more clearly, and in his mind a dim truth began to be visible. Why she had sent him away, why she had been sullen or angry, he did not think, but he began to believe that truly she loved him, and the thought was salt-sweet, like tears; it softened him, weakened him, and made him miserable and happy. At last he pulled his horse round and rode back to the camp.

It was dark when he reached it, so he tethered the horse to a tree, and passed the sentry with a word. The fires had burnt low, and it took him a long while to find Madeleine. When he found her he stood staring down at her, as stiff as a post, for a full minute. Then he went back, stepping softly, to his horse. He rode another fifteen miles that night before he slept.

When he woke next morning with a clouded, confused mind, the sun was already up. He blinked and stretched and rose to his feet, and only then remembered what had happened. He moved quickly towards his horse. He would think neither of Madeleine nor of his hurt and anger of the night before. All that was past, and it was better so, since it set him free to face the future.

When he had looked over the buckles and straps of his own gear, and gone as carefully over his horse's harness, he mounted and rode on, very cautious, very intent, because he knew by now, or thought he knew, the power of the Enemy. Mind and body were as taut as a bow at full stretch, and the arrow upon the string was aimed at a desperate chance.

As he rode, although he was on the alert for any danger among the woods, his mind was busy with plans, even with the song that he would sing to the Young King if he got his chance. He must be ready. Knowing the danger, he did not weaken himself with hope, but setting his teeth, planned to meet the emergency, facing the unlikelihood – almost the impossibility of success, with a set resolve. There was only one thought which he dared not face, and that was the thought of Audiart. Even if – he would hardly let himself think of success – but even if the Young King should show him favour, it would make no difference to her condemnation of him. That was for ever. She was no prize in this game, and he guessed how she would have mocked, if she had known that he was daring to play.

. .

About noon that day he came to a ford on a little river where it ran between deep sandy banks, the higher parts of which were pitted with sand-martens' nests. It was raining and the river ran full, and was dimpled all over with the heavy drops and their myriad shifting, intersecting, fading circles.

Just as he was about to ride down the steep track to the water he saw that a large company was coming down the opposite bank, and he pulled his horse aside to let them go by. A dozen knights passed him first, their wet cloaks hanging heavily on their shoulders, and only a gleam of link mail showing here and there. Behind them came a few monks with the long fat candles wrapped in their gowns to shield them from the rain. After them came a bier, slung between two horses, and over it a great pall of green samite, the finest and gayest thing there. Two men went alongside the bier on each side, steadying it as it swayed and rocked over the river. A mixed crowd of knights and esquires followed, and the servants brought up the rear.

Yves waited till they were all gone, then he went down into the ford, but before he had crossed, another man, riding fast to catch the others, came clattering down the steep bank. He checked when he saw Yves, and they passed each other slowly with a casual glance.

Yves pulled up, and turned, resting one hand on the quarter of his horse.

"Hi!" he cried aloud above the noise of the water.

The other man paused and turned.

"Who was yonder dead man?" said Yves, idly curious.

The other crossed himself.

"Henry by the Grace of God King of England, Duke of Normandy, Count of Maine Anjou and Touraine," he said. "God assoil him."

Yves stared at him for a moment, gaping like a fish. Then he cried angrily, as if the man mocked him:

"It's the Old King you mean. . . . Old Henry of England."

The man picked up his reins again.

"Would God it were!" he said. "Out harrow and alas! It's the Young King."

When Yves had been left alone for a few moments he raised his eyes from the dizzying swirl of the water.

"Ah! It is Thou!" he said softly. "This is Thy play again."

Those who carried the body of the Young King Henry – "the best king ever to bear a shield, the hardiest, the best at tourneying" – towards his grave at Rouen, had gone a couple of miles, before Yves, riding like fury now, caught and passed them.

There was only one thought in his mind beside a bruised and enduring anger. He would get back to Madeleine. He did not reason, nor doubt, nor remember the proof of his doubts, but from the malevolent

Enemy he turned to her. What did it matter to him if she were faithless or wanton? The Enemy could not touch him there.

He was so eager to achieve the discomfiture of the Enemy that, having slept a few hours and waking in the half darkness of the summer night, he decided to push on again, and found himself before long riding between cultivated fields, fenced because the corn stood high, and through the street of a little village. Ahead of him a great bell began to shout, deep and open-throated, and mechanically he began to count the strokes, but they went on far beyond twelve. As he drew nearer a black mass loomed up cliff-like; the road turned by a clump of dark elms, and he saw on his right hand five tall coloured windows, glowing, sombre and rich in the darkness, along the flank of a great church. As he stared, the bell stopped ringing, and he knew that now, at two o'clock in the morning, the monks were shuffling down the airy windows, sweet with the scents of summer, to their candle-lit church.

He rode slowly on, then drew rein to stare up at one of the windows that rose above him, and saw, in a cloudy glory of blood-red, dull gold, green, and a blue that was almost black, a huge saint enthroned, with stiffly crossed feet, and a sword in his hand. His face was great and awful and there was a halo about his head.

For a moment Yves looked. Then he laughed, stood up in his stirrups, and, lifting his clenched fist, shook it at the lit window.

At Nexon next day, when all the bells were clamouring their thankfulness for a deliverance and a victory, a man rode through the little town, asking his way to Feytat. He interrupted a group of talkers with such a scowling face that they told him the worst way, and nothing of the great news they were discussing. When he had ridden on they went back to it.

"Aye," said one, a thin, fair man with a cast in one eye. "And mark me! When thieves fall out there's soon an end. It was Count Richard's Routiers caught the Baker and his lot yesterday and rid us of him. . . . Very soon the Peacemakers will sweep up all . . . yea, even the husks."

Someone grumbled, half to himself, that it would take long to clear the Routier swine out of France, since the great lords would still keep them, but the squint-eyed man was confident.

"But the Holy Virgin herself came to this Durand in Auvergne, came to him clear and close, and said she would help harry the Routiers . . . so in course –"

"It's these wandering packs that are the worst," broke in another. "The Baker has done us more harm in a month than Count Richard's fellows in a year."

Someone laughed. "Well! The Baker won't do no more hurt!" he said, and everyone joined with him. Then the group broke up, still laughing, each man calling out jokes and farewells over his shoulder.

Meanwhile Yves rode slowly out of the gate on his way to Feytat. The stir and bustle of the town and the dancing clamour of the bells annoyed him, so that he rode with his eyes on the peak of his saddle, looking neither to right nor left. Had he looked up as he left the gate behind, he would have seen hanging there, like dead rats nailed to a barn door, the head and hands of the Baker.

Outside the town he came on more signs of rejoicing. Beyond the bridge, in the open country, a crowd of children danced, whirling in noisy circles across the road, their heads crowned with garlands of summer flowers, their linked hands clasping leaves and branches, while, on the grassy bank beside the road, a boy blew shrilly on a pipe. They were not afraid of the dark-faced rider coming from the town, but shouted and laughed at him, spinning their circle unbroken before his horse's nose, until he cursed them, and spurred forward. Then they scattered, screaming, but when he had gone by they rallied, and followed him up with a volley of stones that rang on his steel cap and on the shield slung at his back. Halfway to Feytat Yves came upon a beggar. Yves saw him first in the distance, going slowly along the track, and when he drew nearer, saw that the man's hands were out, groping, and that he stumbled now and then. Yves overtook him, glanced over his shoulder, and pulled his horse back on his haunches.

It was Fat Jehan, with raw red pits where his eyes had been.

Not far from Pierre Buffière in the Limousin there is a high plateau, lifted among higher, sharper hills, and covered in some places with dark swamp and brown grasses, in others with heather, while here and there are jagged, tumbled rocks, red with iron, and so gaunt that no moss nor weed softens their harshness. It is a desolate place of sour earth and barren stone, lonely and of an evil reputation. On that June afternoon it had not even the alleviation of sunshine, for there had been rain from heavy, low, loosely textured clouds, and as evening fell, these were touched first with purple, then with a dull crimson like blood among grey ashes.

To a man startled from his sleep in the heather by a sudden thunder of hoofs, the whole world seemed steeped in the ugly red, so that the air itself upon his tongue almost tasted of blood. He looked about and saw, riding down on him, too close now for escape, a horseman on a red horse. The rider had a dark leather coat the colour of an old blood-stain, hair black as death, and a parchment face. He carried, bare in his hand, a great sword that shone red in the sun from the hilt to midway down the blade, and was red without shining from there to the point.

The man who had been sleeping put his hand up to his breast and began the sign of the Cross, but checked himself, and as the horseman drew up, stood glowering at him from under his shaggy brows, but his eyes were so sunk that their sharpness was hidden. He was as brown and hard and bitter as the rocks of that barren place, as thin as a man may be and yet live, and his clothes hung in tatters about his lean arms and shanks.

Yves' horse, its forefeet wide apart as it had planted them when checked in its blundering gallop, drooped its head and shivered, while the sweat ran down its shaking legs, and steam went up from its sides.

"Who . . . are you?" said Yves at last.

"What do you want?" replied the man.

There was another pause, then:

"Somewhere to sleep. Something to eat," said Yves.

The man lifted a hand like a claw and pulled at his straggling beard.

"Who have you killed?" he said, and pointed at the drawn and bloody sword. Yves looked down at it as though he remembered it for the first time.

"It was. . . . Oh! Some of Count Richard's Routiers. . . . I rode through them awhile back."

The ragged man looking up at him saw that he sat very stiff in the saddle and that his face was very still though there was nothing in it of repose.

The ragged man dropped his eyes and took the bridle.

"I'll guide ye, if it's Routiers ye've killed," he said, and started off, away from the beaten track by tiny twisting paths between black bog and jagged stone. As they went he talked, never turning his eyes from the track, nor waiting for Yves to reply.

"If I could kill a Routier I'd eat him . . . raw or cooked, it's no odds. . . . Vermin they are . . . devils. . . . They'd be better than churchyard food to a starving man. . . . I've eaten that sometimes . . . in winter . . . gone down at night." He broke off again with a sound more beast-like than human and was silent for a few moments. Then:

"I was a free man . . . had a croft over yonder," he pointed towards the red disc of the low sun. "They came, the Routiers; first it was the Count's Routiers – Count Adhemar's – then it was them of Poitou . . . then . . . whose? . . . No-one's but the devil's . . . or. . . . Anyways, there's nought of that village now but nettles. . . . Lords? What use are they? They run . . . we stay and die like beasts . . . or live."

He pulled up suddenly so that the horse stopped and Yves looked down, slowly, and as though it was only with difficulty that he spared a moment's half-attention from some strenuous effort.

"Get on! Get on!" he said.

As the ragged man started off again he cursed the strange rider whole-heartedly, although he guessed that he would hear this as little as he had heard the rest.

They came at last to a great mass of stone, greater and more impending than any they had passed. The man stopped.

"Hobble y'r horse," he said, "and come within," and with that he seemed to plunge into the solid rock. In a moment a spark leapt and died, another followed, then a little flame shot up, lighting the four great uprights and ponderous roofing stone of one of those graves in which the long-forgotten races once buried their dead.

Inside the ragged man was busy with a fire, squatting on his hams and occasionally leaning down to puff at the young flames from swollen cheeks. When he had made the broth – very thin it was, being made of

229

roots and herbs, with only a film of grease on top to show that there had been any meat at all in the pot – he poured half of it into a chipped wooden bowl and held it out to the guest.

Yves took no notice, did not seem to see it. He sat with his back to the wall, his feet sprawling and his hands loose at his sides, a pose of ease or lassitude, but there was nothing of either in his face. The man holding out the broth and staring, remembered something he had seen, when, before the bad days came, he had done service in his lord's castle at a siege. On the wall one day he had watched a fellow standing ready by a mangonel, a hammer in his hand, waiting the signal to knock away the wedge and free the great arm to swing up and hurl its burden of rock. That fellow as he waited had been still, just as Yves was still.

When the man jogged his elbow Yves turned grudgingly; again, it seemed, he disengaged only a fraction of his attention.

"Here!" said the man. "Sup your sup and let me have mine. Ye don't think I've more than one bowl, do ye?"

There was no talking over their thin meal, but at last, as though he was spurred by curiosity, or irked by the silence, the man reached out a bare foot and kicked Yves gently.

"Talk, can't you, you black-faced dog! What are you at all this time?"

Yves' eyes moved towards him.

"Let me alone. . . . I think of mine enemy," he said.

"Your enemy, quotha?" cried the other, forcing his opportunity. "Well, who is your enemy? What's he done to you? . . . I've an enemy too."

Yves sat up from the rough wall, and looked straight at the ragged man. It was as though the fellow at the mangonel had raised his hammer.

"He hath hunted me," he said softly, "for years . . . taken everything . . . and now her too. . . . I met one that told me . . . he saw her hair afloat last thing before they tore out his eyes. . . . They drowned her with all the other wenches . . . and the men drowned or blinded. . . . She had yellow hair . . . he saw it spread out . . . floating. . . ."

He stopped, but the ragged man waited for more. He knew that the blow was not yet struck.

"Who did it?" he asked. "Routiers?" He thought that would bring it, but it did not.

"Routiers?" said Yves. "No. Count Richard . . . again . . . but. . . ." Once more he did not finish the sentence, and once more it was as if the hammer were poised, waiting the signal. It came.

"Ah!" said the ragged man. "It's Count Richard is your enemy? Mine –"

Down came the hammer and the load of hatred was released.

"No!" cried Yves. "Not Count Richard, though I hate him too. . . . Not Count Richard . . . not him. . . . God."

The ragged man jerked up, all a wild stare. Then he came quite close to Yves.

"You too?" he whispered. "And I!"

They peered at each other then in silence, and the quietness of that old grave seemed strange. Except for the flutter of the fire they might have been buried deep in the earth. There was no other sound, no answer to their defiance, no echo even of their stroke.

Yet, though they waited for a sound, when it came they started. The ragged man leapt to his feet, and caught up a long stake, pointed and shod with iron.

"Your horse!" he said, and made for the door. Yves followed, his sword out, but quick as they were, it was too late. A dozen riders came down on them through the dusk, yelling and waving their swords.

Yves sprang forward, then checked, and shouted:

"Hugues! Hugues the Potter. . . . Hold! Stay!"

"Ho!" cried a voice, "it's Yves Ner! What? You got free? . . . We thought we were all." The horsemen pulled up in an irregular bunch.

Yves felt his sleeve plucked, and turned to find the ragged man's face pushed close to his own.

"Who are these . . . and you? Routiers?"

Yves nodded, and the man leapt back.

"One less!" he screamed, and drove the iron-shod stake at Yves' eyes.

Yves did not mean to kill, but he could not help it. The ragged

231

man's knees gave gradually, he sprawled forward, then rolled on one side.

Yves bent over him, and did not even think it strange that he was shocked at what he had done.

"Why –?" he began, and stopped. The man was dead.

XXI

Halts by me that footfall:
Is my gloom, after all,
Shade of his hand, outstretched caressingly?
Ah, fondest, blindest, weakest,
I am He Whom thou seekest!
Thou dravest love from thee, who dravest Me.

FRANCIS THOMPSON.

TWO years, a month and a day later Yves found himself standing with an aching, singing head under the blazing sunshine in a dusty courtyard. His hands were bound behind him with a straw rope that had long ago rubbed his wrists raw, and now he felt the flies settle and crawl on them. The rope that tied him, tied other men on each side of him; in fact the whole crowd of Routiers were linked together like cowslips for a ball. They had been caught early that morning, marched ten miles to this place, and now waited, discussing among themselves the alternatives of death, blinding, and maiming.

The man next to Yves turned a scowling face towards him.

"Damn you to Hell!" he said. "This is your doing, curse you! Who said 'Go north!' when all else said south? And this is where we end! As if there isn't quarrels enough in the south for us to have lived there safe and fat!"

"Yea," cried another who overheard. "And who bade us surrender to-day? What's y'r game now, you that's been a lord?" And he jerked the rope spitefully, but even that brought no answer.

"I suppose," sneered the first man, "that ye look to feast to-day with Count Richard. He's a friend to you, isn't he?"

Yves turned to him with a slow stare, and his lips were moving.

"Let me alone," he said. "There is a line I cannot get."

The man laughed.

"Ho! let you alone?" he scoffed. "What are ye –" He stopped suddenly because two men had come out from a doorway in the courtyard

233

and crossed over towards the huddle of prisoners. They paused, and the elder of the two waved his hand towards them.

"Who are these, fair friend Raoul?" he said.

Raoul, a young knight with an ingenuous fresh face, blushed.

"Prisoners, lord Guilhem," he said, then blushing still more:

"I . . . we . . . we caught 'em this morning. They yielded at mercy. It's a Routier lot has been troubling the country."

Guilhem the Marshall's eyebrows went up.

"What did ye bring them hither for?" he said.

"I thought . . . perhaps the Count would wish . . ." the young man faltered.

"Ha!" laughed the Marshall, but not unkindly. "They're an ill-looking nosegay for the Count. He shall know of it, but there's no need to keep them."

He came a little nearer, then turned back.

"Cast them in the moat, and have them fished out when they're drowned. I see ye've roped them."

That was all. He nodded kindly to the young man, and went away.

Yves did not hear the fresh curses thrown at him, because he was cursing himself. It was for this that he had lied and cajoled to keep the band from going south, and for this had counselled surrender – so that he should choke in the green slime of the moat without a chance to watch Count Richard's face as he listened to the song, that song that had never been, and now never would be sung.

They were already being pushed and herded towards the gate. A few moments only – and then! Oh! for the chance! the chance! Would not the devil send Count Richard even now?

There was a stir at the gate, and in tramped a company of cross-bowmen. The Routiers were thrust back against the wall as the court-yard filled, into a shade as sudden and cool as the water they would drown in. Then through the gate came a score of knights, fully armed except for their helms, magnificent in silk surcoats, with the painted shields jogging at their shoulders.

Yves craned his neck to see, and he saw.

In front of all rode one on a light bay horse. His hair was burnished brown, waving on his head and bristled in his beard. It did not need the golden lion on the red field of his surcoat and on the housings of his horse to tell Yves who it was, and he could have shouted for joy; but instead he waited till all had ridden in and an esquire came forward to the Count's bridle.

Then he cried, with all the strength of his lungs:

"Count Richard! Count Richard! Before you drown me listen to the song I have made!"

The Count turned in the saddle. His quick eyes seemed to find Yves in the mob of prisoners without having to search, then he threw up his head and looked hard at Yves down his nose, like a hunting dog snuffing up wind.

"Sing it!" he said calmly, and held up his hand for silence. The stir in the courtyard died, and men turning to stare left a clear alley along which Yves could look. He fixed his eyes on the Count's face and began the song – "Oi Deus! volh un sirventes far. . . ."

> God, I will make a song Thou shalt not say
> "I will not hear it," for there is no nay.
> See ! here are two men whose live souls are Thine,
> One soul is Richard's and the other mine . . .
> And mine is lost.

The Count's face was as still as a steady flame, only a flush had risen above his reddish beard, and his eyes sparkled. Yves paused; there was no hurry, for this song should be well sung. He drew his breath for the next verse.

> Well wot——— he began.

His neighbour, the man who had cursed him, moved suddenly, whether by accident or for malice, and jerked the rope; Yves, stumbling back, lost his note and stopped.

Richard leaned from the saddle.

"Can ye not be still – beast?" he cried, and motioned Yves on. As though the Count had rebuked every man there, the silence grew deeper, till it seemed something which listened.

Yves sang:

> Well wot I, God, how deep Thou hatest me,
> Wilt burn me with Thy fire eternally,
> Yet I can laugh, since for my soul Christ died
> And lacking it Thou art unsatisfied,
> Thy labour lost.

And, since Thou art the Judge, do justice now.
For my lost soul exact the forfeit, Thou!
For my soul, Richard's, driving him to Hell
Because it is by him, Thou knowest well,
That I am lost.

When he had done, the silence waited. Richard was the only one to move. He turned away from Yves, stared absently at his horse's mane, flicked a lock of it with his gloved hand, and then suddenly swung up, and out of the saddle. Still he did not speak, and nobody else dared. He held out his mail gloves for the squire to unlace them, stamping and shaking his legs to free them from the clinging heat of the chain mail, and only when the gloves dangled free from his wrists, did he turn his head over his shoulder.

"Separate me that man from the rest," he said, and then, to nobody in particular, "What are they?"

It was the young knight who answered, and he spoke in an unnecessarily loud voice because he felt inclined to whisper:

"Only Routier cattle, lord Count," he said.

"Ah!" said Richard casually. "Be done with them! Take them away!"

Yves, his hands still tied, but cut loose from the rest, turned to watch them go. He had sung his song and now his mind was as empty as any sieve. Someone hit him sharply in the back, and whispered urgently:

"Go! The Count beckons."

"Who made that song?" said Count Richard, looking down on Yves from his great height.

"I did."

The Count frowned, considering.

"How can I know it?" he said.

Yves shrugged his shoulders, but said nothing.

"Y'are surly!" said Richard sharply.

Yves looked up.

"I am not fain to answer your questions," he said.

His indifference persuaded the Count. He turned to an esquire.

"When I have eaten," he said, "bring him to me . . . and . . . yea . . . bathe and wash and clean him. Give him fresh gear. Savary's should do . . . I could not bear him else."

He turned and swung away, humming a snatch of Yves' song as he went.

Bathed, shaved, and reclothed in clean linen and a tunic a little too narrow in the shoulders, Yves followed a sergeant into the room where Richard sat. The Count's eyebrows went up when he saw him, but he said nothing, and waved his hand for the sergeant to withdraw.

The man turned to obey, then stepping aside, swept up a dagger that lay upon a carved stool.

"Thomas?" said Richard, very sharply.

The man looked dogged.

"He might . . . use it," he said and jerked a thumb towards Yves.

The Count turned to look at Yves, and the man took his opportunity and got away. Richard looked Yves over steadily from head to foot.

"And would ye?" said Richard.

"I would," he answered.

"Ha!" said Richard, very deep, and his face shone. Then he stood up. "Here! Take this lute – where is the plague thing? Oh! here. Sing that same song again. Take your time if you need. Or have you sung it before?"

Yves took the lute unwillingly.

"I've sung it to myself for . . . for five years," he said. "The tune is the same. The words –" He broke off, took, and tuned the lute. Then he sang, while Richard beat time with his hand.

When he finished Richard said "Yea" softly, several times, as though to himself. Then:

"It is good!" he said. "I like the way your tune goes. This part –" he broke off to hum a few bars.

Yves interrupted him.

"Count," he said, "do ye think the song's a jest, no more?"

Richard straightened himself in his chair, and with his altered position he put on something of majesty.

"No," he said, "I did not. But I am myself a troubadour. No. I had not forgotten. I had ye here to ask. Say me now –" His chin went up and again he looked at Yves down his nose. "What are your griefs against me?" He leaned forward a little, perfectly still, his hands clasping the smooth carved balls on the arms of the chair.

237

Yves laid the lute down and came nearer. Then he stopped, and because this was his moment, and he must collect all his rage and hate, he shut his eyes, the better to prepare, and found that, even so, he could not clear his thoughts.

He opened his eyes, saw Richard's intent face, and began to speak, jerking the words out.

"I. . . . That song. . . . I began it five years back. I told you that. But it was only a year ago that I found out . . . how. . . ." He broke off suddenly. "Oh!" he cried. "That is not what I would say!" His voice shook as though he were a child that had forgotten his lesson, and he bit his lip.

"I was of Angoulême," he began again, speaking quickly and without any expression. "Rifaucon was my fief. You took it. Raymond of Scorbé Clairvaux has it. I was nothing after that. What's a man without land? I would not go with the Old Count when you drove him overseas – I jested at the Count that is now and he . . . I had to get me away. I've been Routier since . . . I could have . . . but always. . . ." His voice changed and grew strained. "Between you – God and you – there was nothing I could keep. Not even the wench. . . . Since then I've. . . . You drowned her . . . you drowned her two years back." He stopped abruptly, and there was silence.

"Who was she?" said the Count, speaking carefully.

Yves gave a sharp laugh.

"Oh! a drab – a common drab . . . but she was enough for me."

"Since then?" said Richard.

"Since then . . . since then I've found out what I said in the song. With her – I forgot . . . but since. . . . Listen. I've lain in the woods – we've been like wolves . . . I have thought . . . I knew He was just – I had to – I must believe it. And I found a way . . . a way . . . to get my debt from both of you. . . . But I must never forget what I was or I'd forfeit it. . . . If I remembered always – every minute – I could claim your soul. And as for Him – He's lost mine. I did it . . . every minute . . . every minute I knew what I was . . . to get your soul. I said to Him, 'Look at me! Look at me! This is what I am! This. . . . Oh! Merciful God! This is what I am!'"

With a startling and sudden violence he lifted both hands to his throat and tore his tunic open to the mid breast. He stood a minute, dumb, as though it was his soul he had laid open; then he let his hands fall, and there was a muffled pause in which was no unrest, but only a spent and heavy languor. At last he spoke again:

"Sometimes," he murmured indistinctly, "sometimes I forgot ... and then I would remember that I . . . that I was even forgetting to hate myself. That was worst." There was no anger in his voice now; he might have been speaking to a friend, and when he ceased there was another pause, during which neither looked at the other.

At last the Count moved in his chair, sighed, and stood up.

"Hearken thou!" he said, speaking quickly, as though his mind was made up, but after that he stopped, and when he spoke again it was slowly, picking his words.

"I cannot undo –" he said. "No man can. But what I may I will. Yea – by God's Throat, as I hope for His mercy . . . I must needs do it." He raised his eyes and looked at Yves, weighing his words. Then his voice quickened.

"Kneel down!" he said. "What was your fief? Rifaucon? Yea then. Raymond can have another. Kneel down! I'll give thee seisin – now! How is it given? A sod – a branch – a staff? How?" He spoke like an eager boy, his hands spread wide as though his generosity was large enough to include the world in his gift.

Yves went back a few steps.

"No!" he almost shouted, shaken out of his lassitude. "No! No! No!" he repeated in a quick whisper.

The light went out in Richard's face.

"Why not?" he said.

Yves did not know. He was like a man so blinded and deafened by the fury of winds and sea, so maddened by noise and tumult that he cannot think, though life depends on it. He only knew that he must refuse.

"No! I will not! From you? I will not! . . . No, nor that's not why . . . I cannot . . . I cannot. . . . No, I cannot."

He would not look at Richard's eyes which dwelt on him, frankly troubled.

"I pray you, say 'Yea,' " said Richard very gently.

239

Yves shook his head, and now all that he wanted was to get away quickly. He must get away . . . could not bear any more of this. He looked round almost furtively, and heard Richard sigh again.

"Messire," said the Count, and the word was another buffet, "if ye will not, then go free. But first –" he began to unclasp the jewelled morse that crossed his breast and held his mantle in place – "take a gift. Nay, I will have it so." He came down on Yves, flung the mantle over his shoulders and fastened the clasp again.

"I will have it so!" he repeated, and pulled Yves' hands away. "And for your arms that my men took, and armour, I'll give others. Silence! I give largesse for the song. It is my pleasure."

He had become so amazingly haughty that Yves hardly knew him for the same man. The audience was clearly at an end.

"I may go, lord Count?" said Yves.

"Ye may go," said Richard coldly, and turned to shout:

"Savary! Savary!" The eldest of the esquires opened the door.

"Give Messire here, horse, arms, all the rest."

He waved his hand, and Yves went slowly out, confusion in his mind.

Savary armed Yves, and then, being a thoughtful youth, fetched food and wine and set it before him in the small tower room. Before Yves had finished Savary had to leave him, as the Count had called for his esquire.

"You will find the horse in the yard, Messire," he said before he went. "A varlet hath it ready."

Yves nodded. He was afraid of the boy and would not speak.

When he was ready he went off down the twisting stair, across one empty room, smelling of dust and mice, down another stair and into another room, darkened by the wooden shutters across the windows. Someone in the shadows cried his name, and he stopped because he could not move. It was Audiart.

She came towards him, and he could see that she held something in her hand, but not much more till she was quite close. Then he stared at her woodenly, because he feared her more than he feared anyone on earth, and would not show it. As for her, she saw more than enough in his face.

"Yves of Rifaucon!" she cried, and he heard the shrinking in her voice.

"Yea, even so!" he sneered. "And what are you doing here, Domna Audiart of Rouilac? Or are ye wed these days?"

She answered his questions mechanically:

"Yea, I am wed . . . I'm here because –" She could not say "the Countess" to him, but instead: "Lord Vulgrin's little lass is here . . . and a many from Angoulême . . . and I'm wed to Lord Raymond of Scorbé Clairvaux."

She was speaking with her eyes on his face, not thinking once of what she said, but only of what she saw there, and before he could speak she cried out again:

"You're not! You're not! . . . Yves of Rifaucon!" The name was like a shuddering incantation to call up a departed soul, and Yves smiled, a travesty of his old smile, for he understood what she meant.

"You think I am even worse yet than I used to be?" he said, and turned aside to see what it was that she had suddenly flung away like an unclean thing.

He stooped and picked it up, an old glove, darkened and rubbed across the knuckles. On the back there was a device worked in red and green, but the threads were frayed, and when he turned the glove over, there was a clean slit across the thumb. He knew it then.

"Mine!" he muttered. "How came you? . . ." He grew desperate, remembering many things at the sight of that small, forgotten, once-familiar thing. "By the Cross! I believe it's you that hath kept it! You must have loved me well, Domna!"

The charge was preposterously absurd, but he did not care, any more than he cared that it was himself whom the words lashed, so long as their impudence drove her away; only he dared not look at her.

She stood perfectly still for a moment, then stepped back.

"Go! And God may forgive you, but I'll not!" she said.

As he reached the door she came after him.

"Stop!" she cried. "Give it me! Give it me!" and held out her hands

He turned back, and dropped the glove into them without a word, but, as he did so, she saw the raw red circles about his wrist, where the rope had cut him. That broke her, and both hands went up to cover her mouth. For a moment she could not speak, and already he was on the stairs.

"Messire . . . Messire . . ." she faltered, while her heart cried nothing but – "Child! Oh, child!"

He made no answer except a backward jerk of the head. Next moment she heard a horse move slowly away in the yard below.

When Yves had ridden a mile or so he pulled up because he realised that he did not know where he was going, and then, since he could find no answer, rode on again, as the horse chose, and did not care at first that he was aimless, since he was busy with his thoughts.

He did not think of Audiart, though he felt her as a man feels the pain of a flogging after his mind has ceased to torment itself by recapitulating each blow. There was no new thing, and so nothing to be thought of with regard to her; he had known it for a long time, even known it dimly the first time she had spoken to him, that day in the orchard. He was no good for her. That was all.

He thought confusedly of the amazing offer which he had refused, and he knew now why he had refused it. He, lord of Rifaucon! He almost smiled at the thought, but Audiart and her scorn crept in by that door, so he shut it.

He tried to think instead of what he would do now, and found himself face to face that instant with something which had been lurking unseen in his mind, and again he forgot the practical question. He had hated Richard. . . . Now – he beat his fist furiously on the saddle – he . . . almost . . . loved him. Richard had held his hands wide with Rifaucon between them; he had been – Oh! small and simple word for a thing so irresistible – he had been kind.

For a moment Yves thought he would turn back, then, almost with relief, knew it was impossible, and, as though it were a familiar landmark to a lost man, he remembered the enmity of God. That enmity was implacable, an eternal and immovable thing – and as he considered it, doubt shook him so that he dared not think, dared not even lift his eyes, lest he should see something which he feared. He rode, staring at the horse's mane, knowing only that he was in open country where dark gorse-bushes lined the track, with here and there a splash of gold where they flowered late.

The tail of his eye caught a gleam of something white, so that he must look up, and what he saw was what he had feared to see.

It was a wayside Calvary. The agonised and drooping head of the Christ was greened by weather down one side, and the shaft of the cross was splintered and rotten; but to Yves it was his doubt made certainty.

He let the reins drop and clutched the saddle like a wounded man. As the horse moved slowly, head down, cropping the short heathy grass, he stared, never moving anything but his eyes, and keeping them fixed on the Christ. He groaned once, and something twisted his face, but there was no one to see or hear him in that wide and silent place.

This was the Enemy from Whom he had fled; this was the harsh justice, the untiring vengeance, the hate. He twisted his head stiffly over his shoulder, and stared at the hot gold of a little sceptre of gorse, pushed up towards the sun by a straggling bush, but there was no respite there. His eyes went back to the Cross.

This God Who was beauty, Whom he desired, this appalling, present love, in which the huge sacrifice of the Cross was only an incident, this love that he could not, that he must escape –

He snatched at the reins and drove the horse on, shouting, and striking with the spurs till they dripped blood. He was the quarry, and the Hunter was very close.

XXII

Na he that aye has livit free
May nocht knaw well the propertè,
The anger, na the wretchit doom
That is complit to foul thraldome.

JOHN BARBOUR.

DOMNA ALIENOR of Cahuzac, called by her neighbours the Bitch of Cahuzac, climbed up the winding tower stair behind the clumsy lad who carried the torch, and after her came her son Jehan, stepping unsteadily, his hands on the walls to keep himself straight. In the swaying light, caught and flung aside at every arrow-slit, the stairs seemed to slide and leap, and the walls themselves to rock, so that Jehan of Cahuzac, with the hot, spiced wine in his head, swore several times before the lad pushed open a heavy door and passed inside the room.

The light, dissipated now through a greater space, lost its fierceness and strength, and shadows crawled beyond its borders, till the lad, taking another torch from its ring in the wall, held it to the lighted one he carried. It sputtered, crackled, then caught, and a single flame shot up from the two of them, and a few sparks dripped. He stuck both in their rings and went out, looking over his shoulder nervously.

Alienor of Cahuzac went to a high-backed chair which stood by the fire, and taking the limp hand which drooped over the side, she shook it. The man who dozed there sat up, his mouth agape, his straight, thick, straw-coloured hair disordered, and his eyes vacant, as though he was still mazed by sleep, but as he stared no gleam of returning intentness came to his face, for he was an idiot.

"Go to bed," said Domna Alienor, speaking slowly as if he were a child.

He answered by a whimper.

"What were ye at, down there?" he complained. "I heard someone crying out. I don't like it. I don't like it. It made me cry." His voice shook, and tears began to trickle down his cheeks.

Jehan, who had straddled awkwardly over to one of the windows, drew his head back from the narrow opening and slammed the wooden shutter.

"Oh! get you to bed, Cousin," he said testily.

His mother turned her head slowly towards him, and her eyes were as hard and dark as two black stones in clear water.

"Let him be," she said, but she pulled the elder man to his feet.

"Come. . . . Come to bed," she coaxed, and he went with her to the door, still whimpering.

When she came back Jehan was on his knees before a big chest strengthened with iron clamps which were forged in the likeness of a hawk's claws. As she sat down by the dying fire, he lifted out a chain hauberk and let it fall in a jingling heap beside him; and all the while she watched the back of his straw-coloured head, with its straight thick hair.

He seemed to feel her stare, for he dropped the lid of the chest with a clang, and picking up the mail, came across and stood facing her, his feet planted well apart, his face flushed with wine.

"See here, madam mother," he said, speaking more loudly than was necessary, for she was watching him still. "Why do you keep this fellow? . . . Curse you, you –! Don't look at me like that! I'm Cahuzac! I'm not that poor devil. But why do you keep him?"

Domna Alienor dropped her eyes.

"Oh! him?" she said softly. "I thought you meant. . . ."

"Cousin Ebles?" cried Jehan with a loud laugh. Then he frowned. The idiot man was the cause of a mute but unappeasable rancour which he dared not discuss. He returned to the other question.

"What's the use of keeping him – the fellow we caught? If he says he's landless and penniless after what ye did to him to-night, he'll say it ever – because it's true. Why keep him then?"

The woman's thin lips stirred before she answered.

"He lies," she said. "What could he be but a knight? You're a fool. Look at his mantle ye wear, and the hauberk! It's fit for a great lord. You can wager your life he is a great lord. That chain –" she pointed suddenly at it as it lay across Jehan's breast. "That chain is fit for a king's son."

She was right in that, for it had belonged to Richard of Poitou, and Jehan glanced at it proudly, but he was not moved by the argument.

"Pooh!" he said. "A gift," and he was right too.

She smiled a little.

"And the horse? And the arms?" she asked, but he did not answer, nor speak again till he had settled himself on a cushion beside the fire, his legs sprawling, and the hauberk over his knees. Then he looked up at her with an impudent smile.

"I know why you would go on with him even when there was no sport left in him. By God! though, he was stiff. He bore more –"

She interrupted him.

"He'll be the humbler next time I have him out. You'll see it," she said and laughed softly. "He's broken now," she murmured.

"Broken?" said Jehan. "Nigh dead! But I know why. Because he called me ill-born!" He watched her face, and laughed when he saw something change in her guarded eyes. "You've sworn to me over and over that Gilles of Cahuzac was my father. Well! I hope so. I've no will to be a bastard son of Cousin Ebles."

He laughed again, but she made no answer except to say softly to herself: "It's his courage is broke."

For a while Jehan dozed there before the fire, his head nodding on his chest, and sometimes the woman looked at the top of his yellow, untidy head, and there was a strange unwilling intentness in her eyes.

There is a pine wood not far from Cahuzac, and she was thinking of that, and remembering it very well, though she had not seen it since one evening in August twenty years ago, when she had been married to Gilles of Cahuzac for six months. She remembered the grey-green mist of needles above, the grey-blue mist of bare twigs below, the sound of the wind, very soft like the sea heard far off, and the sad crooning of the wood-pigeons. It had seemed strange that everything should be calm and quiet when she and Ebles were so buffeted with storms, so shaken by the beating of their own pulses. She remembered the tumult, and the joy, but now her only thought was that Ebles had always been a fool. He had been gentle, whereas Gilles of Cahuzac was not gentle; but he had always been a fool.

He had been a coward too, for six months afterwards she had con-
trived to send for him, and she had begged, her hands held out shaking
towards him, that he would take her and keep . . . keep her safe from
Gilles of Cahuzac . . . because she could not. . . . Oh, God! dared not
stay . . . Gilles watched her . . . watched her. . . . She would rather he
did . . . the things he had done at first . . . anything rather than this
watching. He was waiting – she hid her face in her hands – waiting to
see whose child it was. So Ebles must keep her.

She had looked up then and seen the answer on his face, and cursed
him, and gone back to Cahuzac, sick with fear.

In April Gilles of Cahuzac had set off on the first foray of the season,
for the pilgrims and the merchants were taking the road once more.
Although she had watched him ride off with his men she was too
broken by fear to realise her temporary deliverance, till the long slow
hours of peace made her understand that he was really gone; and then
a fresh fear came as she saw time slipping by, and knew that he must
return. Evening of the second day found her at the top of the tower
watching for the first sight of him, because she must know at once
when he was near. Yet, when she saw the little clump of spears, she had
to press both clenched hands to her mouth to stifle a cry, and as she
went downstairs, wild-eyed and shaking, she wished to God she had
left herself one half-hour more of uncertainty.

It was to this room that she had come. She turned her head slowly
and unwillingly, as if the old fear was still there, and stared at a closet
in one corner of the room. The door stood open and she started up and
slammed it angrily.

The sound wakened Jehan; he got up, stretched with a sleepy snarl
like a young animal, and staggered to the door.

"I am for bed," he said. "A good night to you."

She made no answer, but waited till the door was shut, and then
opened the closet again and peeped in. The stuffy smell was the same;
Gilles used to hang his armour there, she remembered.

She had come to this room because she dared not be anywhere but
where he would expect her, and then because she dared not meet him
she had crept into the closet and pulled to the door.

At last he came. There was the sound of trampling feet crossing the room. One man stumbled against the bed as they laid something on it; then they went out, and there was silence. A terrible hope, and the fear of fear drove her out of hiding. Her knees shook and her mouth gaped as she gasped and sobbed together, and it seemed an age before she reached the bed. It was so dark that she could not see without peering closely, and as though she bent over a snake she clutched her breast while she looked down at him – and saw. A spear had struck him full in the throat, tearing through the steel links and the leather gorget, so that now he seemed to have two mouths, both bloody and both gaping.

All that was long ago and fear had died with Gilles of Cahuzac, but not before it had made her cankered like old iron. Gilles had done his work well, and left a wife who could take his place – the Bitch of Cahuzac, the cruellest beast in France. There were only two men in Cahuzac who need not fear her; Jehan and Ebles. Two days after Gilles had been brought home dead she had sent for Ebles, desiring, even while she despised him, and he had come and served her well enough as protector till she had established herself and the child. As time passed, however, he grew strange and dull, and at last quite an idiot. Then her desire died, leaving only a sort of contemptuous softness.

Every evening one of the Cahuzac men would climb the ladder to the empty stable-loft, unbolt the trapdoor, and thrust in a jar of water, and a hunk of bread. If they took the trouble to peer in, they could see the prisoner sitting slack and inert, always in the same dim and dusty corner, but for the most part they did not even put their heads above the flooring of the loft.

When they were gone, Yves would come out of the corner, fetch the food, and go back again to his old position, the urgency of his fear subsiding, and the mists settling down once more upon his mind. There were indeed only two clear instants in his day. One, the time when he listened to the footsteps on the ladder, shrinking back into the shadowed corner lest "she" should be there, the other, when fear caught him by the throat in the moment of waking.

It was always the same fear to which he woke. He would lie there, not daring to move a finger, while his eyes, wandering and straining, would search for the thing he feared. When he saw nothing on the one side he would begin to turn his head, but very slowly; then, not able to bear the suspense, he would roll over suddenly. She was not there! For a few moments he was almost happy in the huge relief.

Between these two moments – his morning and evening terrors – there was only a grey interval of time. The loft was a twilight place even on a sunny day, a dreary space, full of dust and cobwebs, across which his thoughts passed, a monotonous procession of half-dead thing, as grey and cheerless as the place itself. They were all hateful, and their passage tortured him, but he knew that unless they passed, time would stand still, and never bring him to the sleep which was his only desire, his only escape from the heavy wheels that ground slowly through his brain. And yet even in sleep there were dreams.

That, for how long he never knew, was his life; an age of confused and aching thought, of bodily pain that passed gradually into weakness, and always, shutting him in on every side, pitiless fear at which he dare not look.

One day he was disturbed from his torpor by sounds he could not but hear though he kept his hands over his ears and drummed with his heels on the floor till he set the horses stamping in the stable below. It was not that he had any pity to spare for the people outside, but each scream wakened his own fear till he sweated and shook; when they ceased he lay down again, and hid his face on his arm.

It was quite dark in the loft when red-headed Jaufré opened the trap-door and poked his head up, peering round. Yves stirred in his corner, and the man turned towards the noise.

"Come out, thou spider, thou!" he cried very loud, and beat with a huge hand on the dusty floor as if to rouse Yves. "Come out, God rot thee! She wants thee to make sport."

There was only one "she" for Yves, as for the men of Cahuzac, and his heart gave a great jump and then seemed to stop. He got up without a word and shambled to the trap-door, his knees shaking, and Jaufré jeered at him as he crept down the ladder.

At the door Yves stopped. Between the low lintel and the posts he saw an oblong patch of evening sky, coloured faint blue, unstained by cloud, clear and perfectly fair. He had almost forgotten that there was

249

any world but a grey dusk, and the sudden sight made his fear more unbearable. There was something in that beauty that would have protected him if only he could have got to it, but he could not. Jaufré, swearing heartily, thrust at him from behind and drove him on.

The Hall seemed just the same as on that evening when they had brought him here. He cast a fearful glance towards the fire, and saw with terror that it was burning red and fierce; then he looked for her. She was sitting, as before, at the high table, and beside her was Jehan, his long legs sprawling as he lay back in his chair and swilled his wine clumsily so that it trickled down his chin. There was another man there, Ebles the idiot, blinking and mowing, but Yves had no time to notice him.

He stopped where Jaufré bade him, and tried to keep his eyes on the ground; and Alienor of Cahuzac watched him, smiling, because she knew that he would not be able to do it. When they came up to her face, flinched away to see her watching him, and then crept back, she smiled the more.

"What is your name?" she said.

He gave a great start.

"I am no knight. I'm a landless man," he cried.

"Ah!" she said. "You have not forgot?"

He could only mutter again: "I am no knight. . . . A landless man . . . no knight."

"What is your name?" she said sharply.

"Yves. Yves Ner. But I am no –"

"Peace!" she chid him, and he was silent. "Whatever you are I remember you said ye were a jongleur. Perhaps I'll believe you if you sing better than ye did that night. If ye don't. . . ." She let her eyes wander off down the Hall, and he knew where she looked.

Ebles interrupted suddenly by clapping his hands.

"A jongleur!" he said in a high voice. "Oh! brave! Here, jongleur, eat some of my meat. Poor fellow, you look hungry."

Yves dared not move till he saw the woman nod, then he crept forward and took the meat. The idiot laughed vacantly and made faces at him while he ate it, but the Lady of Cahuzac was impatient.

250

"No more!" she said to Ebles, with a hand on his shoulder, and then curtly to Yves – "Sing!" Someone put a lute into his hands.

He did fairly well, singing softly because he had little voice, and when he had sung two songs Jehan lurched up to his feet and held out a cup.

"Drink, jongleur," he said, and when his mother snatched at his wrist he put her by.

"Let be!" he cried. "Why not? My Cousin gave meat. I give him wine."

There was a sneer in his voice when he spoke of poor Ebles, and because of that, and of his opposition, the woman turned away sullenly, biting her lips, while Yves drank uneasily, watching her from the tail of his eye.

The wine was potent; it was the spoil of the wretched Tolosain merchants who had wished for death that afternoon; and Yves was weak with fasting. When he took up the lute again he broke out into a rapid jigging dancing song that they sing at the Fairs in the Angoumois when the torches are lit round the booths, and the dark corners hide the lovers, and down the trampled lanes of the Fair the wild fellows and wilder women go reeling hand in hand. He was no troubadour now, but a drunken jongleur of the people.

It was Ebles who clamoured for more songs, and while Jehan began to fret with his feet among the rushes, Aleinor of Cahuzac kept Yves at it, but at last even she began to yawn, and breaking into the middle of a song, called loudly for Jaufré.

Yves stopped short so abruptly that a string broke with a discordant sad jar. The idiot stared about, his face puckering, then he began to cry.

"No, no," he cried in a thin, high voice as dreary as a rainy wind. "Do not let him go! I want him to stay with me and sing more and more. Many songs," and he half rose from his chair, leaning his big soft hands on the arms.

Jehan stood up.

"Take him off, Jaufré," he said, laying a hand on the idiot's shoulder. He pushed him down, and with a laugh swung out through the door.

That settled the matter. Jaufré had not moved two steps before the woman said: "Stay!" and she turned to wipe away the tears from

Eble's face with her long sleeve. When she had done, she beckoned to Yves.

"Ye've heard," she said, and he had to look at her eyes. "He wants you, so I'll have you out. But if ye don't do what he wills, in every smallest thing, or if harm comes to him – the least – then fear me!"

Yves bowed his head.

"I . . . I . . ." he stammered, "I'll do whatever he wills."

When Jaufré had fixed a rusty pair of gyves joined by a short chain about his ankles, Yves was free to shuffle after Ebles, who was delighted with his new possession. He took Yves off to the tower room, bade him sing again, and then, fortunately for Yves, fell asleep.

Whether the days that followed were worse or better than the grey time in the loft Yves would have found it hard to say. His strength came back by degrees, for foraging dogs find scraps where no one else would look, and so did he. The men, too, were sometimes sorry for him and would give him what they did not need, and Ebles was kind in his foolish way.

Strength was a clear gain, and he had escaped the monotony of those awful days which had driven him near to madness, but he paid for it in fear. There was now no moment of the day at which she might not come upon him, and she took care not to let fear die for lack of nourishment. The courtyard of Cahuzac was small; you could cross it, if your feet were not shackled, in twenty strides, but Yves, when he must go from the Hall to the stables, would keep close under the eaves of the kitchens, follow the wall of the barns where they ran back, and so, having doubled his journey, would reach the stable door. He did it because if he went thus he was not so easily seen from the room in the tower where she usually sat.

One day in spring he was set to shovel away the filth that had grown during the winter to a high, unsavoury pile before the door of the Hall. He worked slowly because it was pleasant in the sun, and because so long as he dug at the hither edge of the heap he was out of sight of the tower windows. Even when he had cleared to the ground level he went on digging, unwilling to move out into the open.

Six more idle strokes with the spade and then he would move forward, since he dared not linger too long. At the fourth, his spade struck something hard; he drew it back, thrust in again, and lifted. In the dark soil a thin, hard line showed. He looked about, stooped down fumbling with his hands, got it clear, and dropped it with a start.

No one was watching. A couple of men stood in the gateway, but their backs were turned towards him. A cripple woman, a sour creature with a face like crumpled leather, and a sharp tongue, sat in the sun with her distaff on her knees and dozed with her mouth open. There was no one else, for before daybreak Jehan had ridden out with nearly all the men to catch a company of pilgrims.

Yves stooped again and snatched up the thing. It was an old hunting-knife very rusty and without a handle; below the quillons there was a metal band – all that was left of the sheath – and from a ring in the band a thong of leather.

He tested the steel on his hands and found it still supple for all its rust. With another quick glance about he slipped the thong over his head and pushed the knife inside his tunic, pressing the cold edge against his flesh, glad at the prick of the point.

Something he had not dared to know before, had leapt, full grown, from the darkest corners of his mind. He could hate now; he could hate as much as he had feared. As he returned to the digging his hands shook and his blood was hot with fever; then he heard her voice behind him, and he grew suddenly cold.

He straightened himself, and turned to face her, since he could not bear to have her behind him. She came close and stopped a few paces from him, looking him over, while he tried to keep his eyes on the buckle of her belt, and count the holes in the long, hanging tongue. Then he lifted them and met her eyes, and the hidden knife was no weapon now for him, but only another cause of fear. It was all he could do to keep his hands from going up to hide it more securely, so he put them behind him.

"What are you going?" she said. He nodded sideways at the heap of filth.

"They told me carry it," he muttered, and shifted his feet.

She stared at him again, then turned away.

"Get on then!" she said. "Or there are stirrup leathers."

He did not even dare to watch her go, because fear must strangle hate, and if he looked, hate might break free.

He thought no more of killing her, knowing now that he could never do it, but something came into his mind instead, a hope that made the day very long. He had the knife. He would wait till darkness came, till he could hide from her so that she should not see him die, and then he would set himself free. He felt that if she saw him dying she would somehow catch his soul, and then, even dead, he would not be free.

That evening he tended the idiot with a frantic patience, was serviceable, sang when he was bidden and at last saw Ebles fall asleep in his chair. Then he slipped out, and crept down to the courtyard to find the friendly darkness, but there was none.

Jehan had not returned, and they had set a bonfire on the tower, and torches on the gate. As Yves came out of the empty Hall he saw in the shifting glow the four men whom Jehan had left, and Alienor of Cahuzac herself, wrapped in a cloak and sitting on the horseblock beside the gate. He shrank back into the shadows.

A shout, and the note of a horn came from outside. She sprang up, the men turned, staring hard into the darkness and listening. Then one pointed, another put his hands to his mouth and yelled. A faint answer came; Yves saw them snatch the two torches and move forward into the darkness.

For a moment he stared at the empty gate, then leapt forward and almost fell, having forgotten for the first time that he was hobbled like a horse. The gate was free; if he could get out of Cahuzac he could die safely, but the chain held his ankles. He stood for a moment twisting his hands together, then shuffled off towards the smith's shop. It took him perhaps three minutes in the thick and choking darkness to file and hammer and wrench the links apart, but it seemed an hour.

He had just finished when someone came to the door.

"Where are you, Yves?" said Ebles fretfully. "I never said ye to go. Are you there?"

Yves hands went up to his neck; he slipped the thong over his head and stepped forward.

Hate had broken free.

The idiot, with a small cry like the squeak of a bat, took the knife in his throat, and Yves laughed. Then fear came back. He leapt over the body and ran, blindly, making for the gate. If they had been there waiting for him he would have run straight into their arms, but the gate was clear. There were lights before him and laughter and shouting; he turned aside and bolted like a rabbit into the darkness, caring nothing how the chains lashed his ankles. Then he tripped, fell headlong, and lay still, too stunned to move.

"Stop!" cried a voice – hers. "What was that. Search, Jaufré! To the right!"

The moving lights halted, then Jehan's voice came.

"Rot thee! No! Let be. It's nonsense. Get on!"

There was a stir; the torches streamed back again; a few moments more, and the gate slammed heavily.

Yves raised himself up, and groped for the knife. He could die safe now.

XXIII

Which way I fly is hell; myself am hell;
And in the lowest deep a lower deep
Still threatening to devour me opens wide,
To which the hell I suffer seems a heaven.
O then at last relent; is there no place
Left for repentance, none for pardon left?
None left but by submission.

Paradise Lost, Bk. IV, 75–81.

THE watchman at Murat stared out into the rushing blackness of a midnight storm and was very much afraid because he had several black sins to his account. Each alternation of intolerable noise, light, and darkness shook him afresh so that he only kept his place because he dared not move. There was no need of a watchman on such a night as this, or else no use, he thought, in a longer interval of peace; and then heaven and earth were split once more with a cold live flame, and he saw before the gate a dirty, soaked, black-haired fellow, sitting on a tired horse, with nothing in his hands but a knife, and with broken ends of chain dangling from his ankles. The huge shaking flicker of the lightning lasted long enough to show all that, then darkness swallowed everything except a single shout, which was gulfed immediately by the thunder that burst overhead. The stranger was gone as though he had ceased to exist, blotted out of sight and hearing.

When the long mutter of thunder had died away his voice came again, a feeble gnat-like sound after the august anger of the heavens. He demanded to know if Eschiward the Bearded had place for another man in his band; said he had heard that Eschiward had lost two or three lately and supposed – He was interrupted by lightning so vivid and fell that he stopped for a moment, and the thunder came again. The watch, his wits all astray, let him in without further talk, forgetting any danger except that of the imminent wrath of God; but when he told the tale afterwards, no one who heard it could doubt that in those few seconds Hell itself had gaped with a horrid light, spewed forth its master, and shut again with a clang that shook the world.

"Where's your horse?" he said when Yves stood by him in the shelter of the gateway.

"Dead," said Yves. "It was of Cahuzac," he added.

The porter did not understand nor care; the beast had looked over-ridden, and anyway, it was no business of his, and no time to think clearly. The thunder shook his wits again.

Yves turned from him for a moment. The horse had served his turn. It had come up to him, riderless, its bridle trailing, as he had groped for the knife on the hillside. It must have lost its master in the fighting and followed the others home, and being scared of its loneliness it had let him catch it easily. So he got free, rode the poor beast unmercifully for three days, and now, being safe, he wiped its blood from the knife. It had been of Cahuzac.

Murat lies between Auvergne and the Limousin, in the debateable land, and conveniently near to two great roads by which travellers go about their business to and from the various parts of France, so that, being a careful man, Eschiward prospered. He sent a ring and a loyal message to Old King Henry, another ring and the same message to King Philip. The ransoms of the merchants and travellers were his chief source of wealth, and when he lacked corn and cattle he did not plunder his near neighbours, but went further afield, herded and harvested, and returned home rejoicing. He was especially careful to stand well with the holy women of Saint Radegonde at Treignac, and never hurt the hair of a cow's tail belonging to them or even to their serfs. He was therefore undisturbed by the vengeance either of Saint Radegonde or of his secular neighbours, living the life his father had taught him, a shrewd man of business, and no monster of iniquity though he lived by robbery and was sometimes as cruel as a boy. In Murat, high up in an inaccessible and barren valley, he was obeyed and followed by a mixed and disreputable band made up of a few born serfs of his own and a riff-raff of masterless men who drifted to him by uncertain chance ways.

Eschiward received the new recruit without asking many questions. It was enough for him if a man was useful and a good fighter, but Yves' new comrades were more interested. From the first he was not popular.

After a few nights they threw him out of the barn where they slept, and barred the door against him, because he would scream in his sleep and waken everyone up; and from that time onwards he had to make his bed in a rickety lean-to beside the granary.

He had been at Murat for three or four months when the story of the watchman who had let him in began to be talked over among his companions. One day three of them were discussing it in the stable.

Said one:

"I think he is, by —! The dogs are feared of him. Did ye see old Pol snarl at him this morning?"

The second man nodded but the third laughed.

"Well! If he's a devil the sooner he's away back to his place the better!"

He laughed the more because the first man crossed himself, and as he laughed, turned to reach down some harness from a peg. His hand half-way to the harness faltered and dropped, then moved in a clumsy, unaccustomed gesture. Yves, lounging in the darkest corner of the stable, was staring at him, staring and smiling. The three men went off quietly and together.

There was one among Eschiward's men who called himself Robert of Joigny. He was the practical joker of the band, a great ruffianly fellow without either malice or kindliness, and very proud of his reputation of fearlessness. His fondness for practical joking got him into trouble at times, and that autumn he was particularly unfortunate, for one of his jokes led to the burning down of a small granary, and to a sound whipping by Eschiward. As a further punishment he was told off to do servant's work for a time, to carry wood and water and such degrading services. He was not pleased.

One chilly November evening he came into the barn-like place where the band ate and slept, bearing on his shoulders the wooden yoke from which hung two buckets of water from the well. There was the usual crowd round the fire, and he looked at them mistrustfully lest they should be laughing. Then his eye fell on Yves, who, as usual, had allowed himself to be crowded out from the fire, and sat apart, his head nodding on his chest, and his eyes closed. That morning Yves, sitting on the steps of the barn, had watched Robert carrying wood, and had been witty at his expense. Robert remembered it now.

He set his burden down carefully, beckoned to the group by the fire so that they should watch, and pointed at Yves. Then he picked up one of the buckets and slung the water full at Yves' face. There was a roar of laughter. Robert of Joigny slapped his thighs and rocked backwards and forwards on his feet, laughing louder than any, as Yves leapt up, blinded and drenched, shaking the water from his eyes.

The laughter only died when Yves, without a look to any, had gone out, shutting the door softly behind him. Robert picked up the empty pail.

"I'll have to get more for that," he said, still chuckling. "But by the Mass! it was worth it." He waved his hand to the men at the fire and went out.

They found him half an hour afterwards lying on his face three paces from the door, with his own knife in his side.

"Why didn't he shout?" said someone.

"Would you shout if a man's throttling you?" cried another, and turned to look at the Hall doorway.

"He must have jumped on Robert's back as he came out. And look!" he pointed his finger at Robert's neck below his ear.

"By —" said a third, "he's mauled him with his teeth. Pulled him down like a dog with a buck!"

Someone standing in the background spoke suddenly in a high and hurried voice:

"My grandam," he said, "saw a man a devil had killed. It was in a wood she found him. The devil had bitten his throat out."

There was an unpleasant silence and then some else said:

"Let him lie here till morning. This torch is no good. It won't burn but smoky. Let's get back."

Robert of Joigny spent the night staring, indifferent and sightless, at the dark sky.

Eschiward, when he heard of the occurrence, tugged at his beard for a few moments. Then he said:

259

"Robert of Joigny was an accursed fool. That granary –" He left his sentence unfinished and that was the end of the matter.

Eschiward had good cause to be angry, for the loss of corn was serious, and made necessary a hazardous winter expedition to a manor fifteen miles away. However, the raid was successful, and they returned with a string of carts full of grain, and a dozen head of cattle into the bargain.

They got the corn in the nick of time. That afternoon a bitter, slow wind came up and brought with it sulky clouds and a sure promise of snow. The first flakes fell when they were still five miles from Murat, and by the time they reached the gates they could see only a few yards on either side, because of the blinding snow that choked the air. Eschiward saw the creaking carts in, and the oxen, then went off to the tower, well pleased with his plunder. The last man to ride in had other plunder of his own, which Eschiward did not see. Before him on the saddle, held tightly so that she could not fall or struggle away, was a woman, a pale wisp of a thing with a terrified face as grey as the darkening obscurity of snow, bareheaded, and wrapped in a cloak.

Eschiward knew nothing of this unofficial spoil till nearly a fortnight later. The snow continued to fall, night by night, so that all traces of the day's business were softly effaced, and a new world was ready for use each morning. Then for two nights there was no snow, and late in the afternoon of the second day a priest came up to the gate, called aloud for Eschiward, and was taken up to him in the tower. It was the priest of the Nuns of Saint Radegonde, a big man with a sour face and plenty of courage; the porter knew him well.

Half an hour later Eschiward, bareheaded and very red, saw him out of the gate. The priest went off with a warning gesture in place of the usual blessing, and Eschiward plunged across the yard to the tower, biting his nails, and torturing his long beard. He did not come out again till it was dark and all his people were gathered in the big building. Then he came straight to the door, stood staring into the lighted room for a moment, and at last, in a great voice as sudden and harsh as the crash of a falling tree, he cried: "Which of ye have ravished this nun?"

All the noise ceased, and every head turned towards the door. Eschiward pulled out his sword with a rattle and swish.

"By Saint Radegonde, and by all the devils of hell I'll have it out of ye! Which of ye did it? Answer!"

A man sitting by the fire jumped up quickly and edged towards the door, with a glance over his shoulder. He had been Robert of Joigny's friend.

"I know," he said. "I know. I saw him. He brought her in. The night we came back from the raid. We passed three nuns on the road –"

Eschiward broke in.

"Fool! I know all that, and so do they. Who was it?"

The man swung round and pointed.

"It was Yves Ner. I saw him bring her in. He rode back after we'd passed them."

Yves got up slowly and Eschiward turned to him.

"Is it true?" he said and jerked a thumb towards the other man.

"It's true," said Yves. "But what of it?"

"What of it?" cried Eschiward. "Do I want Saint Radegonde for an enemy, and their curses on me? You fool! You fool! May your soul rot! I said the priest it was a lie, but they won't believe. I said it was one of Red Guilhem's men did it, but they'll put their curses on me and I'll never prosper. Where is she now?"

Yves shrugged.

"Ask otherwhere. She said next day she'd rather have an ape than me, so I turned her out to the others. Ask them!"

"It's sacrilege! And Saint Radegonde will never forgive!" Eschiward's veins swelled and his face grew redder. "It's sacrilege! By God's Blood! I'll have yours, ye slinking, evil ruffian! If ye don't fear God nor Saint Radegonde ye'll fear me. I'll soon know if ye're a devil as they say. Yea, by —! I'll see how ye like the fire!"

"Fire?" – Yves jerked the word out, and his voice cracked. Then he flung himself down before Eschiward, clasped his knees, and burst out with a torrent of arguments and desperate pleadings.

It was surprising how eloquent he could be, and how cogent were his reasons. The snow had covered all tracks that day so that they could not know for certain. If Eschiward denied it stoutly they would believe him because he was always dutiful to Saint Radegonde, but if he admitted it they would blame him for every mishap ever after. As for himself –

261

he was a poor fellow not worth ... not worth spending time and trouble over ... but he could be useful ... he would do anything Eschiward bade him do ... anything! And if Eschiward thought to make his peace with the Saint by ... by ... in that way, there were others had committed the sacrilege as well as he. He knew which of them had had her since. What would Eschiward do with them?"

Eschiward listened, growling in his beard. He looked down at Yves disgustfully, for he himself had never learnt how to be afraid. Then he cuffed him away.

"Get up, you swine!" he said. "And get away!"

Yves slipped past him, and out into the yard.

The dark had fallen, but no snow. Instead of the blank clouds that had blinded each night since the snow first fell, the sky was clear, and the moon had risen in a vague mist which diffused rather than dimmed her light. As Yves came out of the Hall the great vast of cold light and cold clean air closed over him as though he had dived deep into clear water. It was very silent, too, as it always is with heavy snow. The noise coming from the Hall behind knocked on the door of the great silence but could not enter. Yves stood perfectly still for a moment, pulled up by the physical shock of cold, and by another shock which he did not yet understand. Then he moved on, stepping softly; the snow under his feet made no sound except a little crunch and squeak. Without looking to left or right he made straight for the stockade, for there was something outside which he must see. It was everywhere outside and nowhere within, but he did not know yet what it was.

When he reached the stockade he laid his hands on the top and looked over, while the snow fell away and melted under his fingers. Then he saw what he had come to see – the night, all alone by itself.

The moon stood in the colourless sky behind him; the stars were thick, and the laden trees at the foot of the slope stood out clear yet veiled; the hooded, waiting shapes of the hills had only a light mist on them. All these things he could see, and yet there was only one thing – the night, all alone by itself.

As he stood there his mind seemed to crumble into confusion as suddenly as a breaking wall, and left him in an immense quietude in which there was no thought, only something which stirred and groped, while he clung to the stockade as a drowning man to his spar. Then, but not through the sight of his eyes, came knowledge. It seemed at first like a little wind that wakened in his mind, a mere breath, less than the least wind of summer, and it soothed and consoled him. His eyes rested, and contentment grew. Here was no more fear, nor hate, nor the ache of anger, but peace, refuge, surety, and kindness. Here he need not fear Eschiward, he need not fear himself. Himself! That was the fear – what he was now, and what he would be soon.

The peace was gone – shattered to fragments. He knew himself, and he knew the refuge to which he had yearned. It was the breast of the Hunter.

For a time he stood still, and the moonlight took all colour from his face, so that he seemed rather a dead man watching the kindly doings of the living, than a living man staring at the emptiness of the night. Then he turned back from the stockade. He dared not surrender. A hell of self-torture lay that way, and the intolerable pain of love. He dared not, and he must escape, but his only refuge was the other hell. So it was. Hell lay either way, but to one he must climb, to the other he need only fall.

He crossed the yard towards the shed where he slept, walking slowly since no speed would save him now. At the door he stopped, for just inside, in the shadow, the woman who had been a nun was waiting. She came forward, peering into his face.

"I have come back," she said at last, and smiled horribly at him.

He stepped back.

"And why?" he said. "Do I want other men's leavings? Get out of my way!"

She did not move till he was close to her, then she caught his hands.

"No. It's not that . . . but I came. . . . You've a knife. I'll shut my eyes. I won't scream." Her throat jerked, and she stopped.

Yves shook her off.

"Why come to me?" he said.

"Because . . . I know you don't want. . . . And they say you kill for sport." Her voice grew shriller and more frantic. "I've been a nun ten years," she cried. "I've been clean. Ah! Holy Mother of God! Pure

263

Virgin! Your knife. . . . Make me clean again. . . . I won't scream. As you hope for pardon!"

"Pardon?" said Yves stupidly. "And if I do not?"

She misunderstood him.

"Ah! Only one stroke. I will not move. You must. You will. Oh! if you do not, surely God will turn His face from you!"

Yves' head went back as though from the threat of a blow.

"Ha!" he cried wildly. "Will He? Is it so easy? Is it? Away then! I'll not kill you."

He pushed past her, slammed the rickety door, and shot the bolt. Alone in the chill dark he flung himself face downwards, and bit his fingers till the blood dripped through them into the straw.

XXIV

If I go down to hell, Thou art there also.
Psalm cxxxix.

ON the afternoon of the day which Eschiward the Bearded chose for his first foray of the spring season, two knights sat together in a comfortable tower room in the castle of Puy Saint Guilhem on the borders of the Limousin, drinking their wine at leisure, and talking of this and that. Roho of Puy Saint Guilhem was an old man, but strong enough still to carry his armour. His face was melancholy except when he spoke or smiled, his cheeks were deeply channelled and sunken, but when he laughed his face folded into humorous wrinkles from which his eyes looked out, mischievous and delighted. He sat now staring at the floor and slowly twirling his thumbs together.

His companion was a much younger man, very tall, with great shoulders, a broad bronzed face, and a pair of very calm and honest light blue eyes, bleached by the sun and puckered about with tiny wrinkles. He was talking while Lord Roho listened; telling tales of the Holy Land and of the happenings there during the last seven years or so, and in particular of the doings of Baudouin of Puy Saint Guilhem, Lord Roho's younger brother.

"Nay. Did he so really?" said Puy Saint Guilhem, and laughed as the other paused and sipped his wine. "That's a good tale. I'll remember it." He chuckled again, and then looked straight at the younger man.

"And so, Messire Pons," he said, "when ye've pledged Jarnac to your brother ye'll return. But what will the two Counts in Angoulême say to that?"

"They will not care," replied Pons. "In truth they . . . they do not love me much. When I came back, four years ago, I had words. . . ." He paused and stared absently out of the window. "Nay," he roused himself, "they will not care. They had rather my brother held Jarnac than I." He paused again, and laughed as though he was a trifle embarrassed, then turned to the older man.

"Lord Roho," he said, "did you ever in all France hear of a man called Yves of Rifaucon?"

Roho considered for a moment in silence.

"Nay," he said at last, "I cannot remember him. What like was he?"

"A small man . . . short and strong . . . black-haired. But he should be known, because Guiraut of Cabreira taught him to rhyme and sing. . . . But though I have asked. . . . Have ye never heard nor seen him?"

Roho shook his head again.

"Nay . . . Nay," he said.

Pons seemed to think some explanation necessary.

"He was my friend in Angoulême. When I went back he was gone. Guilhem – you know him – he's a hard man, and he had – Ah! well. It's an ill tale." He frowned. "It was over that we had words," he added.

Roho looked at him keenly, twinkling and yet serious.

"Ye're a good friend, Pons of Jarnac!" he said.

Pons blushed all over his face.

"Na! Na!" he protested. "But I. . . . We were brothers in arms. We swore it on the pyx."

He turned again to the window and sank into a reverie, forgetting his half-empty cup. Lord Roho drank his wine in small sips, savouring it, and watching with his keen and kindly eyes Pons' thoughtful face.

There was a sudden trampling of feet on the stairs, and a man-at-arms burst in.

"Lord," he cried, "if it please you there's rievers broke in – two score or more, and mounted. Down by Seven Springs they are."

Lord Roho stood up a trifle stiffly.

"Peire, my lad," he said. "It does not please me. I do not see well why it should," and he turned to Pons laughing, his face crumpling up into kindly merriment, and his faded eyes gay. Pons rose slowly, but he said nothing, and waited while Roho went over to a window and leaned out.

"Holà! below there!" cried Roho. "Make ready! Saddle in haste! Arm all!" He swung round again on Peire as brisk as a boy.

"Send Raoul to arm me," he said, then turned to beam at Pons. "Sit down again. This is only a brush. I will be back within the hour. There

266

will never be two score of them. Twenty maybe, and their shadows. Sit down."

Pons shook his head. His slow voice caught Peire at the door.

"Send my esquire too – and my arms."

Puy Saint Guilhem laughed, shrugged, and rubbed his hands together. He went back to the window, and leaning as far out as he could, he shouted up to the watchman above:

"Keep a watch on Magpie Hill!" he cried, his voice sounding strange and far away to Pons. "Blow the horn if you see anything move there." He drew in his head and came back into the room. "If they come there," he explained, "we must out as we are, ready or no, or they'll have the corn, and we the famine."

They armed as quickly as possible. Puy Saint Guilhem, glaring round as his head came out through the neck of his mailed shirt, saw Pons' half-empty wine-cup.

"Ah!" he said. "The wine! Better drink it before we go."

"No time," said Pons, slipping his hands into the leather-palmed, chain-backed gloves, while he bent his head for the squire to pull the mail hood over it. "I'll drink it when we come back. I'll be thirstier." He laughed softly. "And it's too good a wine to haste over."

A noise very much like the braying of a donkey, only of a deeper note, filled the room. It was the watchman on the tower blowing his cow-horn.

"Lo! There!" cried Puy Saint Guilhem, snatching up his sword and shield and leaping for the door. "We must go."

Pons looked about to see that he had everything, slipped the shield strap over his head, and picked up his steel cap.

"I can fit that on myself. No time for the big helm." He nodded to the squire and was gone, charging down the narrow stairs like a bull, so that he caught Puy Saint Guilhem at the bottom.

As they rode out Lord Roho turned quickly to him.

"You said?" he asked.

Pons laughed.

"Nay. I was singing. . . . It's more like a raven, I know."

The old man laughed too. "I thought . . ." he began and Pons nodded.

"Ye might well." He began to croak softly to himself again, and then broke off to say: "It was a thing that man Yves of Rifaucon was always singing. It was an old tune – I don't know what. He put words to it about the Old Count Guilhem, and he would sing it everywhere. 'Twas not courteous to the Count neither, and he – I mean the old man – was ever listening at doors. Still, he never heard it, or if he did he cared nothing. . . . A strange man." He smiled at his memories and was silent.

A few moments later Lord Roho saw him cross himself carefully three times.

"That is done!" said Pons cheerfully.

Roho nodded.

"I'd forgot. A man never knows his hour." He bent his head for a moment; then looked about him and pointed forward.

"There they are!" he cried. The man who had watched upon the tower blew his horn like mad, till the whole quiet countryside seemed full of the absurd and heart-rending lament.

"It's an homely trumpeter," Roho shouted to Pons in the midst of the din, as they quickened their horses. Pons only turned his head and smiled.

The two lines met with a shock, steel ground on steel, men shouted, and now and then a horse would scream shrilly in pain, anger, or terror. Puy Saint Guilhem was no general. He knew only, as his father had known before him, to ride at the enemy and strike and strike, till one line or the other broke; so the battle was nothing but a random confusion of blows.

Pons had a long sword and a long arm. He fought in a business-like way, guarding his head well with the black shield of Jarnac, feinting often, and when he did hit, hitting very hard. His strokes seemed never to be hurried, never to fall too late, and never to miss their mark, so that for the most part he kept a little space clear about himself.

Out of the confusion a fresh enemy came at him – a short, broad-shouldered man riding a big grey. He bore no shield, but used his sword so that he hardly needed one. Pons stiffened as he felt the jar of sword on sword, for this was to be a fight. Their eyes had grappled and each had struck and guarded before Pons' straining gaze changed.

268

His sword checked in the middle of its swing, and he dropped his shield.

"Yves! Stop! I'm Pons. Stop!" he cried above all the din, and even as he cried, saw recognition come into Yves' face, then blank fear, then a desperate fury.

With a little grunt Yves struck upwards, stabbing with the point.

Pons saw the shining thing leap at him like a snake. It caught him full in the mouth between gorget and nasal, tore through teeth and throat and brain, and drove him down through roaring pain into utter darkness. . . .

So ended that very noble and true knight Pons of Jarnac, lord of el Amar in the kingdom of Jerusalem; and Yves' horse trampled on over him in the press.

Not three minutes after Pons fell the skirmish was ended. Eschiward had his left arm slashed so that he bled like a pig, and slackened his strokes. Most of his men were wounded, four were down among the horses' hoofs, and if not dead already, at all events as good as dead. So, rumbling curses, he must needs draw off, and what was worse must leave the cattle, already well on their way to the hills under the charge of three men, to fall again into the hands of their owners. The only chance now to save the whole band from destruction lay in reaching a narrow grassy valley which wound up into the hills; once there, he would have Puy Saint Guilhem at a disadvantage. He gave the signal to draw back, the remains of the band shook themselves free, scattered wide according to orders, and hurled themselves up the slight slope towards safety.

Behind the irregular line came a single man – Yves of Rifaucon. He rode with his eyes fixed before him, staring at nothing, though the pursuers were only a few yards behind. He did not turn because he dare not. In front of him danced the face of Pons of Jarnac with a gap where his pleasant mouth had been, and he could not take his eyes from it.

There was an ash tree ahead, a couple of hundred yards before the valley walls began. He could see it as he looked aside, and Pons' face jogging about in front of it. He tried to look through the face and see only the tree, and as he rode he muttered to himself again and again:

"I will not turn. I'll get to that tree and pass it. I will not turn. When I've passed it I will not turn."

He reached and passed it at a gallop, and then, seizing his reins with both hands he hauled on the bit. The horse shied, plunged, and maddened by the wicked spurs that tore his sides, swung round, and fled full at Puy Saint Guilhem's men. They were slackening already, for they saw the danger of chasing Eschiward up that narrow space, and Yves was on them before they could draw together. He went through them yelling, his sword whirling about his head; only one man tried to stop him, and went down with Yves' sword grinding through bone and brain.

When he reached the place where the fight had been, there was neither sight nor sound of any pursuer. They had not troubled to turn after one man who was probably either mad or a fiend. The green meadow was very quiet, and the trampled muddy grass, and five or six sprawling bodies alone showed that it had ever been otherwise. The only sound came from one of these bodies – an occasional whimpering cry, like that of a neglected child.

Yves dismounted, tied stirrup and reins together to keep the horse, and crossed the field, peering at each of the untidy figures which lay in that utter abandonment which is so different from the repose of sleep. He looked at two of them, then went over towards another, but before he reached it he knew, and came up walking stealthily, though his feet made no sound on the grass.

It was Pons, who, lying on his back, grinned up at Yves through that bloody gap, and glared past him with sightless and staring eyes; yet all that Yves felt was relief. The face was less terrible than that shadow which had danced before his eyes ever since he struck the dolorous stroke. Pons, even so mangled – and Yves' eyes slipped away from the red ruin he had made – Pons was too familiar to fear, too dear to hate. Yves' thought swung strangely round to the opposite pole.

He sat down by Pons, laid a hand on his breast to feel if there were any stir of life there, though he knew well there could not be, and then, drawing his knees up to his chin, he clasped his hands about them, and fixed his eyes on the ground beside Pons' head. His sword still hung from the strap about his wrist, and he began idly to poke at the daisy roots with the point, because, if he watched that, it was easier to keep his eyes from the face.

Sitting there he felt strangely happy, sheltered now, because so near to Pons, no longer alone but comraded once more, and so his thoughts slipped back into long unfrequented ways, and to the old times at Angoulême – Pons' favourite hawk, and what a business they had had to choose a name for it; a morning at tilting when Pons had sneezed just as they met and missed his stroke badly; a day when Yves had taken Pons' horse to the farrier, and Pons had been grateful – the pleasant, sad, inconsequent memories drifted through his brain, and he forgot that Pons was dead, because he seemed so near.

He had so utterly lost himself that he actually turned to speak.

"Do you –" he began, but the sound of his own voice in the silence woke him. Pons was dead. That meant that he was gone – would never come back. Yves' eyes flinched away from the face, then with a gasp, as though someone had planted a knife in his back, he staggered up to his feet.

"You kept me here! Out on you! Untrue! You kept me, to let Him creep up behind!" he cried, and standing over Pons, he kicked the poor head. It rolled slowly over, so that Pons seemed to turn from him, patiently and without anger. That was horrible, but it was not the worst.

A hand fell on his shoulder. He stood perfectly still because he could not move, and because he could not scream he was silent.

"Oh! man of blood," said a human voice.

It freed him. He swung round and saw a monk, a small, shabby man with a straggling beard and a pinched face, who gave him back look for look. In his hand he carried the pale silver of the Pyx.

Yves saw it, and saw his way of escape. He leapt back, catching at the sword that dangled from his wrist.

"You have Him there?" he cried. "Then He'll not hunt me again!"

He struck, laughing like a madman. The blow almost fell short, but the point caught and shattered the Pyx. Yves looked down at the ruin on the ground, the torn silver, the flakes of bread, and the dwindling pool of wine.

"He's dead," he mumbled, and raised his eyes. When he tried to free

271

them he could not. The monk's face was perfectly still, but it was not calm.

"Fool! He died once –" the monk began, but Yves broke in.

"No! . . . but He must turn back now. . . . He'll not hunt me now. . . . I've tired Him out."

The monk's eyes changed. He stepped forward and caught Yves by the wrist.

"I told you before. I told you years back. He never tires. He has you now . . . This is the mort."

Yves stood perfectly still till the monk released his wrist. Then, moving very cautiously like a man in extreme physical pain who must keep every muscle rigid, he raised both hands and covered his face.

The monk saw his throat work, but neither sound nor word came for a moment. He waited.

"Yea . . ." said Yves.

XXV

Saviour. "That is all: If that I could
Get without repining
And my Clay, my Creature would
Follow My resigning –
That as I did freely part
With My glory and desert
Left all joys to fell all smart – "

Man. "Ah! no more, Thou break'st my heart!"

GEORGE HERBERT.

WHEN the monk had gathered up the broken Pyx and the scattered fragments of the bread, he went about the field to each of the still figures, but he never took his eyes for long from Yves, standing quite still with his face covered. The one man still alive – his whimpering was weaker now – took five minutes more to die; then the monk came back to Yves, and touched him on the shoulder. Yves took his hands from his face.

"Leave me," he said, and shuddered.

"No. Come with me. This is no place to stay."

"I will not," said Yves, and hid his face again.

"Come!" said the monk. He took Yves' arm and brought him to the horse. "Lead the animal," he said. "And follow me."

Yves moved to obey, then checked suddenly, his head twisted stiffly over his shoulder.

"Pons!" he said.

The monk held on as though he had not heard that pitiful, lost cry, and after a moment Yves turned and followed him.

They left the open country and plunged into the woods. The pale, bright beech leaves were full out on some branches, on others the buds were bursting like little pointed green flames from the dainty upturned tips of the twigs. They mounted higher. The woods grew bare, a mere veil of branches except where the polished holly, shining against the

273

sun, seemed to be covered with white flowers. At last the trees failed, and they came out on the bare slopes below the jagged heights, and half a mile further on, to the mouth of a cave.

The monk took the bridle from Yves and began to unsaddle the horse. Yves stood still, not even raising his eyes, and the monk, after a quick glance, began to talk. He knew that Yves was not paying the least attention to what he said, but in some gulfs the mere sound of a human voice is a slight comfort.

"This is where I come at times . . . when I want to be alone. . . . Like the holy Peter Damiani . . . his 'sweet solitude.' " He was silent a moment, loosening the girth.

"Eymoutiers is over there . . ." he went on, with a nod towards the sun. "Yea. . . . I've been abbot since then . . . how long? Ten years . . . nay, more." He tethered the horse neatly, laid his hand on Yves' shoulder and led him into the cave.

The inside was very bare. The floor, dusty and dead white like ashes, was swept clean. There was a bed of bracken in one corner, a three-legged stool, a blackened patch in the ground ringed with stones, with a pitcher standing near, and one thing beside: a small carved crucifix – ivory on ebony, the work of some Greek craftsman – hanging on the wall.

The monk picked up the stool, set it by the wall beneath the Crucifix and sat down. He reached up one hand and took the crucifix from its nail. With the other he pointed at the ground before him.

"Kneel here, my son," he said.

Yves knelt down stiffly, and turned his head half away. The monk watched him a moment, compassionate, then he spoke.

"Sic enim Deus dilexit mundum," he said. "So God loved the world," and he held the crucifix before Yves' eyes.

Yves flinched from it with a cry like that of a man who, racked already to the last limit of endurance, is torn by another sudden and appalling wrench. "Ah!" he cried, "that is the worst –" Then he began his confession.

That night the monk watched, and when the sun rose he wakened Yves.

274

"Get up," he said, "and eat."

Yves ate, because he dared not disobey, and the monk watched him, and saw in the cold daylight how last night's work had marked his face.

"I will tell you your penance," he said at last, and did not miss the brightening in Yves' eyes, raised heavily to his.

"The scourge?" said Yves, and looked round the cave.

The monk frowned. "No!" he said. "I've known Penance eat up Penitence that way. I'll have ye do something harder than to kill yourself with that thing . . . and ye would. . . . I saw last night."

He paused a moment. He was taking the greatest risk among all the risks of life – the direction of another man's soul – and he felt hell beneath his feet.

"Do this –" he said at last, and there was no hesitation in his voice. "Get you away to Count Richard. I heard the other day that he was in the Lusignan lands. He is vowed to the Crusade since Christmas, and I think he's the one lord in Europe is sure to go. Go to him, wherever he is, and say this – 'For the pity of God, and as you hope for His mercy, give me the Cross. . . .' Then tell him what you've told me." There was silence. Then at last:

"That is no penance!" cried Yves; but his desperate anger died before the monk's eyes. He held out his hands. "Give me the scourge. Something!" he muttered, but when the monk made no answer he turned away, and went out to saddle his horse.

When Yves was ready the monk came out, and as Yves knelt, gave him the blessing. Yves took it stonily, then turned to mount.

"Stop!" cried the monk, and Yves, turning back, saw that his face was terrible. "Where are your spurs?" The question came at him as fierce as the point of a sword. "Give them to me."

Yves was silent for a moment.

"I must have them. . . . Let me have them . . . it's a small pain. . . . I need it," he said, but while he protested he drew them out of the breast of his tunic and handed them to the monk.

"Coward!" cried the monk and threw them away down the slope. Yves heard them tinkle on the stones and turned almost as if he would go after them.

"I am . . . in hell," he said, but the monk did not soften.

"And you will still run away?" he cried. "Nor abide His forgiving, and the pain of it? It's ease you'll have, and try to miss your punishment?"

He saw a dumb answer in Yves' eyes, and his voice changed.

"Wait!" He turned into the cave and was back in a moment. "Here is something will prick you worse than any spur."

He saw Yves wince as he took the little crucifix and slipped it inside his tunic. Before Yves had reached the trees, the monk was kneeling in the cave, stripped to his shirt. In his hand the scourge whistled and fell, and as he laboured he prayed for a soul in pain.

For three days, from the time the gates were opened in the cool morning, till the time they were shut at soft dusk, Yves sat in the courtyard of the castle of Niort, waiting his chance to speak to Count Richard. Each day Yves saw him pass, sometimes more than once in the day, but he was never able to make himself heard among the crowd of beggars, monks, merchants, and petitioners of all sorts who swarmed about the Count whenever he went in or out. Yves always found himself pushed to the outskirts of the noisy crowd, and as he was too tired to raise his voice, or indeed to make any effort, he just waited for Richard to see him.

On the third day Richard did see him. Yves, staring at him over the heads of the crowd, felt the Count's eyes fix suddenly on his face, and for a moment, as if there had been no one else there, he and Richard looked at each other. Then Richard lifted his hand and pointed.

"I know you," he said slowly, half remembering, and pushed his horse towards Yves, leaving the crowd to save itself from the trampling hoofs. When he was close he pulled up, and sat still in the saddle, staring down at Yves.

"Yea. I know you," he said, and this time he meant that he had remembered all.

"Lord Count –" began Yves, but Richard did not stay to listen.

"Go up into the Hall there," he said sharply, jerking his head towards a flight of steps. "Wait there for me. I'll finish these fellows' business first."

Yves waited for a quarter of an hour, and then Richard came in with

276

a score or so of knights. The Count went straight up to the end of the Hall and flung himself down in a big chair, his long legs and long sword thrust out before him. He looked around and saw Yves, sitting on a bench beside the wall.

"Yves of Rifaucon!" he called in a great voice, and Yves got up and stood before him, but when he would have spoken Richard checked him with a raised hand, and for a long time sat silent, staring. Richard of Poitou was honest, and except in anger or desire, he feared God; he feared now, when he saw Yves' face and remembered the song which he had sung.

"I should have known you anywhere," he said at last. "But you're –" He broke off and began again. "I am glad you have come . . . that is, if –" Once more he did not finish, and those standing about began to wonder why the Count was so strangely tongue-tied with this silent and cowed-looking fellow.

"Why have you come?" said Richard, forcing the words.

Yves lifted his head.

"You go on Crusade," he said, and Richard's face lit.

"Yea!" he said, and looked about as though his army stood before him, ready to march.

"He . . . the monk . . ." said Yves, "he told me of it and he bade me come here and ask in the name of God's Pity – that is what he said – and as you hope for mercy to let me . . . to give me the Cross."

Richard broke in, his voice high with excitement.

"You shall come with me, Yves of Rifaucon! Yea, by God's Throat!" He sprang from his chair and throwing his arms round Yves' neck would have kissed him, but Yves pushed him back.

"That is not all," he said and some wakening pain in the dull voice checked Richard.

"No!" said the Count. "No more . . . let be . . . no more!" but Yves took no notice of him.

"He said I must tell you . . . and I desire it . . . but it's hard to speak. But I desire it . . . and to these lords too."

Before he could say more Richard caught him by the arm and shook him.

"No! I say, No! Am I a priest that I should hear? And as for these –

277

I'll not have it." He turned fiercely on the silent crowd. "Go! Leave me. Don't stay here to gape. Go!"

When they had gone he dropped Yves' arm and went back to his chair. He spoke in a changed and troubled voice.

"Perhaps you had best tell me."

He listened with his hand shading his eyes, and when Yves finished, and turned his face away from the light of the windows, there was silence.

Richard stood up, hesitated, then came quickly to Yves and putting his arms once more about his neck, kissed him on both cheeks.

"Ah! Yves," cried the Count, and caught him by the shoulders. "Ah! Yves, Yves, Yves," and broke off. Yves looked up at him, and saw that his face was wet with tears.

"These sins –" cried Richard suddenly. "These sins are mine."

Yves shook so much that he could hardly stand, and caught at the Count's arm.

"It is not so," he said.

"But yea!" persisted Richard. "You sang it."

"Nay," cried Yves wildly. "I chose my way after that. You had no part nor lot in it . . . only I."

Richard turned away with a sigh and stood a moment. Then he swung round again.

"Listen to me!" he said. "I'd have given you Rifaucon before, and ye would not. Take it now. Raymond that had it is dead without child, and it's escheated to me. See, I give it you." He held out his hands with the same wide and lavish gesture that Yves remembered. "You must take it, or I'll have these sins for ever on my soul," he added.

"No, no," said Yves desperately, catching at his wits that seemed to be leaving him in a blank of weariness. "My sins are mine."

Richard came close again.

"But you'll have Rifaucon. I'll take no nay."

Yves said nothing, and that was enough for Richard. He swung off to the door, and threw it clattering back against the wall.

"Ho!" he roared. "Come in to me. You, Guilhem! Jaufré, find me Messire Hugues Archevesque, and Guy of Thouars – and the steward.

. . . Get me ten witnesses or so, and a clerk of my chancery. Oh! thou art there – good!"

He strode back into the room and waved the clerk to a place at the table. "Sit there," he said, "and write quickly."

The clerk took out pen, ink-horn, parchment, and thin-bladed sharp knife.

"Oh! hasten," said the Count. "Now write."

The clerk looked up sidelong. "What shall I write?" he said.

"Throat of God!" cried Richard. "Am I to teach thee? The usual thing – 'Ricardus Comes Pictavie –'"

The clerk still paused, his pen balanced fastidiously over the virgin parchment. "Is it to be charter, or letter patent or close?" he said calmly.

"Oh! Charter! Charter!" said Richard and laughed.

The monk fell to writing, laboured with pursed lips for a few moments, then stopped.

" 'Sciatis quod,' " he read aloud. "What now, Lord Count?"

"Know that I have given the fief of Rifaucon to Yves of Rifaucon. . . . Make it out in the best way . . . full fee simple. . . . As ye know – roads and paths, pools and fisheries . . . all the rest. Was there –" he turned on Yves, "was there aught beside Rifaucon?"

Yves stammered at the sudden question.

"A . . . a . . . a matter of some manors. He . . . my father had bought them just before – I have forgot . . . I never knew well what they were."

"Hm!" said Richard. "But how many, say? Five, ten, twenty?"

"It was five as I think," said Yves.

Richard pondered a minute, tugging at his beard.

"Write down the fief of Scorbé Clairvaux," he said to the clerk.

Yves was too deadly weary to resist. He was slipping down into a state of dull indifference to which there came no more than the echoes of all the trouble and desire of life. Every scratch of the clerk's pen was giving him back Rifaucon, and it meant nothing to him.

The Count's voice roused him again. Richard was angry.

"Why have you not the wax? By God's Cross! Am I to come after you with your wax and your parchment and your cords? If you've no green, then use red wax or white, but keep me no longer."

279

The clerk turned calmly. He was not afraid, because he knew that a good clerk, used to chancery ways, was rarer and more precious by far than a good knight. Besides, he belonged by rights to King Henry's chancery.

"The King your father, Lord Count," he said, "will have all his charters sealed green now-a-days. If there were a question the charter might be set aside as –"

Richard took him up, fiercer than ever.

"Set aside? And who will set it aside? My writ runs in Poitou even now, and when my father dies (God keep him), who'll set it aside in France or overseas?"

"All kings die. Every one," said the clerk.

Richard was answered.

"Well!" he said. "Get your wax! Get it! But –" as the clerk rose Richard bore down on him, "get it quick!"

The clerk lost his feeling of security, and judged it best to hurry, so that there was nothing dignified in his passage to the door. Richard watched him fiercely with his head thrust forward, then threw up his chin and laughed like a boy. When the door shut he turned to Yves.

"How is seisin given?" he said, and Yves had to wake to answer.

"By a key."

"And the service?"

"Five knights and ten cheeses and a white foal every fifth year," said Yves, repeating something he had known so well that he need not think what he was saying.

Richard looked over his shoulder to a man standing near.

"And two and a half knights from Scorbé Clairvaux. Is that right, Robert of Montmirail?"

"And two hunting dogs, Lord Count. And seisin given by a straw."

"Good!" said Richard. "Send someone to fetch a key and a straw. He turned back to Yves. "Fair friend," he said, "wait for us a while till our clerk comes back," and waved him aside.

Yves went over to a window and sat down there. The room was full of noise and stir but he was outside it, and his mind drifted, catching now and then at scraps of conversation. Near by a young knight was being chaffed about a woman. Her name was Alais, and she was fond of wearing blue. So much Yves heard, then forgot to listen. Someone else complained bitterly that ten of the draught oxen had died of the murrain in one of his villages, and the serfs had not been able to finish the ploughing. He began to reckon how much he stood to lose at harvest time, but there Yves lost him. Some time after he heard Richard talking with a stockish man with black bristling hair. It was something about the rights over a mill, and the grant of a Fair. Yves could not hear all the bristle-haired man said, but it was clear that Richard was haggling like a Jew. Yves did not hear the end of it, and started when he found an esquire standing by him. He understood after a moment that Richard waited for him, and went up obediently where the esquire led him.

Richard stood, very tall and splendid in his lion-embroidered surcoat, having cast off his scarlet cloak upon the chair behind. Yves came to him, dragging his feet like a for-wearied man. Through all the ceremony he did not once raise his eyes higher than the Count's knees. He took the key that was Rifaucon, and repeated the words of homage. Then came the straw that was Scorbé Clairvaux. He took that as dully, and went through the same formula. Then the Count stepped down and kissed him on the cheek, the clerk thrust into his hand an oblong, neatly creased piece of parchment with a dangling seal of green on woven silk cords of red, green and yellow, and it was all over. He was lord of Rifaucon and of Scorbé Clairvaux, and still he stood silent before Richard; and those who were witnesses watched him curiously and waited.

In some things Richard was as discerning as a woman; moreover he had heard Yves' confession and understood. So, while everyone wondered, and Yves stood stock still and as silent as a log, Richard went close to him again, and though the Count neither touched him, nor spoke, Yves had to look up.

"Go now and sleep," said Richard slowly. "Go and sleep."

Yves nodded.

"Raoul!" cried the Count to a page, "take Messire Yves to a room where he may sleep. Find the chamberlain and bid him see to it."

As Yves followed the boy, all turned their heads to watch him. Then the door closed; all heads turned back to Count Richard, and the business of the day went on.

Outside the door he saw Audiart. She was waiting for him, for she rose as he came out, laying down the pages' dice with which she had been fidgeting.

He stopped with his back to the door, and did not look at her face after the first glance, but kept his head bent, waiting for her to speak. He feared her as a wounded man fears rough handling, and she could hurt him more than any other could, but escape was impossible.

She looked at him a moment. His eyes, when they met hers, had seemed dead, his face was lined and shrunk, and as she looked she saw grey in his black hair.

"I must speak to you," she said; then, pitifully afraid, in spite of the change in him, she hurried on. "Only a moment . . . I pray you. If you will follow me."

He wished to escape, but all he said was:

"Yes, Domna. Where you will."

"Wait here!" she said to the page, and led Yves away to a little room, an odd angle between a passage, the wall, and one of the towers. It was too small for general use, but there was a chair in it with green silk cushions, and one narrow window with a very wide splay in the huge thickness of the wall, which gave a small strip of view to the hills opposite, over which came, more stately than great ships, some high-piled white clouds.

Yves shut the door after him and waited, and it seemed to her that he would never lift his head again. Then because she must say what she had brought him there to hear, she began to speak, hurriedly, since her breath was so short.

"Messire," she said. "I did not mean – last time – I said I'd not forgive. I was mad. There was nothing to forgive. . . . It was I. Forgive me! Oh!" she cried, and wrung her hands together, "do not be angry again. . . . I mean no unkindness. . . ."

He wanted to open the door and go, because pain was coming back like a great tide that runs in before a wind, but he could not move.

"Domna," he said, fixing his eyes on her hands, strained together so

282

that the knuckles were white, "you must not distress yourself for me. You were right . . . always . . . what you said was . . . it was nothing to what I . . ." He stopped for a moment, and suddenly began to tell her what he had told Richard.

She heard him to the end, and then without a moment's pause she said in a harsh voice:

"What is it to me what you've done?"

It was so cruel, and so just, that he was dumb until he forced himself to speak.

"I know it," he said. "I know. . . . Why should you care? I did not think . . . indeed. . . . No . . . I did not . . ." he stumbled into silence.

Suddenly and without any warning she dissolved into terrible tears, crossing her arms over her breast as if she feared that the sobs were too strong for her body to bear. Then as he watched, horrified and amazed, she groped backwards to the chair, and crumpled into it, crouching forward and rocking herself to and fro, her face quivering and the tears running unheeded down her cheeks, far too distraught to make any attempt to hide her weeping.

"Domna!" cried Yves. "Alas! Don't . . . don't . . . Why? What have I said. . . .?"

She sobbed for a while, then tried to check herself and began to speak, but the sobs broke in and made the words incoherent.

"All these years . . . and I had . . . said that . . . and . . . I thought I might . . . never see you . . . again." She raised her head and looked at him, her whole face quivering, and the last words came out very clear but hurried. "Oh! child! . . . child . . . poor child . . . you're hurt."

That was worse than the most cruel justice.

"What do you mean?" he cried. "You hated me . . . you always . . . ."

Her crying stopped suddenly.

"Hated?" she whispered. "I loved you."

Yves broke the long silence to ask a question. With all the intelligence left him he had been trying to understand, trying to believe, and remembering everything she had ever said to him. The question concerned the past alone.

"When?" he said, and she hid her face in her hands.

"Always, always, always," she wailed and began to cry again, but with her face covered.

He turned his head away and looked out of the little window. Then, because he could not help himself, he jerked out:

"But . . . now. . . ."

She shrank back into the chair as if he had struck her.

"Oh! cruel!" she said and the words were so muffled that he could barely hear. "Haven't I said? Oh! go away!"

The full flood was on him then, and he was choking in it, drowning in pain, but with no hope of death. He went out, groping for the door latch.

XXVI

"Let my shame
Go where it doth deserve."
"And know you not," says Love, "who bore the blame?"
"My dear, then I will serve."
"You must sit down," says Love, "and taste my meat."
So I did sit and eat.

GEORGE HERBERT.

ONCE out of the town he ran. The few people he met may have stared, but he did not care; only, when he saw a little clump of trees at the side of the road, he left the track and plunged in, past the scented box and pale elder bushes, to the heart of the wood. Then he dropped.

He lay so still that after a while a squirrel came linking over the bare ground on its way between tree and tree. It stopped short half-way, considering the possibilities of danger, then leapt back and scuttled up the tree it had left, pausing at the first branch to peer down at the enemy who had scared it. Yves had raised his head and now he beat it upon his clenched hands. He had run away from pain, but here it caught him again, and there was no escape.

It was mere blind suffering at first; then out of the dark came pity for her, a new pain and terrible. He found himself muttering her name, and stretching out groping hands to find and care for her. From old habit he checked himself, trying to put her from his mind, then realised that there was no longer any need, since she loved, and had always loved him. With a great bound his heart leapt to catch at joy so strangely and suddenly close.

He lay still for a moment, afraid for no reason, but knowing that there was something to fear. Then he remembered. This joy was the gift of the Hunter. He shrank back from the sharp torment of so immense a bounty, and fumbling in his breast for the little crucifix,

285

held it out before him with stiff unwilling fingers, as far from him as he could reach.

"No! No!" he whispered. "For pity! Pardon is hard enough to bear – yea, bitter as a thorn. But to give joy . . . to me . . . to me! Oh! God, I cannot take it. I will not. Oh! God, Your love tears me . . . I will not!"

He threw the crucifix from him and covered his head with his hands, shrinking even now from the last submission. Then suddenly his heart softened to helplessness like that of a homesick child. He laid his face on the ground and wept.

His sobs did not slacken; they stopped. Sleep had come down, silent, swift and irresistible.

When he woke he was very cold. He rolled over on his back and sat up, wiping the dust and mould from his face. The wood was full of small rustling noises and dainty tappings, for the evening breeze was touching the crumpled edges of the fallen leaves, and swaying the lighter branches. In his mind there was a deep, blind silence, and he was interested only in the fact that he was cold. He shivered, and began to rub his hands together to warm them. As he sat there, looking vaguely about, a sound came drifting to him through the trees, like incense between the pillars of a church, but fresh and clear – the sound of men's and boys' voices singing in the open air.

He got up, shook the dust from his clothes, pulled his sword round to its place, disentangling the hilt carefully from a strap that caught it awry, and picked up the crucifix; but he did it all without any thought or intention in his mind. The sound drew him back to the road, and when he reached the edge of the trees it was close; deep and shrill, hollow and full, like all lovely things it partook of opposites. Yves came out into the open.

There were a dozen or so monks and as many novices who led the procession and the singing. At the head swayed a great rough wooden cross, obviously cut from the trees by the wayside. After the monks came a crowd of men, shepherds, ploughmen, a craftsman or two with leathern aprons and grimed faces, and here and there a knight or an esquire. All, as they went, sang the Crusading Song:

286

Lignum Crucis
Signum ducis,
    Sequitur exercitus,
Quod non cessit
Sed praecessit,
    In vi Sancti Spiritus.

Yves went close to the road-side and knelt down, shutting his eyes. The first boys passed, and their fluting notes were swept away by the deep-throated tide of the men's voices:

Cum attendas ad quid tendo
Crucem tollas, et vovendo
Dicas, Illi me commendo,
    Qui corpus et animam
    Expendit in victimam
Pro me moriendo
    Lignum Crucis.

Yves heard it with a blank and quiet face; they passed, and the singing died slowly and indefinitely, as smoke drifts to nothing. When it was gone he opened his eyes with a little sigh like a child waking, and looked about him. He saw that he held the crucifix and wondered mistily why he did so, staring at it for a moment; then he raised it to his lips and kissed it, lightly and simply as a child kisses. It was his submission, yet, when he started off along the road to Niort, walking slowly, and dangling the crucifix by its ring from his finger, there was nothing in his mind but a child's interest in the little wild live things among the grass and the bushes.